WORTHY OF TRUST AND CONFIDENCE

AN HISTORICAL THRILLER

J.A. BALLAROTTO

Worthy of Trust and Confidence

First Print Edition: February 2013

ISBN 10: 0615772250
ISBN 13 978-0-615-77225-7

Published by Pirate143 Press.

Editors: Harry Dewulf (densewords.com)
and Laurie Skemp (authorsea.com)

Cover and Formatting: Streetlight Graphics (streetlightgraphics.com)

FOREWORD

This novel suggests an interpretation of a historic episode that is shrouded in more mystery and is the subject of more debates than probably any other single event in the history of the United States. While I have alluded to some actual historical figures, their conduct is a product of my own alternative and hypothetical theories on the assassination of President John F. Kennedy. Any similarity to other persons, living or dead, or actual events, is purely coincidental. The story or opinions expressed here are not approved, endorsed, or authorized by or associated in any manner with, the United States Secret Service , the FBI, or any other government entity.

CHAPTER 1

ON THE JOB

Las Vegas
Late September 1963

It was late September and I really should have been back East—anywhere back East—most preferably Newark. Although almost any place would have been better than sitting in this wheelchair in the hottest place on the planet. That's only on the outside though, because somehow the mega-egos who built those tombs managed to make all of the great indoors about as frigid as a Catholic girl on a blind date with a chimpanzee.

Although it was only September 1963, I found myself, for the moment anyway, about 70 years old, completely gray, wearing a hearing aid and confined to a wheelchair. Some spot for a young man in the prime of his life. I really didn't give it much thought—I was just too damned uncomfortable because of the inane chatter in my earpiece and the Model 19, Smith & Wesson .357 Magnum gouging into my lower back. A smaller-frame gun would have been nice, until I tried to drop a bad guy, that is. Carmine, the Newark counterfeit squad leader and my mentor in so many ways, said anything smaller was strictly for a lady's handbag. And a handbag wasn't in my repertoire that day. So there I was.

Every special agent was required to carry the same Model 19

without any modifications whatsoever. The theory was such that, in a shit storm, any agent could pick up any other agent's gun and handle it as if it was his own. No hesitations—grab, point and put six shots high in the chest. Those were the important considerations in my life back then.

I was relatively new to the Secret Service, and although the organization didn't always feel like a glove-fit, I was very happy working in Newark, New Jersey's most metropolitan city. I was comfortable in that environment, even if I often felt like I didn't exactly fit into the mold of a special agent. It was a time when cops were cops, college grads were kids, and the two groups just didn't play well together. But hey, things were changing. They expected us to grow, everything except our hair, that is.

I was only 22, going on 23, and although I had all the powers Congress could give, I was in limbo—between the role I was playing in the Secret Service and everything I had ever been or ever would be. I guess I really shouldn't have made a big deal about it. I had suffered through such a haze for most of my life anyway. High school was nowhere, just a place to be before college. And college was just more high school, but with more hair and more sex. I simply couldn't control the urge to dash through the years, the books, the girls and the rides. It became a way of life that whenever I changed either girlfriends or cars, I would inevitably change the other. Some say it was a sign of the times—maybe it was just no sign at all. I was always going somewhere, but I was never fully anywhere. No matter what I was doing, I always felt that it just wasn't important enough, big enough or dangerous enough. There was always something on the other side. One of my closest friends once told me, "Hey, remember, no matter where you go, there you are." I clearly never quite got there—I was just passing through on the way to somewhere else. I had hoped that the Secret Service would give me more presence. The jury was still out on that.

Being in Las Vegas made no difference at all. It was the '60s, and I was immune to the Vegas charms because no matter where I was or what I was doing, I still couldn't wait to get back East. It's like they say, "You can take the boy out of the jungle, but you can't take the jungle out of the boy." And if there ever was a jungle in America, it was Newark, New Jersey. But it was home to me. Some of us, even in three-piece suits, are merely jungle animals, no matter where we are standing at the time. If you looked closely at an escapee, you might have been able to catch a hint of the Newark-land jungle behind the veil of normality. In my case, it was all there in beads, boots and hair.

Under it all, I was always proud to be a Newark Italian. But the glitter of the jewelry or the shine of the fine, smooth leather often found on various appendages of the Goodfellas back home never impressed me. The most recognizable uniform of the day for most young *paisani* was a fine, hip-length, black leather jacket, worn with only a snug fitting "guinea tee" shirt and a pair of fine, black, Italian-made slacks that had just the right Armani break at the top of the shoe—usually a Ferragamo loafer. More recently, however, you started to see more and more of the guys wearing those blue cotton cowboy jeans—cheap stuff. But hey, the girls looked great in them, even if they were a bitch to get off in a hurry in the back seat of a Chevy.

For me, I always liked jeans and wore them before they were fashionable, back when they were called dungarees. And frankly, I only ever owned one pair of Salvatore Ferragamo loafers in my life. They were overpriced, undersized and lasted all of about two weeks. They went into the back of the closet when I pulled on my first pair of real all-American cowboy boots, a gift from my friend, Viet Nam Tom. He was in the army, in some special combat unit that trained American boys to kill other boys in some far off place in the world that the "DC Dicks" somehow thought was important to America. They sent Tom to Viet Nam, where he met a kid from Texas who brought the boots with him. He gave them to Tom when he went home. In the final days of his third tour, Tom received a gunshot wound to his left ankle that forced him to come home. Because of the wound, he couldn't wear the boots anymore, so he gave them to me. Nice elephant hide, they are. They must have been ten years old by the time I got them. I still wear them because they're much more comfortable than most people know, and it's also a great “fuck you” to the Secret Service old guard. I carried around this contempt for almost all authority since I was an early teen. I knew that one day I was going to have to give it some thought. I had no idea that day was just over a stormy horizon.

Nevertheless, there I was in Vegas, wearing that disguise and wheeling myself around the slots floor, trying to get close enough to the surveillance targets to get a look at the $100 bills they were pumping into the bill validators on the slot machines. Caesars was always trying to stay ahead of the curve, and the bill validator was the latest technological advantage they implemented to speed up the rate of play. Play, however, was really a misnomer. They should just skip play and go directly to pay, because there was very little play, but lots of pay.

It all reminded me of visiting one of those Philadelphia Horn and Hardart Automats. They would entice you into buying a three-day-old piece of apple pie because you’ve got to slip your money into a shiny stainless steel and glass thingamajig they called a vending machine. Until that moment, I never really appreciated the similarity between a cafeteria vending machine and a one-armed bandit in the casino. The end-result from an encounter with either one was the same: you walked away with a bad taste in your mouth.

The success of the bill validator turns on a closely guarded fact that few know: The ink on the face of a $100 Federal Reserve Note is magnetic. Small flakes of metal in the ink reveal a magnetic signature pattern. The bill validator can scan a $100 bill and read the magnetic signature that distinguishes it from a counterfeit note printed by some unsophisticated mope who either doesn’t know about the signature pattern or isn’t able to reproduce it. Frankly, this was the first time any counterfeiter had been successful in beating the casinos. It made you almost want to root for them. As resentful as I was of those machines, I knew that someday that equipment would be everywhere, even on coke and candy machines. But for the moment, they were experimental only at Caesars and a few other casinos in Las Vegas.

When a gambler slid a genuine $100 bill into the validator, he would receive a credit for 100 one-dollar plays on the slot machine.

Therefore, he could empty his pockets into the machine lickety-split, without any unnecessary interference from his conscience, or his good judgment. He could lose his money by playing the machine just as fast as the little electric lights and bells could flash and ring. It was a beautiful thing for the casino. On the outside chance that the gambler might win, the counter kept a running tally of the number of plays left to his credit. On the rare occasion when the gambler came to his senses before he blew through all 100 plays, which was very rare, he could hit the "cash out" button, gather the silver dollars from the tray and walk away.

It was a fine plan—not perfect, but pretty damn good. The pay-off for the casino was the unbreakable chain of mesmerizing lights, bells, and shiny, colorful, moving parts that kept the gambler focused on the play. The only dull, uninteresting part of the entire experience was the counter itself. It almost disappeared, and only became noticeable when it reached "0" and the entertainment stopped, signaling that it was time to feed it again. The process seemed familiar to me, yet not immediately recognizable until I remembered that it was just like a girl I used to date at the Jersey Shore. She always looked real good and was loosy-goosy, lots of fun and almost as shiny as the slots. But boy, when she needed attention, everything ground to a halt until I peeled off the cash. No matter what it was, I just couldn't resist giving it to her. The sight, the sound or even just the smell of her weakened my knees and my willpower. I'd give her almost anything, in the short run anyway.

My friend Peter—black as the ace of spades, with a much more cynical attitude toward women—once summed it all up for me while I was recovering from a bankrupting weekend.

"You know Jake, there's lots of fine pussy in the world, and a good man should not be afraid to enjoy as much of it as he can. But you gotta stay away from that 'hypnotic' stuff." I stood there, completely bewildered, waiting for a punch line, but there wasn't one. Instead, there was only Peter's sage advice.

"There are," he continued, "just some women who have something different. They got this 'hypnotic pussy' that takes over your mind and makes you do whatever it wants. It will focus on you, make you feel so great that you forget all your problems. But then it decides it needs attention, and it will break you down and crush you if it don't get what it wants. And you gotta give in to it because you're hypnotized by its power. Boy, you got to stay away from that 'hypnotic pussy', no matter how fine it looks."

Peter figured it out quicker than I did because I'm a romantic with a searching heart, and such notions weaken a man's resistance to its hypnotic power.

On that day in 1963, however, I was stuck in that wheelchair as part of a surveillance team watching a group of players that included a smokin' hot chic. It was the first time I ever laid eyes on her. At the time, I only knew she was a magnificent *testarossa* (red head) with startling strawberry blonde highlights. She was with three guys and two other women. They were dancing with four slots on the east-end floor of Caesars, and it was apparent they were not falling prey to the enticing foreplay of the machines. The men were completely uninterested in the alluring overtures of the one-armed bandits. One of the guys, tall and skinny who kept pointing to the ever-so-dull counter was clearly preoccupied with something other than the obvious talents of both the slots and the *testarossa.* The women, while there and certainly participating, were observers more than movers and shakers, with an element of window dressing to their presence. The *testarossa* stood by pouting, waiting for them to finish up so she could go somewhere else and play. While I knew they weren't Italian, I couldn't help but think of the *testarossa* in terms of my own culture. She wasn't wearing a ring, so I concluded that she was a *goom.*

The term *goom* is a shortened version of the Sicilian slang *goomad* or *goomada,* a bastardized form of the word *madrina*, which means Godmother. It evolved over the centuries as a term of endearment for the illicit status given to a married Italian man's girlfriend-on-the-side. It's not intended to be disrespectful; it's used to designate a special relationship between them that goes far beyond casual sex. Such relationships often last for years, or even decades, sometimes in full view of neighbors, friends and even wives, who are relieved another woman will take their often-problematic husbands off their hands for a while and entertain them in ways they aren't willing to do anymore. However, in the end, it's not unusual for the *goom* to create the same relationship pressures as the wife. The Italian male often finds himself an emotional and financial slave to both women. As far as I'm concerned, it's just another version of the "hypnotic pussy" syndrome.

It didn't take very long to figure out what was happening. Somehow, this gang-of-six figured out the magnetic code on the $100 bill. As a result, they were pumping eight or nine queer $100 bills at a time into a bill validator slot. They tried to look enthusiastic as they played a few games. But then, with 800 one-dollar plays left on the machine, while trying not to look to conspicuous, they would cash out. It was a great scam. They were virtually "washing" the queer for genuine silver dollars. In just a few minutes, the six of them could easily wash $10 or $15,000, and no one would have ever noticed until shift change six hours later, when someone opened the slot to empty the cash. By that time, the counterfeiters would be off like the James Gang, gone with a fist full of genuine cash. Too bad they picked the wrong set of slots, on the wrong day, to launder all that worthless queer.

Caesars' security had been watching a certain slot repairman for about two weeks. Seems he figured out a way for slot repair to pay off in a big way. Every time he opened a slot that needed repairing, he lowered its profit margin by a few hundred dollars. "Surely, no one would rely on the counter of a broken slot," the misguided repairman thought.

The casino did, however. When they caught on, they put a tail on him, and just minutes after he would leave a machine, they would recheck it. Unfortunately for our counterfeiting mutts and luckily for the Secret Service, the industrious repairman targeted one of the counterfeiters' machines when they shuffled off to a new slot to continue their scam. The legitimate follow-up technician noticed a texture variation in the notes on top of the $100 stack in the machine and became suspicious of their authenticity.

The situation just couldn't have been any worse for the crooked but enterprising repairman. He made the mistake of taking two

$100 bills from the top of the stack in that slot. Naturally, they were as queer as $3 bills. When casino security grabbed him, they showed him the security video, and he had to cop-out to palming the notes from the slot—not knowing they were counterfeit—merely to avoid a federal beef for possession of counterfeit money. Once casino security figured out the notes in the slot and the notes in the repairman's pocket were counterfeit, they called us, and here we were.

The Secret Service Las Vegas Field Office became keenly interested in what was happening at Caesars because the notes taken from the slot were brand new counterfeit notes. That is, it was the first time counterfeit notes like these, made from the same specific set of counterfeit plates, were passed anywhere in the world.

Over its one hundred year history, the Secret Service discovered that close inspection of a counterfeit note would reveal specific imperfections that can be associated with every other counterfeit note printed by the same set of counterfeit plates. Every imperfection on the bogus printing plate transfers to the exact same spot on every note printed from that set of plates. As a result, the Secret Service assigns a circular number to each new set of counterfeit notes printed by the same set of plates. These notes were designated c.4161.

When a new note hits the streets in your district, the Special Agent in Charge (SAC) gets all excited because a new note always gets the attention of headquarters. My guess was that the group we were watching would be moving from slot to slot over the next few hours, hoping to score big and then get out of town, fast. Little did I suspect the shakedown of the slots I was witnessing that day was part of an intended shakedown of the entire Western World.

CHAPTER 2

YOU NEED A PROGRAM TO TELL THE PLAYERS

THE DAY BEFORE THEY SENT me to Las Vegas, I was in LA doing a hospital survey for PPD (Presidential Protection Division). So, less than 24 hours earlier, I was dressed in a suit, flirting with nurses and interviewing hospital administrators and doctors. It was a tedious job, but PPD now has the route to every hospital in nearly every city from almost any location POTUS (President of the United States) would ever visit. We have the names and telephone numbers of the best doctors in every specialty at every hospital. If POTUS gets anything from a gunshot wound to gonorrhea, the Secret Service knows where to take him and the fastest way to get there. With that assignment complete, headquarters decided to send me to join the Las Vegas posse and ride the range looking for this new note, instead of just letting me go the fuck back home to Newark. Some job.

So I sat in that wheelchair, listening to all those cops-turned-Secret-Service-Agents squawk in my ear. I knew most of our guys were walking around with hard-ons, just thinking about arresting those mutts and ruining their day. I, on the other hand, was still freezing. My legs were all pins and needles from the Magnum pressing into the small of my back, and my head itched like no tomorrow from the powder they used to gray my hair. I was bored and aggravated like 400 motherfuckers, and all I wanted to do was go back to Newark and get an Italian hot dog, with peppers and potatoes, on a nice fresh "torpedo" roll.

In spite of my physical agitation, the real root of my discomfort was the Secret Service policy that the local office, no matter how incompetent, was in charge of the investigation. It made no difference that headquarters sent three Newark guys out there in the first place because the Washington brass knew it was extremely unlikely that a gang of local cowboys would be busting out a new note in Las Vegas—without the intervention of wise guys from back east. It would just never happen that way. Even though the local field office was way over its head, they simply refused to listen to anything we had to say about how to handle the situation.

As soon as the casino called the Las Vegas Field Office, the SAC put the surveillance team together. Did they do any real investigation or try to learn even a little about who they were fuckin' dealing with before they decided to crawl all over them? No! You might think they would have wanted to know a little something about where the note came from and who might have printed it before they got into the game and played blind. Instead, the SAC had us all just watching these guys pump notes into the slots while hoping that when we busted them, they would crumble like a cheap suit and give it all up. Maybe it would work that way in the wild, wild West, but never in Jersey. Hell, there wasn't a single dago in the entire gang—and that's some bullshit. It just couldn't be right. There had to be one lurking in the shadows someplace.

Here's all we knew at the time. We had three guys and two chics, and a woman who clearly looked like anyone's grandmother. Besides the skinny guy and the *testarossa*, there was also a middle-aged guy, another young girl who looked like his daughter, and then, there was grandma. The third guy was a small slime-ball. He spent a lot of time whispering and plotting with the skinny guy. I didn't get a good look at him because he was both careful and apparently pretty skilled at staying in the shadows.

Casino security already decided that the tall, skinny guy was the source of the notes because four hours earlier they followed him to a car in the garage. They suspected he picked up more notes from under the rug in the trunk. That wasn't surprising because it's typical for a counterfeiter to carry a limited number of counterfeit notes mixed in with genuine notes, just in case he got caught. With the counterfeit notes in your pocket, mixed in with several genuine bills, it was easier to claim you were the innocent victim of someone passing them on to you.

When the Newark guys arrived, we decided to look at our hole card and do a little background investigation. The plate on the car in the garage came back to Hertz. The local rental agent told us the car was rented to Nicolao Fostou, who was 57 years old and lived in a working class neighborhood in Brooklyn. He had to be the middle-aged guy. The Brooklyn Postal Inspectors told us that Nicolao and five others got mail at a poorly-maintained, one-family home in a declining east side neighborhood. The five were Mrs. Nicolao Fostou, obviously the mother and wife; Julia Fostou, the daughter; Social Security recipient Mariposa Fostou, the granny; and last but, not least, Azzimie Zalouco, who was receiving mail recently forwarded from various addresses, including a penitentiary in Arkansas.

A quick trip past the house by a couple of New York Field Office Agents found three cars in the driveway. They took it upon themselves to do a little old-fashioned detective work and employed a tried and true favorite—the old "Fuller Brush Man" knocking at the door. Mrs. Nicolao Fostou enthusiastically responded. The old-world woman, dressed in black—including her socks and shoes—turned out to be friendlier than you might have thought. She probably lived decades in that house where no one talked to her except to ask her to do something for them, probably something in the kitchen. Nicolao most likely had a *goom* on the side, in a bedroom far away, who gave him whatever he needed.

Mrs. Fostou very much enjoyed our little Fuller Brush visit and answered all our questions. She was happy to discuss her family and their escape from the communists in Eastern Europe. She explained how Hungarian tradition requires that the entire multi-generational family stay together in one house. She was at home caring for the house and dog while her husband Nicolao, daughter Julia, nephew Azzimie and Julia's friend from work, LJ, took her aging mother-in-law on a little trip to Las Vegas. Mrs. Fostou didn't mind at all staying home, because she enjoyed the quiet time and the opportunity to catch up on her household chores. Her gentle spirit was a reflection of generations of women not being important to anyone unless she was busy satisfying some member of the family's immediate needs. After thirty minutes of almost non-stop talking about the family, she ordered two toilet brushes, a kitchen mop and a brush for the dog hair that seemed to be everywhere. I hope she wasn't too disappointed when they never arrived.

In a matter of only an hour or two of old time deception, we got a pretty good idea of who the players were, except for the third guy with Nicolao and Azzimie. Nicolao was easy to spot. He was wearing a black turtleneck, with black pants and a black sports jacket, none of which were the same shade. Shoes that hadn't been polished since WWII and a Chesterfield King continuously burning between the fore and middle fingers of his left hand described his most notable characteristics. I was confident that if I got closer, I would have found that those fingers were nicotine stained from years of box car smoking, and that his hands bore the calluses of a man who has spent his lifetime working very hard. And, although he was in the middle of the commission of a federal felony, he had the face of a gentle soul, one who never laid a hand in anger on his wife or kids. He was clean-shaven, and his black and graying-at-the-temples hair was not short, but neatly cut by a barber, who I'm sure was at least two decades older than he was. I didn't see him put a single bill in the validator. But he watched all the counters with more amusement than greed to be sure they credited 100 plays for each counterfeit note inserted. His eyebrows rose slightly and simultaneously with the corners of his mouth when the validator accepted each note, as if to say, "Wow, this really works!"

The tall, skinny guy had to be Azzimie, the nephew. While Nicolao displayed near-childlike fascination at the lights, bells and whistles of the slots, Azzimie was all business. The two men bore similar facial structure and coloring. They were both clearly members of the clan, although Azzimie possessed none of the warm and charming attributes of Nicolao. His shiny, three-day-unwashed hair, together with a shirt and pants that had to fit better on almost anyone else, was the giveaway. He didn't have to wear stripes to signal he was an ex-con. I could almost catch a hint of the aroma of an old t-shirt that got left in the bottom of the hamper when the rest of the laundry was done. I was instantly repulsed at the prospect that the *testarossa* would ever get as close to him as she did, but that was a story I only later understood.

Azzimie was working with purpose. He would pump several bills into the slot and chunk it up to 800 or 900 plays before cashing out. Unless there was another play, the slot showed no reaction—no bells and whistles—other than the spinning of the counter. Even the cash-out was relatively calm, except for the clang of the silver dollars hitting the bottom of the steel tray. He seemed to bloat in harmony with the spinning of the play counter, displaying all the characteristics of an anaconda who eats its prey whole and then expands its intestines to hold it until it could be digested. As the counter number increased, he raised his shoulders and expanded his chest, while his feet shuffled and the whites of his eyes brightened. When he achieved the target number of play credits, he hit the cash out button with a lightening-like jab and then turned away in a three-quarter spin, as if to say, "who did that, not me," just in case someone was looking. Once he felt safe again, he would casually gather his booty in a large casino bucket. With a full bucket, he would melt away from the slot and begin to digest his prey, eventually slithering to the cage to cash out his silver dollars.

The third guy, who I just couldn't get a bead on, often went with Azzimie to the cage to cash out. He was a white guy with dark, angular-cut hair and a slight build, wearing a crumpled suit with an open-collared, yellow shirt. I felt slimy just watching him slither around the casino like a centipede on a wet kitchen floor. I didn't get a clean look at his face that day because he intentionally stayed in the shadows. He remained an enigma to me throughout most of the caper.

Then there was Granny and Julia, who were simply having a good time. They would load up the slot with one or two bills and then actually play. They were childlike in their playful interaction with the machine and amongst themselves. When the slot would hit, even modestly, they would quickly clap their hands together in front of their breasts, with their fingers pointed straight in the air, as if they were preparing to say a prayer. Their glee certainly annoyed Azzimie. To him, this wasn't playtime—this was all business. I'm sure he felt the playful antics of the "girls" would bring unwanted attention to them, when it was really just the opposite. If he weren't so self-absorbed, he would have realized that their behavior was the norm in the slot room. He, on the other hand, was acting like a snake in the grass.

Julia and Granny were kindred spirits. They were both obviously from good peasant stock. While they weren't sophisticated, they certainly were not stupid nor unattractive. In fact, while I was immediately captivated by the *testarossa*, Julia was certainly attractive in her own right. She and her grandmother both had the large nursing breasts and the childbearing hips that were at the top of any old world Eastern European man's list of desirable attributes for a prospective wife and mother. I was sure that Julia knew all the cooking and cleaning techniques of her granny and mother but was completely unaware of the bedroom talents necessary to land an all-American boy. The Hungarian man her father will eventually choose for her to marry will teach her those skills. Even the payment of dowry was probably not entirely out of the question. All that being said, however, they both seemed like kind, loving souls. I took no pleasure in what I knew was about to happen to them.

The wild card in this high stakes gamble was the *testarossa*. It was unclear how she fit in, except that every once in a while I would see Azzimie looking at her like she was a cold beer after tarring a hot tin roof on a July afternoon. I couldn't blame him. This chic was certainly not a member of the family—no peasant stock in her bones. Bright and shiny she was, even though she tried to hide it. There was also the look and polish of education about her. Not the kind a chic gets from her mother or from working in a diner or factory, but the real, sitting-down-with-a-book kind. I had to wonder why she was trying to hide it. In spite of her polish, she and Julia seemed to be genuine girlfriends. She had to be LJ, the girlfriend Mrs. Fostou described to the New York Agents. All I wanted was to get close enough to smell her perfume. There was something alluring about her. At first, I thought it was mysterious, but then I decided that wasn't it—she was a chic. Although still in my tender years, I knew lots of chics, and frankly, I had no luck understanding any member of the gender. They were all a mystery to me. This chic, however, was different. I actually felt like I knew her, yet every move she made was a pleasant surprise, like first time sex with a pro. I was certainly interested in getting the details of the saga, but at that moment, there was a different game afoot.

CHAPTER 3

AND THE GAME WAS ON

"OKAY, EVERYBODY, IT'S TIME TO move."

"Jake, keep your cover," the Vegas SAC instructed over the radio.

"Shit, I gotta stay in this chair?" I unhappily said to myself.

The boys were off and running, looking like "G" men in a Hollywood movie. This is why some affectionately called us the "Secret Circus."

It was actually funny how no one even noticed them as they moved through the slot room floor in a pack. A white man in a suit, with the correct hair length, can make all kinds of threatening moves and everyone still feels completely comfortable, even the perps. Not me, though. Those guys made me feel squeamish, like looking in the rear view mirror and seeing a police car. It's an instant, "Oh fuck."

Six, eight, nine suits were all moving in unison. All of them in that familiar position—reaching in the right breast jacket pocket with their left hand for the Secret Service Credentials while their right hand reached for the Magnum on their right hip. It was a real study in individual perception. Granny completely ignored the ruckus, while Nicolao realized, just as he saw the guns and cuffs, that the jig was up. Azzimie didn't give a fuck—he wasn't going without a fight.

Fax Walder, Secret Service poster boy, got to Azzimie first. He quickly showed Azzimie the patented Fax One-two: One, you hit 'em; two, you yell "Secret Service" and then hit 'em again. You had to admit, it was always a crowd pleaser. Once they've seen it, no one is interested in seeing it again. Nicolao and Julia quickly put their hands up, almost as fast as Azzimie hit the floor. However, to everyone's amazement, especially Fax's, Azzimie bounced up like a licorice square off the kitchen floor and "beat feet" toward the emergency exit. By that time, there was so much confusion that I didn't see Azzimie again that night. I don't think anyone else did, either. LJ had all my attention.

LJ was the first to know something was up. She seemed to know even before the nine sluggers moved in for the arrest. It was as if she felt a change in the air currents as soon as someone started to move. It wasn't fear, or even inquisitiveness, though. The only thing on this chic's mind, other than avoiding breaking a nail, was how to exit invisibly. Her entire aura changed. If I were close enough to smell her, I would bet dollars-to-donuts that her scent also immediately changed, like a jungle animal on the hunt. Now she was the most dangerous animal in the jungle, and she was on the move.

Her head was in high gear, while she put her body in motion. The lights went out for everyone in the room, except her. She wasn't scared—not even a hint of alarm—just, "gotta go and don't get in my way." To Julia, LJ vanished between blinks. She must have uttered a half dozen words before she realized LJ was gone, and she didn't have an inkling as to why she left or where she went. Unbelievably, there wasn't a guy with a badge and a gun in the room that even noticed, except for me. She was a specter to everyone else, an unrecognizable shadow. I was moving on pure, uncontrollable attraction; I couldn't really see her. I was relying on instinct—feel and smell more than anything else. It was as though there was a string connecting us and she was trying desperately to break it. I, on the other hand, was doing all I could to keep even a single thread intact. Her destination was the set of interior stairs. Caught in the wake of her charms, I couldn't just let her get away.

Although I was doing my best to keep up with her, the roll of the damn wheelchair was no match for her athletic strides.

"Fuck it," I said aloud.

I dumped the chair and took off like a starling being chased by a pickup truck on a country road. She slapped the door to the stairs with the palms of both hands. As it closed on my face, I felt like I had been hit in the face with a shovel. The sound of the door slamming one flight up rang in my head. Of course, she didn't predictably go down to the street, but rather up the stairs. Following the clicking of her heels, I ran up one flight, through the closed door, and into the middle of an empty hallway. Having no idea which way she went, I guessed left and soon ran smack into an elevator with a sign on the door—"service personnel only." I was sure it was locked.

I was thoroughly lost and about to back track when the elevator door unexpectedly opened. At first I thought, "That's luck—someone must be getting off here." But then I realized no one was on the elevator. It stopped because I pushed the button. It wasn't locked after all. I just assumed so.

Seeing no other alternatives and feeling dejected and convinced I lost her, I stepped onto the elevator, intending to make a decision about whether to go up or down. No choice was necessary. My spirit perked as the elevator only went down to the kitchen, one floor below the street. When the elevator opened, there in front of me was the reason she went that way—an emergency exit propped open by the kitchen staff to let in some fresh air. I immediately dove for the door, knowing for sure she went that way.

The heat on the street side of the steel door was painful—like being scalded by a cup of hot coffee. I burst through the door and immediately ran to the middle of the street, spinning in circles, hoping to get a clue as to her direction. Luckily, I caught a glimpse of her as she crossed the street adjacent to the Flamingo Casino. I lingered just long enough to notice pointing from people on the street. I guess it looked pretty remarkable to see such an apparently old guy come through that door. I had completely forgotten that the only part of that stupid disguise I shed was the wheelchair. In all other respects, I was an old guy who had no business bouncing around the street the way I was. Except, maybe, if he was chasing a young girl whom he suspected could explain the secrets of the universe to him. I immediately took off after her.

"Forget about it—get your mind off the chic and back on the felon," I tried to remind myself.

After only three steps, she did something she never did before or would do again. She looked back and glued me to the pavement for a full second or even two, with nothing more than an almost casual glance. It could have made me love her, except for the fact that she was a federal felon who, with a clan of criminals, was passing counterfeit $100 bills. I reached to be sure I had my handcuffs because I was planning to use them. Then I took after her like a little leaguer chasing a fly ball that everybody, except him, knew he couldn't catch.

She knew I was coming. For a second, she may have even thought I was gonna catch her. She took two steps to her right, circled completely around the traditional red, white and blue freestanding mail box on the corner and then, after an unexpected pause behind the mailbox, she made a hard left turn. I was sure she did that because she made me and wanted a second to consider her options. Like the fox of the hunt, she headed straight for the Flamingo's grand entrance. What a fitting destination for this *testarossa*—the casino shrine that mob Jew, Bugsy Siegel, built for his *goom*, Virginia Hill, also a devastating redhead.

I followed her through the enormous glass revolving door into the Flamingo. I was hot on her trail. As I crashed through the door, my focus immediately began to circle. I felt like it was impossible to travel in a straight line in any direction. The feeling was remotely similar to being drunk, but with a much deeper intensity.

I was a housewife, standing at the kitchen sink, watching the dirty dishwater as it desperately sought the drain, hopelessly doomed to circle the opening, until the vortex finally released it to continue its journey down the pipe. Panic set in. Although she could see the movement of the water, it was all so cloudy. She was overcome by a desperate sense of impending tragedy as she automatically reached for her third finger, left hand, for reassurance that her diamond ring wasn't lost in the muck and headed down the drain into oblivion.

Like the housewife, I was dazed, anxious and feeling fogged. But unlike her, I couldn't simply grab the third finger of my left hand for the reassurance that I wasn't about to lose my most prized possession. I was forced to endure the uncertainty. I knew LJ and I just came through the same door, yet somehow I wasn't convinced we were both still on the same planet. I felt like Alice falling down the rabbit hole, completely isolated from the world outside, with no reference to time and place. I'm sure that was not by accident, but part of the grand design of the casino.

I knew I had to stop and figure out where this *testarossa* went. I had no idea where to begin. "Come out, come out wherever you are," I playfully muttered to myself, knowing there was no way that was going to happen.

CHAPTER 4

THE RHYTHM WAS PERFECT. THE PLAN WAS PERFECT. LJ WAS PERFECT.

LJ WAS SURPRISED THAT HER moves inside Caesars didn't shake the hound on her tail. She tucked her purse under her left arm, as if it were a battery pack for her pumping heart, and stutter-stepped between cars to the front door of the Flamingo. As she entered the casino, she knew a simple foot race wasn't going to be enough to spring free from the hound on her tail. LJ was going to have to outsmart him. She dashed across the blackjack floor, hoping no one would notice that she was "dashing," and realized that she needed somewhere safe and invisible so she could evaluate her alternatives. She calmly caught her breath, placed the palm of her right hand over her heart and willed it to slow. Like an unruly dog commanded by its master to sit, it immediately began to obey. She then casually walked right past the ladies room door and confidently headed for her only alternative.

With a subtle, but unmistakable smirk, she pushed open the men's room door. Although the door was a steel slab of inorganic matter the size of a small elephant's casket, it moved silently with ease. She wasn't sure how she would react if, not surprisingly, she found a man inside. It really didn't upset her that she might be in the same room with a man while he was urinating. In any event, it had been her experience that when a man has his Johnson in his hand, he is generally oblivious to the rest of the world. Indeed, that's exactly what happened. And, just as she suspected, the two men standing at the urinals to her right as she entered were in deep concentration, with their heads bowed, as if in prayer, but with their eyes wide open.

"Why do men have to look at it when it's operational?" she thought.

Gliding past the urinals, she slipped into the middle of three stalls, turning slightly in order to fit her body and purse through the door in a single movement. As she turned to her right, a chubby, middle-aged man looked up into the mirror on the wall over the urinal. You would have thought he suddenly saw Mickey Mantle walk into the room. LJ caught a glimpse of his face in the mirror just as he began to pee on his shoe. His face was punctuated by the sheer size of the whites of his eyes, followed only by the size of the almost perfectly round hole formed by his wide-open mouth. As she looked back into the mirror, LJ just couldn't resist giving him a little wink. Suddenly conscious that reality was in the opposite direction, he quickly turned his attention away from the mirror and looked directly toward the stalls, only to find all three doors neatly closed and uninteresting. Not entirely sure of what he saw, he decided it was now more important to tend to his soggy shoe, eternally grateful that he missed his sock.

LJ felt reasonably secure in the middle stall, with the exception of her CFMs ("Come Fuck Me" heels) that she feared were visible under the door. She secured the latch with the stealth of a church mouse and responsively sat on the toilet seat, assuming the pondering "thinker" position. She elected to ignore any speculation about the source of the liquid that she felt through her jeans. It really made no difference, however, because although she was physically stationary, her mind was bobbing and weaving like a New York taxi enroute to Idewild with a $20 tip in the balance. She knew, however, that she couldn't just continue to sit there. Not only was she concerned for herself, she was also worried about Julia. Besides, her curiosity was running wild.

"Those guys have to be the law, but who are they and how did they catch on?" she wondered, nearly aloud.

She knew with certainty that getting arrested would seriously complicate her current situation, even though she provided for that very possibility just minutes earlier. If she could get loose, then she could reestablish contact with Julia and the others back in Jersey. If these guys grabbed her, she would probably be stuck in Vegas for a long time, at least until she could make bail and get out of town. She couldn't help wondering who would actually step up and get her out of jail. There were several possibilities, but her money and her freedom were on Julia. In fact, she briefly considered giving up and letting the old fool catch her. At least then she could get off her feet and out of those torturous CFMs.

"Enough of this stupid stuff—he obviously got a look at me, so it's time he saw somebody else. Can he really be that old? Can't be," she said, thinking in scattered notions of the hound chasing her while closely inspecting her strong, but delicate fingers for broken nails.

Confident she was the only person remaining in the room, LJ swung open the stall door, laying it flat against the adjoining stall. This enabled her to look across the narrow room into the mirror running along the opposite wall over the three sinks. It wasn't exactly what she needed to get ready for a night on the town, but it would have to do.

Whether she would admit it or not, there was a beautiful woman starring back at her in the mirror. She was just the perfect height and weight, 5 feet 6 inches and 120 lbs., with tits that, while certainly more than the required mouth-full, gave a supple curve to her shirt. Her skin was the color and texture of a vanilla and peanut butter milk shake—mostly white, but with the perfect brown tint that made even the most distracted male emotionally hungry. Then, the entire picture changed. With a broad sweeping motion, she raised her left hand to the right side of her face and gathered the long locks of her hair. She twisted them around and firmly piled them atop her head. With the help of a bobby pin and rubber band, her *testarossa* with those gorgeous strawberry blonde highlights was gone. Where just a second ago was a spiraling, twisting maze of curls, was now a short, curt and sassy Italian look, still with the tantalizing highlights, of course.

The immediate effect was startling, to say the least. The entire structure of her face changed. The angles now appeared sharp and muscular. Where the once soft curls of a golden, reddish hue delicately framed her features, an angular passion-flame now accentuated her perfection. It was like the burning embers of a fine cigar. It wasn't merely fire on the end of a tobacco stick. It was the culmination of a perfect blend of nature's gift from the finest Caribbean soil, rolled, twisted and wrapped in perfect symmetry to create a tantalizing combination of appearance, feel, aroma and burn performance. The scent alone was enough to cause both man and boy to salivate and break almost any rule to consume. "Hot" wasn't nearly adequate enough to describe what she was.

Her beautiful, nearly exotic skin lacked the deeper and harder tones of so many southern Italians. Indeed, such striking angles and rich skin tone were extremely unusual for a natural *testarossa*. Her Irish mother clearly took credit for her red hair, although it wasn't as easy to credit anyone for her exotic combination of skin color, facial features and shape. Sometimes, when she looked in the mirror, she felt lucky for those gifts—other times, not so much. Since college, she learned that how she looked wasn't nearly as important as how she saw. Her striking appearance amplified her sex appeal, and it was often an advantage with men, sometimes even with women, regardless of their sexual preference. The dikes wanted to get close to her to get in her pants, just like the boys, and straight women wanted to be close to her because they were hoping that whatever she had might rub off on them. Her mere presence in a room enhanced the sexual tension in all directions. This was both good and bad. She couldn't help wondering if her aura was hindering her ability to shake this cop. She was going to find out real soon.

While it was a good start she knew razing her hair alone wasn't going to shake her loose from the hound in the corridor, and so she forged ahead. The water was cold and the soap harsh, but eventually she scrubbed off what little makeup she was wearing. She rubbed off what the soap couldn't get with her fingernails and the second joint of her forefinger.

Next, she shed her black leather jacket—the one she loved so much because it was exactly like the one Marlon Brando wore in the '53 classic, "The Wild One." It was perfectly broken in. The cowhide had become supple with wear as the ends of the sleeves and the creases in the leather had begun to fray just enough to eat through the black dye, revealing the natural tan color of the skin. The jacket was covering a crisp, white cotton, long-sleeved, man-tailored, button-down oxford. You couldn't really tell if it was made for a man or a woman, although there was definitely no confusing who was wearing it now. All the bulges were in the right places. Exposing the white shirt without the jacket gave LJ a completely different appearance—a much softer, even feminine look that was an alluring contrast to her newly revealed angular haircut.

As she pulled the biker jacket down off her shoulders and long arms that were accentuated by the exposure of the long-sleeved white shirt, she noticed how heavy the jacket was. It amused her a little because she never before considered the jacket heavy. It killed her to peel it off and scrunch it into the garbage can. LJ knew she was fooling herself when she whispered to no one, "Once I shake this guy I'll come back and get it." She doubted she was ever going to see it again.

Then, in a moment of uncontrollable sentimentality, she made a decision that would later change the course of the rest of her life. LJ just couldn't "trash" the jacket that was her namesake and so intertwined with her persona. Helplessly, she reached into the garbage can and snatched the jacket from the bottom as if she was saving a drowning child from a foamy brine. It was her first intention to toss the jacket onto the counter surrounding the sinks, hoping someone would pick it up and give it a good home. She was fine with that until she remembered that she was out of her element, in a men's room. Hence, it was most likely that a man would get the jacket and because it was so small, it would probably wind up in the trunk of his car.

LJ stood openly in the middle of the men's room, realizing that she just couldn't leave the jacket in any room containing a urinal. Confident in her decision, she reached into her purse and grabbed a small bottle of her favorite and, in fact, only perfume—"Tarantula"—

an alluring scent named for the female spider that eats its mate after sex. LJ wasn't certain if she knew of the sexual proclivities of the scent's namesake before she started wearing it. And it really made no difference to LJ when she learned of its arachnological relevance. She simply felt the sweet aroma, enhanced by a hint of danger in the scent, perfectly fit her personality. And, as I learned later, she was absolutely correct.

LJ emptied the entire bottle all over the jacket. Most women would simply use a fine leather jacket to look good. There's even an off chance that some might use it to keep warm. But LJ was keenly aware of the mystique of black leather, shiny silver buckles and an unmistakable feminine scent, all mixed in one package. It was like sweet and sour soup, or smooth blue cheese dressing on the rough, tangy skin of a buffalo wing. It's tantalizing, confusing to the senses and oh, so irresistible—like LJ.

She knew she was going through all this trouble because she desperately wanted a woman to have the jacket rather than have some guy toss it into the trunk of his car. Or worse yet, wind up in the hands of some skinny fag. So, she scented it up and walked right out of the men's room and across the hall to the ladies room, where she didn't bother to set foot across the threshold. She just opened the door, sighted the vanity across the room and tossed the jacket into the corner where the wall and mirror met, just under the paper towel dispenser. All she could hope for was that some woman would find it and be selfish enough to keep it rather than try to find the owner or hand it over to some fool in the lost and found office. She let the door swing closed at the same rate as she walked away from it. She confidently headed back to the casino floor.

She was so impressed with herself that she decided to swing her arms, keep her head high and walk straight through the door she came in through earlier. She didn't look for that old prick who was chasing her, not even once. She merely pretended he didn't exist. LJ didn't even remember seeing or hearing the slots on the casino floor; she only recalled feeling the blast of hot air when she walked out the door and onto the street. She hailed a cab and rode off into the sunset, already planning what she was going to tell Azzimie.

The rhythm was perfect. The plan was perfect. LJ was perfect. Too bad she didn't remember the counterfeit $100 note in the left inside breast pocket of that leather jacket. She would, later though, when it jumped up and bit her right in that sweet, perfect ass of hers.

CHAPTER 5

HE FELT LIKE A CIRCUS LION TAMER USING HIS WITS LIKE A CHAIR AND A WHIP.

Havana
Late September 1963

CUBA. MOTHER CUBA. "COLORFUL" SIMPLY doesn't say enough to describe the island, the people or the classic '50s cars the Cubans drive. The natural beauty of the island has colors even Crayola would envy. In some parts of the world, the poor are so isolated and unaware of the wonders of the planet's privileged inhabitants that they're merely happy surviving from day to day, with the help of a little pussy, passion and plunder. Such was not the case in Cuba. Why? Because the American Mob introduced the Cuban people to a lifestyle of fine Italian suits and well-preserved women with nice soft hands and oversized glands. It didn't take much book-learning to realize that if the gringo's have it and the church forbids it, it has to be good.

While most of the Cuban people have only the natural wonders of their Caribbean island to cherish, and little else by way of modern conveniences, that isn't the case for Castro and his band of thieves. The presidential residence in Havana is hardly a revolutionary hovel. The colors and extravagant interior decor rival the finest Cuban beach or rain forest. The rooms are so large and spacious that you're never sure if you're inside or out. And the windows give little guidance because they're always covered with heavy sun-suppressing draperies that help keep the rooms cooler, but do little for the humidity. Not to mention their negative impact on a would-be assassin's aim.

On that day in the late summer of '63, the presidential office was virtually empty. In fact, the Cuban National Baseball Team could have held practice in the office and never even noticed the two figures on the sofa, engaged in surreptitious conversation. So secretive was their discussion that there wasn't even the slightest gesticulation between them.

Both sides of the discussion were similar in almost every element of an objective description. Both were middle-aged men in khaki uniforms that were accompanied by the customary spit-polished black, high-top, leather combat boots. No tattoos were visible, and short haircuts were evident under the fatigue caps. While both men were also similar in size and color, each was most distinguishable by his choice of facial hair. The younger of the two, who was also clearly the subordinate, sported a full but nicely manicured mustache. The older and superior male sported a full beard and was so immediately recognizable that he almost appeared as a caricature of himself. Fidel Castro, the Cuban dictator, was certainly doing all the talking. The mustache was listening, trying to conjure responses to the intermingled litany of questions, ravings and orders barked in one running breath by the beard.

"No. I don't want him dead. Not just yet. Dick-less would be better. Can you arrange that for me?" The unlit cigar in his mouth bounced in cadence with his words, like a conductor's baton. Castro bellowed in such a huff that you could almost see the huge drapes quiver.

"Well, Excellency..." Miguel, a well-placed Cuban revolutionary who always knew how to play Castro to his own best advantage, always began a sentence with a groveling phrase, followed by a distinct hesitation because he never planned to finish his statement. And he never did.

"Well...! Why are you looking at my teeth?" Castro snarled.

"No, your Excellency, I am not looking at your teeth," Miguel responded, in a rush of self-preservation.

Miguel might have been telling the truth because it wasn't Castro's teeth that caught his attention. Rather, it was the color and texture of the inside of his mouth. It looked like burnt bacon with a texture akin to day-old oatmeal brown, crusty and truly grotesque. Castro knew all too well what Miguel was looking at.

"This is the result of their latest frolic in my bathroom closet," Castro mumbled, as he fully opened his mouth like a hooked salmon. It was a close call as to which was worse—the grotesque, ant farm tunnel-like ridges running throughout his gums or the rotten fish smell of his breath.

If you didn't know better, you might have even felt sorry for him. How was his Excellency to know? It tasted like regular old Crest; brushed on nice and easy with that, "I'm ready for sex now, dear" aroma and taste. He was getting fucked all right, but not as he'd hoped. The toxic acid secreted in the toothpaste slowly bonded to his teeth. As it ate through the enamel, it began to work on the bone itself. At first, he had that, "oooh, fresh and minty cool" sensation. Then suddenly, the entire inside of his mouth felt as if he bit into a scalding hot sugar coated charcoal briquette. He could smell and taste the sweet sugary coating, but it didn't disguise the odor of the burning flesh of his lips and gums. In 48 hours, all of his teeth were beyond salvation. Implants were impossible. The pain was so intense he could concentrate on nothing but revenge.

The toothpaste assault was only one of several attempts by the United States Government to destroy Castro's influence in Cuba, with something less than a bullet to the head. When the Kennedy Administration realized it couldn't outright murder him because the Soviets were just too unpredictable, especially after the Bay of Pigs debacle, the only alternative was to drive him from power using his own momentum. The American plan was to undermine his Caribbean virility. Castro was seen as a real-life superhero to not only the Cuban people, but also the rest of Latin America. So, instead of pursuing assassination, the Americans set their sights on his lifeblood instead—powder to make his beard and hair fall out, numbing agents to affect his speech and make him appear as a falling down drunk. It all fit very nicely with the eye drops that wreaked havoc with his otherwise fine vision and the acid-laced toothpaste that blackened his teeth and destroyed his gums. Try giving a three-hour speech in that condition.

The US knew Nakita and the boys in Moscow took a superior, self-righteous attitude toward *El Presidente* from the start. To them, the Cuban Revolution was a gutter fight between two whores, lacking the heroic ambiance of the great people's struggle of the USSR. Cuba was never going to achieve the super power status of the Soviet Union, and therefore it would always be just an "also ran" in the history of the proletariat's twentieth century struggle against capitalism. Everyone, including JFK and even Castro himself, knew the rest of the world looked upon Castro and his island nation revolutionaries as a band of syphilitic cutthroats with no class, let alone a moral initiative.

Castro realized that waging his struggle for legitimacy on the field of Central American geopolitics was futile. He was convinced there was only one way to achieve political and historical significance. He envisioned himself as the embodiment of Michelangelo's heroic David—standing tall, with only a meager rock and slingshot to do battle with the evil Goliath. And there was only one Goliath in the western hemisphere, and he lived in a big, white house. It was Castro's intention to humiliate JFK and destroy the greatly anticipated success of his presidency. There would no longer be a Camelot—only economic confusion followed by the finger pointing of blame at the new president.

"Excellency," Miguel began anew, "we have much to consider."

He didn't say to what or even to whom he was referring. He didn't have to. It was unnecessary, even unacceptable, to utter his name or even his initials in the presence of Castro. JFK was nearly all Castro thought about—there was nothing more important. Some would speculate that all the CIA poisons, while failing to kill his body, killed all of his motivations in life except one—revenge. You could raise the topic with him at any time or place and find that he was an enthusiastic listener of new ways to satisfy his appetite for retribution.

Unless you had real insight into Castro's intellect, you wouldn't know he was convinced the pages of history were the only residence of eternal salvation. His vision of that salvation was one of a very small, one-room shack, with space for only a select few. Everyone else was an interloper seeking mention in the limited number of pages that the history gods would dedicate to this miniscule period of the planet's life. Erasing JFK's pages from history and replacing them with tales of Castro's revolution was his real objective. He dreamed of standing at the threshold of the shack of historical salvation and slamming the door in JFK's face, who would then plead with Castro to share just a few pages of his history with him. He would beg for even a mere footnote. But *El Presidente* would reject his pleas. Instead, he would leave JFK on his knees on the dirty wooden porch, soiling his thousand dollar suit while looking at his gold Rolex, for all eternity, hoping Castro would reconsider, but knowing he would always be nobody, nowhere in time.

With this fantasy firmly etched in his imagination, a new plan of revenge emerged that captured Castro's attention. It was never clear who dreamt up these ideas, but if Castro liked it, you could be sure everyone would give him credit for thinking of it.

The latest idea, while not historically unique, was at least not more of the typical bang, bang. This idea had real promise of a broad, hurtful effect on America and maybe even a little positive spillover effect for the revolution. Not surprisingly, Miguel was also able to figure out a way to make this latest effort pay off for him personally. He was at the palace this day to report to Castro only what he wanted him to know.

"I have explored your glorious plan to destroy the gringo greenbacks," Miguel whispered as he leaned into Castro. He sat so close to him, an observer might think they were both smoking the same cigar, only from opposite ends, if that were possible.

"We have begun to make preparations to obtain the skills to do this. We have friends that will help us, although they do not know it is your Excellency they are helping," he continued, still filtering the information he was providing.

"Yes, I like that idea. But we must succeed beyond the Nazis.

I also want him to know that I did this to him, his family and his country," *El Presidente* replied.

Castro pulled up and away from Miguel, claiming the space between them, leaving room enough for his fantasy to expand and engulf the entire area between them. Miguel had no idea what was happening in Castro's head. He wasn't privy to *El Presidente's* fantasies, only his rantings and ravings, and occasionally a tale of some extreme sexual exaggeration.

The value of a nation's currency is tied directly to the vitality and stability of its economy. The ability to prevent the unauthorized production of paper currency is critical to maintaining its value in the market. Conversely, the ability to counterfeit a nation's currency successfully is tantamount to destroying its navy, or stealing its natural resources, or even depriving it of the benefit of a great leader by death, or even better, disgrace. The Nazis counterfeited the British Pound during World War II with substantial success. The object of the endeavor was not a simple profit motive, but rather the eventual destructions of the economies, as well as the societies themselves, of Great Britain and their Allies. The plot failed along with the German war effort, although some suspect there are still some undetected Nazi-counterfeited five-pound notes still undetected and in circulation today.

Counterfeiting a nation's monetary standard is not a new or ingenious endeavor of the criminal mind. Ever since societies decided that it was too cumbersome to carry twenty-five chickens to market to buy the food and tools necessary to run the farm, they have devised some way to ease the barter system. It all started with coins that had intrinsic value based on their size and composition. The value was directly proportionate to the amount of gold or silver contained in the coin itself. For example, Spanish silver doubloons were minted in large round coins called an "8." If you went to the market and bought a chicken worth something less than an "8," you would actually hack off an agreed piece of the coin and use it to purchase the chicken, therefore having the remainder of the coin to divide further for other commerce. Hence, the term "pieces of 8." All this ended with the development of paper money because there is no intrinsic value in the paper—the strength of the economy and the stability of the nation it represents control its value.

El Presidente was convinced that if he could succeed where the Nazis failed and undermine the free world's economic standard, the dollar, not only would the Americans suffer, but this accomplishment would win him great praise from the Soviets. He would be a president of stature and a hero of the world revolution rather than merely a bagman and lightning rod for "*Nakita Gordo*" (fat Nakita), as Castro often referred to the rotund Nakita Khrushchev.

"When can you begin?" Castro asked, without caring to know any of the details or even vaguely appreciating the complexities of such an operation.

"We have already made preliminary contacts in the States. The plates can be ready in just a few weeks, and a test run can give us $100,000 in perfect $100 bills. We can then test these bills in both the American and foreign markets for their acceptability. If our expectations are realized, we can flood the world markets in a matter of weeks," Miguel nearly promised.

"Make it happen," Castro commanded.

What *El Presidente* did not know was that Miguel was already well down that road. Three months earlier, when his own spies in the Palace leaked to him that Castro was hatching this idea, he began to explore the possibility of securing his own place in history—not as a hero of the revolution, but rather as a well-financed Latin land developer. Miguel's first allegiance was to Miguel. His second allegiance was to Miguel, and so on and so on.

Nearly two years ago, long before the Bay of Pigs fiasco, Miguel learned of a small Mexican island of Cozumel. It was a dry, mostly deserted island just off the coast of the Yucatan Peninsula of Mexico—perfect for a gringo resort. It was amusing to Miguel that while the superior self-image of the American gluttons was directly linked to their Northern European ancestors, they would never think of adopting, emulating or even possessing anything that represented the ignorant, dirty people of Latin America—other than a servant, naturally. He knew, however, that those fragile complexions, now belonging to mostly wealthy Americans, were always in search of the bronzed tint of the Latin people.

"The only real status symbol coming out of Latin America is the Cuban Cigar. And the only reason the fat blubbering gringos suck on these babies is so they can consume them, turn them to ashes, and then crush and step on their remains. They then throw them in the gutter the same as they do to the Latin people, after they scrub their floors, wash their toilets and become lifetime slaves for them. Why do you think they call the end of a cigar the 'butt,' a synonym for ass? They look at that small, brown, exhausted stump of tobacco the same way they look at those small, brown bodies that swim the Rio Grande. But the gringos all want that bronze tint. They want the sun-drenched movie star look that they have to get in either Miami or even deeper into the Caribbean," Miguel often told anyone who would listen to his philosophy.

He also knew that no self-respecting socialites could ever say they were in Mexico simply to sit in the sun and tan their soft pampered asses. Maybe that was okay in the '40s and '50s, but this was the '60s, a new era of activism and social responsibility. Such endeavors got you no invitations to the dinner party circuit. But an excellent cover story was available that enabled the gringos to both socially and intellectually justify their jaunt south of the border. "A real stroke of genius," thought Miguel. The cover story, although there for thousands of years, was one no one thought to take advantage of before.

The beautiful bronzing of their skin would not be the object of the trip, but merely the resultant evidence of the adventure, opining, "It really couldn't be avoided." They could go home and pooh-pooh any notion that they were simply sitting in the sun drinking *piña coladas.* Instead, they were working hard in the archeological ruins of the revered Mayan civilization. They joined the righteous struggle to preserve the ruins of one of the planets most advanced, intellectual and cultured civilizations. It was a substantial sacrifice on their part, but hey, they were willing to suffer the consequences, no matter how difficult, while they unavoidably acquired their exquisite new color.

All this dovetailed perfectly with Miguel's contempt for the gringos and his overwhelming desire to make big money. A social resort in the Mayan ruins of the Yucatan Peninsula in Mexico was the perfect solution. He could take those fat, old or fat, young gringos to the ruins at Chiza Nitza or Uxmal or even Tulum in fancy English jungle Land Rovers. They could fantasize about being real adventurers, and he could charge them a fortune to gaze at the archeological remnants of a brown-bodied civilization that accomplished light-years more than the European white man could have ever hoped for, or so Miguel thought.

Of course, such information would never be discussed on the tour. There wouldn't really be any intellectual or sociological goal to the enterprise. It would be much more akin to taking the gringos to the zoo and showing them the cave where the big, black, brutally ugly, unsophisticated grizzly bear lived. But it would surely make Miguel a very rich brownie. All he needed was a little capital infusion, which *El Presidente's* hatred for the American President was going to provide.

So Miguel saluted *El Presidente* and snappily turned on his heel. As he headed for the huge double doors leading from the inner office of the palace to the rest of the outside world, Miguel felt like a circus lion tamer, using his wits like a chair and a whip to get the big cat to do exactly what he wanted. If only he knew that at that very moment, his best-laid plans were unraveling at a casino in Las Vegas.

CHAPTER 6

ON THE AVENUE

Newark, New Jersey
3 months earlier, June 1963

Miguel was an astute observer of people, especially their dynamics. He knew enough about the States to know two things. First, if you wanted to get anything even remotely shady done, you needed to see a guy whose name ended in a vowel. Second, the best place to do that, without unbridled organized crime complications and entanglements, was in Jersey—specifically North Jersey, and more precisely, on the Avenue—Bloomfield Avenue, in Newark. Long before *El Presidente* ever gave the order to begin this latest tango-in-the-dark between Havana and Washington, Miguel knew where to go, who to see and what to say in order to find the guys who could make all this happen for him. And that's exactly where he went, in the June heat, just three months earlier.

Bloomfield Avenue was to the Italian immigrants of Newark what the overland pass was to the white settlers of the old west a century or so earlier. From the physical and social boundaries of the North Ward of Newark to the sprawl of the emerging 'burbs in Belleville, Bloomfield, and the more prosperous Montclair and

Mountainside, no one on their way up the Avenue ever gave a thought about those left behind. The Portuguese, Hispanics, Blacks and all the others combined were of no significance to those who moved up the Avenue and out of the ethnic ghettos. No one really cared. Why should they? Near the turn of the twentieth century, the Italians arrived in America in droves and took their place at the bottom of the heap in the city ghettos. By the middle of the century, they began climbing out. The Irish, who arrived at nearly the same time, weren't doing so badly either. Although, make no mistake about it, the Italians and the Irish hated each other. It made no difference what the Pope said. You just can't put olive oil on a boiled potato or mix *vino rosso* and beer. It just didn't happen, and both sides liked it just the way it was.

Although Miguel knew very little, if anything, of the social history of the area, when he arrived on the Avenue in June of '63, he instantly knew he was the wrong guy, but he was certainly in the right place. The street was teeming with activity, even in the middle of the day. The problem for Miguel was that any activity anyone suspected his brown Cuban body of being involved in was only bad news for him. But the sights on the Avenue were delicious, even compared to the view in Havana. He couldn't help notice the new jeans phenomenon. He also knew, however, that it was very dangerous for a nice, Spanish boy to look too hungrily at the sweet ass of some *paisan's* girlfriend or even worse, his sister. But, they were everywhere—gorgeous, dark-haired, long-nailed, gum-chewing, purse-swinging chics.

Aside from the girls, the Avenue had a certain personality all its own. Clearly, it was overwhelmingly Italian in its ancestry, but it also had a certain diversity, albeit mono-colored. Unless you grew up in a twentieth century inner-city, street-corner society, you might not have noticed. For someone who was a part of that culture, the difference between the micks and the dagos was as clear as black and white. Thank God, the Italian boys all had Italian mothers. As a result, the boys knew that they could never spend their entire adult lives married to women that were like their mothers—not in their houses and not in their beds. And thank

God, the Irish girls grew up with Irish fathers who unknowingly convinced them that they certainly deserved better than the back of the hand of some smelly old drunk, like those their mothers married. As a result, the dagos were happy to find a sweet Irish lass to wed, and the girls were just as pleased to have a man that was unlike their fathers and brothers. All and all, it worked out because it mended a lot of fences between the Italians and the Irish. They also built a wall to hold back the next groups trying to climb over—the Blacks and the Hispanics.

Although Miguel couldn't help noticing all the attributes of the subculture, he really couldn't give a flying fuck about all those "wops and micks." He believed the pure Spanish ancestry of his family was far superior to the mongrel races of the Italians and the Irish. The fine, high society of Spain referred to the Irish as the "niggers of Europe," and the Italians were always just the greasy people who got their hands dirty because they would subject themselves to the menial tasks no fine Spaniard would ever perform. This even included the great artisans of the Renaissance like Michelangelo and Leonardo da Vinci. However, just like his noble ancestors, Miguel was about to take the big step down into the proverbial gutter and join ranks with a dirty Italian who held the key to his financial future.

Miguel knew exactly who he was looking for. His name was Tuscolano, although everyone called him T, and his game was counterfeiting. Having all the information he needed, Miguel found him exactly where he was told he would find him—sitting in his office reading the *Star-Ledger*, Newark's leading newspaper. It was the best office on the Avenue—the corner booth, with his back to the wall and a full view of the front door, at the Uptown Diner—the spot where all North Jersey dagos went to make the right contact. The FBI often occupied an office there also, although it was usually in the form of rats and informers, all trying to get in on the next score so they could sell the information to The FBI. And naturally, since the relationship between the informers and The FBI was a pay-as-you-play arrangement, if they couldn't find a crime-in-progress, they would do their best to initiate one. And of course that was just dandy with The FBI, as long as the guy they grabbed was on their hit parade. The wise guys on the street knew this was happening, and as a result, The FBI earned the ignoble nickname of the "Federal Bureau of INSTIGATION."

If the truth were known, The FBI was much less interested in prosecuting wise guys than it was in grabbing them and rolling them over to work as informers. That kind of government intervention could never be called law enforcement, even though that's what The FBI called it. It was more akin to the government's approach to a hostile foreign dictator, like the Shah of Iran. The FBI, like Uncle Sam, wasn't so interested in going to war and killing everybody or even putting them all in jail. That might have put an end to all of the suspense, and then who would need all those "G" men running around spending all those taxpayer dollars? It was much more effective for The FBI to prop up an organized crime family, rather than bring it down. This process worked well for everybody. The FBI was able to fortify its value and justify its existence, while the mob guys got to continue making a living, either from crime or The FBI, whichever was paying better at the time. In most cases, however, cooperating wise guys only fed The FBI what they absolutely wanted to feed them anyway. If an informer ever took any heat from the other wise guys for talking to The FBI, he would simply claim the guy he gave up was the real rat who was bringing "bad blood" into the family.

The "blood" thing was an old country approach and was one the old timers liked to use. It goes back to the roots of *La Cosa Nostra* (this thing or affair of ours), and the myth that you had to keep the blood of the family righteous and true. They used this reasoning when they wanted to whack a guy, but had no real reason for killing him—other than he was in some other guy's way, a guy wanting to move up in the family and was better connected. When it came right down to it, everybody on the Avenue and at the Federal Building was playing both ends of the game. It was real Americana—nothing personal, just business. It's like Calvin Coolidge once said, "The business of America is business." And so it was with the cops and the wops.

The Uptown Diner was to the wise guys what The Federal Building was to The FBI—home plate. The diner was located in the 800 block of the Avenue and appeared to the uninitiated as a typical Jersey eatery. But it was nothing of the kind. When Miguel entered the Uptown Diner, he knew he just walked into a place very few Cubans, if any, ever went before. Some aspects of it, however, reminded him of Cuba. The turquoise and salmon colored prints reminded him of the beautiful flowers in the Caribbean. Only here, these colors were imprinted Naugahyde seat cushions and place mats that uncannily and occasionally matched the colors of a patron's best Italian-silk tie. On the other hand, the abundance of stainless steel, in sheets on the walls and in tubes holding up the perfectly round, extra-diameter, dago-ass-accommodating stools at the counter, was completely unfamiliar to Miguel. It was a stark contrast to the natural fibers of home. To Miguel, it was more akin to a combination of operating room décor and a pile of very cheap ties you would find on the table of a street vendor.

In spite of its inorganic surroundings, the Uptown Diner had the perfect aroma. It was a combination of perfectly brewed coffee and homemade pies. Pies, pies, and more pies, all in geometric portions of a circle, were stored in huge, mirror-backed cases. Some revealed both the rippled frosting and the multi-layered bleeding colors of the delicacy inside, while others looked so solid and fortified you could take them outside to jack up one of the huge Cadillacs parked at the curb in front of the place. In fact, after a quick look at the entire picture, the casual observer might conclude one of two things. Either the inside of the diner was bleeding out into the street and all over the Cadillacs, or somebody drove one of the chrome-covered, leather-clad dago rides into the building—and they liked it so much, they decided to build a diner around it. It really made no difference how it happened. The effect was the same. Everybody knew what was outside, what was inside and what was happening in both places.

"Business negotiations" should have been at the top of the menu. In fact, Joey "The Loop," the owner of the place, should have rented the booths out hourly rather than by the food consumed. It would have been much more profitable, although considerably more dangerous to his health. While there was an occasional patron who actually came to eat, usually because they just didn't know better, most of the tables, by far, were occupied by those who were there to do business. In that case, all you would find on the table was a cup of coffee, a pack of cigarettes and a very expensive lighter being sensually caressed by a well-manicured hand adorned by a large diamond pinky ring. A gold ring, that is, with only a single large diamond—none of that black onyx shit with a tiny diamond in the center. In addition, there was always a fine but unset watch on the wrist. Why would a man with all the time in the world need to keep track of a useless commodity? The watch itself was the mark of membership, especially because a true *paisan* would only wear an Italian Panerai.

An important rule of conduct: no one ever took their jacket off and hung it on the chrome racks attached to each booth. The real tools of the trade were always either in that jacket, or under it, in a very comfortable and accessible place. The reason no one would dare hang anything on those hooks was everyone required a clear view of the entire diner. A coat, or even a sport jacket, hanging in the line of sight, could cause just enough insecurity and confusion to initiate a very dangerous response to an unanticipated occurrence from a nervous "businessman."

While even a casual visitor couldn't avoid being struck by the elevated colors in the room, it didn't take long to discover the second most colorful and eye-catching items. For this delicacy, you had to lower your gaze all the way to the floor. While the floor itself was only simple *terrazzo*, it was on the floor that you indeed found *piedi di colori* or "colorful feet"—shoes and socks like you never saw before. No simple black or brown leathers here—only exotic alligator, ostrich or supple calf, and often in at least two colors. Every pair was immaculate and perfect in every respect. After all, they weren't for transportation. That's what the Cadillacs parked outside were for. These shoes weren't intended for walking; they were *arte Italiano* to the last, and not a lace to be found. Wrapping a shoelace around your Ferragamo loafer would be like wearing a piece of clothes line around the waist of your Italian-silk pants—a mortal sin.

Miguel knew he was in the right foxhole; now he just needed to make contact with the right fox. And it didn't take long.

CHAPTER 7

NO HANDSHAKE, JUST A NICE PIECE OF PIE

MIGUEL HAD ONE NATURAL ADVANTAGE when he walked into the diner. He had that smooth olive oil complexion most unaffectionately described by the cops as that "grease ball" look. Nonetheless, Miguel, while he could never pass as Roman or Calabrese, could pass for Sicilian, until he opened his mouth, of course.

He had much harder edges than the *paisani.* His suspicious, insecure manner of walk reflected his revolutionary jungle time—his head oscillated in jarring movements, left and right. A real *paisan* would never move that way. It would disturb the fall of his Italian-silk tie and communicate fear and unfamiliarity in a place that should be like home. In spite of his ambulatory disability, Miguel was, without attracting too much attention, able to saunter across the diner toward T's office in the corner booth. The trip was not unlike getting off the elevator in a high rent office building. With receptionist reflexes, Louisa, the waitress as well as the first line of defense, intercepted Miguel as he approached T's booth.

"You wanna sit, hon?" she very politely asked, while at the same time telling him he would have to sit someplace else without an invite to sit here.

T, without even looking up, knew that Miguel was hovering. It was an instinctual talent, partially inherent and partially learned.

If you ever owned or hunted with a genuine American hound dog, you would recognize the trait. While most people utilize their senses one at a time, T and others of his species operate on a different plane. When going into a dark room, the average guy would desperately search for the nearest light switch and immediately turn on the light. Then, if the room remained too dark, he would look for another light and turn it on, and so on, until the room was sufficiently lit so he could see, and therefore feel safe and secure. T and guys like him wouldn't do that. They wouldn't immediately focus on restoring their sense of sight. Instead, they would rely on a completely different set of senses. They would never grope for a light in a dark room and possibly get a small caliber bullet in the face just as the light went on. Guys like T would remain in the dark and listen for the stressful breathing of another animal in the room, or sniff the still air for a hint of dago cologne or even the distinct aroma of Marvel Mystery Oil, the preferred lubricant used on almost all handguns.

The ability to remain calm in the face of sensory deprivation while reaching for another tool in your head enabled a guy like T to sit confidently in his office at the Uptown Diner. He could read the newspaper, compute the day's baseball line and hear not only nearby conversations, but he could also feel the movement of bodies in the room. This included the ability to smell the presence of someone in close proximity, someone who hadn't been there before, someone who had an unfamiliar aroma about them. That was how T knew Miguel was there. He "saw" him before he even opened the door to the diner. He couldn't actually hear him skip up the six steps to the top landing of the front door, but nonetheless, he knew he had.

T knew this guy wasn't a local *Goodfella,* even if it was only from the squeak of his rubber soles across the terrazzo floor of the diner. He also knew exactly what he wanted, and that had nothing to do with his finely-honed sense of survival, but rather everything to do with a telephone call he recently received from Chicago.

It was less than 24 hours earlier that T got an early morning ring from a guy he didn't know—he never uttered a word to him before. He could never identify him nor provide any description of the guy whatsoever. That's what he didn't know. What he did know was that whoever this guy was, he was speaking for a man he described as a "friend of ours." Those were the magic words. If someone introduces a guy as his friend, that meant he is simply that, a friend. However, when a *paisan* introduces someone or even refers to a guy as a "friend of ours," an entirely different relationship is implied. A "friend of ours" means that the guy is a made member of *La Cosa Nostra,* better known to outsiders as the Mafia, in spite of J. Edgar Hoover's denial of its existence.

After the caller got all of T's attention by identifying the person he was speaking for as a "friend of ours," he told T that this friend knew T's mother was ill and, in a few minutes, this friend would call to extend his concern and inquire about her health. T knew his mother was in fine health, getting ready to celebrate her 77th birthday in two weeks. He also knew his mother had nothing to do with either the conversation he was having with this shadowy figure or the subsequent telephone call he was going to get. It was , however, the *bona fides* of the request he was about to receive that would be confirmed shortly by a subsequent call from their mutual "friend." The caller then got to the point.

"Our friend has asked me to request that you speak to a friend of his," the caller respectfully but firmly stated. He obviously knew he spoke for a very powerful man, and he had authority to assert that power and authority, but always respectfully when speaking to another made man.

He went on to say, "This acquaintance will present what could be a very lucrative business proposition that you are very familiar with. Our friend asks that you consider this proposal, and if it goes as well as he hopes, the usual respects will be paid, *capisce*?"

"Yeah" was all T got to say when the customary "*Ciao*" salutation was abruptly given, followed by the very certain click of the telephone hanging up.

The entire conversation took less than two minutes. The remarkable ingredient of this episode is that such a short, out-of-the-blue contact could have an extraordinary impact on T's life. It was like God calling Moses to the mount and then using a burning bush as a "beard" (wise guy slang for an alibi). God didn't want to blow his cover either, and he certainly wouldn't make a phone call to Moses. He probably felt the same way T did: "the fuckin' FBI is listening everywhere."

To the uninitiated, it might have all seemed just too bizarre to be taken seriously. But you could be very sure these were very serious people discussing very serious issues, with even more serious consequences for disregarding the protocol. *La Cosa Nostra* has a very rigid structure and set of rules, with absolutely no tolerance for violators. In two minutes, T was reminded of a lifetime of dedication and obedience. He understood clearly that a Mafia *Capo* (captain), was contacted by a non-family member who had a money making scheme he wanted T to check out and make happen. And that the "usual respects" would be paid, meaning the capo expected 20% of the gross. That was all okay with T; he just needed to know a couple of things.

He learned the first just a few minutes later, when an old friend called and was very concerned about the health of T's mother, and said not a single word more. That follow up call, which came from a very well placed friend that T knew for decades, confirmed the legitimacy of the initial request from Chicago. The second thing T needed was a complete understanding of what was expected from him, and he knew he was about to learn that from the "spic" nervously approaching his corner booth at the Uptown Diner.

"Hey, Louisa, how 'bout a cuppa coffee here, huh? This booth does come with service, right?" T bellowed, thereby informing her that Miguel was welcome.

T instructed Miguel to sit across the booth with nothing more than a slight movement of the *Star-Ledger* he held firmly in both hands, shielding his face and all of his vital organs as if it was made of bullet proof Kevlar. Miguel slid into the booth as told, without any reaction to the vulnerability caused by sitting with his back to the door. He thought he was okay because he was in a public place; he would have been safer in a dark, rainy jungle.

While mildly interested, Miguel wasn't at all impressed with all the guinea shine. He couldn't care less about silk ties and Ferragamo shoes. He would trade it all for a sturdy pair of combat boots and a full canteen. He was, however, impressed with one aspect of T's appearance—the slight hint of ink permanently imbedded into the cuticles of his fingers. That was the confirmation he was looking for, and he got it even before he got his coffee.

It was a fractured journey to this meeting for Miguel. He had to hug a lot of necks and sit in the suicide, front passenger seat of more than just a few Cadillacs to be able to slide into that Naugahyde booth with "The Printer." The cup of coffee Louisa was about to drop in front of him already cost Miguel, or rather Mother Cuba, 5 giolas ($5,000), and he hadn't even had a piece of pie yet.

Speaking from rote memory, Miguel emotionlessly said, "I was very saddened to hear your mother has taken ill. I hope she is feeling better."

It was true. He memorized those words exactly as he was instructed. As he uttered them, he had a familiar feeling he couldn't immediately identify. He had just slid into a bench seat, prepared to ask a complete stranger he knew was very well connected and whose face he had not yet seen, to help him attain salvation. All of a sudden, Miguel realized why it all felt so familiar. "Bless me father for I have sinned." That's what it was. It was the required preamble to a Catholic confession. They were the operative words that signed you onto a direct line with God. No "bless me father for I have sinned" meant no chance to ask the priest to hear your plight and then guide you to salvation. Yup, that's it. Realizing he had now made the required connection, Miguel could relax and get down to business

"Can we talk here?" Miguel asked in a businesslike tone.

"Sure we can, Mr. ...?" T said, while lowering the newspaper and dousing Miguel with a stare that could have flash frozen his coffee.

"Miguel. Please," he responded, attempting to thaw the chill.

Louisa returned and literally dropped the coffee cup in front of Miguel before turning on her heel, not bothering to ask him if he wanted anything else. Miguel clearly knew he wasn't giving anyone any orders here.

"How can I help you...Michael?"

Miguel immediately got the message. T felt uncomfortable speaking to a "spic" on such hallowed ground.

Miguel wondered to himself, "Didn't anyone tell him I wasn't Italian?" He was sure that would have been discussed with T before the meeting, even though he was confident that no one knew whom he really worked for, at least almost no one.

Miguel was okay with "Michael." He really didn't give a shit about how T felt. It was about the move he was planning. He needed a printer, and according to everyone who should know, this chubby dago was the guy who could make it happen. Miguel decided to get right down to business. He slowly leaned in and began to make his pitch.

"Sir, I represent some very capable people who have the ability to move a great deal of your...art...so long as it's fresh and completely original." A cool stare and a slight tilt of an eyebrow made it clear what he wanted—new bills from fresh, new plates.

T folded the newspaper and set it on the table.

"What do I look like, fuckin' Michelangelo? That's a very hefty order from a guy with no track record and no upfront money," T said in a voice just above a whisper, almost as if he were talking to himself, informing Miguel that such a suggestion didn't even deserve a direct response.

At that point Miguel felt he was about to lose the only opportunity he was going to have to make a deal with a printer like T, someone who could really make it all happen. He was warned when he set up this meeting that "these" people were neither patient nor friendly. It wasn't like he didn't have experience dealing with impatient and unfriendly people. After all, he was a revolutionary. But this was somehow different. In Miguel's world, everyone's status, and therefore their levels of power and authority, was evident. They all carried obvious symbols of their rank and position around with them. Indeed, almost anyone who was anybody in Cuba wore a revolutionary military uniform. In those cases, it was easy to spot the brass and the ribbons. As for anyone else, you could usually tell their status just from their smell. Anyone who could afford to launder their clothes and bathe with soap and water on a regular basis had to be someone important.

Miguel didn't know how to handle T. He saw an average-looking, middle-aged guy wearing a $1,000 suit, with shoes that were ripped from the bones of some exotic and therefore very expensive animal, while sporting a huge watch he didn't recognize but could probably trade for a new car in Havana. Miguel would have recognized a Rolex much quicker. But little did he know that he was looking at something much rarer than a Rolex. If he asked, T would have told him that any Jew knew enough to wear a Rolex when trying to impress and goad their Jew friends as well as the WASPS they did business with. T and his ilk wouldn't get caught changing the oil in their car wearing a Rolex, not that he would ever even think of doing such "nigger" work himself.

T was wearing a Panerai GMT, a handmade work of Italian art, class and ingenuity. Designed and built in a small factory in Florence, Italy, by a family of famous Italian sailors, Panerai is the choice of any wise guy who wanted to make a statement to his brethren that he knew where he came from, and that he was proud of it. It would not have surprised T that Miguel didn't recognize it. Rolex made as many watches in a single year as Panerai made in the past 100. T at one time would have killed for that watch. In fact, he might have. Nevertheless, Miguel knew that he was quickly running out of time and he had to up the ante.

"Your friends, I assume, have assured you that I am a capable man, or you wouldn't be talking to me. I have $10,000 up front as a down payment toward 25 points on the first $100,000 test run. If your talent is what they say, we will order big—very big. But we want all the notes, with no strays given to your friends. And we get the plates." Miguel was getting into form now. He was beginning to push T aside and start driving this bus, he foolishly thought.

T continued to look straight ahead without making eye contact, although now Miguel certainly had his attention.

"How big?" he asked.

"Twenty million, and we pay 20 points, all on delivery," Miguel said, now also whispering while leaning over the table as if he was going to spit right into T's cup of coffee. In fact, he might have, but T didn't notice or even care when numbers that big were being discussed.

"We'll pay 25 points on a test run of $100,000, and I'll sweeten your coffee by paying it all up front," Miguel more than whispered while guaranteeing good money on the table, not just idle chatter of a big deal down the road. He knew guys like T—with their big cars and fancy clothes and even fancier women—always needed cash.

In a normal situation, T would have immediately suspected that Miguel was a cop, maybe even a Fed, but not with the connection he came through. If he were a rat or some kind of a cop, then everybody was in deep shit. On another hand, T couldn't just blow him off, not without doing a lot of explaining to a *Capo* who stood to make almost as much as T would on the deal. An initial run of $100,000 put $25,000 on the table for T and his guys, with a nice piece to the *Capo* to pass up the chain to the bosses. Good business for everybody.

Besides, what the "spic" didn't know was that T did it all, from making the plates to printing the queer. In fact, he already had a fresh set of plates stashed safely away. It was almost like a hobby for him, almost therapy. T, however, had no idea he would be helping Castro in a plot to punish his President. Being a hood wasn't un-American. In fact, it was in the finest tradition of American capitalism; helping those commie pricks was another thing. But who knew? That question would only be answered much later.

T was well aware that Miguel was here in front of him because he was told T had skills that were very rare, even in his neck of the underworld. Making counterfeit plates was a skill not easily replicated. Counterfeit plates are not made like genuine currency plates. The real thing is printed from hand-engraved, hardened plates that take years of talent and technology to produce. Counterfeit plates are made from a photo-offset process. The skills for both are considerable, albeit entirely different.

The counterfeiting process starts with a new crisp $100 bill tacked on the wall. A large format camera, usually a Hasselblad 2 ¼ square format, is used to make a high quality negative of the bill, both front and back—the easy part. These negatives are then used to burn the metal plates that actually print the counterfeit notes. T put the photo negative into a large wooden box he affectionately called Lucille, after his girlfriend. Lucille's reverse air compressor would suck the negatives tight against the printing plate, which is a thin metal sheet coated with light sensitive acid. When just the right amount of cool, white light passes through Lucille and over the negative, the acid on the metal sheet is activated, and it etches a very workable printing image of the $100 bill. The process, done once for the front and once for the back, renders a basic set of plates.

The most important aspect of the process is to create just the right amount of suction necessary to hold the negative tightly against the acid-laced metal plate. Too little suction will create a plate with wide, soft lines lacking the necessary crispness, and too much suction will result in lines that were too thin and frail to last for a full run of printing. Thus, Lucille's talents were obvious. If you were fortunate enough to spend just a single night with T's inspiration, you would know why. She was no square box by any stretch of the imagination. She was a middle-aged woman who had honed all the required skills and still had a blouse full of goodies to share. Why do you think he named a sucking machine in her honor?

The fact of the matter is, at that time, the US $100 Federal Reserve Note was one of the easiest in the world to counterfeit. Once the all green, single-colored back was printed, there was nothing left to do other than to align the modest two-colored front. Queer, as it was often called on the street, was usually printed in sheets of twenty-four notes, similar to genuine currency. Cutting the sheets with any ordinary office paper cutter was no problem. Even genuine notes have uneven white margins. Just peek at any note in your pocket.

The art and endurance of the printing process comes in the masking of the green serial numbers and the Treasury Seal on the front of the bill. This tedious and very difficult task is done on the photo negative before it's placed in Lucille to burn the metal plate. If the negatives are left unmasked, when Lucille does her magic, she will burn the green serial numbers and Treasury Seal into the plate along with the basic black image of the front of the note. That plate will then print the serial numbers and Treasury Seal at the same time it prints the basic front of the note, all in black, despite the fact that genuine notes have a green Treasury Seal and serial numbers. To make the task substantially more difficult, the green Treasury Seal is printed over a large black "100." To achieve perfection in deception, the counterfeiter must artfully mask the green Treasury Seal and serial numbers on the negative so they are not burned into the basic front plate. A second plate, consisting of only the serial numbers and the Treasury Seal, needs to be burned. These plates could then be used to print the green serial numbers and the Treasury Seal over the basic black front of the note, completing the counterfeit. That was the heart of T's art. He had the unwavering hand as well as the confidence and patience of a Sicilian salami slicer—ever see what happens to those guys if they miss? Brain surgery requires no steadier hand.

T's talents were known throughout the counterfeiting world—he was unsurpassed. T could climb into a negative with nothing more than a five & dime magnifying glass, and a brand spankin' new, sharp as the tongue of a pissed off mother-in-law razor. He could mask the Treasury Seal image on the negative so only the crisp black edges of the "100" remained. Two espressos with a generous jigger of anisette were all that were required before repeating the process for the green Treasury Seal and the serial numbers on the second negative. A perfect alignment on the press and you're ready to spend like a $20 hooker on her first night out with a brand new sugar daddy.

The choice of paper and ink is also crucial. Uncle Sam closely watches the production of all paper used to print his precious little works of art. The paper, manufactured at the perfect weight, has as an added precaution—small fibers of red and blue added to the mix during the manufacturing process. If you look closely, you can see them imbedded into every bill. With a very sharp razor, you can even successfully remove one or two. While a well-connected counterfeiter could obtain Hammermill Double Eagle Gold Bond paper, similar to genuine paper, the absence of the embedded red and blue fibers is always the nemesis. There is only one exception to this rule and that was accomplished about ten years ago by an unknown counterfeiter who simply vanished after printing nearly perfect $20 notes. T and his guys figured somebody wacked him in a back alley when a deal went bad.

While almost all good counterfeiters try to follow these techniques, T steps over the threshold when he mixes his own special formula ink. He is not only able to hit the color dead-on after running the finished product through the Maytag on gentle wash—with the right combination of tea bags and old shoes—he also mixes in just the perfect amount of metal flake to render a convincing shine to the bill.

T knew full well what was required for him to hold up his end of the deal. He not only heard the proposition made by Miguel, but he already computed the material cost, the spread to his guys for helping, the gross profit and the net after all "respects" were paid. It was a big number, but that number was always big, and it was the easiest number to identify. The more difficult number was the risk factor—in this case extremely difficult to determine because the guy sitting across from T was a complete unknown. However, he came with such a high nod. How could T go wrong, especially if he got all his money up front? Even if the big print didn't happen, T and his guys would make a few bucks, and he still had the plates.

T and Miguel parted company that afternoon with a clear understanding—no handshake, just a nice piece of pie. The deal was set. T left the diner assured that $25,000 in cash would show up just as promised. So, less than 12 hours later, a shoe box with $25,000 in crisp, new, genuine 100 bills was dropped into the unlocked trunk of T's '59 Cadu, right on Bloomfield Ave, in the middle of the day. Just a short time later, Miguel returned to the same trunk and picked up $100,000 in first class, counterfeit $100 bills. It was business as usual on the Avenue.

CHAPTER 8

HE GOT ALL THE ANSWERS HE NEEDED FROM JUST A LITTLE SQUEEZE

Washington, DC
Late September 1963

AT FIRST GLANCE, THE OFFICE looked like it could belong to any high-ranking business executive in almost any city in America. However, a closer look revealed that this wasn't just any business office in any city in America. This office was an integral part of the business of America in the only city in America that really made a difference.

The first hint of peculiarity came from the desk. It was a good size for the room, but it was oddly placed. The room had a broad bank of windows overlooking the city—being on the fourteenth floor, the view was pleasant on a clear day. Most would have positioned the desk to enable the occupant to appreciate the view, or at least be able to look up from his work and gaze, or even engage his daydreams or fantasies, but not this occupant. The desk, scrunched in a corner as far from the windows as possible, with the front pinned up against the wall, required that the chair and its occupant also face the wall. It was peculiar indeed. Did the occupant feel as though the room was full of peepers who would look over his shoulder at the papers on the desk? If you didn't know better, you'd also think he was afraid of someone peering in from the windows on the fourteenth floor and therefore positioned his body between the secrets on his desk and all else in the outside world.

No mahogany or cushy chairs or sofas for this tough guy. Both the desk and the chair were made of a sturdy gray/green metal only a shade or so lighter than GI green. The desk was clad with a green-flecked Formica top, without a single thing on it, not even a piece of paper. The sturdy chair glided on tiny rubber wheels that flared out from the bottom in a five-spoke pattern that provided ample support for rolling in any direction. It was, however, a better fit on the assembly line at General Motors than the office of a business executive. Even the work posture was more blue-collar. The back and arms were directly vertical and horizontal, respectively. You would be hard pressed to describe the style or décor of the room and there was certainly nothing inviting or relaxing about the furniture. It was all business, actually more like all hard work and laborious.

There was only one other stick of furniture in the room—a six-foot-tall, straight, gray metal coat rack with four, flat, protruding feet. It held only a long, wooden-handled umbrella, wound tightly closed, much like the human inhabitant. It was clear that this room extended no invitations to anyone. The design and function of the space was surely intended to make all visitors feel like they were in the waiting room of a dentist, one who wasn't referred to by the nickname "Painless." It certainly didn't see a lot of laughs.

The walls were empty of any family photographs or even a hint of a life outside the four corners of the office. There was, however, one large color photograph that hung over the desk. It was in a plain black frame, covered with clear glass such that when the sun shined in through the windows on the opposite wall, the glare made it almost impossible to focus on the picture. While you couldn't see the full image behind the glass, you were sure it was looking at you no matter where you were in the room.

When the reflection was subdued, you could see that it was an 11" x 14" photograph of a powerful in all respects, balding, pig-eyed, middle-aged man. He was sitting on the end of a highly polished mahogany conference table that captured all the elegance lacking in the room in which the photograph currently hung. The comparison was jolting. He was dressed in a suit and tie, a white shirt with French cuffs of a style that you were sure never graced the torso of the worker occupant of the present office. Neither a signature nor a caption graced the picture. It was clear, however, that this person was extremely important to the office occupant. The only other object in the photo was the reflection of a red, white and blue seal that was visible in the sheen of the conference table. It must have been hanging at some strategic location in the room where the picture was taken. Although it was difficult to read in its entirety, three words were legible: "fidelity, bravery, integrity." They're wonderful words, and a powerful motto. You would think that someone who went to all the trouble to have them hang on his wall would want to live by them.

This all might have made a modicum of sense if it were readily apparent that the office was on the fourteenth floor of a building located on K Street in the nation's capital, but it wasn't. The view wasn't particularly remarkable because no recognizable landmarks of Washington could be seen. But despite its mundane and spiritless décor, it was certainly one of the most important tiny gray offices in America. This was the office of the Special Agent in Charge (SAC) of the Foreign Counter Intelligence (FCI) desk of the most powerful, oppressive, egocentric, gun-cultured organization in the free world. This was The FBI.

It was 7:30 a.m. and SAC Tom Ritter had been at work for more than an hour. He, however, was just walking into his own office because, as usual, it took him almost an hour to review and synopsize the overnight foreign and domestic teletypes that came into the FCI desk while he slept. Part of his job, as the SAC, was to know everything that was happening in counter intelligence investigations in the free world as well as the Iron Curtain countries. It was also his responsibility to synopsize the activity and prepare a 30-minute-maximum briefing for The Director every day, seven days a week, come hell or high water. While this day began routinely, it was about to take a twist similar to the one you'd find on a tool used to open a bottle of fine French wine.

Just minutes after he walked into his office with the remainder of his coffee and hung his trench coat on the coat rack standing in the corner, his assistant, Alan Piper, knocked on the door. Ritter could tell it was Alan from the timidity of the knock. Alan really was a brave soul because practically no other employee, special agent or not, would dare walk up to Ritter's door and knock like a school-aged trick-or-treater. That's because no one at The Bureau knew much, if anything, about Ritter. He wasn't married, he had no children and he didn't seem to date. The only FBI gatherings he ever attended were those given by The Director—he was obligated to attend. Although he was a complete mystery to other Bureau employees, everyone knew that SAC Tom Ritter was somehow different than all the rest, and he always had something better and more important to do than casually speak to anyone in the office. Today, however, was a little different, and Alan Piper knew it. Since Ritter's secretary wasn't in the office yet, Piper took the risk and tapped on the windowless door.

The light brown, windowless, two-inch thick wooden door stood in the middle of a solid beige wall. The construction of the wall and door emphasized the definition of being on the "outside," only in this case, not even any "looking in" was permitted. Both the door and wall were as solid and impenetrable as the Berlin Wall and it was no accident they were that way. Both had been erected to keep away the uninvited and, just as importantly, to quell the peering eyes and the imaginations that accompanied them.

So Alan Piper stood behind the slab, waiting for some response to his audible overture, without the slightest inkling as to whether or not he would get one. It wasn't as if he didn't know Ritter was in there. He knew he was. He was always there. The question was whether Ritter would respond or not. The answer was soon apparent.

Ritter's voice carried through the thick slab, "You may open the door, Alan." How he knew Alan was out there—every time—was a constant mystery to Alan.

Alan Piper, all 6 feet 2 inches of his solid muscle frame, opened the door with the same timidity as a small boy would open the door to the woodshed, fearing his father was there to give him a beating. Slowly pushing the door open was as far as Alan would go. He didn't dare cross the threshold because Ritter only gave him permission to open the door, not to come into the office. Piper made that mistake once before and suffered an intensive and degrading lecture about assuming more authority than he was given. So on this occasion, Piper literally obeyed the instruction, opened the door and stood on the precipice of the threshold, as if standing behind the guardrail at the Grand Canyon. Crossing it would require much more daring than he was prepared to exhibit.

SAC Ritter was sitting at his desk in a suit, white shirt and tie, jacket on, reading glasses down on the end of his nose. He didn't look up at Special Agent Piper when he opened the door. Even that being true, he still knew that Piper had a package in his hand.

"I hope that's important," Ritter said in an agitated tone.

"Well, I don't really know, Sir, so I thought I should ask if you knew anything about it," Piper confessed.

"And?" Ritter asked, still not looking up, now seeming less agitated and more bored.

"A postal inspector just dropped this off and I'm not sure how to handle it," Piper said, lowering his voice to an almost whisper, trying to hide his confusion and fear.

Ritter was obviously annoyed that he was being bothered during the most productive hours of the day for anything that had to do with the Postal Inspection Service. He believed it was a substandard, bogus law enforcement agency run out of the Post Master General's Office. It reserved high paying civil service jobs for political hacks that The FBI wouldn't even let wash the windows, let alone join the ranks of the special agents.

Piper reached out, trying to set the 8" x 10" envelope on the desk without crossing the door threshold—a physical impossibility. Even so, he truly hoped to drop it and make a clean getaway. Ritter nearly leapt to his feet when Piper reached into the office. It wasn't clear if he did so because he didn't want him in the office and was simply expediting his departure, or because he just then realized there was indeed something important about the contents of the envelope.

Now, nearly fully erect, except for a slight, forward bend at the waist so he could look at and check the length of his tie, he held out his left hand, silently demanding that Piper place the envelope in it. His right hand was fully occupied with the task of attempting to close his jacket by securing the second button with only his right hand, a feat accomplished only by those men who have practiced such a maneuver on countless previous occasions. One could see that a substantial portion of his concentration was devoted to that task with an increasingly urgent nature about it. It was as if he had just walked into a fine restaurant with his fly wide open and was trying to close it, casually, before anyone noticed and he would die of embarrassment.

Even after Piper placed the envelope in his left hand, Ritter continued to ignore it, concentrating more and more on getting his jacket buttoned. But just as he was about to succeed, he instinctively squeezed the envelope, revealing the shape and semi-soft nature of its contents. Ritter immediately let go of the button and its intended hole, and for the first time, looked directly at Piper with wide eyes and a hint of alarm. His expression wasn't one of confusion or even inquiry. He had all the answers he needed and didn't need Piper anymore. Seeing a nod of the head that motioned toward the hallway, Piper, still standing on the threshold, gleefully grabbed the door and closed it in his own face.

Ritter, now more comfortably alone, continued to squeeze and lightly bounce the envelope, delaying its opening like a highly anticipated Christmas gift, but without even the slightest hint of joy in his expression. However, he didn't need to open the envelope. He got all the answers he needed from just a little squeeze. He finally dropped it, still unopened, onto the desk and picked up the telephone. By this time, his dutiful secretary was at her station outside the door and promptly picked up the receiver on her end.

"Tell Mr. Whitaker I need him here immediately." Ritter spoke in a very precise and demanding tone that she understood was tantamount to a less disciplined man screaming at the top of his lungs. She instantly set out to find Mr. Whitaker.

CHAPTER 9

AL WHITAKER GETS INVITED TO THE PARTY

Senior Special Agent Al Whitaker wasn't in the gym. The in-house gymnasium that even had a mini thirty-five-laps-to-a-mile track, was new to FBI headquarters—an addition Al Whitaker didn't approve of. Al was classic old school. A special agent should come to the office in a suit and tie, and stay that way throughout the day. He shouldn't be sweating in the middle of the day, and he certainly shouldn't be showering at the office. The intimacies of The Bureau should be intellectual and psychological, and those of the flesh should be left to other venues.

Al Whitaker was older than most of the special agents in The FBI. Even at Headquarters, he was very near the top of the age list, only three months behind The Director himself. Whitaker was born in a small steel town, Carbondale, Pennsylvania, and while his mother was Italian, his father's German heritage dominated his youth. His influence helped Al develop some of his most successful personality traits. However, he learned the skills that best prepared him for his career with The FBI from his mother. While his father thought he ruled the roost with an iron fist, it was his mother that set the family course with an iron will. She was a woman decades ahead of her time, so much so that she ruled by a term not even invented yet. Indeed, Francesca Travertino ruled the Whitaker house by stealth.

While her husband, Adolph, thought he was the king of the

castle, Francesca, because she knew that embarrassing a man was counterproductive to controlling him, quietly called her husband "*il capo del gabinetto*" (the boss of the toilet). In fact, her control and undetected influence enabled her to name their only child after her grandfather, Alfonso, all the while letting her husband think their precocious male offspring's namesake was his father.

Because men of that era felt religion and schooling were best left to the mother, Papa Adolph went off to the coalmine every day, without the slightest inkling that his trusted and beguiling wife was raising their son a Roman Catholic. Francesca Whitaker worked tirelessly preparing him for life in a society she was sure was going to hell in a hand basket. She helped him develop and hone the skills of deceit, treachery and self-preservation, which he practiced every day on his unknowing father and school friends. But Al Whitaker also learned to honor and respect loyalty and personal devotion. He grew to be a good man.

It's no wonder Al Whitaker was a natural for the new federalized law enforcement agency when The Director took over the reins in 1924. Whitaker and The Director, both graduates of the George Washington School of Law, became fast friends and more importantly, trusted confidants. While Whitaker simultaneously pursued a wife and family, The Director only had The Bureau, until 1928, when a newcomer arrived. An intimate and very secretive relationship developed between The Director and his new Assistant Director, who became known to all as simply AD. They became inseparable and assumed central roles in each other's lives as well as the life of The FBI. Even though The Director was personally devoted to AD, The Bureau was his first love, and Al Whitaker was an essential gatekeeper to The Bureau. While The Director and his loving AD would flit around cross-dressing at the Plaza Hotel in New York, someone had to be trusted to mind the darkest secrets of virtually the entire world—even if it had to be a healthy Catholic heterosexual like Al Whitaker.

Hence, for the last three decades, Al Whitaker was only one of two men who had access to The Director twenty-four hours a day. He thought he knew The Director's every secret—professional, personal and political. He was, however, wrong. He never would have dreamt, even in his worst nightmare, what he was about to learn. Al Whitaker was about to become an unwitting participant in what most would describe as the century's most diabolical conspiracy. Or maybe the planet's last chance at salvation, depending on who you asked.

On this day, Whitaker was sitting on the sofa in his office when Ritter's secretary appeared at the open door. His office was a great contrast to Ritter's, starting with the open door.

"He's looking for you," she said breathlessly, her eyebrows arched high into her forehead, almost touching the top rim of her pageboy haircut.

Al, married for thirty years to a woman he loved almost as much as his mother, had known Grace, the poised and elegant woman standing in his door, for almost that long. He still got a hard-on nearly every morning when he saw her. When he was younger, he would have to contend with that rod in his shorts all day long. But as he got older, he only felt that cold, rolled steel in the morning when he first saw her. The rest of the day he would keep his mind on the increasing responsibilities of his job.

"What's the problem?" he asked, knowing there was one, from the crook in her neck.

"I don't know, but I think it's something important. He has that look that only you can fix. I think you better come quickly."

Al never saw Grace sweat. He couldn't even imagine that possibility, until now.

Al Whitaker set the newspaper he was reading on the sofa cushion next to him and rose to his feet without the aid of his arms, using the strength of his quads alone. He was standing in front of Grace and had he been a less disciplined husband, he would have taken her into his arms, swept her in a semicircle around his superb torso and kissed her with all the passion he could muster. But he didn't. Frankly, Grace had a curious look on her face, one of almost disappointment that he didn't. It was as if they simultaneously realized they had the same fantasy and neither wanted to leave the room. But duty called. Grace turned on her heel and left the room, leading the cavalry to the rescue with Senior Special Agent Alfonso Whitaker in tow. As he followed closely behind her, not taking his eyes off her ass, he couldn't help thinking how he always hated to see her leave, but loved to watch her go.

Just a few short moments later, Grace was back at her cubicle desk outside Ritter's office and Al Whitaker unceremoniously burst open the perpetually closed door. He displayed a hint of irritation, probably residue of the sexual frustration he just suffered. He stood in front of the now sitting Ritter, silently demanding an explanation as to why he was there. Technically, in an FCI matter, Ritter was the ranking agent in the room, but he clearly was not the more powerful man, in any respect.

"What's up?" Whitaker eventually barked, more for effect than out of genuine irritation.

"This needs to be run down," Ritter commanded in a voice Whitaker didn't recognize. "A Postal Inspector just delivered it," he offered.

Ritter had never, ever before spoken to Whitaker in that tone of voice. Whitaker was the one with the direct line to "The Director," not Ritter. Big and strong Al Whitaker was greatly puzzled and quite confused, but only for a minute. He quickly began to piece it together.

Ritter was uncustomarily vague and unspecific in his command. Al had known Ritter for more than two decades and knew that his tone wasn't an accident—Ritter was in a quandary. He was confronted with a situation he couldn't reconcile alone, but he didn't want to share its intimacies with anyone, even to allay his growing concern. Al quickly concluded that Ritter had some reason, yet unknown to Al, to fear there was an FCI pot boiling at The Bureau, and Ritter wasn't invited into the kitchen. It there was any credibility to Ritter's assessment, Al knew there were only two possible chefs, and they were both at the very top of The Bureau. All this analysis went through Whitaker's mind in the 30-second interval between the execution of Ritter's command and his response.

"I'll get right on it," Al casually said as he picked up the envelope in a swift sweep of his right hand, as smooth as a Mantle home run swing and probably equally as powerful.

Whitaker was halfway through the threshold of the door when Ritter finally looked up. It was all over in a brief moment. Whitaker could see Ritter's dilemma in the corner of his eye as he passed through the door, grabbing the doorknob with his dangling left arm, tugging it shut behind him. He had to be careful not to pull on it too hard because the last thing he wanted to do was slam the door and give Ritter even the slightest impression that he was frustrated in the least over the incident. Whitaker knew that the noodle had now twisted.

Ritter was left starring at a blank wall, not knowing what to do next. He was now completely convinced that the only way Whitaker would have scooped up that package and run off with it was if he knew what it was and why it was important. How could he know, was the ever-looming dilemma now on Ritter's mind. As a result of not being able to react quickly enough to Whitaker's maneuver, Ritter just sat there. His only play was to see what Whitaker returned with over the next few hours. He already began to regret his decision to call Whitaker in the first place.

Big Al was taking strides like a thoroughbred stud leaving the stable with his dick still wet. As he walked past Grace's desk, he confidently tossed her a wink that weakened her legs. He knew Ritter was at that moment reaching for his hankie to wipe the sweat from his skinny, treacherous upper lip. And he was.

Whitaker didn't return to his office because he didn't want to take the chance that Ritter would slither after him. He also didn't know how long he could continue the charade of showing confidence in a matter when he didn't have the slightest fucking clue what was happening. He was about as confused as a virgin pulling a Hell's Angel train. But like that sweet young thing, Al Whitaker was going to learn fast. He headed for the only place he knew he could find complete security—some place, any place he had never been before—and he needed to get there fast, before Ritter could put a tail on him. He didn't even stop for his jacket. He always wore long sleeves with gold cuff links bearing the great seal of the United States. He didn't need a jacket; he was carrying an adrenaline warmth as he headed down the elevator and out the front door onto Fourteenth Street. He got into the first taxi he could hail.

"Hey bud, take me to Virginia and take any route you like," he barked at the driver. The taxi headed through Georgetown, over the Key Bridge, and was in Rosslyn, Virginia in about ten minutes. As soon as they crossed the bridge, Al told the cabbie, "Take me to your favorite restaurant, bud."

The cabbie smiled as he looked over his right shoulder and told him, "My favorite restaurant is in San Francisco, bud," obviously not embracing the term as one of affection.

Annoyed because he was anxious to get out of the cab and open the envelope still clenched in his right fist, Al spotted an Italian Restaurant right there on Route 29.

"Maybe next time, bud. Drop me at that place, Nero's, just ahead," Al commanded, still calling the driver "bud," but not intending to piss him off. He thought that a joint called "Nero's" couldn't be all bad. He might even be able to get something Italian to eat other than pizza, which Al considered only mildly better than low grade dog food, unless of course it's old world, thin-crusted tomato pie, crisply baked in a *forno di legno* (wood burning fireplace).

Even though it was still early, the front door was open. It wasn't but minutes later that Al was sitting at a nice corner table for two in the back of the cozy dining room, his back naturally to the wall. While he was holding the menu, he was looking at the government issue yellow 8" x 10" sealed envelope that seemed to soil the nice white table cloth like a urine stain on a pair of brand new jockey's. When the waiter came to the table, Al placed his hand, which was probably no bigger than a big league catcher's knuckleball mitt, on the envelope as if somehow the waiter could see through it. Al hated any breakfast food, so he asked the waiter if he could make him a nice *antipasto* and a *pranzo* (lunch) serving of rigatoni in Bolognese gravy, even though it was still long before the usual lunch trade would arrive. The young, handsome, Italian waiter was both gracious and accommodating. And, as he was turning on his heel, Al added, “and a nice glass of Chianti.” He decided he needed one even at that early hour.

That taken care of and now feeling safe and un-surveilled, Whitaker turned his attention to the envelope like a brunette with a new box of peroxide; what was inside could lead to a new beau in a ’55 light blue Thunderbird convertible or just a head full of orange hair and a tub full of tears. Some men would have carefully unsealed the envelope at the sticky overlapping top edge—the butter knife on the table would have worked perfectly—not Al Whitaker. He was the kind of guy who wouldn’t get caught dead cutting the end of a fine Cuban cigar with one of those guillotine-like cigar cutters. No, he bites the end off like a real man—it’s all part of the ceremony. He still loves to pull his wife’s panties off with his teeth on an occasional Saturday night.

Before he actually opened the envelope, Whitaker grabbed it and squeezed it gently. He already knew its shape, its approximate size and weight; in fact he was fairly certain what it was. You could already see him begin to ask questions. It wasn’t like receiving an unmarked gift and trying to figure out where it came from. No, there was a much more ominous, almost audible tone to his thoughts. It was more like finding a new pair of expensive Italian gloves in a nice box in the top of your wife’s closet. Obviously a gift for a very lucky man, only there was no way in hell those gloves were going to fit you. Sure, there might be an innocent explanation, but not one you could easily arrive at. It was going to take some hard questions and answers and very few of them with your wife. He was also well aware that Ritter knew what was in the package when he gave it to him.

So, as he sat there, he knew that the first step was to identify the first step. Whitaker also knew that if that package was what he suspected it was, the place to begin was not at The FBI. So, now it was time. In one casual twist of the wrist, he tore the envelope practically in two. The contents now lay on the table, half on the hand-painted Italian charger plate and half on the tablecloth.

There were no surprises there for Al. It was exactly what he thought. Six inches by four inches, no more than half-an-inch thick and couldn't weigh more than six ounces. As he looked at it, he still couldn't help feeling it appeared cheap. He tried several times over the years to upgrade The FBI's credentials, but no one thought it was important enough to change. Low-grade leather covered both the front and back of the horizontal book-like ID. The gold embossed letters on the front—US DEPARTMENT OF JUSTICE, followed below by FEDERAL BUREAU OF INVESTIGATION—usually wore off in the first year of service. Other than immediately recognizing the contents of the envelope as a set of authentic FBI Credentials, the pristine state of the gold lettering told him these creds belonged to a very new, very special agent. The outside of the creds is generic. Only upon opening the horizontal flip-up could you see the special agent's name and photograph, along with some official language giving the agent authority to enforce the laws of the United States. The important question was why these particular creds were sitting on that table, at that moment, distracting him from the beautiful, multicolored antipasto the waiter just delivered.

Normally the attractive antipasto would have enticed Al Whitaker to started eating it by hand, first picking a single hot pepper. Only then would he casually open any reading material he brought with him. But this situation was different. Al looked at the antipasto, eyeing the plate for the location of the hot peppers, which should never be on top of the other ingredients. Their placement should be strategically correct—near the outside perimeter of the requisite large oval plate. It's essential, after all, for a good antipasto to keep all the ingredients separate and never mix the tastes. It's not a salad—there should be no mixing. The green hots were right where they should be. Seeing them properly located heightened his expectations for the pasta Bolognese to follow. With his mouth watering in anticipation of the first bite of the hot peppers, he picked one up with his right hand and holding it by the stem, bit the entire pepper off, seeds and all. He simultaneously picked up the creds with his left hand and flipped open the horizontal ID. What he saw on the inside was enough to make him stop chewing the pepper, but only for a second, because while the contents were indeed shocking, it also gave him a great deal of information.

In a flash, Al had lots of answers but still more questions. Before he even read the complete name on the creds, he knew why Ritter was so hinky about asking him for help. It was clear there was an operation afoot and only the highest authority in The Bureau was aware of it. If it was a mystery to Ritter and now Whitaker, there were only two people left at The Bureau who would know, and they were both at the very top of the heap. Evidently, however, something had gone awry and Ritter unceremoniously found himself lost in the loop and was too "fraidy-scared" to question The Director or anyone else about it. Instead, Ritter decided Whitaker was the only person he could turn to because he knew that Whitaker, while often internally critical, was so dedicated to The FBI, it was nearly a spiritual, symbiotic relationship. Al Whitaker would be able to find no place in our society to reside comfortably, other than The Bureau. As a result, even the myopic Ritter knew that whatever had happened in this fiasco, Whitaker would fix it. Even if Whitaker believed the operation was bad for The Bureau, he knew the only thing worse than a bad operation was a bad operation gone public. He would fix it and then raise hell inside the walls of The Bureau, where it would forever stay.

All that being said, however, little did Whitaker know that his faith was about to collide cataclysmically with the only bulwark of principles he otherwise recognized—The Constitution of the United States of America. But, at that moment, Al Whitaker knew exactly what he was going to do next. He was going to eat that antipasto—mostly with his fingers—and a nice piece of semolina bread, enjoy the pasta Bolognese and definitely drink the Chianti.

CHAPTER 10

THERE'S ONLY ONE CIRCUS ANIMAL THAT DATES A GIRL LIKE THAT

Las Vegas
October 1963

Eastern Flight 330, the nonstop red-eye from Las Vegas to Newark, was a typical Eastern Airlines trip. They always had the best-looking stews in the sky, nearly all of them members of the mile high club and most likely with an agent. They actually weighed the stews every month in those days. Management claimed they did it for weight limitations on the plane, although I never saw them weigh one of those fat coach passengers that nearly took up two seats. It was just a scam to keep the stews looking good, but who was I to complain. It would be like complaining if the Dunkin Donuts man put a little extra cream in my donut.

Agents flew a lot in those days. There were only about 600 of us worldwide, and we seemed to be getting busier all the time. The stews were a welcome sight in an environment that wasn't really all that friendly to us. It generally started off bad when we showed up at the ticket counter with a GTR (Government Travel Request). We would give it to the ticket agent, they would issue a ticket and the Government would pay. The GTR required extra paper work, so unless you smiled and flirted with the ticket agent, it was an altogether unpleasant experience. It went from bad to really shitty when you told them you were with the Secret Service and armed. I always thought that just one of those chics would be impressed enough to treat me like a real paying customer, but not a chance. I think it was because all the ticket agents really wanted to be stews and fly around looking edible in their little outfits, but they just couldn't make the grade.

Airport security in 1963 was nearly nonexistent, that is unless you were carrying a loaded .357 Magnum under your jacket and the world's most sophisticated hand-held automatic machine gun in a very clever briefcase. At that time, everyone was so much more relaxed and actually excited about flying. In those days, no one demanded you disrobe before you even got within sight of an airplane. Most people got all dressed up to fly, especially the chics. The last thing they wanted to do was take off their hats and jackets and open their purses before they got the chance to get on the plane and show everyone they could look as good as the stews, which rarely happened. I guess someday we'll all get more comfortable with the process.

I knew this trip was going to be difficult, but I never really thought it would go as bad as it did. I was expecting trouble because Fax "look at me I'm a Secret Service Agent" Walder left directly from Las Vegas to take some vacation, and therefore asked me to take the Uzi back to Newark. Why he brought it in the first place was a mystery to me, other than the fact that some guys have a little dick and they need to carry a spare around in case someone wants to see it? There were plenty of those guys in law enforcement. I always thought it was because so many of them were micks, but I'm not so sure now. Maybe it was just a badge and gun thing.

The Uzi, affectionately referred to by most Agents as "hot stuff," was the weapon of choice for the Secret Service. It's an Israeli-made 9mm submachine gun first designed and built in the new nation of Israel in the late '40s. If an agent really feared trouble, this light weight, fully-automatic, boxy-shaped, foot-long weapon could easily be concealed under an agent's jacket or trench coat by using a sling over his shoulder. It was, however, usually carried in a very low profile briefcase.

"Hot Stuff" fit perfectly into what appeared to be an ordinary briefcase where she was held in place by a strong magnet built into the bottom of the case. An agent would carry the case in his left hand with the lid facing toward his body. When it was time to rock and roll, he would push a lever near the handle and the lid would fall off. By simply raising the case, he could reach across his body with his right hand, grab the Uzi and pull it away from the bottom half of the case that would then just fall to the floor. The lemon-squeeze safety on the back of the pistol grip was usually taped down so she could be fired without worrying about holding her so as to disengage the safety.

She was an excellent offensive or defensive weapon, a great date to take to a deadly party. Whenever she came out to dance, everyone got real shy and demure. The best thing about "Hot Stuff" was her ability to go fully automatic and empty a 30-round clip in three seconds, with hardly any recoil at all. In fact, while "Hot Stuff" was a nickname that the bosses tolerated, most of the guys who used her regularly called her "Dead Fuck"—a description the bosses definitely didn't approve of. But, hey, as the guys would say, "You could bang her as hard as you want and she never moves a lick."

Getting on a commercial flight with an Uzi, however, was always an interesting experience. Airline procedure required that I show up at a security table just outside the gate corridor to show my ID. Airport security would then usually walk me to the gate where I would be introduced to the captain and then be shown to an assigned seat. Things usually began to go sideways when the rent-a-cop security guys decided they wanted to try out their brand-spankin'-new portable X-ray machine. A tabletop metal box, with an old-fashioned latch refrigerator door on the front, was the latest thing in "automated security." Actually, it just proved there was no such thing as "automated security."

The best way to avoid an incident at the airport was to call ahead to a special number the airline security people gave to federal law enforcement agencies, thereby forewarning them that we were coming with guns. At least then someone would meet you at the gate and know how to handle the situation. Keeping the fact that some guy was getting on the airplane with a machine gun from the passengers was of paramount concern to the airline. Naturally, the Las Vegas Airport had no such procedure, and the Las Vegas Secret Service Field Office was no help at all. I didn't know what the local agents did when they had to travel with weapons. Maybe they just carried their six-guns on the plane with all the other local cowboys. Naturally, an obvious *Gindaloone,* as they called us Italians from New Jersey, wasn't going to get the same courtesy as a local boy.

Knowing I had no other choices if I wanted to go home, I took my chances. Hoping for the best, but fairly confident that this was going to be a cluster fuck, I sauntered to the security table and handed my credentials to the geriatric rent-a-cop and told him I was armed. His reaction was just as I suspected.

"Boy" he said. "I ain't never seen one of these before, I'm gonna have to search ya."

I simply couldn't argue with him, and I was sure he would never understand that searching me wasn't the problem. I already told him I was armed. It was the twelve or so passengers milling around the adjacent gate that I knew were going to freak out. But, hey, "No problem," I said as I put my brand new Lands' End carry-on bag and the briefcase holding the Uzi on the table. I thought things were going to improve when a middle-aged supervisor just happened to come by, but as my Vegas luck was consistent, it didn't.

First they X-rayed the Lands' End bag. That was no problem. It got real interesting, however, when they put the briefcase in the X-ray machine and no one even noticed "Hot Stuff" was there. It really instilled a great deal of confidence in the security system, especially since you didn't really have to see much to figure out what you were looking at. It reminded me of the night Marilyn Monroe sang happy birthday to JFK. You didn't have to see much at all to know what was in that dress. "It was a night, oooh what a night, it was, it really was such a night," as Elvis said.

No one saw the Uzi because all three rent-a-cops were too busy looking at my creds and then at me and then back at my creds again. The situation remained mildly uncomfortable until the overly self-impressed supervisor decided to pick up the briefcase and fiddle with the lever under the handle. I guess I could have said something quicker, but sometimes you just want to see them sweat. Well, he did all right.

When he ever-so-slightly touched the lever, the case operated exactly as designed. The lid fell away, fully exposing the Uzi in all her blue-steel glory. Unfortunately, the fool handling this cold steel man-eater had no idea what he was doing. As bad luck would have it, he was holding the case with the lid facing away from his body so that when it fell, everyone in the terminal got a good look at the Uzi; they reacted with predictable horror. Naturally, the only person in the room that didn't have a clue as to what was happening was the fool holding the proverbial "bag." As I stood there thinking that things just could not get any worse, and feeling very smug that I made sure "Hot Stuff" was unloaded before I walked into that airport, I was quickly deflated as the situation deteriorated dramatically.

When the passengers by the gate got a glimpse of what was happening, they audibly gasped. The fool holding the briefcase immediately turned around, and as he did, he banged the case on the side of the X-ray table. The magnet holding the Uzi, luckily, was strong enough to hold it in the case. That wasn't true, unfortunately, for the 30-round ammunition clip that hit the floor with a clang as the case hit the table. To make matters worse, the clip hit the floor at just the right angle to squeeze a 9mm round out of the top, which then squiggled across the floor and landed right in front of the right toe of my Lucchese Caiman Tail Boot. By instinct, I stepped over the round and tucked it away in the space just in front of the forward edge of my 1½-inch cowboy heel and the leather sole of the boot. I quickly realized that unless things didn't improve immediately, I would be doing a lot of explaining and writing when I got back to Newark, if I ever got back there. It was at that instant that I got my first and only break—ever—in Vegas.

"What da fuck are you doin?" I heard from behind me. I'm sure no one else in that airport knew why I was smiling in the middle of that shit storm, but I knew. While I didn't recognize the voice, I certainly recognized a Jersey accent. And sure enough, standing behind me was a certain Jersey dago. He was about 5 feet 9 inches, built like a Ferrari—slim, strong and very fast. Shoe-polish-black hair in a widow's peak, and a three-day shadow that I am sure grew almost as fast as he talked—my kinda guy. He was about ten-to-fifteen years older than me, and although I wasn't immediately sure of his position, I was certain he was substantially up the food chain from the minnows I was currently swimming with.

"There's only one circus animal that dates a girl like that," he said, looking over my shoulder at the chaos continuing to erupt. "You gotta be Secret Circus," he said in a more than mildly sarcastic tone.

I knew enough to keep my mouth shut, especially as he walked over to the frazzled rent-a-cops and simply raised his right hand, palm forward. Everyone knew it was time to shut up. They obviously knew him, and he certainly had some authority. When all quieted down, he calmly picked up the briefcase and lid and politely but firmly took the ammunition clip the supervisor was now holding in his hand. From the forced smile on his sweating face, I'm certain the guy was greatly relieved to give it up and let someone else handle it.

"Sal Giullio, Customs," he said, walking toward me with his right hand out. When I shook it I could feel callouses on his palms from lifting weights. While his hand wasn't bigger than most, it was like shaking an old 5-lb. sledge hammer, from the working end. He squeezed my hand as if he was trying to make orange juice. Sal was a genuine tough guy. I was glad he was on my side, at least I hoped he was.

"Do you have any other luggage?" Sal asked while now holding both the re-assembled briefcase and the dislodged banana clip in his left hand

Without saying a word, I raised my right boot and revealed the hidden 9mm round I was hiding between the heel and sole. Sal just rolled his eyes and very slowly bent over and picked it up with the index and middle finger of his right hand, immediately covering it with his fist. I never saw that round again, nor did I ever see him again after that day. He walked me to my gate without saying another word. When we arrived, I stuck out my hand and tried to say thanks. But as he shook it with just two powerful strokes, he cut me off and simply said, "You'll do better back in Jersey. Don't write or call," he said sarcastically. "I left all that behind."

Then he simply turned and walked away, raising his left arm, with his elbow at a 90-degree angle, and gave me an open handed "so long" wave. It was only then that I noticed the 44mm Panerai Pam 24 polished stainless steel submersible on the back of his left wrist—my kind of guy for sure. "Maybe someday I'll be able to get one of those," I thought to myself.

CHAPTER 11

"WHAT SHOWER, JAKIE?"
"THAT SHOWER, BOOKIE."

AFTER THE AIRPORT DEBACLE, THE flight home was uneventful. Getting out of an airport was a whole lot easier than getting in. So when I arrived at Newark, I was able to get my bags and cruise through the airport. I jumped into a cab for the short ride to the Weequaic Park Tower Apartments on the edge of Weequaic Park in Newark. It was a stone's throw from the airport, which made it a haven for dozens of Eastern Airline stews. The place was a single agent's paradise with all the benefits, including an indoor swimming pool that was often referred to as the swinging pool, for obvious reasons.

When the cab dropped me off, I knew Bookie and his girlfriend Ava would probably be home and surely be in bed, not nearly sleeping, just in bed doin' the horizontal mambo. Bookie and Ava are black, and as genetics would have it, they have that extra muscle. You know the one. The jump, dance, rhythm and screw muscle that most white people don't have, but would kill for—except for Italians of course. We have our own special muscle. Bookie and I spent hours in intellectual debate over who first developed this muscle—the Africans or the Italians. The other is simply the beneficiary of human migration from one continent to the other.

"Bookie, I'm home." I would always yell when I came into the apartment to avoid any embarrassing moments, not that I had ever seen him embarrassed.

"'Sup, Jakie?" Bookie would always respond, exactly the same way, with strong emphasis on the S and the J.

Our apartment was perfect for a pair of single guys. It had a large living room, dining room and kitchen, with separate bedrooms and baths on opposite ends of the apartment. The mostly empty rooms were perfect for the Olympic weights and Smith Machine in the dining room as well as the enormous artificial Christmas tree perpetually standing in the living room. In fact, there were lots of "perpetuals" in that apartment—poker chips and cards on the kitchen table always ready to play, and clothes on the floor everywhere. We would rationalize it all, especially the clothes. It was kind of a failsafe system. Neither of us was particularly fond of doing the laundry, so just in case one of us couldn't find clothes in the drawer, we could always scavenge the floor and find something to wear in a pinch.

We did have a cleaning lady, naturally, because after all, we didn't want to live like pigs. But she was forbidden from removing the clothes on the floor, except for panties, bras and other female accoutrements. They all went right into the trash just to be sure they wouldn't cause any embarrassment to an unexpected houseguest. That was all before Ava, of course. Since she arrived on the scene, life became more settled. She became our guiding light. I loved living with them. Bookie is a man of honor and integrity, and he and Ava are a perfect couple. I didn't realize then what a complicated future Bookie and I were going to have.

I'll never forget the day Bookie first came into the Newark office; it was a watershed in my previous "White" life. Because I grew up in the Chambersburg section of Trenton, I had very little interaction with Blacks, who we all called yaams. The term yaam, while clearly derogatory, is a short reference to "*mellanzane,*" the proper Italian term for eggplant. As with most of the Italian language, the Sicilians crucified it. This particular epithet was shortened, of course, not only to refer to one of their favorite vegetables, but it was also a quick description of the black/purple skin color of the African people who began to populate the surrounding neighborhoods.

Chambersburg was the Italian ghetto of Trenton that emerged during the early years of the twentieth century. By the '60s, it had developed into a solid working class neighborhood with great Italian businesses, especially restaurants. It was also, unfortunately, very insular, although both Black and Hispanic neighborhoods were beginning to emerge on the fringes. It wasn't a time of conciliation between the races. In fact, the Italians still got along with the micks only mildly better than they did with the yaams. As a result, I had very little positive experience with either group. When I think about it, I'm sure that made it easier for me to develop a relationship with Bookie while other white agents would not. For the other agents, especially the southern guys, there was a very bright line between their world and that of almost any minority, especially one of color. I, on the other hand, just saw Bookie as a colorful Irishman.

When a new, single agent came into the office, it was customary to invite him to bunk up with one of the other single agents until he could get settled into his own place. That didn't happen when Bookie arrived. The bosses made no advance arrangements for him with the other guys and just left him to fend for himself. It was pretty awkward when, at the end of his first day on the job, with his bags still standing near the entrance of his new office cubicle, he wasn't entirely sure where he was going to sleep that night. Being the nonconforming rebel of the office, I wasn't sure if they expected me to do something about it, but I did. I liked Bookie from the start. He was very smart, and his sense of humor was like a neon light. It flashed on and off repeatedly throughout the day, often completely undetected by the other agents, some of whom already started to mumble about the need for another bathroom.

That was how Bookie and I hooked up, much to both the relief and horror of the bosses. He slept on my Belleville apartment sofa for a month or so, and then we decided to get a bachelor pad together at the Park Tower. The move only served to isolate me a little more from the rest of the office, but at that point, I didn't give a fuck. I was already reaching my full potential of office rabble-rouser.

Bookie and I had a healthy but quiet relationship. Then

Ava arrived. My first encounter with Ava at the apartment was unforgettable. I had just returned from a temporary assignment out of town. Not expecting anything unusual, I opened the apartment door and gave my customary "Bookie, I'm home" announcement. Hearing no response, I dropped my bag and went to Bookie's side of the apartment to see what was up. As I stood in the doorway of his bedroom, the closed bathroom door was directly to my left. Bookie was in his familiar pose in front of his dresser mirror, wearing only his boxers, with his knees slightly bent and a modest curve in his back. "Bookie's bend," as I called it, permitted him to see the fluffy crest of the almost perfectly round ball of black fur—eventually to be known as the "Afro"—that surrounded his chocolate brown face.

"Bookie, who's in the shower?" I casually asked, really thinking that he was just wasting water because he was in front of me while the shower was clearly running.

"What shower, Jakie?" he replied in a flat tone, his eyes never straying from the mirror, continuing to fluff his hair with a black pick only modestly smaller than a home gardening rake. At that very instant, I could hear the high-pitched squeal of the water being turned off and the ring of stainless-on-stainless as the shower curtain was yanked across the rod.

"That shower, Bookie," were the last words I spoke as I saw my career as a Secret Service Agent flash before my astonished eyes. The bathroom door opened wide. I broke into a cold sweat, as if a stranger pulled a gun on me. It was an absolutely breathtaking, nickel-plated, hand-engraved Smith and Wesson .357 Magnum—a gorgeous weapon that you just couldn't take your eyes off. While it would have been impossible not to admire its beauty, you knew you were in very, very big trouble.

Well, it wasn't a S&W .357 that dried all the glands in my mouth this time—it was a set of perfect, drop dead double D's. The chic that they hung from was about 5 feet 5 inches with an Afro about half the size of Bookie's. She had perfect creamy, light brown features, with a broad smile surrounded by full, supple lips that you just couldn't avoid fantasizing over. And the towel—well, the towel, perfectly placed, surrounded only the holiest of her most holy, from just above her nipples to just below her ass. It hung as a drape over the rest of her, never touching any other part of her luscious body because the largest, fullest, roundest, most horizontal parts of her were holding it up.

All this was the good news. Unfortunately, however, the bad was almost as bad as the good was good. The luscious creature holding up the towel was Ava. She was the SAC's confidential office administrator, the person that knew more about the secrets of the Newark Field Office than probably The Boss himself. She was the custodian of all the top-secret files in the office that included not only official government secrets, but also the personal secrets of both Secret Service personnel and its protectees.

I immediately recalled my first days on the job. One of the very first lessons a new agent learned was that there were two things you just didn't fuck with: government cars and government secretaries. In this case, I knew we were in trouble on both counts. See, Bookie didn't have a POV (personally-owned vehicle), so there was no doubt in my mind that he drove Ava to the apartment in a GOV (government-owned vehicle). I also knew that "We" were in trouble, not just Bookie, because The Boss always saw us as a team, and I, by simply knowing what was going on, was as guilty as Bookie. So we were both fucked—the only difference is that Bookie gets kissed when he's getting it from Ava. I would just get The Boss's foot up my ass. Naturally, Ava was bulletproof. The Boss would never expose her. She held the key to the security safe, where all those mysterious accident reports and other alcohol, chic and gun-related screw-ups were hidden from headquarters.

"Hi Jakie," Ava said with strong emphasis and a wide, bright eyed smile that would make a drag racer stand off the accelerator just shy of the quarter-mile post.

Ava slipped past my quivering legs, took the rake-like pick out of Bookie's hair and slipped back into the bathroom. I tried to be respectful and shield my eyes as not to stare. There were definitely no flies on that girl.

"Bookie, what the fuck are you doing?" I asked breathlessly.

"What you mean, Jakie?" he responded with extra emphasis on the "J."

"I mean, have you lost your fucking mind?" There was no response from Bookie. He just kept playing with his hair as if he still had the pick.

"Bookie, The Boss will cut the balls off both of us for this."

"What you mean, Jakie?" he repeated in the exact same tone, emphasis and cadence.

By that time, I realized there was no point in trying to continue this discussion with Bookie. I could only recall the little dog story they told us in training.

During Secret Service training, knowing they had a room full of young studs they were about to give loaded guns to and then unleash on an unsuspecting public, they told us this story:

"A little dog was standing too close to the railroad track, when a train came along and chopped off the end of his tail. He got so excited, he whipped around and the caboose chopped his head off."

The moral of the story: "Never lose your head over a little piece of tail." I just lowered my head, shaking it from side to side, as I slowly shuffled off to my room on the other side of the apartment, not knowing how to feel about it all.

Over the following years, I learned that Ava wasn't just a little piece of tail to Bookie. They were genuinely in love. I lived in that apartment with both of them for nearly two years and loved them both as family. I often think of them and hope all is well in their lives.

Bookie and Ava risked it all to nurture their relationship. I admired that, and while I never saw myself as a safe player in the game of life, I'm not sure I would have had the courage they did. At that time in my life, I was still a very young man and thought I was hot shit. I still had lots of life's lessons to learn; many of the most important were yet to come. I hadn't yet learned the difference between folly and a risk worth taking. That lesson, unbeknownst to me, was on the very near horizon.

However, at that moment, as far as I was concerned, the only risk I wanted to take was oversleeping the next morning. I was exhausted and still quite bothered about my unsuccessful romp through the casinos in Las Vegas. At the time, I wasn't quite sure why I couldn't catch that *testarossa*. I was certainly disappointed and felt like I failed miserably. However, another part of me admired her, or was maybe jealous of her independent spirit. She made her own decisions and took responsibility for her own life. I was sure she didn't have to worry about the length of her hair, or the shoes she wore, or even who her roommate was screwing. I just had the feeling that if she were in my Luccheses, she would tell The Boss and all the rest of them to kiss her ass. And that thought was the best part of my little fantasy. I had to get her and her ass out of my head because it wasn't the kind of thought that would help me sleep. So, I let her and the entire fiasco go, and with the help of a nice cold beer, I slept through the night for the first time in a very long time.

CHAPTER 12

A SHORT RIDE ON THE NEW JERSEY TURNPIKE

AT THAT MOMENT, LIFE ON the Avenue was good for T. It had been a productive summer for him, and after a little something for his guys for their help with the print for Miguel as well as respects paid up the line, T had more than just pocket money to keep him in pasta, *vino*, ass and gas for a while.

The summer heat had lifted and it was one of those most treasured autumn days—perfect time for a road trip. The sun was bright and strong, with just enough chill in the air to demand the Cadillac's heater to pump a hint of warm, fresh air onto the floor under the boat-like dash of the '59 ragtop. As the huge whitewalls rolled over the pavement on Stuyvesant Avenue in Newark, the entire car heaved up and down in a gentle to-and-fro rocking motion. If he didn't know better, T would have believed the car was a living, breathing animal. Although he never rode an elephant, it was as he imagined.

T, with his little, very blonde goom, jumped into his black Cadu ragtop and took the New Jersey Turnpike south for a little vacation, with lots of shoes, several tiny bikinis for Lucille, a very large pack of rubbers, and almost $15,000 in good walkin' around money—and oh yeah, a little something extra in the trunk. You have to ask yourself why he just couldn't take the cash, buy his *goom* Lucille a nice piece of jewelry and take the Cadu on a cruise to Florida for a week or two. Why did he have to print himself an additional $5,000 and then not even destroy the plates? Did he think he was going to need them in a pinch to run more notes to pay for dinner? There was no need to keep them. He could always make new ones for the next print, if there was going to be a next print.

If you asked T why, he wouldn't be able to give you a straight answer. He would probably tell you this story:

"Hey, did you ever hear the story 'bout the turtle and the scorpion? There was a turtle and a scorpion on a riverbank and the scorpion wanted to get to da other side. So he said to the turtle, 'how 'bout I get on your back and you give me a ride to da other side?' The turtle said, 'hey, do I look stupid? If I let you get on my back and swim out into the river, you'll sting me.' The scorpion said, 'Why would I do dat? If I sting you and you die, then we both drown.' This made sense to the turtle so he told the scorpion to climb on and he started to swim across da river. In the middle of da river the scorpion stung the turtle and dey both started to sink. In complete astonishment the turtle turned to da scorpion and said, 'why diya do dat, now we both drown?' The scorpion had only one answer, 'hey what can I say, that's just the way we are.'"

Wise guys usually reserved that story to explain why they called Jews "Scorps." However, in this regard, as well as many more that neither side would admit, both cultures were, oh so similar. The point being there is just no rational explanation for T's decision. It's just the way he was.

Lucille had been T's main squeeze for almost a decade now. Most of his prior girlfriends were named Maria. Now that might sound incredibly coincidental and improbable to the uninformed, but not to anyone who grew up on the Avenue. The fact is, it wasn't hard to date a girl named Maria when seven out of ten girls on the Avenue were named Maria.

It's an Italian thing. Almost every *paisan* has a mother or grandmother on one side of the family or the other whose name is Maria. As a result, the first daughter in almost every family is also named Maria, after somebody's mother or grandmother. No one focuses on the fact that its Latin origin is Mary, Mother of Christ.

The important fact is that the proper respects are paid to the family member who carried the name in the previous generation. In reality, Maria is the divine being most often called upon by all Italian men for help and guidance. You hardly ever hear a *paisan* call on God or Christ for divine intervention. When the shit hits the fan, it's inevitably, *Ave Maria* (Hail Mary) who he will turn to. But hey, the prayer does ask for the Mother of God to "Pray for us sinners, now and at the hour of our death." Why not turn to her in the hour of need, any need, even if it's just to catch a fish.

Lucille was a perfect *goom*. First and foremost, she was not only Italian by blood, but she was also Italian in spirit. Lucille fully understood the old-time Italian man. It was important that she was able to distinguish from the old world and the new, even though she was nine years younger than T. Had she not been properly prepared at a young age by her parents and siblings, especially her older sister, her expectations for a relationship with a man would just not have allowed her to be with a *paisan* like T.

Italian culture expects that she show her gratitude to her parents by dedicating the first two thirds of her time on the planet to honoring them and providing them with all the expected gifts. As she matured and became a beautiful young woman, she recognized her duty to family, culture and even religion. Everyone in the neighborhood knew her as a "good girl." This meant that her brothers never had to worry that they would run into a guy in a local bar and have to give him a beating because he was bragging that he fucked their sister. This didn't make Lucille a cold fish, though. She just had to be very discreet and careful about with whom and where she conducted her love life. In time, she did what was expected of her—she married a nice Italian boy in St. Philomena's Roman Catholic Church. She was pregnant within three months of the wedding and gave both her husband and her father a beautiful and healthy baby boy. Who could have asked for more?

No one asked for more, and that's where it all just came crashing down. She was desperate for someone to want more, much more, in so many respects. Lucille, like so many other "good girls" of her generation, became a non-person. It was an empty life, and as middle age crept up on her, she knew her chances of finding happiness were virtually over—divorce was simply not an option. So it went until the day she got the call to come to the hospital—her husband had been hurt at his job. She never really thought that working in the ironworkers union was dangerous, but evidently, it was. In just a blink of an eye, her life veered off course and she was a free and independent woman as she had never been before.

After the funeral and a modest six month mourning period, Lucille sold the house in the Brookdale section of Bloomfield and moved into a very small apartment on the east side of Manhattan. The move completely shocked her family. Lucille's focus changed from everyone else's needs to the fulfillment of her own dreams and happiness. Then she met T. It was never a matter of fulfillment, but rather more of an issue of entertainment. T could never truly fulfill a woman like Lucille any more than a Marvel comic book could satisfy a Hemingway reader.

What Lucille liked the most about T was that he was slow, and slow is what she wanted. It wasn't that T was dumb or intellectually dull—he was just slow. He did everything slowly. With T, life not only slowed down, but it was also easier, quieter and smoother. Actually, life rolled on much like T's Cadillac: deliberate, under control and most importantly, it made no sharp turns. He made very few demands of her and was very concerned about her happiness. That's why Lucille was surprised at T's colossal exercise of poor judgment to get involved with Miguel in the first place. Her surprise turned to complete astonishment that he would allow his stupidity to expose her to his fiasco.

Maria had no idea T decided to stash fifty $100 Federal Reserve Notes—all of them as "queer" as the Cadu was long, neatly stacked in a Salvatore Ferragamo box—in the trunk of the Cadillac. Tucking the plates in an empty tomato pie box was also no stroke of genius. T broke Rule #2 that day. Even worse, it was his disregard of that Rule which later precipitated his violation of Rule #1, which eventually rendered all other rules inapplicable.

Rule #2 was "never show your ass." That means never put your ass in a place where somebody could see it has pimples. Keep it covered. Make it look sexy and slim. Never stick it out where someone could bite it. T broke this Rule, and it didn't take very long before someone noticed, bit him real hard and enjoyed every morsel.

The trip to Florida started as expected. There is simply no road anywhere like the New Jersey Turnpike. Sometimes it feels as wide as it is long. It's probably the straightest, flattest super highway in America. You can drive from the Delaware Memorial Bridge to the George Washington Bridge with your eyes shut. And ooh, those Cadus. They just rolled up and down the Turnpike like sofas on wheels. You would never catch a guy like T in anything else. No matter what the big money said about those German-made Mercedes and BMWs, guys like T never forgot that the Kraut's tried to kill our boys with that steel; there was no way T was going to even ride in one, let alone buy one. His opinion of the German cars was mild compared to what he had to say about the Japs. Besides, even all the politics aside, those cars just weren't his style, and he had a very particular style about everything.

See, a guy like T didn't sit in front of the TV watching a baseball or football game, even if he bet a ton of money on it. He didn't bet on the game because he thought he knew about the game and could therefore predict its eventual outcome. He would only bet on the game if he had an inside line, that is, he had it on very good authority that the game was fixed. If there was a score to be made, T and his guys just had to be a part of it. They had to get their piece. That was the game they played, not that baseball or football crap. They played the game of real life, and they always played with an edge.

So there he was, doing 75 mph in a 50, cruising in the left lane, with Lucille's head comfortably on his shoulder, rocking in perfect harmony and cadence with the rises in the pavement. Her presence and touch nicely diverted his attention from the monotony of the ride. If I told you Frank Sinatra was on the radio, I would be making it up, but if he wasn't, he should have been, because otherwise life at that moment for T and even Lucille was perfect. And that's just what the New Jersey State Trooper thought T was thinking when he decided he was going to "ruin this dago's day."

It didn't take long for him to close in on the Cadillac, even with the troop car and his mind starting from a dead stand still. It wasn't about law enforcement. It was personal. The Trooper was sick and tired of "these guineas driving up and down the Pike in their grease ball Cadillacs." They never worked a day in their life, or at least never slept through most of the day and collected a paycheck for it every two weeks like the Troops did. After all, his Pollack father used to kick the shit out of those dagos on the streets of Paterson. It was his obligation to carry on the tradition. Or so he thought.

As the troop car pulled within inches of the Cadillac, the wailing siren seemed to undulate in cadence with the roll of the pavement. But, so did the 4,000 lb. Cadillac, which nicely coordinated with the gentle stroke of Lucille's hand on T's cock. It was a ritual they always practiced whenever they took a long trip. Lucille was happy to go along and T was happy she was there. All in all, T's senses were fully occupied and therefore he didn't hear the siren for three miles. It's a good thing that didn't aggravate the Trooper too much. However, all good things eventually come to an end, even on the New Jersey Turnpike. T ultimately saw the flashing lights, and pulled up the Cadu, and his zipper, in anticipation of the impending visit from some dull-witted flatfoot.

"You wops just think you own the fuckin' road, don't you? Let me see your driver's license, *paisan,*" was the Trooper's salutation to T, when he finally approached the driver's side window of the Cadillac.

His description of their relationship, however, could not have been more incorrect. A "*paisan*" is reserved by male Italians for their most kindred spirits, other Italian males who they consider to be their most trusted planet companions. This Trooper was substantially behind the yaam that filled T's car with gas earlier that morning, and was nowhere even close to a *paisan.*

While most motorists would have been intimidated and even fearful of a 6 feet 2 inch Trooper, dressed in the genre of a 1943 Nazi Storm Trooper, and every bit as cocky, T couldn't give a shit, and he let him know it.

"What's the problem?" he snarled, without even the slightest bit of respect, treating the Trooper as if he was a waiter who just told him there was no more blueberry pie.

Sensing the disdain, the Trooper snapped back, "You got a registration for this wop-mobile?"

As the Trooper was talking, he was already in pursuit of his primary objective. His eyes were all over the inside of the car before T could respond. In fact, there was hardly anyone for T to talk to, because the Trooper wasn't there for his response. His eyes and his head were in the back seat, under the front seat, in the glove box and heading for the trunk.

Without waiting for an answer to either of his questions, the Trooper asked in a flat tone that could never be described as solicitous, "Mind if I look in the trunk?" Simultaneously, his arm, which was about as long as one of those poles used by T's mother to hold up the clothes line when she was drying sheets, reached into the window and snatched the keys from the ignition. He was now in a full Gestapo stride, heading for the trunk of the Cadu.

T didn't sweat his guinea tee. He didn't even protest. He figured the Trooper was just gonna bust his balls for a while and then look for a $20 bill. He figured the quickest way to get back on the road to Florida was to take whatever ticket the Trooper wanted to write and then move on. It wasn't like he was going to pay it anyway.

"Pop" went the trunk. The last thing T remembered was hearing the Trooper's sarcastic voice.

"Salvatore Ferragamo, my favorite dago cockroach killers. Let's have a look at those bad boys."

So much for the trip to Florida.

CHAPTER 13

"I'LL TAKE CARE OF IT CARMINE."

After a relatively sleepless weekend, because Bookie and Ava were up all night banging as if they were the drum line at Texas A&M, I managed to drag my lonely ass out of bed on Monday morning and went directly to the office. That might sound routine to most, but it's generally not how a Secret Service Agent works. Be certain, the Service gets every dime out of the salary it gives an agent. You work all hours of the day and night, any day of the week, including all high holidays like Christmas and Thanksgiving. You only get to take a vacation when there's nothing better to do and, when no other, more senior agent, wants vacation. The only real *bene* in the entire experience is the "sign me direct to the field" option. This option allows an agent to avoid going to the office in the morning like most working stiffs by merely calling the office and signing out "direct." By doing so, an agent represents that he is going directly to some other location to work on an investigation or conduct some other official business. A not-so-clever play of this option would allow an agent to make that call on the radio from his driveway and then retreat back to his bed for another hour or so, for whatever reason.

Since I had no amusement waiting in my cold, empty bed, and no other real reason to live and breathe, I did what so many of my brethren avoided. I went to the office, hoping to find someone who was interested in talking to me, someone who had the same security clearance, so we could actually have something in common to talk about.

My entrance to the Newark Field Office of the Secret Service was somewhat different from most agents. I wasn't permitted unsupervised entry to the office like other agents. It wasn't because I couldn't be trusted with the weapons, counterfeit or government secrets held there, but rather because my hair was too long and I wore cowboy boots. Indeed the basic mindset of the organization was focused more on such superficial aspects as appearance, rather than more heady considerations of national security or integrity. As was often preached to me, "looking like an agent is just as important as acting like one."

The Secret Service, established in 1865 to suppress counterfeiting of US currency, was nearing its 100th birthday. The Secret Service wasn't assigned its most important job of protecting the President until the assassination of President McKinley in 1901. Being America's first national law enforcement agency, the Secret Service is steeped in great tradition. It's shortcomings of character and direction developed over the century as a result of political intervention in personnel selections. At this point in its history, the Secret Service was still hiring former local cops with a high school education, at best. The fact guys like me and Bookie and a few other newcomers weren't former cops but "college kids" only drove a bigger wedge between the old guard cops and those *avant-garde* college kids.

On that particular fall day, I eventually gained access to the office as a result of the "dago conspiracy"—a secret pact suspected by the SAC and his faithful ever since I joined the office. Clearly, this was an internalized fear of all the Irish micks in the office who just couldn't stand to have a self-confident wop around. It reminded them of the guys that used to steal their girlfriends when they were teenagers.

When I arrived at the office, located in an inconspicuous corner of the second floor of the Federal Building on Walnut Street in Newark, the outside door was unlocked. It was always that way to accommodate the general public. Once inside the waiting area, I approached the security window, fully expecting to be told, “Go get a haircut,” by the SAC or one of his henchman, like the Assistant SAC, Pat Flannigan. Instead, the counterfeit squad leader, Carmine Perugia, greeted me by quickly opening the security door and presenting me with a completely unanticipated dilemma.

Carmine was one of the few cop/agents in the office I could talk to without the aid of a social interpreter, although he often communicated in a manner that was only marginally verbal. On that day, when he met me at the front door, I immediately knew it wasn’t by accident. His face was focused with intention. His eyebrows were slightly scrunched and his glasses—an absolute necessity for safe navigation around the office—were in his left hand, while his right hand was clenched in a fist held perpendicular to his face, against his tightly pressed lips. In fact he never even said, “Follow me” or “I want to talk to you.” He just gave me that wide-eyed look and a nod of the head to follow him. I did, because unlike most of the bosses in the office, I truly respected Carmine.

When we reached the counterfeit squad room, located at the very rear of the office, he walked straight through the room to his office in the back corner. It must have been comical to watch because he walked in very large strides with his upper torso lowered, but still very vertical, his arms down to his sides, his head motionless and pointed straight ahead. I was only half a step behind, in full cadence. I couldn’t help mimicking his stride and body posture, half in jest. It reminded me of a Marx Brothers comedy routine where Groucho says to Harpo, ”Walk this way” and they would both stride off in some identically twisted formation.

Crossing the threshold of his office, he turned in a perfect circle, never breaking stride. As he passed the door, he extended his arm and slammed it shut, only after I barely made it inside. Once in the room, all fucking-around stopped. Carmine didn’t have to tell me. I knew that whatever he had to say was both serious and important. While Carmine is a man who has a certain caricature quality about him, he is indeed a very serious man, who serious people take very seriously.

We both stopped moving simultaneously. Now standing face-to-face in the room, Carmine held out his hand and said, "Jake, this was just sent up by headquarters."

It was a $100 bill. While it was as queer as the day was long, it wasn't just any old counterfeit note. It was the same note the perps were pumping into those slots in Las Vegas just a few days before. I was thoroughly confused, wondering why Newark had a c.4161 note that was passed in Las Vegas. Then, as Carmine began to explain, the pieces began to fit together like a great set of tits on a lesbian. You know where they should be, but for God's sake, you can't imagine why.

Carmine leaned in closer and whispered, "They grabbed the printer."

When Carmine told me this, I began to unclutter my mind and even managed to stop fantasizing about the fabulous *testarossa* I chased all over Las Vegas and eventually lost. It still, however, took a couple of stupid questions to focus.

"Carmine this is the Las Vegas note. What's happening? Why did headquarters send it here?"

"Some Trooper stopped this guy on the Turnpike with a shoe box, Ferragamo," he added with a hint of admiration, "full of these notes, together with a beautiful set of plates in a fuckin' tomato pie box," Carmine said, peering through his glasses at the note.

"You mean the Jersey Turnpike?" I questioned, full of astonishment.

"Yeah. The Troopers sent the notes to Headquarters instead of here to the Field Office and Headquarters sent them back to us with more than just a little attitude. The Director's office wants to know why a printer is popped in our district with a shit load of new notes, together with the fuckin' plates and we're out of the loop. The Boss hasn't seen this yet because he's on leave until the end of the week. It would be a good idea to have some answers for the questions he'll have when he gets the news so we can pull him down off the fuckin' ceiling."

The Boss, although a short term for the SAC, wasn't a term of affection, especially since he was German, and based on his personality, we could have just as accurately called him "*Mein Führer.*" He wasn't going to be happy that the Troopers bypassed our office and sent these note to headquarters without so much as a courtesy call to us. He'll certainly interpret it as disrespectful and want a piece of somebody's ass, actually everybody's asses would be more like it, beginning with Carmine's, followed closely by each of the guys in the counterfeit squad. And since I was at the bottom of his favorite personality hit parade, I would get an extra special heaping of shit. So when Carmine asked me to check it out before The Boss got back, it sounded like a good idea to me. I was prepared to do whatever he asked.

"How about you track down this Mr. Tuscolano Di Viterbo and see what he has to say for himself, other than his shoe size and favorite tomato pie toppings."

"I'll take care of it, Carmine," I told him in a flat monotone response, hiding my keen interest and excitement. I was thrilled that Carmine had enough confidence in me to trust me to run this note out. While anticipating a challenging investigation, I had absolutely no idea of the wild ride I was in for.

CHAPTER 14

AND MAYBE HE COULD TELL ME A LITTLE SOMETHING ABOUT THIS NEW C.4161 COUNTERFEIT NOTE, TOO.

I GRABBED THE $100 NOTE AND headed for the door and my "G" car parked in the garage downstairs. Other than the official black limos and familiar black station wagons used as follow up cars in protection movements, all other cars used by Secret Service Agents at the time were undercover cars. These cars, used for surveillance and undercover operations, were Cadillacs, Lincolns and other un-cop-like cars. In my case, The Boss thought he found the perfect car for me.

About six months earlier, a kid at Rutgers University was head-over-heels in love with his high school sweetheart, but her father, in an effort to weed the seeds of love from his daughter's garden of higher education, packed her off to the University of Kentucky. However, the lustful young boyfriend would not be denied. He burned up the telephone lines from New Jersey to Kentucky, along with his monthly food allowance and college financial aid. About the time the first semester ended and with still five more lonely months ahead of him, our young Romeo decided a few hours in the school metal shop would render him a bag full of quarter size slugs. These would keep him and his squeeze in oohs and coos until the summer wind returned her to the backseat of his 1958 VW Beetle.

It didn't take long for the Secret Service to find the common denominator for all the pay phones jammed with the homemade quarter-size slugs; the sweet "thang" in Kentucky was the only possibility. The truly heartbreaking part of the story was that the girl gave the kid up in a New York minute. Apparently, she found a new love in Kentucky and didn't even bother to make the trip home to Jersey at the end of the year. Our lovesick pup not only discovered a new way to love in the Federal Detention Center in Newark, but also lost his Beetle as an instrumentality of the crime. Unfortunately, for love, he made the mistake of using the Beetle to carry his slugs from pay phone to pay phone. It was hard to tell which loss was more heartbreaking for the kid—the chic or the car.

No one in the Secret Service would even consider driving the Beetle except me. The crazy thing about it was that I really loved the car and drove it with enthusiasm. No, I drove it like I stole it. The speedometer only went up to 85 mph, this in the day of the emerging muscle car. I would often push it until I buried the needle and it would just keep on keepin' on. I always prayed that I would never run into that kid again because it would just break my heart; I might have even given him the car back. The combination of the hippie character of the car, the length of my hair and the demented way in which I drove it was cause for many interesting experiences with local cops.

Take for instance the day not too long before when Carmine asked me to take about $100,000 of queer to Newton, a small town in the northwestern-most corner of New Jersey—the nuclear war relocation site for the Newark Field Office. Someone must have figured that if the idiots in Washington or Moscow ever let their "fingers do the walking" on the buttons and the world went "Boom, Boom, Ka-boom," some of us might survive and be stupid enough to drive two hours to Newton to die of radiation poisoning.

As a semi-dutiful special agent, there I was, driving my Beetle through the back roads of Sussex County, in the wee morning hours—with a sample of every known counterfeit note seized in the Newark district for the past twenty years in a briefcase on the passenger seat—still burying the needle. I was expected to deposit the sample notes in a secure safe in the Newton Post Office just in case we ever had to operate from that location.

During those days, it was neither surprising nor unusual to look in my rearview mirror and see those oh-so-familiar flashing red and blue lights. As a teen, it was the same familiar "oh fuck" that resulted in me losing my license seven times between the ages of 17 and 22, when I joined the Secret Service. But now it was different. "I was one of them. Or was I?" I thought to myself as I pulled to the shoulder of the road and watched the two local cops in the rearview mirror get out of the patrol car.

"Okay, kid. You must have to pedal real hard to get that piece of shit to go that fast," the cop quipped, as he held a two-foot steel flashlight in his left hand up about chin height and rested his right hand on his dick—I mean his gun. Even with the flashlight shining in my eyes I could see he was carrying a huge, chrome, six-inch colt peacemaker strapped in a black leather, basket-weave holster. He was only looking at me with one eye while he was watching for a reaction to his witticism from his obviously junior partner standing on the passenger side of the Beetle.

He noticed the "RUTGERS" sticker on the rear window, a holdover from the lovesick kid who lost the car, so naturally the clever officer offered more sarcastic observations.

"I bet you're a college kid who just don't have time to obey the speed limits. You got a driver's license and registration for this shit box?" he said, this time with a more serious and hurtful tone in his voice.

Now it was my turn.

"Yes, officer," I responded, in a cheerful tone that both surprised and confused him.

Without saying anything else, I reached the short distance to the glove box and pulled out the little cardboard envelope that held the vehicle registration. Every Secret Service vehicle had one, and this one was like all the rest—completely fictitious. And the fictitious registration, in the name of someone who obviously didn't exist, matched the fictitious license plates. This little precaution was necessary because bad guys often had access to the DMV (Division of Motor Vehicles) files. Just in case they did a lookup to burn a surveillance, the car was cool and not registered as a cop car. I also had a fictitious driver's license in my undercover identity that I also carried in the glove box. It didn't match the name on the registration and plates because I just didn't have time to get them in sync yet at the DMV. In any event, it was the same old, same old, all over again. I handed the cop the fictitious license and registration and watched very closely, trying to read his reaction as he shined the light on them. Would it be completely hysterical? I could only hope.

"You Jerry Cella?" he asked with a tone of expectation in his voice that I would confirm his assumption.

"No!" I said with a tone akin to telling a waitress that I didn't want sugar in my coffee. The cop was so oblivious that he didn't even pick up the subtle insult.

"Who is he and why do you have his license?" he asked while squinting at the license. He still showed no sign of real agitation so obviously my job wasn't done yet.

I began to reach down between my legs with my left hand, attempting to get my ID out of the inside of my right boot, where I always kept it. Officer Zucker immediately took a dislike to my unauthorized movement and barked at me in a tone I am sure was reserved for his children, wife and unruly pets.

"Hey, I didn't tell you to move your hands, hippie boy."

"My ID is in my boot, sir," I said.

"I already got your ID in my hand, boy," he barked with the authority he only had on a country road on a dark night in Sussex County, New Jersey.

"Well that's not exactly the case officer. That license is fictitious like the plates and registration. My real ID is inside my right boot, where I keep it until I need it."

Well, that was all the unconventionality Officer Zucker could handle at 2 a.m. from some punk kid in a foreign car who needed a haircut—the kid that is.

"Okay, out of the car kid! Keep your hands where I can see them."

I swung the tiny door open and climbed out of the bug. As I stood there, Officer Zucker continued his interrogation as his young partner kept a watchful eye and began to move around the back of the Beetle toward us.

"Okay, who is Jerry Cella, and what are you doin' with his car at this hour?"

That really was all that I could have hoped for. It was time for me to really fuck with him. After all, he probably never suffered being put in his place since his father beat him with a strap when he was twelve. I should have felt sorry for him and the miserable life his father probably made for him, but I just couldn't help myself. I wasn't in such a good mood that night either.

"This car does not belong to Jerry Cella, and I told you my authentic license is in my right boot, together with my commission book."

You think that would have given him a hint that there was something more to this than a routine traffic stop. Maybe he should have asked, "What the fuck is a commission book?" But no, not Officer Zucker. He needed to be hit over the head and I was ready to oblige.

"What's your license doin' in your boot? You tryin' to make it smell, college boy? What else you got in there, an old pack of rubbers?" he said while only half-looking at me and clearly beginning to worry that this episode was going sideways, and he was feeling powerless to straighten it out, so he turned to crude sarcastic humor as a last-ditched equalizer.

Here we go again. "Only my commission book, sir. I keep my gun in my left boot, officer."

Well, that got his attention. He stood there for a split second as if he just heard he hit the Irish Sweepstakes for a million bucks. It was all he ever wanted from his career as a police officer in the village of Newton, New Jersey. The fictitious registration he was holding in his left hand flew in the air as he reached across his ample belly to hold down his holster so he could draw his revolver with his right. Actually, I would have sworn he had a hard-on—and why not? He was going to get to shoot somebody or at least draw down on him. He had to hold the holster down while he drew the gun because the layers of fat on his belly made it physically impossible to get the gun out. It was more like pulling the holster off the gun than drawing the gun from the holster.

It was at that instant that I realized my folly. While I was commissioned with all the authority the Congress of the United States could give me, these two guys had all the cold steel authority Smith & Wesson could strap to their hip. To them, I was only a hippy kid, with a gun, in a goofy car, and they were just itchin' to prove to everyone that they knew that they were real cops.

Without even being told, I spun around and assumed the position—hands on the roof of the Beetle and legs spread apart. In short order, the younger cop was at my right boot retrieving my black leather commission book, followed by the S&W Model 19 from my left boot. An instant later, I was in cuffs. Just when things couldn't get any worse, they asked me what was in the brief case and I told them.

"About $100,000 in cash, but don't get excited—it's all counterfeit."

They somehow failed to see the humor in that as they proceeded to slam me into the back seat of the police car and we all took a little trip to the station.

As I sat in the back of the squad car, turned half into the corner of the seat because they cuffed me behind my back and my hands were going numb, I couldn't help wonder why I kept finding myself in such situations. I had every opportunity to defuse that confrontation, but I didn't. It was much more important for me to say "fuck you" to almost any authority figure than make life easier for me and everyone else. At that stage of my life, I still hadn't figured out why I was so contemptuous and challenging. It was only years later that I put all the pieces together so I could construct a more relevant self-portrait.

Like most "head cases," my problems started from the beginning. I grew up in an Italian family in an Italian neighborhood, which was a multi-generational experience. As a result, because my generation was the first merger of the Italian, old world culture and the American, new world experience, there were inevitable conflicts.

All four of my grandparents were born in Italy and migrated to the new world during the great European exodus in the early part of the twentieth century. Both marriages were pre-arranged in Italy and my grandparents were sponsored to come to America only after the marriage deals were struck abroad. Arranged marriages, a very common holdover from the old world, were an effort to keep the blood pure and the families united.

I lived with my mother and father, an only child of two first-generation, American-born Italian-Americans. While they were American by birth, their cultural existence hadn't yet caught up with their citizenship. They were Italian by every other measure. My father was born in the Chambersburg section of Trenton. However, his birth certificate and baptism papers were in Italian and he learned English when he went to kindergarten at Saint Joaquin's School. Pop was a toughened 18-year-old when he married my mother in 1940. Some say there was a shotgun involved, but I never did the math to confirm the suspicions. He enlisted in the army on December 8, 1941 and went to war with the rest of the world. He came home to my mother and me in 1945 after being shot twice and badly burned on his right arm and hand. "The war sucked all the piss and vinegar out of him," his friends always said.

I don't know if there was any truth to their diagnosis, but I can honestly say that I never saw my father angry or even threaten to raise his hand to anyone, including me, and certainly not my mother. He was a kind, hardworking soul, with little formal education, but an engaging sense of humor and an inquisitive mind. My mother, on the other hand, was the dominant personality and the ultimate authority in the house. She inherited her pit bull personality from her father, my grandfather. He was a New York City cop and he thought his shit didn't stink. I have only recently discovered that therein was the genesis of my "fuck you" philosophy.

I had very little respect for my grandfather. He flaunted his patrolman's status with the NYPD like a schoolyard bully. It was never discussed, but I knew he began his career with the City of New York as a street sweeper; how he was "promoted" to the police department was a mystery. I'm sure, however, that it had something to do with the fact that the name tag on his uniform read "Larry Camel" rather than his actual name, "Lorenzo Camillio."

Nevertheless, wherever he went, he was the ultimate boss. At the regular Sunday dinner at our house, my mother would not only serve her father, but even her low life, petty criminal brothers, before my father. While to the casual observer her conduct wouldn't seem very significant, in the old world Italian culture it was treasonous for a wife to do so. On the rare occasion that my father's sister was present, she could hardly restrain herself and it was only after a stern look from my father that she calmed down. I now rarely give any thought at all to those days because it pisses me off just to think about it. I often recall, however, that Benjamin Franklin once said, "Never sell your virtue to purchase wealth and never sell your liberty to purchase peace." Hence, I was always ready for a fight, as I was that night.

No one at the station believed I was who I said I was, so Officer Zucker, who I was now calling "Officer Sucker", decided, at the suggestion of his lieutenant, that he should call the Secret Service Field Office in Newark. Just as I was beginning to think maybe I made a mistake playing with these humorless pricks, I overheard the telephone conversation between Officer Zucker and what I recognized as Carmine's voice on the other end. Carmine must have been the duty agent that night, and fortunate for me, he sincerely believes in the history, mission and integrity of the Secret Service. He suffers no fools when it comes to those issues. It was all I could do to keep from smiling. In fact, maybe I did smile, just a little, when I heard Carmine on the other end of the phone setting Officer "Sucker" on fire. Carmine was speaking to the officer in a very clear, loud, firm tone, to describe his behavior modestly. It went something like:

"Just what the fuck about his commission book don't you understand? He is operating with the full authority of the Congress of the United-Fucking-States of America and if you interfere with his mission for so much as another 30 seconds, I'll get a warrant from the United States Attorney and come the fuck out there myself and arrest you, your partner and your fuckin' dog too. Is this clear enough for you officer?"

In short shrift, I was on my way with my commission book, gun and briefcase, along with a nice hot cup of coffee and a donut. God bless America and my luck that Carmine was the duty agent that night, not one of the other suck-up squad leaders.

It was, therefore, with warm thoughts of my last interaction with local law enforcement that I was, on that day in October 1963, on my way to the New Jersey State Police Barracks in New Brunswick. It was here that I hoped to find a printer named Tuscolano—a wise guy who just might be able to tell me more about a woman I was completely captivated by, a woman who I never spoke to, but was somehow connected to, by a long and resilient emotional cord. And maybe he could even tell me a little something about this new c.4161 counterfeit note, too.

CHAPTER 15

"WHAT, YOU NEVER SAW AN ITALIAN 'G' MAN BEFORE?"

EVIDENTLY, MR. DI VITERBO HAD a difficult time with the Troopers. He was either a genuine tough guy or very naive to get into a rumble with the gang of thugs who patrolled the Jersey highways with impunity. I'm sure, as a result of a smart mouth, he was no longer at the State Police Barracks—he "fell" down the stairs and was taken to the hospital. Sure he did. He was currently in the Middlesex County General Hospital prison wing. When the Troopers told me where he was, I was actually relieved to get out of that fortress they called a barracks. I was probably only marginally less uncomfortable than the perps who were there. So, with the c.4161 note in my jeans pocket, I drove directly to the hospital. I knew Mr. Di Viterbo was in custody and he might have a lawyer, but I decided it was important for me to take a run at him before anyone else knew he had been approached about cooperating with us. I didn't even tell the Troopers who I was, other than that I was interested in where he was being held. Besides, they had no interest in talking to some punk kid anyway.

The process of convincing a man to abandon his family, friends and a lifetime of crime requires perfect timing, secrecy, and a skillful combination of threats, promises and lies. A hot cup of coffee, a cigarette or even a nice Italian "torpedo" on semolina bread, with hot peppers and genuine imported, aged provolone, and covered with extra virgin olive oil could break through lots of barriers. The latter, I figured, was the magic formula for setting the proper tone for my conversation with Mr. Di Viterbo. The "torpedo" was the only thing in my brief case when I entered the lockdown ward at Middlesex General.

The lockdown ward at the hospital was not a place fit even for mad dogs or Englishman, let alone a nice Italian boy who just got the shit kicked out of him by the Jersey Troopers. Oh, that's right, a nice Italian boy who accidentally fell down the steps in a single floor barracks.

The walls were a light green color, more in kind with puke than maple leaf green. It was astonishing how similar it was in sound, smell and even temperature to a real jail. Your feet stuck to the floor like an old musty, movie theater at the Jersey Shore. Most of the old, steel-framed, crank-out windows were at least partially open, but still the air temperature inside was at least ten degrees hotter than any remotely comfortable range. It made you sweat, sweat in a way that caused the foul odors in the ward to stick to your body, hair and clothes like cigarette smoke lingers long after you left the bar and began to explain to your wife that you were never there. It was the kind of place that even a Nikon loaded with Kodachrome would only get you a thousand shades of gray—not even any black or white, let alone color. The furniture was gray, the people were gray, even the air was gray, and fitting it was.

It didn't take very long for me to find Mr. Di Viterbo. I didn't even have a picture of him, but I immediately knew he was my guy. Naturally, he was the only patient wearing a $500 pair of Salvatore Ferragamo's and not a hair out of place. I saw him from across the room—beyond the fat nurse sitting at a very gray metal desk with absolutely nothing on it—a perfect communion with the life level of the room, all except for only one guy.

Mr. D was very much alive; he was a real-deal wise guy. No wonder the Troopers never mentioned whether or not any of them were hurt in the tussle with him. It's a wonder three or four of them weren't dead on the side of the road. Even when I got closer, I didn't see any injuries except for the bruises on his knuckles and I knew why. When he closed his hand and made a fist, it couldn't have been too much bigger than a bowling ball. If he ever hit me with it, I'm sure I would feel like I was hit by a small steel safe dropped from a six-story building. Not knowing what to expect, I walked up to him, stood three feet away, and said nothing. He looked me straight in the eye for at least ten seconds, consuming everything he could pull from my soul. Then, in a very casual manner, he examined me from my head to the number five cowboy toe on my ostrich Lucchese boots. It was all without reaction or emotion, until he pressed his lips, forced a sarcastic mini-smile and broke his silence with something less than a warm encouraging salutation.

"What the fuck do you want?" he whispered to me as if to say "I know who you are, now get the fuck away from me."

"Go fuck yourself. I don't want anything from you. I just came here because I thought you might like to know who gave you up," I told him, knowing full well no one ratted him out; it was just dumb luck by the Trooper.

But he didn't know that and I immediately saw the light go on as he began to clench those two bowling balls dangling at his sides. I didn't really know what to do. If he hit me, I'd hit the floor and the investigation would be over.

"Bullshit," was all that came out of his mouth, but that wasn't all he said.

You see, communication with a guy like Mr. D wasn't like chatting with a regular *homo sapien*. This guy was a predator, and like a jungle animal, he used all of his senses as well as his physical presence and environment to communicate. You think he didn't know that if he hit me it would be like a concrete block hitting a plate glass window at Macy's? Sure he did, but he was confused about the final outcome. He knew full well where he was and why he was there. What he didn't know was how he got there, and where he was going. Confronted with any one of those mysteries would not have given me an advantage. However, he was incapable of multi-tasking a resolution for all of them simultaneously because he didn't have the common denominator—me. "Just exactly who the fuck is this kid?" was the question he needed answered.

At this stage of my life, I had very little experience with a guy like Mr. D so my instinct was to tell him, "Let's sit down and talk.... maybe I can help you, la, la, la..." However, I wasn't convinced that was the right thing to say, so I decided that I needed him to want to talk to me more than he thought I needed to talk to him. I could only think of one way to do that.

"Okay, kiss my dago ass," was all I said in a slow, clear, crisp tone, never taking my eyes off his.

I wanted him to know I was Italian, as if he couldn't tell by looking at me. I'm convinced that it wasn't what I said, but rather the split-second freeze, at the very end, before I turned to walk away that got a reaction. In fact, he probably never heard a word I said. He was too busy calculating who was the tiger and who was the lamb, the same as me. I completed my 180 and was taking my first step away from him, that as I look back on it now would have changed my life forever, when he said in a very soft almost tender voice,

"Where's Lu?"

"Where's Lu?" was a very complicated question. It was complicated because you first had to understand that he knew Lu was home in her bed in New York, probably alone. But he wasn't certain.

What he meant to say was, "Hey, Lu's home in bed, probably alone, but I'm not sure. And by the way, I don't like it here—I'm too old to do hard time. I'm not a rat, but if you can make it easy for me, maybe we can talk." At least that's what I heard him say in my head.

I ignored him, and other than slowing the pace of my next step, I just kept moving away from him. It was a feeble attempt to tell him that I was in charge and that if he wanted to help himself he had to follow me, not the other way around. In fact, I didn't stop at all. I walked directly to the ugly metal desk and spoke to the ugly metal nurse. After I told her that Mr. D and I needed a place to talk, she pointed to a white, paint-worn wooden door across the room. As I walked away from the desk, heading for the door, I looked back at Mr. D; he hadn't moved. His head was down, but his eyes were following me, surely looking for a sign. He got it when I looked back at him, so he nonchalantly began to walk toward the same door. I couldn't help but notice that he didn't drop the bowling balls. They still hung from his sides and when he lumbered across the room with his huge gait, they swung like pendulums on an enormous grandfather clock.

I walked into the 10' x 10' room; he was about half a step behind. When I turned and looked at him, he had intentionally moved fully into the room so he couldn't be seen from the outside through the glass in the top half of the door. Immediately upon feeling "invisible" to the outside world, his persona changed. It was like an actor walking off stage and into their inner sanctum dressing room.

I was gratified to see the unclenching of his fists, not an insignificant occurrence to me. It told me a great deal more than the simple fact that I wasn't going to need plastic surgery in the near future. The wall was coming down.

"You're an agent?" he said to me in a flat quiet tone that only hinted at a question.

"Is it that obvious?" I responded with a hint of a smile, as I put both of my hands inside the top portion of the front pockets of my jeans. I was generally more comfortable putting my hands in my back pockets, but I decided it was less threatening to keep both hands in front of me, in clear view.

"Yeah it is. But, you're Italian?"

"Yup, all the way. What, you never saw an Italian 'G' man before?"

"Na, but hey, some girls love it, huh?"

"Some. Most love the Italian part best," I said, knowing that he understood what parts I was referring to.

That was the end of the preliminary. It was time to get on to the main bout.

"Listen, Mr. DiViterbo..."

"It's T. Nobody calls me by my last name except a fuckin' judge, and only my mother ever called me Tuscolano....so it's T... just T."

"Okay T, I'm Jake. Anyway, you're in deep shit here and you know there's only one game in town. You wanna play or you wanna do the time? It's up to you. We both know there's very little chance you'll out-live any federal counterfeiting beef without our help."

T knew I wasn't running a con. It was absolutely the truth. You just don't live very long in jail. The food sucks, the disease rate is astronomical and the medical care is virtually nonexistent. All that being said, T did have a choice, and it was my job to make it clear to him now was the time to make it.

"What choices do I have?" he asked, knowing the answer as he slid onto one of the two gray metal chairs on each side of a gray metal desk pushed in the corner—obviously made by the same gray metal company that made the desk in the other room. While sitting in the chair clearly signaled his willingness to talk, he still wanted to know exactly what the deal was.

"Your choices are to keep livin' or start dyin'—just that simple. You had a fuckin' shoebox full of a new counterfeit $100 note as well as the plates. I don't have to spell it out for you. The real question is, 'what will you do for me?'"

It was my opening salvo. We were on the dance floor now, like two teenagers wondering who was going to put their hand on the other's ass first.

"What do you want, my fuckin' blood?" he said without any real hostility.

When he spoke to me he had his head down, but he still looked me in the eyes like he was seeing through his eyelids. He kept the rest of his body slumped in the chair. He looked like a huge marionette held up by invisible strings. The image became almost comical when he looked up, raised his enormous eyebrows that were bushy enough to do a comb over the rest of his balding forehead and shrugged his shoulders, re-asking the same question. I had to laugh. I also had to begin to like him. He reminded me so much of so many of my father's friends I came to know growing up in Trenton. There was really only one thing to say.

"Djeet?"

"No, Djou?" he replied.

I didn't say another word. I just threw the soft, chocolate-brown brief case on the desk. His eyebrows, nose and lips scrunched together. His whole face seemed to take the shape of a huge question mark. Frankly, I don't understand how he didn't smell it by then. The wonderful aroma of the provolone, salami and olive oil haunted me since I bought it an hour earlier. T didn't move a muscle; he just gripped the arms of the chair and waited to see what I did next. Up until that moment, I was his worst nightmare, but when I pulled out that foot-long "torpedo" wrapped in white butcher's paper with hints of olive oil seeping through, he immediately relaxed. As I unspun the paper wrapper and broke open that sandwich, T and I were *paisani*, at least for the moment.

I swear he ate an entire half of the "torpedo" in no more than four bites. It wasn't that he was without manners or ate like an animal. In fact, he had a certain genteel quality about how he maneuvered his hands, especially when they weren't curled up in a fist. When I saw the artistic dexterity of his fingers, I was sure he was the one who made the plates found in his car, even before I noticed the faint hint of ink in his cuticles. That wasn't, however, what impressed me most. While his fingers and hands were certainly the manufacturers of these near-perfect plates, his eyes were surely the creators.

His eyes were extremely dark, but they didn't approach black. The color quality was vibrant without identifying a specific color. They behaved like the lens of a camera—they absorbed the reflected light of the object of their attention and, as a result, transmitted a sensation of activity and analysis. It appeared that he was not only memorializing, but also colorizing the object. As a result, even while he was surrounded by the vast grayness of the room, his eyes still transmitted vibrant colors and an intensity far beyond the actual quality of his dull and almost lifeless surroundings.

When he finished the "torpedo," he crumpled the wrapper in such a tight, little ball that it was near the size of a golf ball and probably as hard. He held it in his hand so tightly you could see the color disappear from the edges of his fingers. He wasn't even angry, just focused. The object of his focus was the crisp new $100 bill I pulled from the right front pocket of my jeans and now lay flat on the desktop. It was the c.4161 note Carmine gave me. It didn't yet have the customary "counterfeit" stamp on the front and back as do most seized counterfeit notes.

I slid the note across the desk, face up, to T, who looked at it motionlessly for a full ten seconds. It was like a hot marshmallow on a stick right out of the campfire—way too hot to handle. Eventually he reached to pick it up, but before he did, he looked up at me and found me looking right back at him. It didn't deter him from taking the note in his huge hand and drawing it close to his face. A brief smile lit up his face when he recognized that the paper in his hand was not just Hammermill Double Eagle paper, but was truly a work of art—his work of art. He handled it with loving care as he examined it like a mother holding a newborn, counting its fingers and toes to confirm its perfect form.

"Nice work," I said. I got no response so I tried a different tack.

"Well, it really isn't that good when you consider the heavy paper stock and the soft green color of the serial numbers and seal," I told him, hoping to get some reaction to my criticism of his work, although he hadn't, as of yet, admitted it was his. There was still no reaction. He just kept looking at the note without looking up.

"Okay, okay. What the fuck? Are you going to talk to me about this note or not?" I said, giving him a clear message that I was quickly losing patience with his coy approach.

He put the note down on the table with such a soft touch you would have thought it was fine china. He then asked, "Waddayouwanna know?"

"I want to know everything: who, when, where, how, how much, and why in Vegas," I told him in a very matter-of-fact tone, still trying to establish a no-nonsense relationship between the two of us.

"Vegas? What the fuck you talkin' about, Vegas?" he quickly retorted in such a convincing tone that I immediately realized something unexpected was afoot.

It was clear to me that T didn't know about the Las Vegas connection and if that was the case, I wasn't going to blow the whistle until I knew where this freight train was heading. If it was heading for a train wreck, I didn't want to wind up on the bottom of a pile of twisted steel and rubble. I quickly abandoned Las Vegas and moved on.

"Did you print this note?"

"What? Do you expect me to just fuckin' spit this out so you can send me to the fuckin' joint for the rest of my fuckin' life?"

His response made him sound much more ignorant than he actually was. It was a good defensive maneuver on his part. Some people, without insight into his character and culture, might have been taken off-guard and might have underestimated him. His tone and choice of vulgarities allowed him to fit in with his regular crowd. To act otherwise would cause him to be the object of isolation or even suspicion. Even in my relative inexperienced youth, I realized that when you're in the woods with a bear you better walk like a bear or be eaten by a bear.

Hence my response. "You're fuckin' right I expect you to answer my questions. In fact, I expect you to answer all my fuckin' questions and even answer a few I don't ask. And remember, you were caught cold, and I'm the only motherfucker on the planet who can keep you from spending the rest of your fuckin' life in a five foot by eight foot room with a guy named La Roy."

I didn't feel entirely comfortable with the tough guy act, but it was all I had. I thought I was doing a good job until he responded. But then I realized it's not a good thing to act like a bear in the presence of a real fuckin' bear unless you really were a bear, or at least had a very big bear gun, which I didn't.

When I finished, at least three full seconds of silence passed before T reacted. He first looked down at the table, with his left hand spread on the side of his face like he just slapped himself. I sat there still trying to look tough until T looked away to his right. He turned his head more than ninety degrees so I couldn't see any part of the front of his face. Actually, all I could see was the back of his left hand pressed against the left side of his face. It made me very uncomfortable because I felt like he was talking to someone standing directly to his right. It didn't take long before I realized he wasn't speaking to anyone at all. He was laughing.

"Well," was all I could muster. I could see his entire body shaking as he tried to hide his almost uncontrollable laughter. I think I remember being angry at some point, but it's all a blur to me today.

"Okay, okay, you broke me. I'll tell you anything you want to know," he said in only a half-serious but very sarcastic tone as he wiped a tear from his left eye.

I always assumed the tear in his eye was from laughing at me so hard, but as I reflect on it now, I'm not so sure. I don't think I really understood at the time how hard the choices were for T. That's because he made it look easy. He was the kind of man, who once upon a chosen course becomes completely committed. I couldn't help thinking he knew where this encounter was going to wind up, while I was still meandering in the dark. I was completely stunned, but still undeterred.

"Good, then tell me who printed this note," I told him trying to keep some semblance of seriousness.

T became much more serious and asked me, "Com' on, what will you do for me? For real?"

"For real, I can keep you from going to jail for the fuckin' rest of your life. You know you're not a young man any more. Time is running out."

"How long?" he asked in a very quiet voice.

"I can't tell you that because it depends on how well this goes. You just have to trust me and know I'll take care of you."

"I don't even know you," he asked, more than stated.

"You know enough to know I'm right," I said as a matter of fact. "And I know you didn't do this print all by yourself, so I wanna know who the other players are."

When I told him that, you would have thought I told him I wanted to fuck Lucille as part of the deal. A less experienced manipulator would have leapt to his feet and shouted "No, never," but not T. He knew that if he did that he would be setting up a huge emotional barrier that we would have to break through before we could move on. He took a more sophisticated route.

"Na, I didn't need no fuckin' help. Whadda ya think I am, some kinda pussy? I ran the whole job by myself," T said in a soft, calm voice. And, while very convincing, I knew it just wasn't true.

He clearly needed help not only for setting up the press but also for some security during the print. He was printing a lot of counterfeit worth a pile of cash to almost any hood with even a halfway decent distribution network. There was no way he was going to risk somebody stumbling into the plant and ripping him off, not with the "respects" the bosses were expecting from whatever deal he made. No, I knew there were others, but I also knew if I wasn't careful, his cooperation against his *paisani* could be a deal breaker. So I started slow, like foreplay on a first date with a nice girl.

"Look T, I'm offering you a way to cut your losses here and minimize any jail time exposure you have. I'm not really interested in the guys that helped you do this print. I'm mostly interested in the printer—that's you—and the distributor—the guy who ordered up the print in the first place. I'm prepared to offer your guys the same deal I'm offerin' you. And they don't even have to cooperate in the investigation. In fact, I prefer they don't. You can keep them in line until we grab the distributor and then he gets the hard time. You and your guys catch a break at sentencing because of your help breakin' the case. I'll take care of it, guaranteed. If you don't wanna bring your guys into the fold and leave them out in the cold, that's okay with me. But you and I know they'll certainly get busted sooner or later and it's a whole lot better if they have a 'get-outta-jail-free card' in their pocket, even if they don't know how it got there. *Capisce*?"

As I listened to myself explain the deal to T, it sounded better than even I thought. He paused for a very short second and then began to shake his head left and right. The longer he shook it, the more pronounced the movement became, and then he began to unravel a most amazing tale.

"Look...this guy comes to me earlier in the summer and wants me to do a run of fresh, new hundreds. He's paying it all up front. I had a new set of plates anyhow, so I figure I could make a few bucks. I ran a little more for me and that's what I had in the car. That's it."

"Did you deliver the queer to him?"

"Sure I did. He wanted the deal in two runs. The first was a test run and later I would do a full run."

"How big was the test run?" I asked, not prepared to be so startled.

"A hundred and a little extra five for me and Lucille."

"That's a pretty big test," I said, which, in and of itself, was a tremendous understatement.

"That's what he wanted and that's what he paid for—more or less—mostly more," he quipped.

"What was your *vig* on the test?" I asked as I took out a pencil to compute how much good money he put in his pocket.

"Twenty-five points on the initial $100,000 test run, twenty on the full run of...$20 million." He intentionally hesitated on the $20 million because he just realized the enormity of that number.

The numbers were even more astounding to me. I wasn't the most experienced agent in the counterfeit squad, but I knew that no one had ever even attempted a run that big before. All this, while very interesting, did not give me the answers I was looking for; only T could do that, and as right now he wasn't telling. The showdown was yet to come.

We spent the next twelve hours doing the same dance. In the beginning, things were rough. It was like eating bad tomato pie. You would eat it because it was hot and in front of you, but you didn't realize it was bad pie until you had about three slices. Only then did you realize that you ate it even though it really wasn't that good. That's the way it was with T. I would listen for about half an hour and take notes and then realize it was mostly bullshit with a little truth mixed in. Then we would do it all over again getting about twenty percent more truth with each go-round. It was very tiring and very slow, but after about four hours, I was beginning to get the story and he was beginning to get the drill. Maybe it was a ritualistic dance we had to do in order to establish our respective roles and begin to trust each other. Anyway, we were getting there. He even told me a little about his two guys, Frankie and Canevecchio, who helped him with the print, the most difficult part of the story

T also told me about the meeting at the Uptown Diner and the deal they struck. He also told me when, where and even how he made the plates that were found in his car. It was what he didn't tell me, however, that eventually became most important. See, T told me about Miguel, but he never told me he was Cuban. He left me thinking, and I was just naive enough to conclude that Miguel was some run-of-the-mill Spanish drug dealer who decided he would try his hand at something more enterprising. To this day, I'm still not sure how much T really knew about Miguel. T had moxy enough to know that the "good" Miguel was coming up with had to be from some very big players and if the mob was involved with a Spanish guy, let alone a Cuban front man, the crossover had to be sanctioned from the very top. While Carmine never told me, he knew this from day one and, as a result, he made certain moves he never told me about until much later.

Even though I was sure I didn't have all the straight answers from T, I felt I got all I could from him in a relatively short time. So I decided to give him a breather and take it all back to Carmine to see what he thought our next move should be. So I left T in the hospital ward and headed back to the apartment, hoping that Bookie and Ava were out of gas and bodily fluids for at least a few hours so I could get some sleep and get with Carmine first thing in the morning. I was pretty excited about all that had happened, feeling like I didn't let Carmine down. I had no idea this caper was going to throw the rest of the planet and me into the back of an 18-wheeler and drive us over a dirt road on a rainy night.

CHAPTER 16

SEE THE USA IN A CHEVROLET

ALL THE WHILE T WAS cruising down the New Jersey Turnpike trying to get the Trooper to lose interest in Italian shoes, Miguel was on his way back to the US to finalize Castro's plan, and more importantly, to solidify his own future. He already had a $100,000 cache of first rate, counterfeit $100 Federal Reserve Notes hidden in a very special place that was also very close to his heart. He was anxious to get back to the States to finish the print so Castro could get his revenge on America and he could then disappear into the sunset with a pile of cash, completely unbeknownst to Castro.

Getting into the States from Cuba through regular channels was almost impossible since the Bay of Pigs debacle only a year earlier. Therefore, Miguel had to make alternative travel plans. One option was to get a fictitious passport, fly to Mexico City and then get a flight to New York. It sounded a lot easier and safer than it was. Whenever you go through U.S. Customs, especially in New York, there's a risk that some young customs buck will examine your passport too closely and find some bullshit reason to detain you. If that happens, all bets are off. Miguel could wind up in an INS (Immigration and Naturalization Service) detention center for months while they tried to sort it out. It happens all the time to legitimate travelers, let alone to a Cuban spy.

No, Miguel would take the most direct, most interesting—and if you don't attract the Coast Guard—the quickest and most anonymous way to get in and out of the States: a ninety-mile boat ride from Havana Harbor to the Conch Republic, known to those not in the loop as Key West, Florida. Havana to Key West, at ninety nautical miles, is substantially closer than the trip from Miami to Key West, which is over 150 miles on the overseas highway. You could make the trip on a commercial puddle jumper, but the safest alternative for any clear thinking Cuban spy would be to take the all-American mode of transportation and drive. There was a time when a third alternative existed, but the best laid plans of mice and giant industrialists is but a whim in the face of a big blow that at one time only carried the name of a woman, as it should.

In 1905, Henry Flagler, one of America's greatest entrepreneurs, decided to take on the single largest, privately-financed construction project in the history of the world. With only his personal financial might, he commenced, completed and nearly perpetuated the prodigious task of building and running a railroad from Miami to Key West. The steel-laden boulevard snaked through the Florida Keys, frequently resting on so little earth that it barely qualified as an overland route. Hence, it was dubbed the Florida Overseas Railway. The steel links were coupled together from key to key by iron-clad trestle bridge spans, which when reflected in the tepid, light green ocean, resembled prehistoric creatures waiting with open jowls to gobble up any unwary locomotion prey. The train would surely run into the open ocean if it did not successfully negotiate the severe twists in track direction and grasp the few available splinters of dry land. The tracks ran nearly 160 miles southwest from Miami into the Atlantic Ocean and Gulf of Mexico, eventually landing at Flagler's Casa Marina hotel in Key West.

The Overseas Railway was a spectacular achievement and provided a unique and vital service to the people of America until Labor Day, 1935. It was during that holiday weekend that the first Category 5 hurricane of the twentieth century slammed into the United States, nearly dead center of the Florida Keys. Hundreds of local residents and World War I veterans, who were living down there while working on public works programs as part of the depression recovery effort, were killed from the tidal surge. The rescue attempts to save these men is a great story of heroism and ingenuity that unfortunately ended in tragedy and the demise of the Overseas Railway. This tragedy signaled the birth of the new era of the internal combustion engine, prompting the construction of the Overseas Highway that became the artery of life that now feeds and sustains the Florida Keys.

Without knowing much of the history of the Keys, Miguel chose his invasion route into the United States through Key West, the heart and soul of Caribbean America. A quiet motorboat landing on secluded Smather's beach on the east end of Key West in the darkest hours of a moonless night was his choice.

Once he got into Key West, Miguel figured he could slip into mainstream America with not too much effort; he had done it many times before. He knew he couldn't stay in Key West very long without reverting back to an island mindset, which made it considerably more difficult to become a mainlander. Key West has always been unlike anyplace else in America. That's probably why Ernest Hemingway spent so much time there.

From his Smather's Beach landing, Miguel grabbed his duffle and walked to the famed Casa Marina on Reynolds Street. The Conch Republic was probably the only place in America where a man with a duffle bag, Spanish accent and wet feet could walk into a five star hotel and check into a room with no questions asked other than, "Salt on your margarita, sir?" After a long, hot shower that was really only lukewarm, Miguel spent the better part of the night at the Green Parrot Bar listening to some of the world's best blues in a spot Hemingway himself would envy. He also wanted to stop by Sloppy Joe's on Duval Street, but passed on it when he saw the huge crowd out front ogling a new local, blonde hippie-kid folk singer who sang about life at the end of the road in Key West.

Miguel was anxious to get out of Key West and on to making his fortune. The next morning, hangover and all, he grabbed a puddle jumper from the Key West airport up to Miami. From there, he got an Eastern Airlines flight to Newark. Snappy trip for a guy with absolutely no identification, although he did have a stack of $100 bills—genuine, of course.

Miguel had a whole list of things to do, some business and some pleasure, now that he was safely in the United States. Even though Miguel was a cog in the wheels of the destruction of the United States of America, that didn't mean that of all the places on the planet, the USA wasn't the place to live and spend his anticipated fortune. While he feigned dedication to Castro and his communist ideology, he was really a highly motivated capitalist at heart. This counterfeiting plan was his ticket to international independence. With a little luck, CIA would finally either kill Castro or drive him completely crazy. And, because only Castro and Miguel knew of this plan, he was confident he would be the sole beneficiary of $20 million in counterfeit American dollars, which he was equally confident could be easily turned into $10 to $15 million genuine. However, all that being considered, he was a long way from his apartment in Jersey and his long anticipated spin to the Jersey Shore in his new '63 Split Window Corvette that was there waiting for him. Finding his *paisan* printer and getting the final print completed was a close second on his list of immediate priorities.

The reason driving the Vette was so high on his list, even when there were seemingly much bigger issues to resolve, was because Miguel was a greedy, self- promoting terrorist in the vein of a schoolyard bully who beats up smaller kids and takes their lunch money. It's for that reason he enjoyed flaunting his new Vette in the face of all those dirty-handed Americans who would do almost anything to be able to "see the USA in a Chevrolet." The closest most of them would ever come would be to see the TV commercial while watching "Bonanza" on a lonely Friday night. Miguel enjoyed this fantasy as he relaxed in his nice Eastern Airlines first-class seat into Newark.

CHAPTER 17

CUBA, CASH, CHICS AND CARS

WHILE RIDING IN THE CAB from Newark Airport to his new East Orange apartment, Miguel couldn't help reflect on where life had taken him over the past few months. His first trip to the States in June was a success by any standard. He connected with T and secured the test print without Castro even knowing. He was even able to pave the way for his current return to finish the print by getting a nice apartment and even buying a great car to keep him amused while in the States. He was troubled, though, because he couldn't reconcile the fact that he was a Cuban revolutionary, illegally in the United States for the sole purpose of committing a felony that could undermine the free world. He smuggled at least one automatic handgun past customs, but he still needed to forge alliances with characters like T and a mutt like Azzimie to achieve his goals. Back home in Cuba, he wouldn't let guys like that launder his crisp, white, cotton shirts.

It all started just a few months earlier, in June, when he was on the Avenue setting up Castro's plan with T. Miguel concluded that, so long as he had to remain in the States to nurse the deal, he would indulge in one of his life's greatest fantasies: drive the Corvette, "America's Sports Car."

During his youth, American television bombarded his island home with TV ads just like the allies bombed Dresden in the Second

World War saturation. As a result, almost every Cuban male had a hard-on for the American automobile and other than the occasional Chrysler muscle car, the GM beauties from Chevy and Cadillac were the prizes. Every Cuban stud had a calendar of GM pinups hanging in a prominent place so all his amigos knew his lust was properly placed. The only images you could often find on their walls were pictures of Catholic Saints and a Chevy Bel Air. The Corvette was more akin to Jesus himself, rather than a mere saint. And naturally, every car was equated with a hot chic; sex, sex, sex.

Even a tough guy like Miguel wasn't immune to the ass factor of these cars. However, while in Cuba, he could never hope to have a new Vette, so he decided now was the chance to start living in the fast lane, literally. In fact, maybe it wasn't the anticipation of the payoff from taking a slice of *El Presidente's* pie that led to Miguel wanting the Vette. Maybe it was the other way around. Maybe there really was some truth to those GM commercials. It's like the old silk hat they put on Frosty the snowman. It had to have had some magic in it because, "Once they put it on his head, he began to dance around." Maybe once Miguel started to drive around in the "dream machine," he could begin to think he could really make all his dreams come true. Who knows why, but whatever it was, Miguel's obsession to get that Vette and a passable driver's license in the States caused him to commit a colossal fuck-up. He waltzed a completely unknown moap like Azzimie right onto the dance floor of the biggest conspiracy of the century. While Azzimie opened the door of opportunity for Miguel, the same door, unfortunately, opened to an elevator shaft of destruction.

Buying the Corvette wasn't difficult. Miguel had a Chevy dealer on Route 22 in Hillside all set to deliver the Vette for a cash sale with no questions asked, as long as Miguel's Division of Motor Vehicle (DMV) documents could pass the smile test. The dealer didn't give a shit who was buying the car, as long as no one ever came back to bust his balls. When Miguel showed up with the cash and no DMV documents, the dealer refused to deliver the car. And, as smart and cunning and even as ruthless as Miguel was, he was no match for the New Jersey Division of Motor Vehicles. Even with the assistance of the KGB, Miguel didn't have a snowball's chance in hell of getting a license and registration that would get past even a routine Newark Police stop, without help from somebody on the inside at the DMV. So the dealer told Miguel how he might be able to fix the problem; evidently, this problem wasn't so unusual. The drug trade was just taking off in America, and there were lots of Hispanic young men with shopping bags full of cash and a similar hunger for an American "spread machine," as they liked to call America's muscle cars.

The dealer advised Miguel to go down to the DMV on Frelinghuysen Avenue in Newark and just stand around. It all sounded pretty stupid to Miguel. He thought the dealer should at least give him a name to contact and say how much the bribe should be to get the paperwork done. In Cuba, anyone could go up to an official, offer a bribe and get what they needed; it's business as usual. After all, that's the way it was done in Cuba. But as Miguel soon learned, that's not the way it was done in the States. The States had a business pattern to protect. The consumer had to go to a retailer, who would go to the source to get the product. Everybody had a role and everybody took their cut. That's the way it is in a capitalist economy. So that's just what Miguel did. He went to the Frelinghuysen Avenue DMV and, much to his surprise, it quickly became very apparent to him who he had to talk to.

The guy he spied certainly wasn't the kind of man Miguel would normally speak to. He was dirty—dirty in every respect. His hair was brown, stringy and certainly hadn't been washed for a week. His shirt hung from his muscle-barren shoulders and arms without even a hint of starch. His tan cotton pants had dark brown stains over the thighs of both legs, from just below the pockets to midway to the knees, from rubbing his dirty hands on them after God knows what activity. This guy's hygienic practices were compounded by his physical structure. He was simply too tall for his level of coordination and his clothes. He was a clone for a "Gumby" who had been left outside in the backyard for a week or so in the hot sun. Azzimie, Miguel later learned was his name, swung his arms when he walked, with his belt buckle leading the way as his sloping shoulders remained punched back. He was so skinny and his clothes hung so loosely that he appeared two dimensional—completely flat across the front as if he were pencil-drawn on a piece of white Xerox paper.

There was something about Azzimie that even a criminal thinly disguised as a revolutionary like Miguel just couldn't warm up to. It was as if the dirty grease in his hair, the grime under his fingernails and the stains and smell of his clothes came from within, and no matter what you did or how long you did it, nothing could cleanse his body and soul.

Whenever Azzimie spoke, he would lean in and cock his head slightly to one side while holding an unfiltered Camel between the stained index and forefingers of his right hand. He would often simultaneously clamp his thumb and pinky together in an attempt to retrieve an errant piece of tobacco from the tip of his tongue, all this within inches of your face. His foul stench emanated in concentric waves, like throwing a rock into a cesspool. He was indeed a wholly unattractive package, but, as Miguel observed, he was clearly getting the job done at the DMV and that was all that interested Miguel. He concluded Azzimie was the person who could help him. However, he didn't realize that Miguel asking Azzimie for his help was like a surfer asking a shark for a ride onto the beach. He might get the ride, but it was going to be painful.

Azzimie, on the other hand, immediately sensed that there was a score to be made with Miguel and, while he was not only anxious to help him with his urgent DMV problems, he was also eager to keep him close and show him how valuable he could be. The longer Miguel spoke to Azzimie, the more he ignored his appearance and began to appreciate his less than obvious talents. At the same time, Azzimie was pulling a great deal of valuable information from Miguel. It's not like Miguel didn't know this, but Azzimie was very skillful at playing the "something for something game." It took less than a minute or two for Azzimie to completely understand and identify a solution to Miguel's DMV problem. Nevertheless, he stayed perched in Miguel's face for over half an hour, asking question after question while giving only little tidbits of the solution in return. Finally, Miguel had enough of the game and turned to walk away, knowing full well that Azzimie would never let him get away and that now they would finally get down to the business at hand. Azzimie placed his grimy hand on Miguel's shoulder and asked him if it made a difference what name was on the license, to which Miguel replied, "No."

Azzimie walked off and returned in less than thirty minutes with a New Jersey driver's license and car registration in a completely fictitious name that suited Miguel perfectly. Azzimie pointed out that the license was registered to a particular address and that Miguel should wait a month and then do an address change with the DMV, registering the otherwise fictitious license to a specific address that Miguel could correspond from if need be. Azzimie thought that Miguel was like his other clients and planned to use the license in perpetuity. He had no idea Miguel only needed it for a few months because he then would be off to some exotic part of the world that had no diplomatic relations with the US, where he could live a grand life, drive an Italian sports car and run his Yucatan Resort in complete anonymity.

When Azzimie handed the license to Miguel, Miguel gave him a nice, new, crisp, genuine $100 bill. Azzimie was obviously very happy with that arrangement, but he hardly even looked at it. Azzimie knew that, although he was unable to put a dirty finger on the specifics, he wanted to keep Miguel close to him. He sensed, like all good con men, that there was a score there. He decided to cast a baited hook.

"Listen man, you lookin' for a crib?" asked Azzimie.

Not entirely sure what this creature was talking about, Miguel just curled the edge of his mouth and said nothing. Azzimie tried a different lingual approach.

"I know where there's a sweet furnished apartment in a nice building full of yummy babes. You need a place like that, Amigo?" Azzimie tried again.

Azzimie didn't bother to mention at the time that he also gigged as the "super" of the building and just happened to have a key to all the apartments. Although he had no idea Miguel was in need of a place to live, Azzimie figured he would shoot for the works and if he couldn't get him to live where he could keep his sticky fingers in his pockets on a daily basis, he would work his way down to just learning where he lived, for future investment.

At first, Miguel had no interest moving into any building that also housed Azzimie and his like—cohorts and lovers—including several who played multiple roles. However, there were four great loves in Miguel's life: Cuba, cash, cars and chics, and not necessarily in that order. So while he was about to blow Azzimie off and drive over the horizon and never see him again, and certainly be better for it, one of his four loves reared its bodacious head—actually heads was more like it.

Out of the blue—and as he reflected on it later, probably critically staged and timed by Azzimie—two smokin' hot chics sauntered up to Azzimie and perched on each side of his skinny, twisted torso. These chics were so hot that Miguel's eyes started to burn. He noticed both of them before they made their move on Azzimie because they were just the kind of girls Miguel liked. As they moved across the parking lot toward the side of the building where Miguel and Azzimie were standing, you could actually see the emotional destruction left in their wake. They were way too fast for that environment. There should have been a sign like what they have in a marina: "slow down; make no wake." At first, Miguel couldn't understand why they were interested in Azzimie; but it didn't take him long to figure it out.

As they percolated around Azzimie, Miguel realized that while most men would certainly describe these two chics as beautiful, they also had a noticeable quality about them that was a stark contrast to Azzimie—they were clean. One chic had shoulder length red hair with gorgeous strawberry blonde highlights. The other was a sweep cut brunette. Both were full-bodied and wore jeans that fit just right in all the important places while their plain cotton t-shirts were the same color they were when God made the cotton—clean white.

The strawberry blonde had about ten pounds of pure muscle and maybe two inches on the brunette, but both were more than respectable in every dimension. They knew every eye in the parking lot, both male and female, was on them and probably looking in the same places. Neither was shy, as both were engaged in animated conversation with each other as they approached Azzimie and eased in for a very soft landing, up close and very personal. They stood so close to him that Miguel had to wonder why they didn't feel the same revulsion to his stench that he did. But that didn't keep Miguel from leaning in to get closer and hopefully getting noticed by them. When he did, he realized why they weren't put off being so close to Azzimie. The strawberry blonde conveyed a distinct aroma of sautéing garlic and peppers—hot peppers, actually red hot peppers—the kind that make your throat burn before you even eat them. Her aroma and aura completely neutralized anything Azzimie transmitted and left a wonderfully tormenting bouquet.

Once Miguel got over the tease, he began to realize the brunette chic was now doing all the talking and she sure enough wasn't speaking Spanish. It took Miguel a few seconds to realize she was speaking some middle or eastern European language that he just could not understand. Even though the brunette was doing all of the talking and was much more animated, Miguel was drawn, almost magnetically, to the redhead. Even though she stood there quietly, and may have even been in neutral with the parking brake on, Miguel could see from the motion in her eyes and the twitch in her thigh that this chic wasn't along for a Sunday afternoon ride. He was sure, without even a peek under the hood, that she was packin' a racin' motor and it was runnin' hot and revin' high: she was ready to get it in gear and itchin' to giddy-on down the line. It was then, almost simultaneously with Azzimie giving a deliberate jostle of the head for Miguel to come closer and join them, that Miguel put all the pieces together. "Motherland." That was the connection. The brunette and Azzimie crawled out from the same corner of the planet.

It was somewhat unclear to Miguel whether he was more interested in the girls themselves or the fascination of how they could possibly be interested in Azzimie, a character Miguel thought all women would find thoroughly repulsive. In any event, he wanted to get to know these girls better, and sooner rather than later. So, he decided to ante up and get in the game even though he didn't exactly know the rules or even the language. He was hoping that the universal translator, sex, would enable him to bluff his way to a winning hand.

Well, Miguel struck out that day. In fact, the girls seemed to lose interest instantly upon his engagement with them. He barely learned their names. One was Julia and the other, the redhead, he only heard Julia call her LJ. Miguel, however, was tantalized by Azzimie's lifestyle. He thought the ability of a character like Azzimie to succeed both financially and with women like these had to be an American phenomenon. The likes of Azzimie had no chance in the perception and facade driven society of Cuba. In Mother Cuba, all successful men had to have a certain swarthy swagger about them. Azzimie had none of that. Yet, Miguel felt a twinge of jealously, although he couldn't figure out why. He eventually regretted his failure to see that it was all a set-up, although under no circumstance would he have figured out that the set up went all the way back to the Vette salesman who sent him there in the first place. He was completely distracted by the girls. As a result, just minutes after the girls walked away, (if you can call the wiggle they did, walking), Azzimie offered to show him the apartment. And Miguel swallowed the hook.

Even though Miguel wasn't actually in the market for an apartment, he was curious about the possibility of changing his current living arrangement. He was currently staying at the Robert Treat Hotel in downtown Newark on a weekly basis. It suited him fine; that is, until Azzimie made his offer. While the hotel offered maid service in a fairly nice but old building in a high, and getting higher by the day, inner city crime area, it all of a sudden didn't fit-in with Miguel's newly acquired life style. Miguel was getting a new Vette, thanks to Azzimie's help, and the hotel didn't have an adequate garage for such a beauty.

He also knew chics like the two he just saw with Azzimie were not coming to the Robert Treat Hotel. The only thing on the menu there was second or maybe even third-rate hookers who were blowing the doorman before they even set foot in the elevator.

Sloppy seconds were okay for a soldier on leave with his comrades, but Miguel now had higher aspirations in mind for his brief, but hopefully profitable stay in America.

There was even a legitimate and pragmatic reason for Miguel to get out of the hotel. A Spanish guy living in a hotel alone in Newark for an extended period of time was bound to attract questions. He already saw it slowly developing from some of the staff. Their comments were more than just, "Good morning" or "How are you today?" They were beginning to ask small, seemingly harmless questions. They were much too inquisitive for Miguel. He began to hear comments about being especially dressed that day or working late. Simple inquiries began to concern him. The staff in inner city hotels like the Robert Treat made good money from the cops for tips about unsavory characters. With the blossoming drug trade in the States, a Spanish guy driving a flashy new Vette, without any visible means of support, while staying in a marginal hotel, would eventually attract unwanted attention.

Maybe all his observations and concerns were accurate or maybe he just needed some justification to upgrade his lifestyle. But in any event, just a couple of days later, Miguel found himself walking through a large, one bedroom apartment on the third floor of a four-story apartment building on South Munn Avenue in East Orange, New Jersey. While the building and neighborhood were neither architectural nor social masterpieces, they were very respectable and functional.

The apartment was absolutely huge compared to Cuban standards. Back home three full families of four would live in an apartment that size. Miguel was convinced he would be very comfortable and inconspicuous there. A perfect fit, it had lots of room, the neighborhood was quiet and the neighbors seemed to mind their own business. A line of garages in the back of the parking lot was available for rent. It was a perfect spot for the new Vette, which he was picking up any day. In fact, he was holding off picking it up because he was concerned about where he was going to keep it and didn't want any more attention at the hotel.

He knew, in the alternative, he could just forget the entire idea of getting a Vette; just behave like a dutiful agent of Mother Cuba and live like a member of the proletariat. But that was never an aspiration of Miguel's. He also knew that at any time, Castro could get some hare-brained idea and call him back to Cuba for any one of a hundred stupid reasons. He thought it would just be easier to leave the apartment and the Vette in the garage and go. So Miguel took the apartment, and in only a few days he was all moved in, got his new '63 Split Window Corvette settled in the garage and sure enough, he was called back to Havana for a progress report to *El Presidente.*

Miguel was okay with the trip because he felt everything was under control in the States. T already made the first test run that looked very good and he had every expectation that the final run would go just as smoothly. He had his New Jersey driver's license and his new Vette, which he proudly named Marilyn. She was safely tucked away in the garage behind his apartment. To leave him even more assured, Azzimie was the super at the apartment complex. Miguel felt comfortable in that arrangement, not because he had some semblance of friendship with Azzimie, but rather he sensed Azzimie thought that in some way Miguel was a powerful man and he wanted to stay on his good side, either hoping for some payoff or because he sensed his ruthless nature and didn't want any trouble with him. While Miguel believed he controlled the relationship, he didn't trust him enough to leave anything of importance or of value where Azzimie might stumble over it. He mistakenly thought his precautions were adequate.

It was for these reasons that when Miguel left his new apartment for his rendezvous in Cuba, just a week or so earlier, he left with confidence and a sense of calm assurance. Nothing that happened before he left for Cuba could have either tipped him off nor prepared him for the shit-storm that was about to darken his future and crush the enthusiasm of an entire generation of Americans.

CHAPTER 18

AS SERIOUS AS A HEART ATTACK

After sparring with T for the better part of a day and night, I slept for eight hours straight, which rarely, if ever, happened. The next morning I went to the office early and let myself in the back door. This way I avoided all the haircut and cowboy boots bull shit. I couldn't have been there more than thirty minutes when Carmine arrived. He was anxious to hear what happened, so we went into his office and I filled him in on what I accomplished the afternoon before with T. For some wholly unjustified reason, I thought I was going to get an "attaboy" from Carmine. Well, what I got instead was about a thousand questions, very few of which I could even remotely answer.

Here I was, thinking that I was getting the hang of this undercover stuff and even beginning to understand the thinking process of both the bad guys and the good guys, when Carmine, a guy I certainly admired and respected, turned the lights out on me. He wanted to know not only what T said and what I said and why I said it and where I was going with my questions, but he also wanted to know what we both were thinking. All of a sudden, I felt like I was talking to one of those NASA guys about building a fuckin' rocket ship. I was no longer expecting, not even remotely, an "attaboy." I was now worried I had completely dropped the ball and had let the entire case slip away. I couldn't help thinking that maybe it was because I was distracted over the *testarossa*. Boy, how life is tricky. I went from feeling I was so cool—a real special agent—to convinced that I should have been down in the garage using my tie to check the oil in the cars.

I think Carmine got the picture and decided to lay off a little, but he still wanted this thing handled right. What I learned first was that I let T control the interview and the flow of information. As I looked back on it, I realized I gave him too many options and way too much information. That was because I didn't do enough homework before I went in there with him. I didn't really know where I wanted to take him, instead of letting him taking me and the Secret Service. It's not, however, like I was completely outta gear. I knew we wanted to get to this guy, Miguel, and make the next run and then arrest everyone and look like heroes. The only thing was, I just didn't know how to get there.

"Okay, tell me, Carmine. How do I wiggle this bitch back into bed?" I asked, still trying to be cool while admitting that I fucked up. Carmine began the lesson.

"Well, we make a deal with this *paisan* and print the full second run. We play it from the inside out and take all of them down. If we're careful, we can squeeze them, including this Miguel guy, and move up to the next tier. Do you think this guy will roll over that far for us?" Carmine asked, looking me straight in the eye with a slight grimace on his face while he narrowed the space between his eyebrows.

When I responded with, "Sure, do you think we can get him out of jail to do the print," the most respected undercover agent in the history of federal law enforcement looked at me like I was a contestant on a TV game show and missed the "gimmie" question.

At that point, I was totally lost. Carmine silently sat on one of the two steel government-issue chairs in his office and motioned for me to sit in the other. As soon as I did, he scooted closer and shared with me the art and wisdom of a lifetime of undercover work.

When I walked out of Carmine's office almost two hours later, I had a much better understanding of the "undercover life." And, while I still had some questions, I was sure of two things. First, I now knew I could do this if I kept my head and was willing to get my hands dirty; and second, there was no way in hell T was getting out of jail to do this print.

Carmine set up an entire scenario as if he were writing a screenplay, but with contingencies. It all began with T cooperating, heart and soul, and setting up the final print so we could be there every step of the way. We both knew the last thing this old wise guy wanted to do was eat cheese sandwiches with the Feds and rat on his lifelong *paisani*. But when given a choice between that and getting bent over by some yaam in a dark corner of a federal penitentiary the decision became clearer. Besides, we did offer his *paisani* a piece of T's cooperation deal, albeit unbeknownst to them, in order to sweeten the deal for T. Carmine thought that was a real stroke of genius on my part, or maybe he just said that to make me feel better after kicking me in the nuts for two hours. But it was clear, without bringing his guys along, T was not making the trip with us.

Only a few years earlier that choice wouldn't have been so clear because the wise guys had so much influence inside the walls. Serving time then, on a federal rap, was easy time, almost vacation-like. A wise guy could go inside and live in a dormitory with his *paisani* where they could yap about the good old days, play old Italian card games like *Briscola* or *Calabresella* and even cook a big pot of meatballs—beef, pork and veal, naturally—and gravy every Sunday. But things were changing. All the federal joints were taken over by the Federal Bureau of Prisons and are now technically part of the US Department of Justice. And, even though the Attorney General sees the operation of penal institutions as distasteful, he wants to show the public that federal law enforcement can control this *La Cosa Nostra* thing, in spite of The Director's denial that it even existed. Making a move on the mob was certainly easier to do while you had them behind bars. So instead of putting real agents on the street and breaking this thing up, the government decided to be real tough on them in jail by taking away their Sunday evening pasta and even their Friday afternoon visitation blow job from their gooms, who the guards would happily sneak in just to get a look at their tits. Carmine was sure T knew all this and he would cooperate both for his own sake and for his guys' long-term benefit.

Carmine's plan called for T to set up the final print, but he would have to be completely out of the loop. He would identify all the players who worked the initial print, get this mutt Miguel into the mix and then introduce a nice, new, fresh-faced printer to finish the job. Carmine made it painfully clear that the US Attorney would never let T out of custody, even if only to make an introduction—that's just the way it was. Sometimes the agents just have to bite down hard and realize the federal prosecutors made all the final decisions on any subject that could cause the Government bad publicity. The US Attorney wasn't going to risk T giving us the shake after we spring him and then be responsible for losing the biggest counterfeiting case in the history of the union. We needed a serious alternative plan, a plan as serious as a heart attack. And that's just what Carmine arranged.

"As soon as T puts wheels on this wagon and gets everybody on board, he's going to have a massive heart attack. That way we can keep him under lock and key, albeit in a hospital room, and he can then introduce a new printer whose trustworthiness he can vouch for to his guys. His Godson, the son of an old childhood *paisan,* who T stood behind on the day of the boy's confirmation, is the perfect choice," Carmine explained.

The confirmation connection was a good idea. It's a treasured Italian ceremony and custom. The boy even takes the sponsor's name as his own middle name and forever thereafter calls him "Godfather," because it's his responsibility to see to it that the boy grows up a good Catholic.

With the plan laid out, it was time to put it all in motion. The only place to start was to take another trip out to the lock down ward and give the bad news to T. So that's what I did and it turned out better than I expected. T had obviously been contemplating his situation and arrived at the same conclusion we did—both he and his guys had no real choices.

While I was naïve enough to think T was actually on board and he would voluntarily cooperate with us, Carmine, on the other hand, believed in the old adage, “when you got ’em by the balls, their hearts and minds will follow.” He never shared his skepticism with me and it wasn’t by accident that he let me swing my dick around. He didn’t want to quell my youthful and unfortunately ignorant enthusiasm. I actually thought that because I shared a “torpedo” and a little bit of heritage with T, he would willingly help me shatter the fiber and melt the glue that held his life to a collective that defined his reason to exist. I just never considered the personal consequences of T’s cooperation with the Secret Service.

I missed that connection because I was a fairly normal kid who grew up in a mostly typical family environment. I had some good friends and even kept a few from my younger high school years. But I had no idea of the intensity of the relationship between T and the other men he referred to as his “guys.” I knew there was no actual biological connection between them, but what I didn’t realize was that any mere biological relationship would pale in comparison to what they shared. These men were kindred souls. They lived as the men who flew the flying fortresses in the Second World War did. They each had a function or place in the struggle, and while at times some performed more immediate tasks, the mission—life itself—had no chance of success without their combined effort.

As I got to know them, it became clear to me that T wasn’t the leader or “pilot” of their ship because he wasn’t the one who could inspire the others and keep his head cool in times of despair. He wasn’t the navigator either, because he wasn’t the one who could plot the course from start to finish and remain steadfast in its completion when the journey got rough or the night got dark. I learned over the next few weeks that T was indeed the bombardier of this flying fortress. Because, while he couldn’t assume command or point the way, he certainly could make things happen when confronted with an opportune situation; and that’s just what he did here. When Miguel offered him a target-rich environment, he knew how to take advantage of it. And when The Secret Service offered him the opportunity to bail out of a ship in a headlong nosedive, he knew how to pull the ripcord—so long as he was confident that his guys also had parachutes. It was now up to me to keep this ship in the air until the Secret Service decided to shoot it down.

CHAPTER 19

"REMEMBER, A GUY ONLY HAS TO SUCK ONE COCK AND HE'S A COCKSUCKER, AND THAT'S THE POINT."

"YO, FRANKIE, IT'S T. HOW'S it hanging, son?" T began his telephone conversation.

"I took the goom for a little road trip. I got some sun and pussy, great combo. Ha, ha. Yeah. Well it worked for a while, but I ran into a little unexpected trouble. No, no nothin' like that. No, I didn't get pinched. I got a little trouble with my ticker they say, fuckin' thing. My old man had the same bullshit. Yeah, he always told me to stay away from that young stuff. He swore it would kill me. Yeah, I should be so fuckin' lucky."

"Listen I got this problem...we gotta finish paintin' that guy's house, ya know what I mean?"

"No, I didn't hear from him yet, but I expect to, any day. It's gonna be a rush job so we gotta be ready and with me with this fuckin' problem I need to talk to ya."

"St. Michael's, seventh floor."

"When? Okay."

"Listen...don't tell our friends about this yet. I don't want anybody losin' confidence in my ability to get the job done."

"Okay. *Bene, domani a sei. Ciao*"

T hung the receiver up in a gentle, pensive move. He held both parts of the telephone in his hands as if it were a baby. He stared at the cord dangling across the floor as if he wanted to quickly cut it to keep his words from ever leaving the room and influencing his lifelong friend to get in his car and come to him like he asked.

Listening to his words, you would think T was in the room alone, but he wasn't. Standing next to him, I took the phone from his hands and walked around the bed. Watching so the cord didn't get tangled, I put it back on the rectangular rolling service table standing at the foot of the bed. Nothing else was on the table except a plastic pitcher of iced water, cold and sweating on the outside, much like T was.

"He'll be here alone, right?" I asked in a voice that tried to be calming yet official at the same time. I knew enough Italian to know that the meeting was at 6 p.m. tomorrow. I was trying to get T to relax and not feel so bad about what he was doing and at the same time remind him that this was important business and needed to be handled as such.

It was only about a week since T's entire world had come crashing down. Before that he had been a happy-go-lucky guy, cruising the N.J. Turnpike with a great looking *goom* next to him, looking forward to sun, sex and a change of scenery. Well, he got the change of scenery all right. But instead of being at the Miami Beach Fontainebleau, he found himself locked up by the Troopers, held in some podunk jail where he ate the big cheese sandwich and turned into a rat. Now he's in Saint Michael's Hospital, where he was born and always hoped he would die—between nice clean sheets—rather than in a pool of blood on a street corner in some strange part of Jersey. Being there now with a kid he hardly even knew, who will now be instrumental in the preservation of the rest of his life, was just a bit mystifying.

With Carmine's help, I was able to get The Boss to convince the US Attorney to let us move T's custody from the lock down ward in New Brunswick to Saint Michael's in Newark where we would all be close to the action. My ass was on the line, but I was confident it would work. We put T in a private room on the seventh floor so there was no possibility of him doing a swan dive from the window, unless it was a dying swan. He knew that and I didn't think he was suicidal. Now that we let it out to his guys that he was in the hospital after suffering a heart attack, we had to be careful not to ruin the entire set up by them showing up unannounced and blowing our cover story. In order to avoid just such a catastrophe, we put T in the intensive care unit where the visiting was limited; we only needed to be concerned about specific hours each day and we could also claim to the US Attorney that he was still technically in our custody. We locked his door whenever we were not in a visiting window, and for good measure, we put a very medical looking desk and chair about twenty feet down the hall, with a clear view of his door and the elevator. Sitting at the desk 24/7 was a scrubs-clad young man, with a stethoscope around his neck, looking like a hard working intern. In reality, he had no clue how to use the stethoscope, but was very proficient with the .357 Magnum under those scrubs.

The Boss was able to convince headquarters to send us an EPS officer from Washington to babysit T, while we tried to pull this charade off. The EPS, formally known as Executive Protective Service, is the uniform branch of the Secret Service. It's composed of lots of young men who are trying to become special agents. In the meantime, they sit at the gates of the White House while going to school on their off-duty time. They're an eager bunch, always ready to help out a field office in need. Trying to get some egocentric special agent to sit out there would be painful at best. I felt confident, all in all, that T wasn't going anywhere; whether the investigation was going anywhere, I still wasn't sure.

"Okay, T," as I started to call him in order to establish a more personal relationship between us, "we've got a day to get this show on the road," I told him like I was the guy in charge.

"Sure, sure. Whadaya want me to do?" he replied while sitting on the side of the hospital bed wearing the same clothes he was arrested in. I'm sure he wasn't happy about that. But hey, there weren't any bars on the windows or some guy named Chico dying to shower with him.

We were lucky to get a room at St Michael's on the ruse that T had a heart attack. He was admitted by Doctor Vesputti for tests and follow-up care. One thing I learned during my short tenure with the Government is that you can't always rely on official channels to get things done. I always remember watching those old World War II movies where every company had a scavenger who could beg, borrow, steal or trade for the equipment his unit needed. And, that's just what we did. T certainly hadn't had a heart attack. But nonetheless, the good doctor—also Carmine's cousin—was happy to help us get T into a room and forge a treatment chart for a little excitement and, oh yeah, four New York Yankee box seats that somehow Carmine always seems to be able to get for almost any Yankee game. Some guys are convinced that Carmine knows or somewhere along the line did a very personal favor for Yogi Berra, but there's no confirmation of that. Someday maybe I'll ask him about it.

Responding to T's question, I began to tell him exactly what we needed from him to make this thing work. "I need for you to give me all the details on these guys Frankie and Canevecchio."

"Listen to me kid," he said. "I'm gonna do what you say, but who's gonna do this print? I get the bullshit story we're gonna give 'em, but these guys ain't a couple of pussies. If it don't smell right, they'll shut you down and walk away like you were sittin' in a port-o-potty in a junk yard in Port Elizabeth. Get the guy who's gonna do this print down here now, kid," T bellowed, adding the kid reference at the end just to piss me off.

"Relax," I told him. "The printer is ready, *mio Padrino*."

My words froze T in space and time. He got a look on his face like a 16-year-old boy who was just caught his father wearing nylons and heels. He just didn't know whether to shit or go blind. "*Padrino*" is Italian for Godfather. The message was as clear as a shot of Sambuca, and T understood.

"Listen kid, I like you, even though you're a fuckin' cop. But what the fuck makes you think you can pull this off? These guys are the real thing; they ain't no fuckin' Hollywood mobsters. This is business to them. Only thing, unlike those jerks on Wall Street, they also take it very personal. They get a hint you're a cop and the jig is up for both of us. You know what I'm sayin' here? Besides, you can't fuckin' print for shit anyways," he told me as he took a full step backward, like he needed room to wind up his words and swing his arms without us actually getting into a fist fight.

"That's the deal T. You know, you think the only smart guys, whose names end in a vowel, are in the mob. Some of us on the outside have a few good ideas, too," I firmly told him as I closed the space between us as if daring him to take it to the next level.

It was important for me to let him know that even though he called me "kid" I was "the kid" in charge here. We were going to do this and do it my way, and he was going to make it work, no matter how much he moaned about it. He looked down, closed his eyes and shook his head from left to right, but he wasn't saying no. He was scared and I knew it, and I think he knew I did and he didn't like that. I needed to get us back together on the same page.

I lowered my voice and moved away from him half a step, giving him space and respect. Then I explained it again.

"Look T, I worked this out with Carmine. He's done this for a long time with pricks a lot meaner than your guys. With a little luck, this will all go real smooth. We may never even get to the printing part. We just have to get it set up to print and then the sky will fall on everybody, including you and me. Nobody will know how it happened and with just a little luck we get the buyer and he gets the blame for bringing the 'blue'" (a less derogatory term for the cops).

"Just work with me and get me ready to run the bluff for a few days. That's all you have to do. Then you and your guys get a sweetheart letter from the US Attorney and a short stay at a minimum-security Club Fed. We'll throw in a one way ticket to Timbuktu where you and Lucille can relax and spend the rest of your days squandering all that ill-gotten cash you got stashed... that we're never gonna ask you about. *Capisce, mio Padrino*?" I gave him that little speech, making it clear there was nothing more to talk about and it was now time to get to work. But, as always, he had something to say.

"Your hands are no fuckin' good. It's the first thing Frankie'll look for," T said in a rough voice while still looking at the floor, but clearly telling me he was now ready to make it happen.

It was just the sign I was looking for. I certainly didn't expect him to apologize or even act like he agreed with me. I got all I was going to get from him, but more importantly, it was all I really needed.

"What do we need to do?" I asked in a very deferential tone.

T grabbed both my hands like a couple of jelly donuts. He first turned them knuckles down and then knuckles up.

"These hands are for playin' with yourself when you get bored being a fuckin' dago 'G' man. These ain't workin' hands, and they sure as hell ain't the hands of a printer. If you're a printer, you ain't never gonna get all the ink outta your hands. The ink seeps into the cuticles and the calluses and ridges in the skin of your palms, dries 'em out like three-week-old salami left on the kitchen floor. You got none a those things, let alone ink in 'em."

At least this time when he told me all the things I wasn't, he looked me in the eye like he was looking for an answer, rather than just blowing me off. He continued.

"When Frankie meets you, he's gonna grab your hands like this," he said as he grabbed my right hand like he was going to shake it. He also squeezed it the way he probably wanted to squeeze my head for making him do all this.

"And then he's gonna turn your hand over like this and look at your knuckles and cuticles looking for ink stains. When he don't see 'em, he's gonna talk about the fuckin' weather and maybe some dames, but fugettabout any printin' shit," he said, while still squeezing my hand so tight I was sure he ruined my future career as a concert pianist. Hell, I wasn't sure it would ever go back into shape. I couldn't help thinking that maybe I was lucky when he backed down a little while ago. I wasn't entirely sure I wouldn't have to shoot the son of a bitch if we really got into it.

"Okay, okay...look...we have about 24 hours to get ready for this meet. I know you can't teach me to print in that time, but you sure as hell can teach me to talk it real good. I know you can. And as far as the hands, well, leave that to me. So what else?" I asked, giving him a challenge that I knew he couldn't resist.

It's what a guy like T lived for. He wasn't like the rest of us. He didn't get up in the morning and go to work and struggle through the day to come home to wife, kids, supper and sex, all lashed together in a nice neat bundle by three hours of television—no, not this guy. A regular Joe thinks boredom is what life is. He has no idea what it can become. He lives every day just to avoid conflict, uncontrollable situations and unpredictability, especially in people. But that kind of existence for T just didn't work. To T, life was an exciting adventure every day, or it was nothing at all. Some guys satisfy this need by performing physically challenging feats, like mountain climbing or sky diving. But even that kind of challenge wouldn't satisfy T. He'd figure any dumb son-of-a bitch could jump out of an airplane or climb a mountain. T, on the other hand, got his excitement from an intellectual and psychological challenge. Of course, he liked a little danger once in a while, but not like sky diving—more like getting chased by the psychotic husband of some lustfully lonesome woman who he had fucked hard and sent home to her husband wet. That was his call of the wild.

"And another thing is your language. It's ignorant. I gotta teach ya everything?" T blurted out in response to my challenge.

When T told me that, I laughed right out loud. But he didn't laugh back. In fact, he didn't even smile. He was dead serious when he called my language "ignorant."

"Yeah, sure it is, T," I snapped back, thinking he was just busting my balls and trying to show how inexperienced I was. Then he explained it to me and made me feel like I should be looking for a job as a mouseketeer rather than working as a Secret Service Agent.

"*Ascolti,*" (Listen to me) he said in a stern voice because he knew I was making fun of his criticism. I guess he thought it would impress me. It did. I was impressed with myself that I even understood what he was saying. In reality, I only knew a few curse words and anything edible or having to do with sex. Other than that, I would just shake my head and smile.

"...There's a few rules that every friend of mine knows, and if ya wanna parlay, you gotta know 'em, okay?"

While he was speaking, T tilted his oversized head slightly down as if he were looking at me over the top of his eyeglasses—if he was wearing any, which he wasn't. As soon as he stopped talking, he pressed his lips together tightly, and then puckered them just enough to emphasize that he had just said something important that I might have missed; but not enough to make me fearful that he was going to kiss me. I didn't miss anything and I told him so.

"I got it T. They're friends of yours, which means they're Made Guys, but they're certainly not friends of mine or ours. I got it. I got it. And by the way, *paisan*, someday we're going to have a long talk about this Made Guy stuff and just how you and your guys got that way. You know there's no statute of limitations for a 'hit.' You did know that right, Mister, 'I-made-my-bones'?"

T immediately recognized the expression and was maybe even a little surprised that I knew what it meant and even said it right out loud. It's a very serious subject. When a guy "makes his bones" it means that he has actually killed for the "family" and as a result is eligible for full status as a "Made Man" in *La Cosa Nostra.*

Boy that really got his attention, although I wasn't entirely sure it was such a smart thing to bring it up just then. I found myself enjoying the intellectual jousting with T, but I may have gone too far with that "hit" stuff. I didn't want to scare him and make him think that when this was all over I was going to punk out on my promise to go to bat with the US Attorney for him and then try to pin some thirty-year-old hit on him. Or possibly even worse, do that to Frankie or one of his other guys. I do have to admit, however, that the issue did creep into my mind now and again. Even though T had an affable nature, I always had to remember he was in fact a "Made" member of the Mafia and historically there is only one way a man achieves that status, and it's not by making a good pot of pasta gravy. Even knowing that, it was very difficult to see T as a cold-blooded killer. I wasn't so sure if I was going to have that same difficulty with our anticipated visitor.

I realized that it wasn't the time to talk to T about the past, but rather try to keep him focused on his future—his future out of the joint when we finished our work together. I needed to get his head off it quickly.

"Fugettabout it," I said, trying to imitate him. "You're such a pussy. I'm sure they made some kind of an exception for you because you're such a good looker and probably got all the guys laid, huh, T?"

"See...that's just what I'm gettin' at here. You just called a guy a pussy without knowin' the fuckin' rules," he bellowed. "Are you ready to listen to me now, or are ya just gonna fuck this whole thing up and then blame it on me and throw me back in da joint?"

I'm certain T could have been a captain of industry if he chose to do so. Instead, he was a Caporegime in the Mafia—same skills, maybe different rules—maybe not so different. Quite a manipulator T was. I just had to hope he was able to manipulate me into this dark inkwell and back out again without too many lasting stains. He began to lay down the rules.

"First rule is that you can use the word 'fuck' or 'fuckin' all you want. You can even call a guy 'a fuck,' a 'fuckin so and so' or even a 'no good fuck' so long as you never, ever combine it with certain other forbidden words," the lesson continued.

"Never, never call a guy a 'Motherfucker.' Yeah, I know lots of guys talk like that but not us. You call a guy a 'Motherfucker' and you'll catch a beatin' for sure, *capisce?*"

As I listened to him, although I never quite focused on it before, it became perfectly clear and surprisingly logical. "Mother" is a word reserved for the most sacred of all beings in an Italian man's life, probably a more important and more revered word even than "Christ" or "God." Mother is the giver of all life and even in the undeniably patriarchal society of *La Cosa Nostra*, your Mother is the most important, protected and respected person in your life. And that goes not only for your mother, but also for the mother of all your *paisani*. If you call a guy a "Motherfucker," it's not what you are calling him that gets you the beating; it's the reference to his Mother that does.

As T went on, I was listening like a ten-year-old standing at mom and dad's bedroom door on date night.

"Now, you can refer to your cock, anybody else's cock or any cunt or pussy you want. The minute you start putting 'em together you get your ass in a jam. *Capisce*? So, you never call a guy a 'cocksucker.' Get it? Remember a guy only has to suck one cock and he's a cocksucker, and that's the point. Listen, alotta guys have done time and some of it was hard time. What a guy does in the joint is his business and he gets a pass for it. A 'Made Guy' would never do somethin' like that, but some of the guys around him might, and he has to protect his 'earners'...understand? It's somethin' a guy who's been around 'Made Guys' knows; so watch your mouth. Frankie'll pick up on it right away."

That concluded the etiquette lesson. We then turned to the critical discussion of getting me ready to talk a good print. Secret Service School gave me a shallow understanding of the technique. And conversations with Carmine helped me understand the subtleties. But listening to T was downright illuminating. It truly was art. I listened for almost four hours and memorized his instructions, the lingo and even his incredibly detailed drawings on an old sandwich wrapper.

I left the hospital about 3:00 to make the final preparations for the biggest and scariest evening of my life. We figured Frankie would probably show up around six or so, stay an hour or maybe two, and then leave to go eat. I figured that a low dose of exposure on the first "date" would be best. It would give me a chance to catch my breath and talk to T afterwards, in order to straighten out any fuck ups I made. I couldn't help think what strange bedfellows we were. I also never gave a thought to the fact that, no matter what I thought or how I prepared, the course of the night could not have been more out of my control than if I had a date with a vampire.

CHAPTER 20

SAINT CHRISTOPHER, HERCULES AND DAFFODILS

When I left the hospital, I only had about three hours to get home, get prepared and get back to initiate the charade. The drive home was quick, so I had just enough time to handle the last minute, but important, preparations for the meet at 6:00. I figured I didn't need to be there at six sharp because I had a feeling Frankie wouldn't be there "on the dot." I made a quick stop at the local lumberyard for a single 19-cent item. I cooked up a little surprise for T that I thought would impress him and at the same time help me make my own "bones" with his guy Frankie. I knew it wasn't going to be fun, but if Frankie was going to examine my hands, he was probably only going to do it one time and that would be today, while he was trying to decide if I could really print. As I was preparing, I couldn't help wonder if it was all really worth it. I decided it was and bled a little more.

After a hot shower, I realized that the clothes on my back would be almost as important as all the other stuff T and I discussed. He never mentioned how I should dress and it never dawned on me to ask.

"What the fuck do I do now?" I kept thinking.

I didn't have a single pair of cuffed, sharkskin pants with a perfect Armani break at the instep of a pair of Italian loafers.

Furthermore, I didn't then, nor did I ever expect to own a three button, Italian-knit, pull over sweater. It was too late to build a costume that I thought would fit, so I had to go with what I had. Luckily, I did have a couple of things that might help me show some legitimacy; if I could give them enough play to hold Frankie's attention on them, instead of on the jeans I was sure to wear.

First, I had an authentic 14k gold Saint Christopher medal given to me by my own Godfather when I was confirmed. I wore it all the time because I always felt I was a bit lost in life and I figured wearing the patron saint of the lost traveler around my neck couldn't hurt. The thing I never did, though, was wear it outside my shirt. I was taught that a Saint's medal wasn't jewelry and should never be worn as an adornment. In fact, when I was a kid, I took a couple of cracks in the head for just being sloppy with it. From then on, I kept it quietly tucked into the top of my guinea tee. But this day was different. I figured I would follow the lead of a lot of guys my age in the Italian neighborhoods and wear it prominently displayed over my undershirt. If I wore a regular shirt with a collar, I could leave the top two buttons open and it would sparkle nicely, like a fishing lure to a trout. I've often seen guys wearing nice silk t-shirts, even turtlenecks, with the medal completely outside the shirt like a chic would wear a heart or some other such thing. There was no way I could do that and feel comfortable. Besides, where was I going to get a silk t-shirt?

The second play I had was a gold ring made from a great silver Roman coin minted in 50 BC. I got a tingle looking at a silver coin that over 2000 years ago was in the purse of some Roman Legionnaire. The coin is about the size of a nickel and has an image of Caesar on the front, but that's not the important part. It's the back of the coin that holds its significance. There are lots of coins that bear the likeness of Caesar or some other self-important Roman politician playing god. But there are far fewer that actually portray a Greek and later Roman god—Hercules—that men and boys throughout the ages emulate in both body and spirit. Boys and men of all ages, especially those who grew up with the added images of Steve Reeves on the silver screen defeating tyranny and injustice, wish they could rise to adversity in life as Hercules did. The coin I wore was one that commemorated one of the great tests of Hercules—the defeat of the Nemean lion. It's a dramatic image of a mostly naked and heavily muscled Hercules, standing erect, repelling the attack of this mythological man-eater.

The ring I wore then, and still wear today, was once worn by my father. He had two identical rings made and gave one to me when I graduated from high school. He wore his until the day he was buried, after dying a young man. The last time I ever laid eyes on him was when I slid the ring from his finger as they prepared to close the casket. I slipped it on my finger after removing mine, remembering my promise to him that I would pass mine onto my son, until it's his time to wear mine and continue the tradition through the ages. I still wear the ring every day and wouldn't consider taking it off for anything, including this assignment. I always felt my father's presence and believed the ring gave me strength and courage in the mythological tradition of Hercules and the loving support of my father. Indeed, if I took it off for some brief moment and then left in on the dresser or bathroom sink, I would immediately feel vulnerable without it—I would seem to lose my way. I drove sixty miles back to my apartment one day because I left it on the nightstand and just felt I couldn't get through the day without it.

It wasn't until recently, almost two years after he died, that I discovered the secret he never revealed. He probably thought I would have just pooh-poohed it, but now I'm a believer. Just before I went for my interview with The Boss for the Secret Service job, I was in a shop looking at a watch. The salesman noticed my ring and asked to see it. I never take it off to let someone look at it—I just let them gaze at it while it's still on my finger—but this guy was an older Italian guy and I felt like he had a genuine interest in it and he might enjoy seeing both sides of the coin. So I took it off. Much to his glee, he poured over every inch of the ring, even using a jeweler's loupe to see the definition in the coin. When he gave it back to me, he mentioned how captivating it was. As I held it in my hand, I must have seemed confused by his description because he promptly added, "You know, with the inscription and all." Well, I guess there was no hiding the absolute astonishment in my face. "You didn't know?" he quizzically asked. As I was about to confess my ignorance, I suddenly knew.

I grabbed the jeweler's loop and sure enough: *forte, valore, sagezza*, (strength, courage, wisdom) was the inscription on the inside of the ring. I was sure it was on the other ring as well. My head rang as I recalled my father uttering those Italian words to me the day he gave me my ring. But, I had no suspicion that he was handing me the instrumentality to inspire my will to achieve such virtues on a daily basis. It was one of the most profound experiences of my life. I felt like I had just learned that I was adopted by Mr. and Mrs. Kent after falling from the sky, giving rational explanation to my suspected invincibility. I have never again taken the ring off for any reason. You can ask a number of women who will confirm that.

There were just a couple of decisions left since I already decided I would wear my perfectly faded Wranglers, which were at that time just becoming the cutting edge of fashion. The only better jeans were those perfect ass-cut Gloria Vanderbilt's. They were truly amazing. They made every girl's ass look like a seven course meal at an expensive New York restaurant.

As far as shoes went, I really didn't have a choice. If I wore sneakers, even my Converse All Stars, I'm sure Frankie would be convinced I was some kind of college kid, especially when combined with the jeans. The only other choice was my Luccheses. Hell, they got me in enough trouble in the office; I might as well make them earn their keep. I actually had a few pairs, but my favorites were a nice, light brown goatskin that had a talon stitch pattern down the shaft and around the vamp. They looked great with a pair of jeans. I figured that I knew I was going to be nervous and uncomfortable and I could minimize that if I at least had on clothes and boots that let me feel like myself.

In the middle of all my anguish, just to complicate things a little more, I got a call from Carmine.

"Hey kid," as he liked to call me along with almost everybody else on the planet, so it seemed. "About an hour ago we got a call for T from a guy with a Spanish accent on the undercover phone."

While that was good news, it was just another thing to worry about at a moment that was already chocked full of worry. I also knew of only one guy with a Spanish accent that would be calling T, and that was Miguel. Once again, Carmine's experience was essential to this caper. When he moved T into the hospital, he also isolated him from not only his guys, but also from reconnection with the buyer, Miguel. It was easy enough to reunite T and his guys, but we had no idea how to contact Miguel, and that's probably just the way he wanted it. I'm sure he figured he was safer reaching out for T when he wanted to move ahead with the print, which is probably what he intended when he called T's apartment. Only thing is, when he called T's apartment, instead of talking to T, he spoke to the Secret Service. Little did he know that Carmine had the telephone company reroute T's number to a telephone in our undercover room at the Newark Field Office.

Using the telephone to establish a surreptitious connection with a target wasn't unusual. When the undercover phone rings in the office, the closest agent responds to the call. The first thing he does is turn on the TV in the room and turn up the volume. There's a pad by the telephone with some very simple instructions to follow depending on who the call is for. In our case, it just said that if someone calls for T, simply say he's out and get a name and number, if possible. The TV is turned on loud to add ambiance to the situation. Who would ever think they're talking to the Secret Service with the soap operas blaring in the background. The loud TV also gives the agent answering the phone a chance to say, "Hold on a minute while I turn down the TV," so he can quickly review the notes on the pad before he says anything. We had to set it up that way because sometimes there was more than one case going on at the same time and the agent answering the phone may not know anything about the case the call is about.

"When did we get the call?" I asked.

"About 1:00 this afternoon. I took the call myself."

"What did he say?" I was hoping we learned something about this guy, but no such luck.

"Nothing...not even a message. Just a terse, 'I'll call later'." I could hear the disappointment in Carmine's voice.

Now I had to ask, "Are you sure it was him?"

"No!" he quickly replied. "But, he clearly wasn't Italian and it didn't sound like a social call. It could be just a little more homework on the part of the buyer. There's no way of tellin. We gotta be ready for a hook up with T. What's up over there?"

"Well, I think we're as ready as we can be. I'm going back to the hospital around 6:00 and I hope this guy Frankie shows up. We'll break the ice and then later, when we get the nod from Miguel, we'll set up the print." I was trying to give Carmine the information he needed without sounding like I was nearly as lost and confused as I really was. I wanted him to think I had it under control. After all, this was like a first real date for Carmine and me. He was a real pro at this and I was a rookie. I didn't want him to think that after I put on the rubber I didn't know where to put it, so to speak.

"Okay. Call me when it's over. In the meantime, I'll arrange for the TSD (Technical Security Division) guys to go out to T's apartment and hook his home phone line through to his hospital room. This will never go down unless this guy can get T on the phone directly. He'll never leave a number," Carmine explained, knowing just how to make it all come together.

"Roger," I said, confirming my obedience before I hung the phone up, slipped on the goatskin Luccheses, picked out a watch to wear, slipped on my black leather jacket and headed for the door.

The drive from my apartment back to T's hospital room was even shorter than the exact same drive from the hospital to my apartment. I couldn't tell you why—maybe because my brain was spinning like a Ferrari revving into the red—but I'm sure it was. I quickly arrived, parked the VW, walked into the hospital, got off the elevator and was nearly in front of T's door before I realized where I was and why I was there. I think the voices I heard coming from behind the closed door startled me to consciousness. I focused my eyes on the EPS officer down the hall, who was still sitting at his post, looking very medical. However, he did give me the high sign by a little nod of the head, telling me that our guest had visitors and I should be prepared. I wasn't and I knew it. Then to the EPS officer's complete astonishment, I turned on my cowboy heel and, without so much as a stutter step, headed back toward the elevator. He was probably well beyond astonishment when I actually got on the elevator, turned and put my index finger to my lips, shushing him, as the doors closed and the elevator descended to the ground floor.

Thankfully, when I arrived in the lobby there was a men's room directly across the hall from the elevator. You would have thought I was gonna shit my pants the way I hustled through the door. Actually, come to think of it, maybe I was. I stood and stared directly in front of the 8-foot-long mirror that covered the wall over the sinks as if I was looking out an open window, hoping there was somebody out there to talk me off that ledge. My own reflection was that of a complete stranger. I actually startled myself, and it wasn't until I stepped back half a stride and gazed into my own eyes that things began to feel familiar again. I took a moment to splash some cold water on my face and reflect on what was happening to me. It didn't take long for me to face the reality that I was just plain scared. But what was I afraid of? I knew that I wasn't going to get shot by these guys right there in the hospital room. The worst that could happen was that Frankie would make me as an agent and the caper would go south. Once I faced that fact, it was easier for me to understand that I was afraid of my own failure. I was terrified of having to listen to The Boss and the other guys in the office who were just dying to call me a jerk college kid who will never make it as an undercover agent. It would also kill me to disappoint Carmine. He went to bat for me and I didn't want him to strike out because of my incompetence.

After only a minute or two, I looked at my ring and said right out loud there in the bathroom:

"Do you think Hercules was 'fraidy scared of that fuckin' lion? You're wearin' a Saint Christopher medal and a pair of genuine cowboy boots. What the fuck could go wrong? Get up there, you pussy, and make this thing work."

I felt much better. I put some water on my hands and ran them through my hair, just to give it a little grease-ball shine. Another quick look in the mirror and I hit the door and was off.

I was about to get back on the elevator when I realized something else was wrong. I was supposed to be going to see my Godfather in the hospital right after he had a heart attack and my hands were empty—not good. So l looked for the hospital gift shop, which I found just around the corner from the men's room. Naturally, the place was full of stupid little shit and sicko cards that just wouldn't do. They also had magazines, like *Time* and *Newsweek*, which T would never consider even looking at. Then I looked closer and saw the cover story on *Newsweek*—"Bobby Kennedy's war on organized crime." That was it. Of course he would want to read that story. So I bought it and a small vase of daffodils and some other yellow flower I didn't recognize. Now I felt complete. Having something in my hands gave me balance.

I rode the elevator to the seventh floor again, only this time I was in complete fuckin' control and ready to handle whatever these guys could throw at me. Yeah, sure I was!

CHAPTER 21

ELVIS, A RED BRICK AND A SLIDE RULE

When the elevator opened again, the EPS officer was still there. It was obvious that he didn't think he was going to see me again so soon. He looked as surprised as a 15-year-old smoking in the boy's room when the vice-principal walked in and asked for a light. I could still hear the voices in T's room so I stuck my head in the door and said in a soft voice, "*Padrino*?"

"*Giacobbe, Giacobbe, Viene qui*, come here, come here!" T responded in a rather booming voice for a guy who just had a heart attack.

"*Come stai*, how are you?" I asked in both Italian and English knowing that was the extent of my Italian language skills, hoping T remembered that and would stick to English from then on.

As I walked into the room, I focused entirely on T. He was in the bed, wearing a white, tied-in-the-back hospital gown. He seemed to be convincingly playing the part of a sick guy. I, however, was sweating like a farm animal. I leaned over the bed and gave him the kiss of respect on the cheek. It was required. I always kissed my father when I saw him, so the custom was not unfamiliar to me.

"This is my godson that I have been telling you about," T said while still looking at me. I think he was trying to calm me down because he could tell I was shaking like a leaf in a tropical storm.

When I lifted my head from T's cheek, I saw there was someone standing on the other side of the bed, away from the door. I don't know how I missed him when I walked in, but I just did. As I focused on him, my mind immediately began to go into overdrive. My first reaction was one of complete surprise.

"He's nothing like I expected," I thought to myself.

I knew Frankie would be there. I spent the entire day preparing myself physically and mentally for the encounter. It threw me for a loop to be confronted now by a guy that didn't fit the image I had conjured.

The guy in front of me was around fifty. Come to think of it, fifty was the right number. His age was about fifty and so was his waistline, as well as the number of pounds he needed to lose. He was only about 5 feet 6 inches and, naturally, he was wearing a black, three-button Italian double knit shirt. The shirt was pulled down around his belly like a queen size sheet fitted onto a king size mattress. It was so tight you could see the vertical ribs of his guinea t-shirt underneath. He also wore a gold crucifix around his neck and a gold pinky ring. I was unable to see what the ring was because it was so tight on his little finger that it appeared to be screwed on, like a nut onto a bolt. While the crucifix fit around his enormous neck, it did, just barely. There was no way it was ever going to come off over his huge, balding head. Unlatching the gold chain would have also been a near impossible task because most of it was imbedded in the fat of his neck. As a result, the extra-long chain fit like a choker collar and the crucifix was only visible in the relatively small "V" space created by the three open buttons at the top of his shirt.

He looked physically powerful, but he projected a somewhat dull and unsophisticated persona. His arms were huge. In fact, their size, coupled with the layer of fat that looped around the sides of his chest, made it impossible for them to hang perpendicular to the floor. They hung below his "no neck" and hunched shoulders, at a 45-degree angle to his chest, while resting on the protruding flab. All-in-all, he looked like a cue ball stuck in the corner pocket of a pool table.

I knew the confusion must have shown on my face. While I was trying to digest the image in front of me, T said in a calm, clear voice, "Hey kid, meet my *paisan,* Canevecchio."

T made the introduction while my attention was still riveted on the man I was sure was Frankie but now was told is an old dog? I quickly turned to T and found him looking with great intent into my eyes as if to say, "Calm the fuck down, everything is under control."

This was the first thing that made any sense to me since I walked in the door, so I gladly took his advice. I reached over the bed, shook Canevecchio's hand and smiled warmly. Even though I'm sure my heart rate slowed by at least forty beats, I was still thoroughly confused. But at least now my mind was working the problem, albeit frantically.

"Now what?" I kept thinking, when it dawned on me that Canevecchio didn't come alone. It was like a B-grade horror movie. I suddenly realized someone else was in the room, but I didn't have the courage to look. So I turned my head toward T, hoping he would see that I still needed help getting my bearings. He knew exactly what I needed.

He slowly took his eyes off me, directed them to the far corner of the room and just began to speak when Canevecchio boomed, "Yo *Ponte,* come meet da kid."

Even before he finished his short command, I looked across the room toward a chair in the corner, next to the window. I clearly heard Canevecchio call this guy *Ponte*, but there was no doubt in my mind this was Frankie. T Immediately jumped in to straighten out what he knew was a confusing cross-use of names.

"Jake, this is my *paisan*, Frankie," he said ignoring the name *Ponte*.

None of the name calling made any difference to me. I was just relieved to identify the target. Now I had a purpose for being there and I could finally calm down and focus. But I didn't, of course. As soon as I saw where he was sitting, I started to think about the fact that he was able to see my every move and gesture since I walked in the room. Each time I looked at T with that expression of panic, Frankie was in the corner watching. That's probably why he was there in the first place, to observe and probe before having to actually make a move. While this bothered me a great deal, I at least realized that the worst thing I could do would be to compound my initial mistake and show him even more of my ass so he could bite down on it real hard. I had to stiffen up and play the role I was there to play.

"*Ciao. Padrino* talks about you often. I am very happy to finally meet you," I said in a very strong, steady voice as I moved toward him with my right hand extended in friendship. As I got closer to him, I realized he was a perfect combination of Frank Sinatra, "Ole Blue Eyes" and Jake LaMotta, "The Raging Bull"—alluring and terrifying in equal proportions.

Frankie continued to sit in the chair with his right leg tightly crossed over his left, like only a skinny guy can do. He could do that because he didn't have an ounce of fat on him anywhere. I didn't even have to see all of him to know that. He had those perfect genes. His face was chiseled and angular, with deep-set, dark brown Italian eyes that were framed in high cheek bones and full, luxuriant eyebrows.

The window next to the chair was open a crack to accommodate the smoke from the Benson and Hedges cigarette he was holding but not smoking. He didn't stand as I approached to shake his hand. I was surprised; I would have stood. He took my hand, held it with a firm grip and never took his eyes off mine, nor did he utter a single word. He never felt or looked for evidence that I was a printer. I was certain he would and was upset when he didn't. I was prepared to meet the test and became concerned that I had already blown my cover, and therefore he wasn't even interested in checking me out. As usual, I was over simplifying what was happening. I hadn't blown my cover and he certainly was checking me out, only he just hadn't gotten to my hands yet; all that was to shortly follow.

The room became eerily silent as Frankie let go of my hand. At that point, everyone in the room, including me, was staring at Frankie as if to hear a verdict from a jury. He didn't say a thing, but he did reach over to the window sill and put out the half-burned cigarette in a waiting ashtray. He then looked over at T, put his lips tightly together and raised his voluptuous eyebrows that brightened his already piercing eyes. He gave his head a single nod as if to say. "Okay, now what?" Canevecchio remained standing next to the bed, still looking like a cue ball stuck in a corner pocket. Only now, he pushed both of his lips out and shook his head up and down like a bobble-head doll.

Evidently all this meant something to T. He tried to sit up but the flat bed made it difficult, so he looked at me and rotated the wrist of his right hand in a small clockwise circle. I understood and immediately went to the foot of the bed and turned the crank enough to raise the head of the bed so he could sit up. Canevecchio slid up the side of the bed closer to T, and I occupied the same space on my side of the bed. Frankie got up, moved over to Canevecchio's side and stood next to him. It was time to get down to business. T started the conversation.

"Okay. We gotta finish paintin' that guy's house. I expect to hear from him any day now so we gotta get ready. We need to get the paint and brushes and stuff we're gonna need. *Capisce*?" T explained, looking for confirmation that everyone knew what he was talking about.

T didn't know that the buyer was already reaching out for him. I figured I would tell him after the guys left.

"Now," T continued, "I'm not gonna be able to help—that's why I called Jake here. I already spoke to him about how the guy wants us to paint it and he can do it. Ya know what I mean? He's a very good painter. I trained him myself. Ya know what I mean?"

Canevecchio was bobbing his head vigorously. He was obviously already on board. However, all the time he was bobbing, he was looking at Frankie. Clearly, convincing Frankie of my mettle was key. Evidently, however, T was getting vibes from Frankie that he didn't like.

"Listen, *Ponte*, believe me—it'll be okay," T said, using the other name for Frankie that I heard for the first time only a few minutes earlier.

T never mentioned to me that they called Frankie by another name. It unnerved me just a little, so I tried to figure it out. "*Ponte*" certainly wasn't a common Italian nickname I ever heard before. It was clearly Italian, meaning bridge or link. I knew that from the famous *Ponte Vecchio* (old bridge) in Florence, but I didn't understand the reference in connection with Frankie. While I didn't like the fact that T never mentioned it to me, I didn't have the time nor the energy to dwell on it at that moment. I knew it would eventually be important to understand its significance, but I had to just go with it at that moment and find out what it was all about from T later.

"Kid, can you do this? Just tell me the truth," Frankie said, speaking his first words to me while covering me with an icy stare. I felt like we were all on a movie set with Cecil B. DeMille directing a Mafia epic. It took all I had not to yell cut and head for the door. But I didn't. I leaned over the bed to get closer to him in opposition to every instinct in my soul. I raised both of my hands above the bed, parallel to each other and perpendicular to the bed, like a good Italian kid and said, "I can do this *Ponte*."

I was taking an enormous chance by calling him *Ponte*. I figured there was some significance in the fact that his closest friends called him that. It had to be out of respect and even if I didn't know exactly why, I figured I could get on the inside track if I started acting like somebody who deserved to be there. I was counting on T being true to our deal. If I was right, Frankie didn't know what T told me and what he didn't tell me about him. For all he knew, he told me the entire story about why they call him *Ponte* and so it would have been natural for me to use it. I immediately concluded it may have been a mistake when, as soon as it was out of my mouth, Frankie straightened up his torso and turned and transferred that icy stare to T. To his credit, T revealed absolutely no emotion in response and just gave him a little nod as if to say, "The kid's one of us." And then it happened. And when it did, T was about to freak. I, on the other hand, was actually relieved.

Frankie reached across the bed and grabbed both of my hands, pushing them together, palm-to-palm. He squeezed them so hard that it felt like they were in the jaws of a rabid Doberman. I didn't react though. I just went with it as he separated them and then turned them over, and over again, first, knuckles up and then, knuckles down. It was time. He was doing exactly what T said he would do and without any pretense or stealth. He was looking for a printer. And much to T's astonishment, he found one.

It was the first time since I walked into the room that I knew I was prepared for what was happening. The hours I spent earlier in the day smoochin' and cuddlin' with that fuckin' red brick paid off. After T made such a big fuckin deal about my hands, I thought about it and decided he might be right. There was no way I could graft two decades of hard physical labor and printer's wear onto my hands. But with a little ingenuity, I figured I could at least mask my "college" hands and create a couple of mitts that might get by.

Earlier, on the way back to the apartment, I stopped at a local brickyard and bought one, brand new, kiln-fired, red brick. I got a new one because the old ones, which some builders prefer because they have that classic patina that only comes with time and weather, become smoother over the years. The brick I bought was rough and edgy and it fuckin' hurt just to pick it up with my bare hands. I took it home and fondled and rubbed it for nearly two hours. By the time I was done, my knuckles were red and bruised, with chunks of skin torn off, and my palms felt like 80-grit sandpaper. My palms actually weren't as pristine as T made out. I had spent several years lifting weights in high school and college and did develop some calluses. Handling the brick made them look as if they were more recently subjected to manual labor. A special touch was needed to add a printer's patina to them. So I opened the ink cartridge from a ballpoint pen with a razor blade and rubbed a small amount of black ink into the cracks and crevasses created by the red brick, paying special attention to my cuticles because T made an extra big deal about them. It didn't take much ink to leave the impression that these hands had been in places they never actually were.

I was really glad T was on my side in this. He was a great actor. I know that when Frankie was turning my hands over and running the tips of his thumbs over the newly chaffed skin, T was completely astonished at what he was seeing and yet not a single hint of surprise. We, however, did make fleeting eye contact while Frankie was occupied with my hands. I couldn't help giving him just a little "I told you I could handle this" look. As I glanced down, I had to admit my hands looked pretty authentic. After I took a shower, I washed them with Lava soap. It was rough, but unlike the brick, it irritated uniformly. A little hand lotion quieted the redness and made the skin look more permanently scarred, and actually, I think it is.

Just as I was giving myself an "attaboy," I was again caught completely off guard and feared I was caught "red handed" so to speak. Frankie turned my left hand over, knuckles up, and while I was confident they would pass his examination, I was floored to hear that he wasn't looking at my hands.

"Kid thinks he's fuckin' Elvis," Frankie said while turning his head just a quarter turn toward T, keeping both eyes on me. There wasn't so much as a hint of a smile.

I actually felt faint for the first time in my life. What a pussy. I also knew exactly what he was talking about. I was so shocked that he knew enough to make the reference to Elvis that I wasn't even upset with myself for not anticipating it. Never in a million years would I have thought not to wear that watch. And there I was, desperately trying to figure out what he was thinking. Actually, we were both probably facing the same issue. He was probably trying to figure if there was any significance to me wearing the watch and I was trying to figure what significance, if any, he was attributing to me wearing the watch. And how the fuck did he know what he was looking at anyway? Once my ass un-puckered and I started to think again, I started to work out some answers to these new and troubling questions.

I was wearing a yellow-gold, Hamilton Ventura watch. It was the world's first electric powered watch in a new-age triangular shape—a daring design effort by the American watchmaker.

While released in 1957, it was the November 22, 1961 premier of Elvis Presley's latest movie, *Blue Hawaii* that caught everyone's interest. It was a fairly big hit, both in the theater and at the jukebox. But what the average moviegoer didn't know was that in that movie, Elvis wore a Hamilton Ventura exactly like the one I was wearing now. Elvis loved that watch. I was sure that was the reason for the Elvis comment by Frankie. On reflection, it was probably a bad idea to wear it. But the history of the watch never dawned on me. In reality, only somebody that had a real interest in watches or was simply an avid reader would have ever known about the Elvis connection. That realization immediately terrified me because it told me that this guy is way smarter and actually much hipper than anyone has given him credit for, especially me. Frankie wasn't done yet, either..

"So, waddaya think, you're Elvis? You should wear a real man's watch," he said in a sarcastic tone that pissed me off just a little. I wasn't sure where he was going, but I didn't like either his comment or his tone. I felt he was belittling me, and probably testing me to see if I could be a real tough guy or just some pussy kid. I needed to make a stand and take a chance. So I decided to see if he could take it as well as give it. I took a deep breath and went for it.

"Yeah. What's wrong with Elvis? He's a great talent, and besides, he's probably banged more broads than even Sinatra," I responded without mentioning a word about the watch and risking he would take the Sinatra slur personally.

We were the only two people in the room who had any idea what we were talking about, and there was no reason to explain it to the others. It was like we were talking in code, which made me feel that we had successfully connected, even if only in conflict. Besides, I learned something important about Frankie in those few minutes. He was a man of refined taste as well as a reader. He wasn't confined by all that macho dago bull shit like most of the guys of his realm. That made him much more dangerous to me. I had to cover him on fronts that I really wasn't prepared for, like this whole watch thing. So I thought I'd let him know I knew a few things, too.

"I guess you're a fan, too. Did you enjoy the movie or did you go because some chic made you take her?" I said, knowing it would piss him off maybe a little bit, but not too much. And then I thought I would give him a lesson, or at least I thought I would. Because while he was shooting his mouth off, I was making a few observations of my own.

I casually motioned to the watch he was wearing on his left wrist which, by the way, I instantly noticed when I first laid eyes on him, and said, "Breitling, Navitimer Cosmonaute, 809 ,Venus 178 movement; worn into orbit by Mercury Astronaut Scott Carpenter, just last May 24th."

And then I slapped him back a little. "Figure out how to use the slide rule yet?" I said in a very condescending tone that I regretted immediately after it came out of my mouth.

I knew that the bezel on the Navitimer was a very sophisticated round slide rule that pilots could use to perform important functions, like computing their fuel reserves. It was a fabulous watch. I wanted one desperately ever since Astronaut Scott Carpenter designed it, with a twenty-four hour dial, to be worn by the astronauts in space. Only thing about 'em though, was they were made only for pilots and you had to really be connected with the military or maybe an airline to get one. I never thought to consider how he got it. I probably just assumed he stole it. In light of the Elvis remark, I should have known better. I also completely forgot that he was still holding both of my hands in that vice-grip of his while I was busting his balls—not one of my better moves. So I waited for his response. When it came, I was once again surprised, or more like startled, and naturally at a loss for a response.

"Okay, let's go eat," he said, dropping my hands like a napkin after dinner and heading for the door.

Naturally Canevecchio started bobbing again just at the mere suggestion of food. And I didn't know what to do. I was completely dumbfounded. I needed to meet with T. I needed to tell him about Miguel reaching out for him. I also needed advice on how this thing was going so far.

"*Andiamo, andiamo* (let's go)," Frankie said again, only this time he waved his right arm in a semicircular motion, halting it while pointing at the door.

"Yeah, good idea, you guys go. I gotta get some sleep, *domani, domani* (tomorrow)," T said, motioning toward the door and at the same time motioning with his wrist for me to lower the bed.

I took it all as a sign that T thought I should go with Frankie and Canevecchio and catch up with him tomorrow. My head was spinning. All of a sudden, it felt like Frankie hit the accelerator and I just wasn't prepared to go for the ride. I was counting on a nice, short, initial meeting and then some time to regroup. I was afraid my façade would crumble if I exposed it too long to his scrutiny. But I just couldn't think of an excuse fast enough and I was afraid to insult him if I refused without a good reason. So I took the chance.

I lowered the bed, shrugged my shoulders and said, "*Ciao, Padrino, fino a domani* (until tomorrow)." In a complete state of bewilderment and terror, I followed my new best friends out the door, turning off the light behind me.

On reflection,I should have stayed more focused on how Frankie got that Navitimer. If I had, maybe I would have arrived at some answers with a watch on my wrist, rather than with a gun to my head.

CHAPTER 22

MANGIAMO, MANGIAMO

THE EPS OFFICER WAS STILL dutifully outside T's door. I could only sneak a peek at him on the way out to let him know everything was okay. He still looked medical enough not to attract anymore attention from Frankie.

I followed Frankie down the hall to the elevator without anyone uttering a word; Canevecchio was closely in tow. I couldn't imagine where we were going but I was hopeful it was someplace to eat food. Otherwise, Frankie's invitation meant something else and that wasn't good. The elevator was waiting.

We were the only people on the elevator, but it still felt crowded and well over weight. The moment Canevecchio stepped aboard, the entire car bobbed from his presence. It was quite a scene. I almost had to laugh as now his whole body was bobbing in unison with his head; it did help ease my nerves, though. I guess his comedic appearance made him appear less cunning and dangerous. I should have known better.

"Let's go over to Lapanto's," Frankie more than suggested. Canevecchio merely nodded without a word and nobody cared what I thought—I was along for the ride, a cinematic and terrifying thought.

When we reached the first floor, I headed for my car when Frankie said to leave it, we would take his and they would bring me back later. As I was in no position to suggest otherwise, I followed Frankie across the street to, naturally, a black Coupe de Ville. It had to be fairly new and was very beautiful, albeit in the dark it looked like a World War II class submarine. I was okay with all of this until Frankie unlocked the doors. I headed for the passenger side, intending to climb over the split front seat and get into the passenger side back seat.

"Sit up front kid," he casually said, clearly expecting that I would do exactly what he suggested.

I immediately looked at Canevecchio, who bobbing along, was just arriving at the car. I didn't think he could have heard Frankie, but he made a beeline through the passenger door and into the back seat. Now I started to think—I knew these two guys rode over here together and I'm sure Canevecchio rode in the front seat. Considering his girth, it was really the only place for him, unless you tied him to the front fender like a deer you were taking home to make into venison. But Canevecchio unhesitatingly crammed into the seat behind me. His torso completely rounded out and totally filled the back seat. His belly extended forward so that while standing outside the car, even with the door fully open, I couldn't see his legs or his feet. He had to cross his arms in front of him, resting them on his belly because there simply was no place else to put them. I felt bad because he looked so uncomfortable, although not nearly as uncomfortable as I was, getting into the seat in front of him.

If you had ever seen a wise guy movie, and I saw them all, you knew I was getting into the "wack 'em" seat. With my back to Canevecchio, I was completely defenseless. A 22-caliber round to the back of the head was certain and a testimonial to anyone who cared to wonder who did it or why—it safely eliminated suicide and accidental discharge. Or an 18-inch length of piano wire snugly laced next to my nice, gold, Saint Christopher medal would have been just as effective and wouldn't ruin those nice white leather seats. I knew, however, that I really had no options. I either got into the car or hit the bricks running for my life. If they were going to whack me, Frankie would probably shoot me in the back before

I got fifty feet. If wrong, I would have killed the caper and burned T simply because of a set of bad nerves.

I got into the already running car. "Heat wave" was playing on the radio.

"Got enough room back there, Canevecchio?" I asked, knowing there was nothing I could do to ease his pain because the Cadillac had a front bench seat and Frankie was clearly not moving his half.

"Yea, Yea. It's close," he responded, as I wondered if he was referring to the trip or my demise.

"You ever been to Lapanto's?" he continued.

"No, but I've heard about it from T," I casually replied to Canevecchio's question while having absolutely no idea what Lapanto's was, hoping it was a restaurant that T and these guys went to regularly. I figured if this thing was on the right track, they would want to go someplace they felt comfortable talking, because everybody in the place was a friend of theirs. If I was wrong, I was probably very wrong, and it was way too late at that point anyway.

"Yeah?" was the only response I got from Frankie, who kept his eyes forward, diligently on the road.

I figured it was safe to assume we weren't going to a Chinese restaurant, so I expected to see a neighborhood Italian joint filled with wise guys. I was half-right. Instead of driving across Livingston Avenue to Bloomfield Avenue and into Belleville or Newark, we went in the opposite direction to Madison. Although I was concerned that we were driving down streets I had never been on before, I tried not to make it obvious that I was overly interested in where we were going. I assumed Frankie wasn't interested in talking because he left the radio on and we listened to 77 WABC out of New York City. It was the hottest rock station of the day, with some of the coolest jocks like Cousin Brucie and Scott Muni. I was surprised to hear it on the car radio of the vehicle in which these two characters were riding. But I quickly got an explanation.

Canevecchio chimed in from the back, "We don't like dis fag Brucie. Although he's okay when he plays them four wops from Newark. Later on tonight dey play Sinatra."

Now I was completely lost. I knew that even though it was a

rock and roll station, there was always a spot for Sinatra in the Northeast. But what four wops from Newark was he talking about? The comments from the back seat were actually welcome because it gave me an excuse to turn my head and body toward the center of the car to talk and put my vulnerable back against the door.

"Dare they are. Dey play 'em a lot. Turn it up, Ponte."

Now I understood what Canevecchio meant. The falsetto voice was unmistakable, even at this early stage of their career. "Sherrrrry, Sherry baby."

The Four Seasons had recently burst onto the music scene with the monster hit, "Sherry." And sure enough, they were four Italians from New Jersey, and Frankie Valli was actually from Newark. Canevecchio already knew the words and tried to imitate Valli, only to produce a shrill I thought would shatter the windshield of the Cadillac. Thankfully it didn't, and Frankie lowered the radio as soon as the song was over. Cousin Brucie came back on in a tone that I never realized was almost as annoying as a pair of worn wipers navigating a muddy windshield.

The ride was short, along with my nerves. We arrived at a country driveway with a tall, stone pillar on each side, leaving just enough room for the Cadillac to pull through and rumble up the stone drive. There were no lights along the quarter mile stretch. In fact, there wasn't even a sign out at the road, come to think of it. However, at the end of the stone drive was a truly elegant and rather stately farmhouse. I called it a farmhouse mostly because it had a beautiful covered wooden porch across the front. The white, clapboard siding with green shutters on each side of the windows made it especially homey and inviting; it wasn't lit up like a restaurant. There were no outside lights on the building or in the landscape other than a single lantern at the front door. On the other hand, you could see that the interior of the house was well lit by table and floor lamps, and an occasional chandelier. The allure was warm, hospitable and also very disarming; I immediately became suspicious.

Just as Frankie pulled the Cadillac into a spot right in front of the porch steps, Cousin Brucie spun an Elvis tune. Instead of slamming the car into park and turning the ignition off, Frankie flashed me a grin—the first sign of nonaggression, and maybe even friendship.

"Yo, Dog, dinner's gonna have to wait till "The King" is through, eh kid?" he said to Canevecchio, but clearly directed to me.

I didn't respond. I just gave him a genuine smile of acknowledgment, hoping his was equally authentic. We listened to Elvis tell us not to be cruel to a heart that's true, with Canevecchio singing along, getting every third word right. At the end of the song, Frankie snapped the key counterclockwise and yanked it from the dash ignition.

"*Mangiamo, mangiamo* (Let's eat)," he commanded as he opened the enormous door of the Cadillac, slamming it behind him decisively, knowing that Canevecchio would climb over the passenger front seat and out of the door on my side.

It was two steps up to the gray painted porch and only about six or seven feet across to the glossy, black front door. Frankie led the way, with Canevecchio bringing up the rear. Although there didn't seem to be a lot of cars in the parking lot that was unpaved and mostly grass, opening the front door was like snorkeling in the Bahamas. As soon as you slipped your face through the surface of the water, you found a totally different and vibrant world on the other side. When Frankie cracked the door, even just a little, the energy and color from the inside exploded out onto the porch, covering us in a panoply of soft light, chatter and aroma. I immediately felt both successful and safe that they would bring me to a place like this. Unfortunately, my security was relatively short-lived.

The front door opened directly into the bar. There was an old wooden strip of hooks on the wall immediately to the left of the door that was holding several jackets, hats and umbrellas. All the jackets were leather, predominantly black, although there might have been one or two dark brown ones. The variety of hats was of similar distribution. They were almost all black, with a few dark gray ones. None of them had little feathers in the brim like an old Jew would wear, and they all looked like Canevecchio sat on them in the back seat of the Cadillac on the ride over.

I followed Frankie as he sauntered up to the bar. No one in the place even looked at me; they knew who I was with, but they didn't want to personally see or hear from me. I was Frankie and Canevecchio's responsibility. The bartender was a mountain of a man, wearing a white shirt with a white terry cloth hand towel draped over his left shoulder. He never acknowledged any of us when we hit the bar. He just turned his back and reached for the Jack Daniels. He poured three doubles over ice and brought them over to us, never making eye contact. It was clearly a place where everyone was invisible to everyone else, unless you intentionally de-cloaked.

The huge mahogany bar—complete with a brass rail around the top on the entire outside edge—ran the entire length of the room. There was a ceramic tile trough filled with ice cubes around the bottom of the bar, between the base and the oak floor. I had seen ice cubes poured into the urinal in bars in New York, but never anything like this. For a moment, I was afraid some dago would whip out his dick and take a piss at the bar, but I soon dismissed that as an impossible notion. I later learned that in the old days, men would spit in the trough, like spittoons, or use it to get rid of their cigar butts. And much to my initial disbelief, some did in fact, take a piss at the bar, and why not—no women were ever allowed in such a place for any reason whatsoever.

I had never seen a bar like this before in my life. Unlike any other joint I had ever been in, this bar didn't have any stools. This was a two-fisted, stand-up bar. No man sat in this room, and there were certainly no chics in the place, which certainly wasn't by the chic's choice. Even though Sinatra was on in the background singing my favorite song, "Summer Wind," I couldn't for a moment forget that this place was all business. The most telling aspect of the interaction between the patrons was that all the conversations were between only two guys at a time—no group discussions—and there certainly wasn't any yucking it up across the bar. Every once in a while, you might see the bartender give a drink to a guy and whisper in his ear, after which there would be a very deliberate "*salute*'" to a friend across the bar who was obviously buying. That was it. I also saw, on a couple of occasions, guys change places. It was like changing dance partners, but always only two guys at a time in a single conversation, and for a dozen guys in a room, the voices were uncannily subtle. Actually, when we walked in the door, all conversation stopped until everyone in the joint recognized Frankie and Canevecchio and paid their respects with a simple raise of the glass. It all seemed quite predictable to me at the time. It wasn't until much later, however, that I learned the real significance of the salutation we received.

CHAPTER 23

FAMILY DINNER WITH STRANGERS AT LAPANTO'S

THE THREE OF US STOOD at the bar at Lapanto's for about twenty minutes, drinking our "Jacks," listening to Sinatra and not saying a single word to each other or anyone else. Eventually the bartender came over to Frankie.

"You guys wanna eat, right?"

Frankie put his lips together and pushed them out as if to pucker for a kiss, and nodded his head up and down just one time. Up until this moment, I was doing okay. The ride over was less unnerving than I initially feared, and the joint was immensely entertaining. When the bartender asked about eating, I was sure we were going into the dining room that was adjacent to the bar through the door directly to my left. I could see there was a step down to a dining room occupied by basically the same genre of characters as occupied the bar. I was okay with that, but that's not what Frankie had in mind. As soon as he signaled the bartender that we were going to eat, he raised his head one more time and held it in the up position for only an instant. If I hadn't been looking at Frankie at that moment, I would have probably missed it completely. But I didn't, and so I started to sweat again.

As the bartender turned away from us, Frankie said, "Come on, finish your drink. We're gonna eat."

He turned to his left and began to walk around the far end of the bar. Canevecchio followed closely, without even turning to see if I was coming. I gulped my "Jack" and was right behind him as Frankie, and then Canevecchio, disappeared around the wall behind the bar. I knew this wasn't the way to the dining room and from Frankie's nod to the bartender, I figured we weren't headed for the basement either, which was the good news in all this movement. As I turned the corner behind Canevecchio, I could see that my instinct was right. There, in front of me, was an enclosed set of stairs up to the second floor. Frankie was almost halfway up already as the old "dog" struggled with each step, like a walrus getting into a prom dress. While I wasn't happy about this little trip upstairs, I wasn't too alarmed except for the fact that I didn't see any lights on at the top of the steps. I could only hope that Mother Bates wasn't sitting by the window and I had walked into the wrong motel.

Frankie climbed the stairs in short order and was already around the corner at the top, while I was still behind Canevecchio, hoping that he didn't stumble and fall backward down the steps and crush me. I had both arms up the entire way, like I could possibly keep him from falling on me, although I thought I could at least help him keep his balance. We eventually reached the top and, by that time, Frankie, I assumed, turned on the hall light. Canevecchio turned to his left and proceeded down the hall, evidently knowing exactly where we were going. I followed not too closely behind, trying to give myself some reaction time if necessary.

The second floor of the restaurant confirmed that the place was once a real farmhouse and became a restaurant only by economic transformation. The hallway that Canevecchio was traversing was very narrow and, because the ceiling was so low, it felt a little like I was in a cave—Canevecchio being the black bear inhabitant. We passed a small bathroom with pink 1950s ceramic tile and a two-ton steel and ceramic tub that you just don't see in a modern house anymore. Then two small original bedrooms, one on the left and one on the right, with old deco ceiling lights in the center of each room. They were dark except for the hall light spilling into them, revealing three small dining tables in each room. They were all immaculately set with white tablecloths, dinner plates, cloth napkins, and wine and water glasses at each place setting. A bottle of Pellegrino was unopened in the center of each table. When I was able to peer around Canevecchio, I could see the dimly lit third bedroom only about ten feet ahead. There didn't appear to be any tables from where I was, and I neither saw nor heard Frankie, or anyone else for that matter.

When we finally arrived in the far bedroom, there was indeed a single table, set for four, in the middle of the room, directly under the deco ceiling light. There was also a large side-board along the far wall with at least a dozen or more bottles of liquor on it—mostly hard stuff—including Jack Daniels, Scotch, Seagram's and naturally, a bottle of Sambuca. Several tall and short glasses were grouped along one side. The other side of the server, however, was most interesting. Naturally, anyone intending to indulge in any of these potions would certainly require ice. There was an ice bucket sitting on the far side, full of fresh, cold ice. It couldn't have been standing there more than ten minutes. How this could have happened occupied my attention until Frankie said to Canevecchio, "Close the door, Dog."

My mind immediately emptied and my heart leapt into my throat.

"Sit!" Frankie said, pointing to a chair at the table, with its back to the door. Canevecchio was returning after gently closing the door, but not locking it; I listened carefully for the latch.

I sat where instructed to sit and Frankie, not surprisingly, sat with his back to the wall, while Canevecchio went directly to the side table and fixed three double Jack Daniels. He gave the first to Frankie, and brought the other two to the table, one for me and one for himself.

"*Cento anni* (100 years)," Frankie toasted, and we all touched glasses. I already had one downstairs, but I still took a long gulp of this one, hoping it would steady my nerves. I figured this was all going to go well for the caper or it would go very badly for me, personally.

We all sat and drank our Jacks, without much conversation at all, for about fifteen minutes or so. Then, without warning, the door swung open behind me and two waiters I hadn't seen before walked into the room, each carrying an enormous round serving tray chocked full of bowls and platters of food, some steaming hot, some not. As they placed the food on the table, family style, it reminded me of a Sunday dinner at my grandmother's house. A heaping bowl of cappellini in red gravy, accompanied by an equally immense bowl of meatballs and sausage, also covered in a thick, dark, steaming, red gravy, were set in the middle of the table.

While this would have been plenty for any three reasonable men to consume in a single sitting, the pasta was only the *primo piatto*. The *secondo piatto* was three portions of roasted breast of veal seasoned with rosemary and garnished with golf ball sized red potatoes and sweet onions. A platter of fresh broccoli rabe sautéed in first press olive oil and garlic was there for color and aroma. The table was full, leaving room for only the bottle of Chianti that the waiter split into the three water glasses in front of us. I'm sure he used the water glasses because regular wine glasses just wouldn't hold enough to kill the bottle. To help digest all of this, the waiter set a large romaine salad on the sideboard with extra plates and silverware. All old world Italians eat their salad after the meal, not before, like Americans. His final act was to fill the coffee percolator so we could turn it on when we were ready to enjoy coffee and Sambuca with the fresh, *dolce* strawberries.

"Thanks, Rocco," Frankie told the waiter who stood at the table when everything was set, obviously waiting for permission to leave. It was also apparent that even the waiter knew that Frankie was in charge. Canevecchio and I were clearly "tag alongs." This just confirmed to me that there was something special about Frankie that I wasn't able to figure out yet. For all I knew, he was just a regular member of *La Cosa Nostra*. He wasn't a boss or a *Caporegime*, yet he was treated with great deference by everybody he came in contact with, including me. There was something no one was talking about, and I was both anxious, and frankly a little frightened to learn more.

The next two hours were, in some ways, unlike any time I ever spent before and at the same time exactly like so many meals I had with family and friends throughout my life. We ate, drank, talked and laughed right out loud. We talked baseball—the Yankees, naturally—especially the Italian Yankees both past and present: DiMaggio, Rizzuto, Berra and especially the new Yankee bad boy, Joe Pepitone. I thought we would get right down to business, but we didn't. In fact, we never did talk business. On more than one occasion, I tried to bring up the impending "paint job," but each time I got absolutely no reaction from Canevecchio. Frankie would only pucker his lips, shake his head and wiggle his finger, clearly telling me it wasn't time for such talk. I heeded the warning.

Frankie was a surprisingly good listener. He asked me about my family and how I came to have T as my Godfather. Now, I knew he was probing for information to corroborate my story, but he was either very skilled at it or he was genuinely interested in my life. I tried to stick to the story T and I cooked up, but I was forced to adlib in some areas. It was an easy sell that T and my father met in the army during the war because they both served and were in their early twenties when they enlisted. Actually, my father was only 19 when he enlisted right after Pearl Harbor. Men who were survivors of combat together often became life-long friends. Italians who served together often intertwined their families after the war through marriage and other Catholic rituals, like baptism and confirmation.

"How did your father and T meet in the army?" Canevecchio asked between forks-full of broccoli rabe.

"They were both in the Army Engineers in Europe. They were very close in the Army and when they came home, *Padrino* often came to visit us in Trenton. My father was very sick for a long time. He was wounded a couple of times and as a result, never fully recovered. I think that's why T stayed so close to him when they came home. I knew my father wanted T to stay in my life after he died, so I took him as *Mio Padrino* when I was confirmed. My father died shortly after. I was only 13 at the time."

"T never mentioned you before," Frankie said, without looking up, which made me a little nervous. I gave him the set answer.

"My mother married a mick about two years later and we all

got fuckin' Irish after that. Thank God for my Grandmother or I'd be drinking beer and eatin' boiled potatoes now," I said with a sarcastic chuckle.

As I sat there eating and talking to these two guys, a pattern began to emerge. I already noticed that everyone treated Frankie with great deference, but it was how he interacted with Canevecchio that held my attention. Frankie and T were about the same age, somewhere in their mid-to-late forties, about the age my father would be, had he lived. That made them about twenty or so years older than me. Canevecchio, on the other hand, was about twenty years older than Frankie and T. He had to be in his early sixties. While Frankie was clearly in some type of superior position to Canevecchio, either in the organizational structure or just in this particular caper, there was something special about their relationship. Frankie was kind and respectful to Canevecchio, while being keenly observant and very responsive to his situation and needs. At first, I thought it was because Canevecchio was twenty years older and obviously not in good health, but there was something more going on between the two of them. Frankie watched him much the way a parent would a child. For example, Canevecchio was eating at a dizzying pace. He would twirl yards of pasta on his fork and then stuff it into his mouth and swallow, almost without chewing at all. After he did this a few times, Frankie looked at him with his fork raised in his left hand showing him the palm of his right as if to say, "whoa or slow down." Canevecchio immediately got the message and slowed his pace and the size of his twirls. But, there was more.

Frankie was looking out for Canevecchio. I couldn't put my finger on it because I never really saw this kind of relationship before. You would have thought that Frankie made some promise to Canevecchio's mother to watch over and guide him so he would get home safe at the end of the day. At one point, Canevecchio started to choke on a piece of veal and Frankie immediately jumped to his side to make sure he was okay. This just seemed odd, since Frankie was clearly the important one to everyone else. But he was clearly dedicated to the well-being of Canevecchio. Frankie was attentive to him even in a non-emergency situation. Like when we finished the pasta and breast of veal, it was Frankie who cleared Canevecchio's dish and asked if he wanted some *dolce and café.* Frankie brought it to him and put it on the table in front of him. He returned to the sideboard and got some *dolce and café* for us, but only after Canevecchio was taken care of. It felt like this responsibility accompanied Frankie's superior position. His conduct was truly admirable, albeit puzzling.

As we were drinking our *café,* I wanted to continue to talk to Frankie because I felt like the longer I directly interacted with him, the more I learned about his role in all this. Unfortunately, he already made it clear that he was not going to discuss the caper in any form, no matter how cryptic I crafted the conversation. He broke the family background barrier with his questions about my father and T, so I thought I would venture there also.

"So you guys grew up in Newark?" I asked, figuring that if I lumped the two of them together it might seem less personal and I might get more of a response. Frankie pretty much ignored me, but Canevecchio was enthusiastically responsive.

"Yea, we're Vailsburg guys through and through. We were all altar boys, but as you might guess, T and *Ponte* came along after me. We hooked up after the war." As soon as the word "war" came out of his mouth, he quickly diverted his eyes from me and Frankie to the huge, whole strawberry he was about to devour, as if it were his words.

I sensed there was something going on so I pursued it—just a little.

"Were you in the Army during the war, Frankie? I casually asked.

Frankie never looked up from his *café.* Canevecchio quickly changed the subject.

"Hey kid, so how old are you anyways?"

"Well, I'm younger than Frankie and lots mo' younger than you," I jokingly replied, letting my question to Frankie evaporate along with the bullet-sized beads of sweat on Canevecchio's forehead. I got enough of an answer for the time being; I figured I would get more later, either from Frankie, or maybe from T. Naturally, I had no idea the impact it would have on virtually the rest of my life.

Following a short, after dinner conversation that carefully avoided any incendiary issues, Frankie wiped his lips with the cloth napkin and said, "*Andiamo* (let's go)."

"Yup," Canevecchio grunted. He couldn't get out of there fast enough, as they both stood up. There was no check or settling up with the waiter or any of the usual conduct following dinner at a restaurant. We just got up and headed down the hallway to the stairs leading back to the bar. I didn't say a word. I just stood and followed.

I was the last to emerge from the stairway at the bottom of the steps. I was behind Canevecchio, who had almost as much trouble getting down the steps as he had getting up, although I wasn't fearful of him falling on me on the way down. Even though I was right on his heels, we got into the bar well after Frankie did. As I turned the corner, I could see Frankie just completing a handshake with Rocco, the waiter. The mood in the entire bar changed. It was as if by shaking Rocco's hand, Frankie signaled that all was well and he was in the mood to shake hands. It felt like the President working a rope line. Everyone tried to touch him. For the next ten minutes, Frankie circled the bar and shook hands with every swing-dick in the place. In fact, he hugged and kissed most of them. I carefully watched their faces—to a man, they were genuinely excited to be close to him. I couldn't figure it out. These guys were not the sentimental type. There was something special about this guy and I still had no idea. Hell, Canevecchio and I even got a couple of squeezes on the shoulder just for being with Frankie.

When all was settled, we headed for the door and back to the car. I insisted that Canevecchio sit up front after seeing how uncomfortable he was on the ride over. He agreed and I felt much better on the ride back to my car at the hospital. I even sang along with Canevecchio to a couple of his favorites, "Alley Oop" and "Pony Time."

When we arrived at my car, Canevecchio twisted, slid and jostled his way out of the front seat so I could climb out of the 2-door Cadillac. He surprised me with a big, bear hug, send-off; he smelled of Aqua Velva. Frankie, with less enthusiasm, extended his right hand across the seat and said, "See ya kid," with a little nod and a blink of both eyes. I took that as a sign of high approval. I started to climb into my car, but then told them that I should check on *Padrino* before I went home, which they both thought was okay. They drove off while I headed for the emergency room entrance to the hospital. I couldn't wait to get up stairs to run all this by T.

Little did I know that while I was at dinner T was occupied with a mouthful of his own.

CHAPTER 24

MARILYN'S SECRET REVEALED

MIGUEL'S HEAD WAS OPERATING IN overdrive during the otherwise uneventful cab ride from Newark Airport to his South Munn Avenue apartment. During most of the flight home, he was focused on his mission—both Castro's and his own—but as he got closer to the apartment, he began to gravitate toward more personal and even hedonistic desires. He couldn't help thinking about Azzimie's chics, especially the redhead, even though he only met her once at the DMV with that other chic, Julia. He was still frustrated because when he tried to make a move on them at the DMV he struck out in short order. He didn't even get a little foul tip for his efforts. When the two chics were done hanging all over Azzimie, they just walked off without even a wave. He had to be satisfied just watching them wiggle off down the street. That's not what he was accustomed to in Cuba.

The cab dropped Miguel off at the front door of his apartment building, which sat well off the street. It was one of two identical stone buildings that were probably built in the early part of the twentieth century. They both had a certain castle like quality to them in that the front façades of both were covered with huge fieldstones. There weren't any other buildings in the neighborhood that looked quite like them. They were real fortresses. There was a small elevator in each building that carried about three to four people or one person with very little luggage. Miguel was traveling very light. He had only one small duffle, which enabled him to jump on the elevator and be at his apartment door in just minutes.

When Miguel left his apartment to return to Cuba, he was careful not to leave anything that would reveal his true identity. He did this for two reasons. First, he knew that Azzimie was the apartment building super and therefore had a key to all the apartments, and Miguel wasn't entirely confident of his reading of Azzimie. While he was fairly certain he was a common street hustler with just a little more personality than most, if someone told him that, in fact, he was an FBI informer, Miguel wouldn't have been completely stunned. And there was a second reason Miguel took such care when leaving the apartment. Even if he was right about Azzimie, he could still never be sure that he was completely successful in establishing his undercover identity in the States. The FBI and CIA had lots of informers in all corners of the world, including Cuba. If someone was suspicious of his identity and broke into his apartment, he wanted to be sure that it appeared as normal and as innocent as possible. This required that all the little idiosyncrasies of a normal, healthy bachelor's apartment should be there. It needed to have the right amount and type of clothes. Miguel's Cuban heritage left him with a flair for the fashionable. Jeans and t-shirts, which were becoming the standard uniform of the new American youth, were merely work clothes in Cuba. They were the kind of clothes a man used to wash his car on a Saturday morning, not the clothes you wore on a date. It was for that reason that Miguel came ashore with only the clothes on his back. It was critical that he outfitted his wardrobe with only American clothes, both in manufacture and character.

Other requirements included just a little tad of porn with a few packages of rubbers. Rock and Roll was a mainstay of American society, so a Hi-Fi and a collection of 45's and 33's was expected. He left no reading material, except a few outdated *Star Ledger* newspapers and old copies of *Time* and *Newsweek*. A few dirty dishes left in the sink was customary, along with the rest of the place not being too neat. So, when he walked out the door to return to

Havana for his little *têtê-à-têtê* with Castro, he felt fairly confident about how he left the apartment. Even though he was prepared for a look over by either Azzimie or even some government agent, that didn't mean he had no interest in knowing if they had been there. He did, and so he had another plan.

Miguel wanted to know not only if someone had been in the apartment, but also where they went once they were there. So one day before he left, on his way back to the apartment, he stopped at a local stationery store and bought a package of carbon paper and some nice white typing paper. While the apartment had nicely stained oak floors throughout, Miguel strategically placed at least one area rug in every room, the first being in the foyer at the foot of the front door. With the area rugs as perfect cover, Miguel carefully married a nice fresh piece of white typing paper with a piece of carbon paper, placing the blue transference side against the typing paper. He carefully placed a pairing, with the carbon paper on top, on the floor under the foyer rug. He repeated this process under every area rug in the apartment, sometimes more than once depending on how large the rug was. All he had to do then was carefully exit the apartment without stepping on the rugs that lay over the paper and check them when he returned.

Miguel's plan left the apartment cleverly booby-trapped. If anyone came into the apartment, they couldn't help but step on the rugs and therefore unwittingly tread on the carbon-typing paper trap. When they did, the movement and weight of their foot would rub the carbon paper against the typing paper, leaving an unmistakably indelible print of their trespass. Actually, Miguel was rather astounded how clear the impression was. You could almost match the footprint to a particular type of shoe and even determine the size. In light of all these pre-departure preparations, Miguel was very careful as he unlocked the door to his apartment and stepped into the foyer.

A smart side-step, once inside the door, allowed Miguel to avoid the foyer rug completely and then move about the apartment from room to room, easily rolling back each rug to reveal a blue map of the locations the intruder traveled throughout the apartment. In fact, as he carefully analyzed the lines and spaces on the white typing paper, he became more sure that the intruder was in the apartment on more than one occasion. He had no idea, at the time, who was in the apartment, but he had his suspicions. The reality, however, was much worse than he anticipated.

Once Miguel knew that he evidently wasn't as successful as he had hoped in establishing his cover in the States, he surprisingly began to worry less about it. He was almost relieved to know that his next move was now identified. He had to find out who was stalking him and why. Not all the answers were readily apparent, however. While he was fairly certain he wasn't visited by a common burglar, because nothing like the TV, Hi-Fi or even any of the cash he intentionally left lying around was taken. He was also confident they weren't there to only look in his underwear drawers. If they weren't there to steal things, they were there for information, and that's exactly why he felt relaxed. He just didn't leave any hard information or even remote clues to be found. He was, however, more than a little curious about the identity of his visitor.

Unable to resolve anymore questions concerning his mystery visitor, Miguel turned his attention and fantasies to Marilyn, who was patiently awaiting his return in the garage behind his apartment. By the time he got the paperwork straightened out, he barely got to drive her before he had to return to Havana and kiss Castro's feet, so he was anxious to ride her hard, like any absent lover.

He named his Vette Marilyn and always referred to her as a she because a Vette is like a beautiful chic to a man who has one or even yearns for one. Girlfriends and wives often refer to the Vette as a "fiberglass mistress," and for good reason. Naturally, Miguel wants to ride 'er hard, but first comes the foreplay. All the way down the elevator and across the parking lot to his locked garage, Miguel anticipated his first look at her.

A click of the key entering the tight but lubricated cylinder, with just the perfect thrust and a soft responsive twist at the anticipated depth, sprung the legs of the garage door lock. His heart rate escalated with anticipation while the adrenaline rush quivered his fingers, barely enabling him to free the lock from the hasp and throw open the doors.

Inside the small garage, his fiberglass mistress was dutifully poised. She sat backed into the tight space, completely encased in a soft gray quilted cover specifically made to perfectly envelop every gentle, luxurious curve and each hard aggressive edge of her figure. The cover was, however, no mask; her identity was unmistakable. Now came the slow, careful unveiling that would reveal his licentious Marilyn, a name she rightfully deserved. He had carefully parked her shapely rear end so it almost touched the back wall revealing her sensuous hood, which graciously pitched forward from the base of her petite windshield to her covered, yet unmistakable chromed front bumper.

There was no reason to linger. Miguel, now almost in a sweat, with not even a hint of the troubled thoughts he left back in his apartment, stood at her right front corner and reached down to grab a hold of the cover that was tucked inside the wheel well. Standing directly opposite the front passenger-side quarter panel, he carefully slipped his right hand under the cover at the wheel well and slid it toward the front bumper. When he felt the sharp, cold, rigid edge of the bumper, in contrast to the smooth, warm almost supple touch of the woven, sanded, waxed and polished fiberglass, he moved forward, around the wheel. Now, standing directly in front of her, he grabbed the edge of the cover with the passionate hands of a desperate lover. With a snap of the wrist, the cover floated into the air just enough to give a teasing glance at the smooth sheen of her flawless daytona-blue finish and the perfect symmetrical curve to her front fiberglass fenders. The image was, to Miguel, every bit as sensual as the photo of that other Marilyn standing over a New York City subway grate showing off her own curves.

He carefully folded the cover over the hood, up the windshield and down the back revealing the *sui generis* rear split window. “It’s the very first Vette of its kind and who knows, it may also be the last,” Miguel was thinking to himself. Once the cover was completely off, Miguel became frustrated by the dim light inside the garage, even though it was a beautiful sunny day. The deep shadows, especially toward the rear of the garage, defeated the sparkle and glow of her finish. And, while he just couldn’t keep from rubbing his fingertips all over her, he wanted to see her glow as well. Like a lover who turns on a light or candle in the bedroom to enhance the thrill, he started the engine, and accompanied by her subtle roar of ecstasy, ever so slowly pulled Marilyn out of the garage and into the bright sun light where he could see and love every inch of her.

Once safely outside the confines of the small garage, Miguel walked around her, caressing and closely examining every inch of her. Marilyn was perfect in every respect, and why not? She was practically right out of the showroom. Except for a couple of Sunday trips to the Jersey Shore, she was a virgin.

As Miguel was absorbing the thrill, he felt that something was not as it should have been. He wasn't sure at first, but as he walked around the driver's side he noticed that something was amiss with the left wheel. He was shocked to find that the signature five-spoke wheel was missing a chrome lug nut. They were specially made for the Vette, and Miguel was certain she was not like that when he last saw her. His initial reaction was that the dealer didn't tighten it fully and it vibrated off. He immediately looked in the garage, but it was nowhere to be found. Upon close inspection of the tire that was now mounted on the driver's side rear wheel, Miguel became nearly hysterical with regret. He began to sweat like a $2 whore at a cowboy rodeo and trembled in a combination of fear and rage as the inevitable conclusion began to emerge.

"What made me think hiding it here was a good idea!" he kept repeating aloud to himself.

Miguel dove into the car and reached for the spare tire wrench stored neatly under the passenger seat. Because the Vette had no rear access, the spare tire was mounted up under the rear cargo deck. Miguel, wrench in hand and lying on his back on the ground, shimmied under Marilyn's rear end. As he began loosening the long bolt that held the spare tire tight up against the rear deck, he was already thinking about how to fix the mess he knew he had on his hands. He knew there was only one reason for the spare tire to be mounted on Marilyn's left rear wheel; there was only one person who could have done it, and there was only one outcome. When the bolt reached the end of its threads, the tire released and hit the pavement with the thud of a bowling ball rolling off a dining room table. There were no surprises. The tire in the spare well was the original tire that the factory mounted on Marilyn's left rear wheel—only it now had a plugged hole in the tread. Someone had driven her, got a flat tire, changed it out for the spare and then plugged the hole. Taking Marilyn out for a dance without permission was bad enough, but that was only foreplay for the fucking Miguel got, and all without even a little kiss.

Other than the tire, there was nothing else in the wheel well. That's precisely why Miguel bounced up off the ground and began a fresh new task. With a small screwdriver he also kept under the passenger seat, he carefully loosened the six small Phillips head screws that held the driver's side inside door trim panel to the door frame. Once the panel was loose, but not completely off, Miguel was able to reach into the frame of the door and palm the familiar form he was looking for. The Mauser .380, semi-automatic fit into his hand like a Yankee Stadium hot dog. The cold steel quickly warmed to his touch as if it were responding to his anger. For the first time in a very long time, Miguel didn't feel alone. The Mauser was like an old friend who lived nearby, but hadn't visited in a while. But now they were going to catch up on old times and maybe share a nice meal together, and Azzimie was the main course.

Miguel knew that Azzimie was the only possible person who had access to Marilyn's keys with the balls to take her for a ride and, in the process, steal the $100,000 in perfect, new, counterfeit Federal Reserve Notes that Miguel, in his complete stupidity, hid in Marilyn's spare tire well before leaving for Havana.

Planning his next move, Miguel carefully reattached the door panel and replaced the tire and wheel cover under the rear deck. Marilyn, like a good mistress, was returned to the garage as he found her. With a soft brush of the hand and a promise to return soon and stay longer, he bid her farewell.

Confident in the righteousness of his revenge, Miguel slid the tiny Mauser into his jeans waistband and headed for the apartment building like it was on fire and his dog was inside, chained to the radiator. He didn't need the elevator because that fuck Azzimie lived in the super's basement apartment.

Miguel bound down the stairs in gravity defying leaps, landing on the basement floor with both feet together. As he approached the apartment door, he began to shorten his gate and slow his pace. His mind had begun to re-engage and quell his thoughtless rage. He began to realize there were lots of issues that needed to be resolved in the next few minutes. Miguel needed time to sort out an order of resolution and determine what he would be willing to pay for his revenge. He knew he had to reprioritize his objectives and avoid ripping a hole in Azzimie's throat, at least right out of the box.

Miguel now began to focus more on what Azzimie knew, rather than what he had done. Miguel knew he took the counterfeit from Marilyn—it wasn't lost, it didn't fall out, and Miguel didn't forget where he put it. He was certain Azzimie took it, but what he wasn't certain about was whether he still had it or not. Miguel was betting not. He was confident that Azzimie knew it was counterfeit and therefore wanted to turn it into genuine as soon as possible, probably within hours of finding it. He was also confident that Azzimie knew just the right local, small-time scum who would give him five to ten measly points on the dollar just to take it off his hands.

This is where Miguel underestimated Azzimie. He failed to value his resourcefulness and cunning. It never dawned on him that Azzimie would find a way to turn the counterfeit over, dollar for dollar, and launder the good, all in one fell swoop.

He arrived at Azzimie's door still not sure what was going to happen.

CHAPTER 25

AZZIMIE DID THE LAUNDRY

STILL STANDING IN FRONT OF Azzimie's door, Miguel continued to weigh his alternatives. In his mind's eye, he would burst through the door, kick that prick in the nuts for just putting them in Marilyn's driver's seat, grab him by the hair, stick the Mauser in his ear and blow his perverted brains all over the fuckin' kitchen floor. He was sure that would give him instant gratification, but he also knew that killing the little puss pot wouldn't answer his questions nor get the counterfeit back, if that was even possible.

Over the years living in Cuba, there were very few things Miguel learned from Castro and his fool brother Raul. One thing he did learn, however, was that killing wasn't for pleasure, like fucking or smoking or drinking. The fear of death was the strongest link in the chain of slavery. The initiation of the process or even just the threat should be reserved as an instrument to accomplish the end result—bondage. Such terror should not be wasted on mere folly or personal gratification—terrify, enslave and exploit were the smart moves.

With that thought in mind, Miguel knocked at the door with a friendly, almost timid rap. Azzimie opened it so fast Miguel almost feared he was standing there waiting for him.

"Did he already know why I was there and, even more importantly, was he prepared to defend himself and his treachery?" Miguel wondered.

Initially, Miguel felt a twinge of concern, if not fear, that he made the wrong decision and should have just come in shooting; he just desperately needed satisfaction. He decided to temper his instincts, convinced he would eventually just kill the motherfucker.

"Hey, you're back," Azzimie said with a big smile as he opened the door, knowing only that Miguel was out of town someplace, for some unknown reason.

"Yes, my friend. How are you?" he said with a huge grin on his face that he hoped hid the sweat he felt bleeding through his pores, due to his nearly uncontrollable, sweltering rage.

And then it happened—Azzimie gave him that little forced smile with a nervous nod of the head. Leaving the door open, he immediately turned his back on Miguel and walked toward the kitchen. Miguel was now certain Azzimie took the counterfeit and he knew Miguel found out and now this was the reckoning. Miguel realized his next move would forever define his relationship with Azzimie, and because Azzimie had now inextricably intertwined himself in this situation, Miguel's entire future could also be at stake.

Old habits are hard to break. Miguel stepped into the apartment, softly closing the door behind him without turning his body away from Azzimie. He took three giant steps. In concert with the first step, he reached into his waistband and cupped the Mauser with the palm of his right hand. He cut the distance between them in half with step two while raising his upper arm parallel to the floor and his forearm perpendicular like he was on a bicycle signaling a left turn; the Mauser remained in his grip. The barrel was pointing up and the cold steel of the gun frame turned flat in his hand toward Azzimie. Step three answered all other questions.

"Azzimie," Miguel said in a soft, controlled voice as not to reveal the follow-up. When he turned, revealing his unblemished, slightly girlish face, Miguel was in full stride and smacked him right in the face with the side of the steel gun frame, surely breaking his nose and splattering blood across the room. Miguel expected a cry of excruciating pain from Azzimie and was both disappointed and impressed at his silence. Azzimie took it. There wasn't a peep out of him, and certainly no reaction of surprise. He knew exactly why he got that Mauser in the face and probably wasn't even that surprised. He cupped his face with his left hand and turned toward the sink, reaching for the cold-water tap and a dishcloth to hold back the blood. After retrieving the makeshift bandage, he turned to Miguel, gasping a breath through his wide-open mouth.

"Okay, okay!" he said as he sat at the table in submission, obviously ready to talk about what he had done and seemingly thankful for the opportunity.

Miguel didn't utter even the slightest sound. He didn't sit. He just stood there hovering with the Mauser still in his hand. Only now he had the business end pointed at Azzimie. He didn't really intend to shoot him, at least not at that moment anyway, but Azzimie didn't know that. When Miguel didn't move, Azzimie decided it was time to start talking fast.

"It's not what I intended," he said, looking Miguel dead in his dark, shark-like eyes.

"I met this chic and I thought I could get into her pants if I tooled her around in Marilyn. I knew you left the keys in the apartment and I figured I'd just cruise with her through the park a couple of times. And then maybe she wouldn't care that I lived in the fuckin' basement," he explained, like a 10-year-old trying to explain to his father why he had been playing with matches and burned the house to the ground. He wasn't really expecting much forgiveness. So he pumped up the volume, hoping to find a sympathetic tone, and continued.

"She wasn't like the others. She had class and I knew I was getting nowhere without a cool ride. I was gonna tell ya 'bout it. I figured you'd be okay with it because it was for ass. Ya know what I mean? But then I got a fuckin' flat and when I went to change it, well, I just got tanked up over the money. Hell, I didn't even fuck the chic; I just took her home. I didn't mean it," he repeated again.

Azzimie was now pulling out all the stops. He was looking directly at the Mauser, hoping to see any easing of the tension on Miguel's trigger finger. It didn't happen. Instead, Miguel spoke his first words since his sweet little murmur before whacking Azzimie in the face with the side of the Mauser.

"You thought it was okay to bone my ride and then hustle my product? I should just kill you right now and be done with it," he said as he stuck his arm out a little closer to Azzimie's still bleeding face.

Azzimie closed his eyes tightly and hunched both of his shoulders up almost to his ears, as if somehow that would protect his head from the bullet he was certain was now inevitable. However, with inimitable confidence in his ability to talk his way out of anything, he kept chattering.

"*Escucheme* (listen to me)," he pleaded. "I didn't intend to take your product man. It just fell out on the ground. I'm sorry I took Marilyn out, but I didn't look at it like I was bonin' her. I was lookin' after her; I was trying to bone the chic. You know how it is man."

"Where's the product?" Miguel said in a raised and less controlled tone, still pointing the Mauser at Azzimie's head.

In spite of Miguel's intention to keep him "under the gun" in every respect, his question about the counterfeit was like a call from the Governor to a man awaiting the gallows. Azzimie now knew that Miguel wanted something more from this meeting than his blood, sweat and tears. He opened his eyes, lifted his head and inched closer to the Mauser that was now nudging his forehead at the edge of his receding hairline, and baited the hook.

"It was beautiful, man. All this money just fell out. Bro, if it were legit, I would have never taken it man, but when I saw that the serial numbers repeated in each batch of $10,000, I realized it was counterfeit. Then I started thinking for both of us, like we was partners, ya' know? I knew you was too smart to waste it and it just came to me—the fuckin' casinos. My sister Julia, man, just the fuckin' night before, man, she was talking about takin' a trip to Vegas. I thought I would go just for shits and giggles and maybe some pussy, ya know? But when I saw all that counterfeit, I figured if I could find a way to clean it and not for just ten or fifteen points, you'd be okay with it." Azzimie tried to unravel the story before Miguel got bored and his trigger finger got itchy. He started to get worried again when Miguel rolled his eyes at the suggestion that he would be okay with Azzimie taking the counterfeit to Vegas. His ass still puckered, Azzimie continued.

"So I took the package and crammed into the car with all of them and went out there. But I wasn't sure how to play it. I was afraid to try to buy chips with it and then ya shoulda seen man—it was perfect. They got these new things on the slots. Ya don't even need to buy tokens or chips or anything. The slots take the paper and give you plays on the machine. I tried it with a genuine $10 bill and I got ten plays, and ya don't even have to play. You can just cash out and you get genuine silver dollars to cash in at the cage. Ya know what I mean? So I tried one of the counterfeit and it worked like fuckin' magic. The slot took it and gave me a hundred plays. We played a while and then cashed out. It was beautiful man. I wished you were there."

Miguel was now listening, much more interested than he could have ever imagined. "Could this moap have discovered the perfect wash, a fool proof way to launder the counterfeit notes for genuine currency? That's hard to imagine," he thought to himself.

"Who is 'we'?" Did you have a rat in your pocket?" Miguel retorted.

Azzimie was now on the precipice. Does he go all the way and tell Miguel the truth, a maneuver he was completely unfamiliar with, or lie and minimize what happened? The Mauser convinced him to tell it all.

"Me, my cousin, Julia and her friend, LJ, my Uncle, *Nauna,* (Grandmother) and this dude Brus. The girls were there as a decoy. Me, Uncle Nico and Brus banged the machines hard after we figured out it worked. Sometimes Julia and LJ went to the cage with the silver dollars and got cash."

At this point Miguel was completely focused on the wash and less interested in blowing a hole in Azzimie's head, at least until he got all the details. He still had questions. So he slightly lowered the barrel of the Mauser and asked, "You had to bring all of them into this? What the fuck were you thinking?"

"I had no choice man. Once I saw that it worked, there was no point in doin' just a few notes. I decided that we had to bang the machines real hard for a few hours or so, then cash out, and blow before the shift change or a slots boss got curious and decided to open one of the machines. Then we would move to another casino, although not all of them have those bill things." Talking as fast as he could, Azzimie continued.

"Look, the product was good, but not good enough to twist one of those slot bosses. If they spotted a single counterfeit, they would lock down all the slots and call every casino on the strip, and then all the slots in the city would be too hot to scam for months. We rolled through five casinos cleaning hundreds of those notes and makin' piles of genuine in just a day and a half. We should have split, but we tried one more and wham," Azzimie described, now much more animated and energetic with the Mauser out of his face.

"What do you mean 'wham'? What did you do? Where is the product and the good for that matter?" Miguel yelled at the top of his lungs.

The Mauser was back up like a 17-year-old's dick in the back seat of dad's Chevy on a Saturday night. Now Azzimie was terrified. He had come to the end of the good news. It was all bad, very bad, from there on out. All he could do was close his eyes and just say it and hope they weren't the last words he would ever hear.

"Gone."

"Gone?" Miguel quickly retorted in a whisper. He didn't yell. The silence was terrifying. You could almost hear the pounding of Azzimie's heart as his hollow chest expanded and contracted with each shallow, rapid breath. Azzimie could feel the boil of Miguel's anger approach.

Miguel, for the first time in this little colloquy was about to lose control. He actually began to pressure the trigger of the Mauser when he realized that killing Azzimie would get him no answers and certainly bring heat on the building, which he certainly could not afford, especially now.

"Okay, give me the entire story right now, all of it—now," he commanded.

Azzimie was thankful for just another breath, yet he knew there was the distinct possibility that when he gave it all up, his last words would be punctuated by a lead period right through the head. He knew, however, that he had few choices left and decided to stay in the game and hope for a good draw.

"We were doin' great. We busted dozens of slots in five joints. We went through most of the product. We hit the last joint and they must have been waitin' on us. We were there bustin' out the slots when cops came from everywhere. I was holdin' the counterfeit, so I took a chance and beat feet toward the service door. I got away."

"And?" Miguel asked in a piercing tone that curled up on the end.

"I dumped the rest of the product," Azzimie said in a softer tone. When he saw Miguel's eyes widen with rage, he added in a final pitch that he hoped would appeal to Miguel's logical side. "I couldn't take a chance on gettin' grabbed with it, could I?"

"And all that genuine that came out in the wash?" Miguel demanded.

"In the hotel room, hidden in the AC duct. But I couldn't go back. There was way too much heat. I just busted outta town."

Miguel was only mildly interested in the remaining product or even the laundered genuine. At that point in time he was confident piles of product were going to be available to him. He was much more interested in who got busted and who made the bust.

"Was it the local police or the Secret Service?" It made a great deal of difference to Miguel. If it was only the local police, then he had some time before the notes were hot worldwide. If it was the Secret Service, he had to throw his plan into high gear right now. He had more questions.

"What happened to the others? Who busted them?" he asked.

"I don't know," Azzimie said, looking at the floor, not realizing that his answer was about as bad as Miguel could have imagined.

"You don't know? How could you not know?" Miguel screamed at him again.

"I was too scared to ask. I ain't even gone over there since this happened. Man, I'm scared they're layin' for me over there. And no, I never told nobody where I got it from," Azzimie said, answering a question not yet asked by Miguel. But Azzimie was sure it would only be a matter of time until he needed an answer.

"What are you telling me? You're afraid that your sister or your uncle or your grandmother ratted you out? Is that what you're telling me?" Miguel demanded.

"I don't know. I don't know what to do," Azzimie kept saying over and over again.

"Well, I'll tell you what you're going do. We're going over there and find out what happened, and then we're going to figure out what's going to happen next, at least up until the minute I blow your head off, you no good piece of shit. Get dressed. Let's go!" Miguel commanded.

Miguel wasn't sure where this was all going, but he knew he had to get some answers, fast. He also knew that he had to set up the final print and get the entire deal closed before anything else went wrong. And that's exactly what he did. While Azzimie was changing his underwear and trying to stop shaking, Miguel headed for the door. He was originally hoping to get a little more time to work out the details of moving his end of the print, but right now he didn't have time to fuck around. He needed to complete the final print immediately.

Miguel had a number where he could call T. He figured he could at least begin to move this deal over the telephone, although talking on the telephone was something he hated to do. Actually, he simply hated talking to the grease balls even though many of them claim there's a close similarity between Spanish and Italian. Miguel considered that complete nonsense. Spanish is a language of science, a language of precision and function. Italian, on the other hand, tacks useless vowels on the end of every word like feathers on the ass of a cancan dancer; they serve no real purpose other than to fan the imagination. Just listening to Italian gives him a headache, but he really had no choice. Even an aristocratic revolutionary has to deal with the scum ring around the tub sometimes; even if it's just to be sure the servants clean it.

Miguel decided to make the call hard and right to the nuts. There was no time for bull shitting around; the gloves were off with everybody. He would get the print in gear and then go back downstairs and drag that fuck Azzimie out of there to get on with straightening out the mess he made. And then at a convenient and satisfying time he would blow his brains out.

Miguel headed back to his apartment so he could make the call in private.

CHAPTER 26

WHY DO YOU THINK THEY CALL IT THE SECRET SERVICE

I WATCHED FRANKIE AND CANEVECCHIO DRIVE off until I could no longer hear the rumble of the big V-8. Then, with a stomach full of pasta and a head full of ideas, I went directly to the elevator bank and up to the seventh floor. The EPS Officer was still perched outside T's door, but he didn't look so medical this time. His stethoscope was lying on the desk and he appeared a little disheveled. It was clear by the way he immediately jumped to his feet when he saw me that he didn't expect me to return. It didn't take long before I learned just how unanticipated my return was.

I didn't hesitate to push open the door, expecting to see T watching television or possibly sleeping, although it was only 10 p.m.

Well, he wasn't sleeping and I'm sure there was nothing on television that could compete with what was going on in real life. At first, with only a very dim light on in the room, it was difficult to determine exactly what was happening. However, once I focused and realized there were two bodies in that small hospital bed, and not all four feet were pointed in the same direction, I began to eliminate the possibilities. I also didn't think there were any apples between the sheets, so the head-bobbing I saw could only mean a few things. Adding the grunts, groans and slurps to the equation resulted in only one nauseating conclusion.

Just as I was about to announce my presence with a solid throat clearing, the nurse lifted her head and through her red and irritated lips let out a little "Oh oh," followed by, to my astonishment, a little giggle. I didn't know how to react. She was cute, not a day over twenty-five and obviously having just a good ole time sucking that dirty old man's cock. She rolled off the bed. Still mostly clothed, she straightened out her uniform and smiled as she walked past me to the door, which she closed behind her. I wasn't sure, but I could have sworn that she was chewing bubble gum when she walked past me.

"Jeezus T," was all I could get out.

"Hey kid. I'm glad to see you. I was a little worried there for a while. It all go okay?" he said, totally ignoring what just happened as he shuffled to sit up in the bed. I figured it was best to do the same.

"What do you mean you were worried?" I barked.

"Well I wasn't too sure what *Ponte* meant when he said 'let's go eat.' I mean...what the fuck. But everything went okay, right?" he said with that feigned look of concern on his face. I wasn't sure if he was serious or just busting my balls.

"Yeah, it went swell, asshole, no thanks to you. We got a lot to talk about, me and you." I was just getting warmed up when the telephone rang. T jumped three feet into the air.

He looked at me and then moved to pick up the receiver and answer the phone. I was lost for a second and then realized what was happening.

"Don't answer that," I yelled loud enough to startle him a second time. He gave me another of those "what the fuck" looks.

"Just sit tight. I'll explain in a minute," I told him as I raced around the bed to grab the phone, only guessing who was on the other end, let alone knowing what I was going to do about it. Only later did I realize how lucky we were that I was there.

In a pinch, feigning ignorance can usually give you time to think, so that's what I did. "*Pronto,*" I responded to the caller. I was pretty sure who was on the other end so I continued, "*Io non capisco inglese. Uno momento, uno momento, aspetta.*" I then put my hand loosely over the receiver and yelled, "*Tooony, Vieni qui. Telefono.*"

As I was doing that, I explained the situation to T; I only had seconds.

"I think this is Miguel. We had your telephone at the apartment forwarded to this phone. We don't want him to know you're in the hospital yet. We need to play him along for a while. Here, set the deal," I explained in a whisper.

"What? He thinks I'm at home. You can do that?" T asked incredulously.

"Why the fuck do you think they call it the Secret Service? Just talk to him and set up the fuckin' print. Give us a few days," I said, knowing I was running out of time. I held out the phone and he took it.

"Yeah, who is it? Yo, Miguel, howyadoin'?"

I could hear Miguel on the other end, but I couldn't quite understand what he was saying. T continued.

"Yeah. We could do that. Let me set it up and get back to you. Gimme a number where I can get ya, okay? Call me next week sometime. Right. Okay. *Ciao*."

I made very little sense of what I could hear, so I had to rely on T's interpretation.

"Okay, give me the details. What's up?" I asked.

"Well, I can't believe you can cross the telephone lines like that. He really thought I was in the apartment. Boy I'm gonna have to remember this when... never mind." T decided to censor his words on that thought and continued.

"He wants to finish the job. He said the test print was perfect and wants to go ahead and finish the print pronto."

"When and how much?" I anxiously asked.

"Twenty," he said with a little smile.

"Twenty what? Twenty million?" I asked because I just couldn't believe the number.

"That's what the deal was. Some score this woulda been," T confirmed and lamented in the same breath.

"Wow! When? How long do we have to get ready?"

"He didn't fuckin' say exactly; probably a week or so, no more. He sounded in a rush. We're gonna have to wait to hear from him 'cause he won't gimme a number."

T paused for a second while I was absorbing the enormity of the situation, and then he continued. "Why didn't we tell him I'm in the hospital and make the introduction now, like with the guys?" T was confused about how we were handling it. So I explained it to him like it was all my idea, when in truth, Carmine was calling the shots.

"Listen, it's too soon to throw him a curve. He might bail on us. We're gonna have to be the girl. We're gonna cock-tease him until his dick is so hard he'll do whatever we want to get into our pants. We'll bring him right to the brink of the print, and then when he's already counting his money, we'll spring the switch on him. By that time, he'll have no other alternatives and hopefully he'll go along with me doing the print. Besides, remember we're not going to actually print all that queer. We're gonna set it up and get it started and see how it goes. Headquarters likes big numbers, so we'll see how much we can print before we take it all down," I explained.

When I got to the "take it all down" part I could see the remorse in T's face. I'm sure he was thinking about what he was doing to Frankie and Canevecchio and felt lousy about it. Even after only my short time with those guys, I felt lousy about it too, but that's just the way it was. I changed the subject.

"I'm exhausted. It's been a long day. I'm goin' home. You try to get some rest, and let that cupcake nurse take care of some of the other patients, huh? I'll see you first thing. *Ciao bello*," I said and headed for the door, not even waiting for a response.

I had hit the wall. I was completely wrung-out, and just wanted to get into my own bed, even if Bookie and Ava were banging their brains out. I just didn't give a shit. I didn't even have the strength to grill T on all the questions I had after dinner with Frankie and Canevecchio. It would have to wait.

I closed the door behind me and didn't even notice if the EPS officer was still there. I'm sure he was though. I went out the emergency entrance, got into my beloved VW and drove to the apartment. I was so tired and emotionally exhausted that I don't even remember the ride home. Even Bookie and Ava were asleep when I slipped into the apartment. I was convinced I would feel better after a good night's sleep, but I only slept for three hours and then tossed and turned. I just couldn't get those guys out of my mind. I felt like the hangman the night before an execution and I didn't know exactly why. Days later, I eventually figured it out.

CHAPTER 27

23 FOXTROT, NINER, NINER, ECHO

While I was doing the hustle with everybody on my side of this fiasco, there was also quite a dance going on at The FBI. It started when Special Agent Tom Ritter got an extraordinarily unexpected visit to his olive-drab office.

In unprecedented fashion, while he was sitting in his gray steel chair, his office door opened. This unannounced, unauthorized "opening" was of biblical proportion to Ritter; biblical, meaning like the parting of the Red Sea. He was startled at first by the audacity of someone even putting their paws on his doorknob, let alone opening the door. His startle was completely overcome by catastrophic fear when he looked up, wearing his stern face, to see none other than The Director himself standing there like he owned the joint, which in fact he did. The Director had swung the door open until it banged against the little rubber capped door stop screwed into the baseboard trim on the adjoining wall. He just stood there waiting for some reaction from Ritter. Ritter, still in his chair, felt like the door had hit him square in the forehead, rather than hitting that little doorstop.

The Director, as always, was dressed like a mannequin in a Brooks Brothers' window. He was wearing a deep blue, three-piece suit that had to cost $500. A slightly lighter blue silk tie with a small red check and matching hankie was framed by a very crisp, white, straight-collar, Egyptian cotton shirt, and all this was neatly tucked behind a fully-buttoned vest. The jacket was unbuttoned, leaving the suggestion that it might not be able to completely encapsulate his slightly rotund form, making him appear more physically powerful. His shirt collar was just a half-size too small, which gave him a stiff unyielding impression. The flesh of his throat spilled over the top of the collar of his shirt, partially covering the Windsor-knotted tie, thereby softening the separation of man and attire. The white French cuffs, sharply creased and pierced by round, gold cufflinks engraved with the blue seal of The FBI, extended past his wrist joint, covering the base of his smooth, stubby hands. The uniform size, shape and gloss of the tips of all ten of his fingers, evidence of the unmistakable touch of a professional manicure, completed the portrait. These touches of high fashion, and even a hint of femininity, did not diminish the electric twinge of uncontrollable fright that swept over Special Agent Ritter. He knew he was being confronted in a very small space by possibly one of the most powerful and equally ruthless and cruel animals on the planet. He would have felt less threatened if he were cornered by a hungry lioness.

Ritter, recognizing that this was a very serious situation, leapt to his feet, resisting the overwhelming urge to salute or at least stand at attention and click his heals. This was the first time The Director ever came to his office. Ritter never even saw him on the floor before. In fact, in all of his twenty-six years with The Bureau, this was only the fourth time he had ever actually been in The Director's presence. Even when the Public Affairs Director would parade out all the hierarchy of The Bureau for a press release, Ritter was never ever invited to be in any of those photographs. He never knew why; The Director, however, did.

In a relatively short period, Ritter was able to marshal his senses and address The Director. However, it quickly became abundantly clear that he was not there to chat or visit, let alone seek his advice on any subject. All Ritter was able to get out was a tremulous, "Sir," before The Director succinctly stated his business.

"Drop any inquiry into 23 Foxtrot, Niner, Niner Echo," The Director said, looking Ritter directly in the eye. He clearly wasn't expecting, nor wanting, an answer other than a simple "yes," which he stood there waiting for.

"Yes, Sir," Ritter said, taking a short breath at the end as if he were filling his lungs to continue his response.

The Director, after hearing "yes," slightly rocked his head back, raising his jaw as if daring Ritter to hit him with another word. Ritter thought better of the idea and just averted his gaze. He was actually relieved that he could even figure out what The Director was talking about. His presence in Ritter's office confirmed that the package Ritter gave to Whitaker was indeed the credentials of an undercover agent that was at the core of a high level operation that was afoot without Ritter's involvement. While uncomfortable that he was left out of the loop, Ritter was instantly relieved that he no longer needed Whitaker. The Director himself had now put Ritter in the loop even if it was only to stand aside. Surprising Ritter, The Director continued.

"Twenty-three Foxtrot is assigned to a matter of the highest national security. There will be no communications or inquiries unless it comes directly from me. Understood?"

Make no mistake about it. The Director only wanted to know whether or not Ritter understood the simple command to butt-out and go do something else; there was no further discussion. Ritter got the message. He simply repeated his initial "yes" and it was over. The Director turned toward the door by taking four short baby steps as if he was waiting for his robust torso to catch up with his feet. When aligned with the door, he carefully and deliberately walked out and down the hall without another word; his business with Ritter was concluded. He left the task of closing the door to Ritter.

Under normal circumstances, when a human being survives a confrontation with a dangerous and hungry predator, a palpable, even audible sigh of relief is present once the animal turns and ends the face-off. Ritter felt no such relief. Even before The Director was out the door, he was already thinking about Al Whitaker and what he needed to do to get him disinterested in 23 Foxtrot. He knew that he could never do to Whitaker what The Director just did to him. While Ritter was a man who had achieved a fairly high rank at The Bureau, he still was by all standards a "pussy." He carried a badge and a gun, and among his peers, he was a powerful person. But he didn't actually have the intestinal fortitude, more commonly known as "the balls," to actually confront a powerful personality like Senior Special Agent Alfonso Whitaker. Whitaker was just not easily intimidated, actually, he was not intimidated at all.

All this uncertainty was swirling around inside Ritter's head as he reached for the secure line to call Whitaker, still unsure how to pull him off the case. He regretted more than ever that he was so insecure as to bring him into the mix in the first place. Ritter knew one thing for sure. If Whitaker got even a whiff of what just happened with The Director, he'd be on this thing like a stallion in a china shop with the Waterford stacked between him and a mare in heat. Whitaker would never give up until he got what he wanted and Ritter just didn't know what that was. His quest to find out every detail of this mystery and his inherent inability to accept a simple instruction to lay-off, would surely wreak havoc for Ritter. Knowing all this, Ritter had to do something. So, he picked up the telephone and called Whitaker himself—no secretary running interference. He was going to try to do this as simply as possible.

"Hello, Al. This is Ritter. We worked out the issues concerning that package I gave you, so you can get it off your plate. Leave the package with my secretary. Okay, thanks."

That's what Ritter wanted to say to Whitaker, but he just didn't have the nerve because he didn't know how he would handle Whitaker's questions and, he was sure Whitaker would have lots. So when Whitaker didn't answer his telephone, Ritter left no message. Rather, he just hung up and typed out a classified interoffice memo for immediate delivery to Whitaker's office. Ritter then began to brace himself for the barrage of questions he expected. He decided that he would tell Whitaker that 23 Foxtrot was involved in some routine, unspecified, FCI investigation, and was out-of-pocket for a few days due to a communications snafu, but has since been found. That would have been the best Ritter could have hoped for. It just didn't happen that way.

It was still before noon when the envelope with Ritter's message was delivered to Whitaker. The courier delivered it right into his hands. Whitaker nonchalantly opened the envelope; classified and even secret memos were common at The Bureau. It didn't even pique Whitaker's interest until he opened it and saw who it was from. Although the message was short and incomplete, Whitaker now knew that there was an FCI pot boiling with a very unusual undercover agent deeply inserted into the brew. Almost as emotionlessly as he opened the envelope, he plotted his course of action. He saw The Director's squishy hands all over the message, even though it was authored by Ritter. He decided to fuck with them both. He picked up the telephone and called The Bureau's nemesis from day-fucking-one: CIA.

When you've spent more than two decades sniffing around the fancy parties, panties and closets of most of the power brokers inside the Washington Beltway, you can't help but make a few friends and do a few favors for fellow sniffers and back-door-ers like yourself. So he made a few calls, had one quiet conversation in a very dark movie theater, a cold roast beef sandwich on a park bench and something akin to a high school make-out session in the front seat of a very expensive BMW. After just two days, he confirmed his suspicions.

Al Whitaker was now quite sure what was *not* happening. Special Agent 23 Foxtrot, Niner, Niner, Echo was not involved in any authorized FBI or even CIA investigation. While Whitaker was certain that 23 Foxtrot existed—he saw the commission book with his own eyes—he was unable to confirm much more. This must be why Ritter asked him to get involved in the first place. Ritter had no idea what was happening so he thought Whitaker knew something he didn't. Somebody must have also asked the wrong question of the wrong guy somewhere along the way. That's why The Director decided to put it all back in the box. He had no idea that Whitaker was in the loop, otherwise he would have done something much more effective than just telling Ritter to go sit in the corner and be quiet.

"Hell," Whitaker thought to himself. "If this thing was

important enough, that faggot would have had me hit by a bread truck at lunch. He's done it before."

Whitaker decided to let the kitchen cool a bit before he put somebody's cookies in the oven. He dutifully left a message with Ritter's secretary that he got his memo and, "no problem." He locked the commission book in his safe though, just to see who came looking for it.

CHAPTER 28

A RUB, A TUG AND HOPEFULLY A HAPPY ENDING

When The Director left Ritter's office, he sauntered to his private elevator. Not only did he not utter a single vowel to anyone, he didn't even look up. It's not like he was deep in thought or burdened by the heavy responsibilities of his office. No, he just didn't think anyone had anything of value to say.

The elevator climbed three floors to the executive suite. The only offices on that floor were those of The Director, his beloved Assistant Director and their staff. The secretaries at Headquarters were completely under The Director's thumb, mostly as a result of some young, simple transgression that usually involved sex and a special agent who had since been transferred to some remote outpost of The Bureau.

The door to The Director's office was never closed. There was no reason to keep it closed. Situated at the end of a very long hallway, no one in his or her right mind—except AD—would ever enter the hallway without first being announced and granted permission to approach. The fact is that even those granted an audience with The Director, rarely, if ever, got into his inner office.

When you enter the door to The Director's office, you walk into a large room with a huge, highly polished, see-your-face-in-its-reflection mahogany conference table. Ten leather padded chairs surround the table in front of an entire wall of windows that overlook the White House and the Capital in the distance. There is nothing else in the room save for a yellow pad and pencil set at each of the ten places. This is where the public business of The FBI is conducted. At the far end of the room is the large wooden door to The Director's private office that is always shut. Beyond this door is where the vital and real clandestine business of The FBI takes place—the inner sanctum.

On this day, not unlike many, The Director went to his private office.

"Find the Assistant Director," he commanded of a secretary as he walked past, not otherwise acknowledging her existence. She knew, however, exactly what to do.

The Director wanted to see his trusted AD, he wanted to see him now and he wanted to see him in his private office. All this was apparent just from the tone of his voice. She immediately called AD's office, which was only a short distance away—he was never far from The Director. Almost immediately AD came hustling down the hall in a series of quick, short steps, extending his legs as far as he could make them go while still only covering as much ground with each step as a small three-legged puppy. That didn't quell his determination or his enthusiasm though. He was getting there just as fast as his little legs could carry him. He walked past all the secretaries, giving each a warm, personal grin as he went directly to The Director's office with no further announcement.

"What the fuck is going on with that Cuban Rabbit?" The Director barked in an unusually aggressive manner, not that it would make any difference to AD. He understood The Director like no one else and just didn't get upset at his frequent hostility.

"We haven't made direct contact with the target yet, but our agent is in place and I expect we will establish a relationship soon. Why do you ask?" AD replied in a rather calm, unconcerned tone. As he spoke, he looked at the cut of his suit in the mirror hanging on the wall behind a small table near the front of the office.

"Because somehow that stupid fuck's commission book wound up in a mailbox and the DC Postal Inspector sent it to Ritter," The Director said while holding a cup of coffee in a very fine Lenox cup and saucer. He wouldn't get caught dead drinking anything out of a paper cup, and using a mug would be tantamount to moving into a trailer park, as far as he was concerned.

"Wow!" was AD's one word reply, not because he felt one word was sufficient, but because he could see The Director winding up to deliver a diatribe. He knew that whenever he gulped his coffee mid-sentence, he was about to launch like one of those new space rockets they're using to hurl those dumb sons-of-bitches into space. He was right on target.

"Why the fuck would the postal inspector deliver that book to Ritter? Who the fuck is he? He should have contacted The Director's Office. That's the protocol. I'm gonna call over there and have that jackass fired. Who's the fucking Chief Postal Inspector this week?" he asked, not waiting even a split second or half a breath for an answer. He didn't care about that; he had lots more to say.

"And Ritter, he decides to check it out. He puts Whitaker, of all people, on the hunt. Can you imagine what he thought when he saw those creds? And do you think he calls up here? Fuck no. It's only because my secretary got a whiff of it from the secretaries downstairs that I found out about it at all. Envision the entire Bureau running the fuck around like a bunch of cockroaches in a dark kitchen," he continued, knowing AD would sit quietly, admiring his cuticles until he was done.

"You know, I never asked Ritter for the commission book," The Director reflected with a little surprise in his tone. "He never offered it either. He should have handed it up, unless he didn't have it. And, if Whitaker has it we have a real problem," The Director huffed, while looking over at AD who was sitting with his right leg crossed over his left knee, now examining the shine on his wingtip and drinking a hot cup of tea in a matching cup and saucer.

When The Director signaled that he was resting for a moment, AD carefully placed his cup on the saucer and set it squarely on the doily on the table. Setting anything on the fine finish of the furniture would be a capital offense. He then tried to construct a logical and, more importantly, calming scenario to present to The Director, that, while not necessarily solving the problem, would at least quiet the immediate crisis, thus giving him time to work on it.

"Well, I can't immediately tell you what that ass-kiss Ritter is up to, but I can tell you what we have learned in just the last twenty-four hours from our source in Havana," AD told The Director in a rather nonchalant tone. AD knew that the prospect of getting secret information from the inner circle of the Castro Revolution was, to The Director, like putting a clean, dry diaper on a baby. It made him feel loved and very secure.

The Director got that surprised, giggly look that most men save for when they are unexpectedly offered a blow job from a hot babe they hardly know—it just seems too good to be true.

"What do we have, my love?" The Director asked, as he slid with exhaustion into his enormous leather chair.

"Well," AD began, "we know that something recently happened in the royal palace that really pissed Castro off and he called over to the Russian Embassy for a face-to-face with the KGB station chief." So far, The Director wasn't impressed. "But before the KGB Agent arrived, Castro asked for all of the available contact information in the States for The Rabbit we are currently hunting with 23 Foxtrot," he continued. "Since the Cuban network in the States is *Ad Hoc* at best, Castro needs the KGB to reach out to his own agent, probably to issue a change-of-plans order."

"What fuckin' change of plans? What fuckin' plans for that matter? What do we know and what are we gonna know?"

This was one of The Directors favorite managerial questions. He always asked the same question when he felt lost and left alone in the dark. He wanted to know what everyone in the world knew about the subject and then he wanted someone to go way out on a very skinny limb and predict with certitude how it will all turn out. This way, he could rest his mind and believe that all would be right with The Bureau. A child's fairy tale would have accomplished the same result. AD laid it all out for him, again.

"Our kitchen help in Havana (a double agent with good inside information) tells us that Castro sent this Rabbit into the States to initiate a significant counterfeit print someplace in the northeast. That idiot has some ridiculous idea of undermining our currency. The Rabbit is here and a Bureau CI (confidential informer, usually a professional, paid informer) tells us that he made contact with a Hungarian family in Jersey. We planted 23 Foxtrot with the family and anticipate an interception any day now." AD sipped his tea and continued.

"We're not exactly sure where The Rabbit is because some of the host family got grabbed in Las Vegas last month passing a new counterfeit note into the slots at the Casinos out there. We know that 23 Foxtrot was in Las Vegas with the Hungarians, but we don't really know what happened after that, although we don't think there was a bust. The 'kitchen help' seems to think that The Rabbit is out of the hole and possibly running his own operation, maybe alone or maybe with someone with a bone for Castro. It's not entirely clear yet, but it's a good bet that the counterfeit they were passing was the result of The Rabbit's efforts here in the States. We understand that The Rabbit was not in the States when the notes were passed, which is probably why he wasn't busted in Las Vegas and is also why 23 Foxtrot hasn't made an interception yet. The source tells us The Rabbit was in Havana meeting with Castro when it all went down in Las Vegas."

AD delivered all this information in a calm, almost prepared narrative, although he was circumspect to tell The Director only what was necessary to satisfy his appetite and keep him out of the kitchen. The Director was listening closely, but was clearly waiting for the "happy ending." AD took another sip of tea, carefully replaced the cup and continued.

"Now, we didn't notify the Secret Service. We figured we could make much more of this than a simple counterfeit bust and the Secret Service would only get in the way. If 23 Foxtrot can snatch this guy, we can belly him up and send him back to Havana as a hero of the revolution and a dishwasher for us. There's no room for anyone else in the game," AD concluded while The Director listened, without propounding a question.

Everyone knew that it was the legal obligation of The FBI to notify other law enforcement agencies of criminal violations within their jurisdiction when discovered by The Bureau. Everyone inside federal law enforcement also knew that the only time The FBI turned over such information was if The Bureau first determined that it was of no value to The Bureau. Their concern for the professional responsibility of other agencies, the directives of Congress or even the best interests of the country, is insignificant to what's beneficial to The Bureau, its budget, its self-established goals or just simply its ego or public persona.

Well, so far, The Director got a rub and even a little tug, but it was far from the happy ending he was hoping for.

"Okay, you're all a bunch of fuckin' patriotic geniuses. But what about the change of plans? And where the fuck is 23 Foxtrot?" The Director was now less questioning and more demanding.

"We don't know yet," AD responded, knowing never to say that he doesn't know without following it up with a 'yet', assuring The Director that all answers will shortly follow.

"Obviously Castro asked the KGB to pass along some new instructions to his agent, but we just don't yet know what those instructions are. We're also not sure yet if the KGB delivered the message. We don't really know where the Rabbit is at the moment, although we anticipate that he will reunite with the Hungarians and, hopefully when he does, 23 Foxtrot will be there. Our plan is to snatch him and return to our original operational plan with the added bonus of finding out what other hare-brained scheme he had cooking with Castro and the KGB."

While AD sounded certain of all this, he was really operating on a wing and a prayer. But it was still light years better than not having a happy ending for The Director. It wasn't that unusual for The Director to be somewhat out of the loop on a foreign counter intelligence case. This type of case created little or no publicity, and therefore it wasn't something The Director tracked on a regular basis. It was, however, exactly the kind of explosive matter that AD kept from detonating and wreaking havoc in The Bureau.

AD knew full well that there was a bigger game afoot and that Castro was intent on hurting the present administration—a goal The Bureau wasn't entirely adverse to, depending on where it would be when the fallout hit. While he didn't spell it out for The Director, AD certainly planned to use his contacts at the KGB to find out what this Cuban Rabbit was sniffing and where 23 Foxtrot was in the hunt. With a little skillful horse trading, he might even be able to find out the details of Castro's message. If he could get that information, then he had a few moves of his own to make when things shook out a bit. The Director, however, didn't need to know those details at the moment.

CHAPTER 29

SHE'S GOT AN ASS LIKE A $20 MULE

MIGUEL HUNG UP THE TELEPHONE and headed back down to Azzimie's apartment, still working through the trepidation he was feeling as a result of the conversation with T. But he now had a more pressing issue to attend to—like $100,000 in missing counterfeit Federal Reserve Notes.

Miguel found Azzimie on the bedroom floor of his apartment, half dressed. He was able to put a shirt on, but couldn't button it. He also managed to pull on a pair of pants up to just above the knees. At that point, he probably fell over and just didn't have the will or the strength to pick himself up off the floor. Miguel simply wanted to put a bullet in his head and leave him there, but he was cunning enough to know that the entire deal could go south if he did. He needed him to find out what happened to all that product and what agency made the arrests.

"Okay. Get up. We're going to find out what happened. Where are they now?" Miguel growled at Azzimie, as he picked him up off the floor by the scruff of the neck.

"Where are they right now?" Miguel demanded again, in a much louder and more aggressive tone when Azzimie didn't answer the first time.

"They're probably at the bowling alley," Azzimie finally responded, in a breathless voice replete with exhaustion.

"The bowling alley?" Miguel repeated and demanded in rapid fire. "Who's there? Are the chics there? What about the other guy, this Brus guy, is he there?"

"My sister and LJ work there. Brus will probably be there later tonight. He's always hangin' around," Azzimie replied.

"Okay. Let's go. And remember, keep your mouth shut about where the counterfeit came from or I'll kill you dead right in front of everybody. You hear me? You drive."

"Yeah, yeah, sure thing," Azzimie assured him.

Miguel practically pushed Azzimie out of the apartment door as they headed for Azzimie's car to drive the four miles to the Bloomfield bowling alley. It was a silent trip. All you could hear was the shallow, rapid breathing of Azzimie as he drove the car at a slow, deliberate pace across town.

It was getting dark when they arrived. Azzimie parked the car around back because he usually went in through the back kitchen door. Azzimie figured he could come and go as he pleased, being the cockroach that he was. Even though his cousin Julia was only a waitress in the joint, she was clearly the smartest person working there; she was the *defacto* manager. Julia collected the money and made the cash drop every night. That's also why Julia was able to get LJ a job working there with her. They had become thick friends over only just a few months. And besides, the two of them were a torrid twosome and great for attracting business from those hair-pie hungry bowlers.

Miguel insisted on going in through the front door for a couple of reasons. First, he's not the kind of Cuban who goes in through anybody's kitchen door. He expected that someone should be holding the front door for him, rather than him using the back door. Second, he wanted to case the joint before he made any moves inside, just in case Azzimie's family ratted him out, which wouldn't have surprised Miguel one little bit. He had no idea how this confrontation was going to turn out.

There were no bowling alleys in Cuba. It wasn't an identifiable sport in Mother Cuba. In fact, it wasn't even a pastime. There was only one sport in Cuba where a ball and a piece of lumber came into contact with each other and the result wasn't a clumsy thud, but rather a spine tingling "crack." Cuba's sport, baseball—also the great American pastime—couldn't be denied, even by the communists.

Miguel had absolutely no interest in this "rolling ball" frolic. So while he had heard of bowling alleys in the past, he had never been in one before. In fact, he had never even seen one from the outside before.

Initially, the first noticeable characteristic of the building wasn't the building at all, but rather the parking lot, the size and capacity, to be specific. While the one-story, metal-sided and roofed, airplane hangar-like structure was indeed huge, it was dwarfed in comparison to the parking lot. There must have been 300 cars in the lot with still room for more. It was hard to believe that the occupants of all the cars in the lot were in the building. It would have been easier to believe if someone told him it was a bus or train station parking lot; at least then some of the occupants of the parked cars could have been in transit to other places.

Indeed, the parking lot was a trifle unnerving because there was absolutely no activity. In a parking lot this size, you would expect to see some people coming and going, but not here. It wasn't until Miguel understood the drill better that he realized that everyone was there to participate in league bowling. This meant that almost everyone arrived and left at the same time, about thirty minutes before the league began, and then only when the lounge closed at 2 a.m.

The enormity of the building wasn't immediately obvious. It was deceptive because the roof sloped dramatically down toward the parking lot in such a way that the front wall of the building appeared very short and squat. The red and blue neon sign mounted on the roof flashed, "Bloomfield Bowling Lanes" in twenty-foot, red letters with a thirty-foot blue bowling pin positioned on the far right side. The sign was animated so that it blinked on and off while mimicking the pin, first standing and then knocked on its side. The sight was dizzying, partly because in the dark, it was impossible to see where the roof ended and the sky began. The reflection of the neon sign illuminated just enough of the roof to give the illusion that the span was endless.

There were absolutely no windows in the building whatsoever. There was, however, a single glass door right in the center of the squat front wall. Bright, harsh white lights spilled through the naked glass onto the pavement outside. The contrast was stark and the image was not at all inviting. At the far left end of the building was the only other orifice. It was a single glass door with a small, red neon sign over it that said, “Lounge.” There was little or no light coming from the other side of the door. In fact, if it were not for the red neon sign, you would never even notice the door was there at all. Azzimie parked in the nearest available spot, which was three rows back from the center door. Miguel gave him one last warning,

“Remember, watch your mouth. I’ll do all the talking. You just do the introduction,” Miguel instructed as they both walked toward the light.

There was a black rubber mat spread out in front of the entrance. Neither Miguel nor Azzimie wiped their feet before going in; the place didn’t seem to warrant such care. The bright white lights inside revealed a hallway that stretched from the front doors down a long hall to the business end of the building. The linoleum-covered floor caused Azzimie’s sneakers to make a squishing sound when he walked, which announced his presence with humiliation. When they reached the end of the hallway, Miguel felt like he had just crawled through a hole in the ground that opened up into a huge underground cavern. Even the ceiling had a rounded finish to it as it traversed from the front to the back of the building. There was a hefty wooden counter at the end of the hallway, with a chubby, bleached-blonde, more-than-middle-aged woman manning it. Behind her was one of the most curious arrangements Miguel had ever seen.

It was a series of wooden cubby holes that stretched the entire length of the counter and was so high that Blondie had to stand on a small step stool to reach the top row. It reminded Miguel of his local post office in Cuba. Naturally, there was only one post office in the world and that was the United States Postal Service. But Cuba, like so many emerging nations and societies, emulated the American system. No one could ever approach American automation, so cubby holes were the Cuban delivery system. The purpose of these cubicles in the bowling alley was surprising to Miguel because they were filled with shoes, of all things. In his world, shoes were meant to scrape along in the filth and even wastewater of the streets, never, ever to be raised above waist level, unless they were brand new and unworn. It was incomprehensible for Miguel to watch people approach the counter, remove their shoes and give them to Blondie who would place them in a cubby hole. He was actually horrified to see some people even put the shoes down right on top of the wooden counter. Of course Miguel could not fathom any reason for this odd behavior, especially right there in full public view.

Almost all other aspects of the place were equally puzzling to Miguel, everything except where he was. That's because the single biggest thing in the entire building was an American flag that hung from the ceiling over nearly all of the fifty lanes. Miguel hated the harsh image of the American flag, even though it included the same red, white and blue colors of Mother Cuba. He found thirteen red and white stripes too distracting; the five stripes—three blue and two white—of the Cuban flag were perfect.

It wasn't until after he reconciled the shoes issue that he even noticed the constant rumbling of destruction that filled the room. The entire place was chaotic, in both sight and sound. People and objects were moving in all directions with no apparent rhyme or reason. The main room of the building had fifty shiny wooden corridors or lanes as they were called. Many of the occupants, both men and women, stood or sat around the near end talking, drinking and flirting, while others raced forward to a firing line where they hurled a large ball, as fast as they humanly could, down the wooden lane toward a stack of wooden pins. The view was maddening because between each lane was a ramp that carried a similar ball back to the bowlers. These balls were traveling in the opposite direction of the balls sent hurtling down the lane by the bowlers. This chaotic image was intensified by salted explosions of the pins and the dull, heavy, thud of the balls striking the lane upon each bowler's release.

The aural stimulation was the soundtrack for the visual amusement. As soon as the ball left their grasp and control, each bowler began a ritualistic dance meant to somehow control the movement of the ball—a wiggle of the hips, a step to the left or right or a wave of the arms, all accompanied by shouted orders—were typical. The enthusiasm that resulted from the successful destruction of the targeted stack of pins was a celebration of annihilation; a relatively controlled release of violence under bright lights accompanied by an excessive consumption of alcohol salted with just the right amount of sexual stimulation. And it was LJ and Julia who provided two out of the three.

Miguel remained standing at the shoe counter absorbing all the completely unexplainable behavior that surrounded him. But Azzimie, completely unaffected by the utter chaos, walked directly to where Julia and LJ were working. Both girls were waitresses and served not only customers in the lounge, but also served the bowlers while they were waiting for their turn to bowl. The entire building was divided into two levels. The entrance and a wide hall that ran the entire length of the building were on the same level. There was a set of two steps down positioned about every six lanes or so. The bowlers and the lanes were at the lower level. Along a metal railing separating the two levels between each set of steps were long relatively narrow tables. It was at these tables, with LJ and Julia standing on the higher level and the bowlers on the other side of the tables on the lower level, that business was conducted.

Julia and LJ were what most Americans and probably no one else refer to as cocktail waitresses. The meaning of the term alluded Miguel, other than the obvious sexual connotation. They wore short skirts that left a great deal of leg showing and a tiny, tight top that shapely outlined and certainly enhanced their tits and for a kicker left a good three inches of their tight mid-section, including their belly button, fully exposed. Without directly selling sex and probably breaking some archaic American law, Miguel was sure their appearance directly contributed to the sale and consumption of substantial quantities of alcohol.

Miguel followed Azzimie down the hall behind the bowlers to the lounge area where LJ and Julia were filling drink orders. When Miguel laid eyes on LJ, now for the second time, she was standing across the bar in the lounge. She stood tight-legged, facing away from him, with her upper torso twisted to her left. Miguel could see the silhouette of a not-too-petite shape, framed by a layered, full cut of red and strawberry blonde hair—just looking at her created sexual tension and frustration. That was the bad news. The good news was that the remainder of the view answered all Miguel's questions. The leather skirt, low on her hips, packaged the treasure trove. Every man knows how to describe what he saw. It was a perfect ass, plain and simple. Back home, the farm boys would surely say, "That girl's got an ass like a $20 mule," and they would be right.

Miguel could see that both LJ and Julia were very busy. They would scurry about to several tables taking orders for drinks and an occasional order of French fries, after which they would hustle down to the far end of the building where the lounge was located and scurry back to deliver the order. It was obvious that the interaction between the male bowlers and the girls was a highlight of the evening for the men. Whenever one of the girls arrived with an order, or merely passed by, all the men stopped bowling and just stared. It added stimulation to the evening like gasoline at a campfire rally.

With all this swirling in his head, Miguel directed Azzimie to a corner table where he could work out some sort of a plan for the evening. Azzimie was already busy smoking a cigarette and drinking a beer, probably to calm his nerves. It was noticeably quieter in the lounge than it was out in the bowling area. The action was certainly out there and not in the lounge, at least for the time being. Miguel figured, and correctly so, that when the games out there were over for the night, the games in the lounge would begin. It was for that reason he concluded he had only a limited window of opportunity to get Julia and LJ to focus on his issues.

Miguel sat at the table drinking a rum and coke over ice, trying to figure out how to handle the situation. He knew he didn't have much time and needed to know as quickly as possible exactly what happened in Las Vegas. He had neither the time nor the inclination to do a dance with any of these people to get the information he needed. And he didn't really care anymore if they assumed he was the source of the notes. Before they could make another move and, with any luck, he would be long gone.

So, he took another long gulp of rum, another peek at LJ's sweet ass and wondered, "Who is this guy Brus anyway?"

CHAPTER 30

BOWLING BALLS, CFMS AND DER FÜHRER

Azzimie and Miguel sat in that corner for almost two hours before there was finally a lull in the activity—sometime between the end of the bowling night on the lanes and the beginning of the hustle night in the lounge. LJ came over to the table looking tired, complaining that her feet hurt. No wonder they hurt. Both Julia and LJ were wearing spiked "Come Fuck Me" heels that threw every man in the joint into a cold sweat.

As LJ took a seat at the table, Azzimie did the introduction.

"Hey LJ, this is my friend Miguel. He lives in my building. You met him before at the DMV," he said as he pushed his face very close to hers. Anyone could see he found her scent tantalizing.

"Nice to meet you," she said as she put her right hand out to Miguel. Miguel took it and gently squeezed it, but didn't shake it.

"Azzimie told me you guys recently had an exciting time in Las Vegas," Miguel told her, coming right to the point, while looking her right in the eyes to make sure that she understood that he was a man of serious business. She clearly understood.

"Yes, we did. But it's all over now," she replied, giving Miguel a clear sign that there were no lingering consequences.

At the same time, Julia walked up and overheard the conversation. Miguel, unlike Azzimie, never saw Julia coming because he was completely enthralled by the sight, smell and aura of LJ.

Julia just jumped right in. "Yeah, they didn't have nothin' on us because they never got us on tape putting bills in the slots. LJ got away completely and they let me out without even posting any bail. My public defender said that once they realize I ain't talkin' they'll just drop the charges," Julia explained, at the speed of an Indianapolis race car.

It was clear that Julia knew she was traveling with a fast crowd, and like any race car driver, she knew that if she didn't stay ahead of the pack, she could get run over. She also had a pretty clear understanding of who Miguel was; after all, she was Azzimie's cousin and did inherit some of the family instincts. Julia decided to get it all out so Azzimie and Miguel would relax about it. All she wanted to do was put it behind her; whatever Azzimie and his buddy Miguel wanted to do was their business.

"Lucky thing, huh?" Miguel asked in a very dry voice.

"Yeah," Julia pensively replied. With both her eyes were as wide open as they could possibly get, staring right at LJ as if pleading for help.

"Yeah. Stupid flat-foots. They didn't know their asses from their elbows," LJ chimed in with a cocky tone.

"Who were they?" asked Miguel.

"Who were who?" Julia asked back, now completely unveiling her reluctance to think about it anymore, which alarmed Miguel.

"I'm sure they were just local fuzz," LJ quickly announced, sensing that Julia might get them both killed. She could see that Miguel, whoever he was, was no one to fuck with.

"You think?" Miguel asked sounding unconvinced.

"Oh yeah," Julia started to say when LJ interrupted.

"For sure. The old fart chasing me could have never been a fed, if that's what you're askin'."

Miguel didn't respond. He just looked at both of them, nodding his head and taking a sip of his drink. The tension seemed to ease. But to make sure, LJ jumped up and told Azzimie, who sat silently during all this, that she would get them a fresh drink. As she left the table, she gently touched Julia's arm, who now knew enough that it was time to make her get away.

"See, I told you they were cool chics. No problems, huh?" Azzimie said to Miguel, leaning forward across the table, filling Miguel's nostrils with his foul breath.

Miguel hoped that Azzimie was right for everybody's sake. He certainly wasn't interested in another drink, even though he certainly was interested in grabbing a piece of LJ or even Julia for that matter. He had no romantic fantasies about either of them; he wasn't that kind of man. Rather, he just imagined throwing a woman on a bed, tearing her clothes to shreds and fucking her hard and brutal. However, at that moment he knew he had a guinea he needed to talk to, so he reigned in his imagination and was preparing to leave.

Miguel was getting ready to cowboy up and get the courage to push T and his *paisani* to finish the print on his terms rather than theirs. But then a small, skinny guy walked in through the lounge door from the parking lot. When he opened the door, the red neon color from the "lounge" sign hanging over the door cast an amber hue over most of the room. As soon as Julia recognized who it was, she immediately looked at LJ and then wide-eyed at the table where Azzimie and Miguel were sitting.

Azzimie touched Miguel's arm and uttered a single word, "Brus."

Brus couldn't have weighed more than 135 lbs. and stood not an inch over 5 feet 5 inches. He had tiny little hands and feet, a lifeless complexion and color, but with a very serious look about his face. While Miguel couldn't immediately see that he had cold, steel-blue eyes, he was struck by his two most noticeable characteristics—the hair on top of his head and the hair over his upper lip.

Generally, when a man of his stature presents himself, there's hardly ever a thought of power or danger. Being a physical menace just doesn't come to mind unless there's an additional component like a gun or a knife or some other indication of danger or evil. Brus had it as sure as if it were a loaded .38. It was known as a toothbrush mustache—a two-inch vertical patch of hair that sat in the center of his upper lip. The sides were not tapered, like most mustaches, but shaved vertical on the ends, giving it a hard, dramatic conclusion. By this time in the history of western civilization, this postage stamp-sized clump of hair was known as the "Hitler Mustache." Miguel couldn't imagine why anyone would wear the personification of such evil right in the middle of his face. It was tantamount to having a swastika carved between his eyes. To emphasize that the image was not donned in error, Brus kept his thinning, unwashed hair in a high left part, combed straight to the side to complete the evil Hitler look.

Brus immediately approached Julia. He didn't walk up to her and begin a conversation like most people would, but rather he stepped across her body and firmly took hold of her right arm. Bringing his face within inches of hers, he spoke directly into her ear. She didn't speak or even turn her head; she just slowly nodded and looked directly at Miguel and Azzimie's table. Brus then turned to LJ, who was standing nearby watching intently. When he attempted the same maneuver on her, she defiantly turned sharply in his direction and faced him squarely. Brus only spoke a few words before LJ just spun on her heel and walked away, showing no apparent response.

When Miguel saw Brus's connection to both chics he immediately became concerned.

"Why the toothbrush on his lip?" he asked Azzimie as if he already knew the answer.

"That's Brus; it's a Hitler thing. Ya know what I mean?" Azzimie replied, talking through his glass of beer like he was wishing he could jump in it and hide.

"Yeah, I know. How did he get involved with both LJ and Julia?" Miguel wanted to know.

"He just walked in a few months ago and hit on them, like everybody else, I guess. He's around a lot. Julia invited him to Vegas," Azzimie explained.

"Oh yeah?" Miguel said, while trying to decide if it was all just that simple, although he could certainly understand why some putz, who's so insecure he has to try and look like *der Führer*, would chase chics like Julia and LJ.

Azzimie just started to run on at the mouth, probably because he was so scared he wanted to show how helpful he could be; Miguel just let him talk.

"He came in 'bout a couple of months ago," he began. "I guess that was before Julia hooked up with LJ. He just started to hang out. He's here every day, always askin' lots of questions. He's a hustler. He runs a numbers operation in the south ward; Nigs, ya know. Julia's got a thing for him. It's pretty fuckin' weird, if you ask me. I think he's got a stiffie for LJ. Actually, he's got way too much moxie for either of 'em."

"What's the deal with Julia and LJ? They're not dykes are they?" Miguel asked as if he didn't hear a word Azzimie was saying.

"Fuck no," Azzimie said with absolute certainty, but then added, "Shit, you don't think so do you?"

Miguel didn't respond, but just gulped his rum. Several seconds later he asked, "How did they meet?"

"From what Julia told me, I think they met at some store, Bambergers I think. They were fightin' over the same pair of shoes. I don't know for sure. Why?" Azzimie didn't yet understand that Miguel was the one asking the questions; he didn't answer any.

"What do you know about her?" Miguel was more than mildly curious to know.

"You mean other than she's got a great ass and tits that say 'Boom, Boom?'" Azzimie nervously laughed, adding, "She lives in Irvington and drives an old, powder blue Bel Air. She don't got no family, I don't think. I heard her mention Baltimore. She lived there once, maybe as a kid. She and Julia are real thick now. They work most nights here and spend lots of time together on the weekends. That's why they both made that trip. Ya know, can't separate them for nothin'. I think that's why LJ's shitty to Brus; she knows Julia likes him and she don't want to give him no play and upset Julia. But boy she's got some ass, huh?" he said as he was starring right at her best attribute.

"What happened to Brus in Las Vegas?" Miguel asked, changing the subject from LJ's ass.

"No fuckin' idea. I told you I never asked nobody. The last thing I saw was a bunch of cops chasin' him across the slot's floor." Azzimie was trying to explain when Miguel cut him off at the knees and said, "Well it looks like we're gonna find out. Here he comes."

LJ Immediately turned on her heel and left Brus standing there looking like he just missed the last bus home in a snow storm. He turned with a look on his face as if he didn't care anyway, just in case somebody was watching, and headed for Miguel and Azzimie like he forgot that he left his wallet on the table. As Brus approached the table, Miguel couldn't help thinking that he looked more like Charlie Chaplin than Hitler. He had a hitch in his gait that made him bobble left and right as he walked like "The Little Tramp." It made him look—toothbrush on the upper lip and all—comical rather than sinister and evil. Unfortunately, for Miguel, he also saw him as harmless. Maybe it was because he was surrounded by all those low class bowlers and sitting there with the likes of Azzimie talking about ass and boom-booms that he missed the deadly scent of a marauder.

"Hey Azz, what's groovin' man?" Brus asked in hip talk.

"Nothin'," Azzimie said as Brus sat down at the table without an invitation, something that would just never happen in civilized Cuba. Nevertheless, there he was. Not only was he sitting uninvited, but he also immediately launched 1,000 questions like Agamemnon launched Greek ships against Troy.

Miguel just ignored Brus's questions, while Azzimie continued to stare into his beer, terrified of what Brus was going to say next. He didn't disappoint.

"So listen what man, you split clean in Vegas, huh?" hearing Brus verbalize the Las Vegas fiasco terrified Azzimie and absolutely stunned Miguel.

Miguel decided to go right at him.

"What the fuck do you know about what happened in Las Vegas?" This was the hard throw to the plate. Miguel thought he could rattle him right out of the box. He was certain this little scumbag knew who he was, and he wanted Brus to feel the terror right then. He should have tried another play.

"What I know is plenty, aa-mii-goo! I was there. Where were you?" Executing the perfect fade away slide and getting the "safe" call from the ump, Brus curled his upper lip in such a way that his toothbrush mustache almost completely disappeared. Miguel was thoroughly pissed, but he didn't show it. Instead, he calmly stood and Azzimie immediately followed.

"Com' on! Sit and talk to me. We can do business. I can move wheelbarrows of that stuff. It's good stuff. We can make gobs of money. I got all the right connections," Brus pleaded.

The more Brus kept talking, the farther away Miguel walked until Azzimie finally told Brus to shut up. He then literally chased after Miguel, who was already stepping through the lounge door into the parking lot. The red neon light made the lot look like a forbidden radiation zone from a sci-fi movie. Azzimie was on his heels like the dog shit he was.

There was nothing for Miguel to discuss with Brus or even Azzimie for that matter. Miguel had already made up his mind and at that moment, he needed only one thing.

"Find me a pay phone!" he instructed Azzimie.

CHAPTER 31

WHOA, THAT WAS NEVER PART OF THE DEAL, AMIGO.

Clang, clang, clang. T, as sound asleep as he could ever remember, immediately pumped his arms and legs in frantic circles, trying to get the sheet and cotton cover off his body. Even before he fully succeeded in securing his release from the now twisted and tangled bedclothes, he attempted to get to his feet. To complicate matters, his hospital gown—tied only in the back, at the very top—was pushed up and contorted around his neck. In an effort to break free, he literally jumped off the right side of the bed, feeling the familiar cold floor on the balls of his feet. He was relatively awake, but uncertain about what was happening. He stood as straight as he could with both arms down at his side, even though his cock and balls were hanging in the breeze. When he initially hit the floor, he knew his back was to the bed so he therefore knew exactly what he needed to do.

Clang, clang, clang, again. T was now thoroughly confused. There had always been only one edict. Either you responded or you got a beatin'. He ignored the confusion and began to get into position. As he tugged at his gown in an automatic response to the unfamiliar breeze he was feeling, he put his two cold feet together, made a snappy turn to the right and stood straight as an arrow.

Clang, clang, clang, for the third time. Now his confusion scared him. When he opened his eyes, he was facing the soft, calming, light-green wall of the hospital room, not the black, vertical steel bars of Rahway State Prison. He began to sense some relief. He was no longer standing for inspection at 5 a.m., in response to a 300-lb. hack walking the tier while lacing the bars with his billy club as he passed by. T didn't have to fret his return and the prospect of catching the business end of that club in the gut for no reason other than being a wop.

Clang, clang, clang. T, now fully awake, finally understood what was happening.

"It's the fuckin' telephone," he said to himself, although speaking nearly out loud.

The phone sat on the little rolling bed table on the other side of the room. He literally belly flopped on the bed and grabbed the receiver, just as it was completing the third ring for the fourth time.

"Yeah, what?" he said, sure that it was Jake, completely forgetting that the Secret Service had rigged the telephone lines so his home phone rang in the hospital. He was in complete shock to hear Miguel's voice on the other end.

"I want to do that job tomorrow night. Understand?"

There was no greeting or identification by the caller. T still knew exactly who it was. Now was not the time for playing games; T got right to business.

"I understand what you're askin', but I'm not sure we can pull it off," T responded, still doing his best to concentrate and think ahead of his next statement.

"I'm not askin'. If you want to do business, that's what has to happen."

Miguel knew he was running a risk that the deal would collapse, but he decided to gamble on T and his guys not wanting to lose a very big payday. He also knew what kind of organization he was dealing with and that T would have a lot of explaining to do to the bosses above him when there wasn't any more cut for them. The suspicion of a double-cross alone could get T killed.

T was awake now and he was listening to Miguel very closely, and not just to the tough-guy talk. He could feel the tension in his voice. He concluded that Miguel was pushing for the print *now* because things weren't so good on his end. T didn't know what it was, but he was pretty certain it was more than just a tight pair of jockeys. Of course, for the first time, T didn't feel any pressure because he had the whole United States Government on his side; little did he know. He was also worried that this could be a scam Miguel was running to see if T was legit. If Miguel pushed him beyond all acceptable limits, then he might conclude that only a cop would agree to such demands and no self-respecting mob guy would go along. T knew if he didn't play this right, he could blow the entire deal. Actually, he still had mixed emotions about it all, but somehow he felt he was on a team and the fact that this creep was a Cuban made it a lot easier to bury him. He decided to give him a good pitch, but not so good that he couldn't hit it if he wanted.

"Maybe you should watch your mouth, pal. My friends would be very disappointed to hear you give orders like that. *Capisce?*" He took a breath and continued. "Impossible to do tomorrow night. Impossible." And then there was the silence T expected. He let it simmer and then continued.

"Maybe we could get ready and do it Saturday night. That's possible," T continued, knowing that Saturday night was always the preferred time, but he didn't tell Miguel that. Miguel's response was almost immediate and just as he expected, although a little more than he bargained for.

"Okay. Where? I need to be there."

"Whoa. That was never part of the deal, amigo." Now T started to think that this deal might really collapse.

Miguel decided to explain his demand in a much more respectful tone. "Look, you know I'm not stickin' around. We do the job all in one night, everybody's in the same boat for what, ten, maybe twelve, hours. I'll bring the genuine. When it's all over, you get the genuine, I get the product and get off the continent—a clean, profitable deal for everybody, my friend."

T had to admit to himself that it did sound pretty good. Even though they were all in the same joint for a long night, it was over when it was over. There were no risky exchange meets and no transportation of the counterfeit by him or his guys. He already saw how that could go bad.

"I gotta get permission for that. I gotta talk to my guys and some other guys, know what I mean? Call me this time tomorrow. I'll be here and I'll let you know what we can do."

"Okay. Please, my friend, make this happen. You won't regret it, amigo."

That was just what T wanted to hear him say. Now he knew he had him.

T hung up without saying another word. It was well after 2 a.m., he was exhausted and he didn't know how to get in touch with Jake even if he wanted to, which he didn't. He ripped that stupid gown off and got into bed, balls-ass naked, just the way he liked to sleep, even in the joint.

He would fix it all in the morning or he wouldn't. Right now, he was going to sleep. What the fuck—he had a Secret Service Executive Protection Service Officer sitting right outside his door protecting him, just like the fuckin' President. He was asleep almost before his eyes closed.

CHAPTER 32

THERE'S ONLY ONE GUY THAT'S GONNA PULL OUR ASSES OUTTA THIS FIRE

I woke up on Friday morning about 6 a.m., my regular time. I spent about twenty minutes doing some pushups and sit-ups along, with some stretching and about ten minutes playing the bongos. Banging on the twin drums, while holding them between my knees, calmed me down and really improved my hand speed and dexterity. I took a long, hot shower during which I tried to plan my day, the same way a big league pitcher plans to pitch to the Yankee-lineup, merely hoping to survive the onslaught. I only wanted to see two people—Carmine and T. I figured I would first go to the office early to see Carmine before all the bosses came in and broke my balls over one thing or another. I would then drive over to see T and try to move the print along. Little did I know that T and Miguel were working late the night before and made other plans for my day.

I pulled on my jeans and a nice, cotton, long-sleeved, button-down shirt, a pair of Luccheses—naturally—and headed for the door. For some reason, I always looked back at my room just before I walked out the door to the hallway that lead to the foyer. Because the apartment had the bedrooms on opposite sides of the living room, I always felt like I was living alone, especially since Ava moved in with Bookie. While their relationship was a little on the slippery side, it worked for them. They actually shared each other's lives, which was a very difficult accomplishment in a job like ours.

On that morning, I was feeling especially alone. From the bedroom doorway, I was able to look through the open bathroom door into a clean, neat and mostly empty bathroom. There was nothing on the floor or the vanity, save for a single toothbrush hanging in one of the little holes around the ceramic cup holder that was glued to the wall next to the sink. The bedroom had that same clean and empty feeling. I think it hurt that day because my heart felt the same way—empty and alone. I thought of how whenever I went over to Bookie's side of the apartment, his bathroom and bedroom was a brilliant mix of colors and textures that Bookie and Ava created together. My side was just a blank canvas, devoid of human passion and creation. They lived and loved on their side, while my side was simply a place to close my eyes to garner strength for the next work day. I would have given anything to see a pair of red lace panties lying on the floor, stockings or a bra over the back of the chair, even a medicine cabinet or vanity cluttered with makeup, tweezers and eyelash curlers. But it just wasn't so, at least not then. So, with a single swipe at the wall switch next to the door, I shut off the light and watched the room—like my heart—go dark.

For some unknown reason I changed my mind and decided to go see T first. I just couldn't face going to the office and dealing with the narrow minds that think they have the formula for life that, incidentally, they found written on the side of a mostly-empty scotch bottle. On the other hand, there was a certain entertainment value in spending time with T and his guys. They blurred the line between good and bad. So I pointed the little round nose of the VW down Central Avenue, deciding to start my day slow and catch up with Carmine around lunch time, hopefully someplace outside of the office.

I was at the hospital in less than fifteen minutes. I parked the VW in the visitor's lot and walked through the emergency entrance like I always did. On the seventh floor, the EPS guy was still at his desk. As far as I could tell, it was the same unlucky guy, all hours of the day and night. I got no more than a nod of the head, but I was comforted to know he was there and I could at least be confident that T was still there. I still had a frightful notion that he was just playing us and, at the crucial moment, he was gonna scram and leave us holding the bag, literally.

It was only 8:00 a.m. and T was wide awake, sitting on the edge of the bed. I should have known something was wrong. Usually, he's catching his beauty sleep till 11. He led a life of long, productive nights and recuperative days.

"What's up?" I asked sensing something was wrong.

"I got a call in the middle of the fuckin' night," T responded with a look on his face like he had a mouthful of lemons.

"You got a call? You mean a telephone call? From who?" I knew there was a wide range of disasters that we could be talking about. It was like waiting for a hurricane report. The fact that there was a hurricane wasn't surprising; it's the category of the storm that makes all the difference. This storm could have been a Category 1: T's *goom* called and dumped him. Or it could have been a Category 5: Frankie called to tell T that I was an agent and "Oh, by the way you're both fuckin' dead men." I was waiting for the news, never expecting what I was about to hear.

"Miguel called. He's got a bug up his ass and wants to do the print immediately and he wants to be there. How 'bout that shit?" T spit out, all in one breath.

"Wow! I wonder what got him all juiced up. What did you tell him?" I asked as I hunched my shoulders up around my neck, waiting for the answer.

"I think he's on the lam. He wants to shoot the entire load in one night, pay up and get the fuck outta town. I told him maybe we could do it Saturday night."

"Can we be ready? I mean can we get Frankie and the equipment and a place by then?" I asked, not yet realizing we had no choice other than to do it.

My question was greeted with a sarcasm-riddled smile and an affirmative nod of the head that was intended to remind me who was really in charge of this caper. I didn't like it, but just the same, I was relieved at his confidence. To complicate matters, we then got a couple of unexpected visitors.

"Good morning, fellas. How ya feelin', T? Hey kid, what's up?"

I actually heard the heavy breathing even before the door opened. I immediately had mixed emotions because I really liked Canevecchio. He was a man and a half in many ways. And, if Canevecchio was there, it was a good bet that Frankie was right behind him. Even though I hadn't figured it out yet, there was an admirable quality about Frankie that made men, including me, seek his company. This was all extremely confusing because they were the "bad guys" in this caper and I'm the guy that's gonna arrest them and throw them in jail. I didn't even think about the other possibilities, like what do I do with the .357 in my boot if one of them tries to resist or run away. I could very well find myself faced with the possibility of shooting one or both of them or failing to keep my oath as an agent. I didn't want to think about any of it, so I just did what came naturally.

"Yo, Canevecchio, my main dog," I said as I walked over to him and we exchanged hugs. I spent a total of about ten hours with this guy and now I think he's my favorite uncle.

As I suspected, Frankie was just on the other side of the door. I stepped into the hall and was troubled when I saw him looking hard at the EPS guy sitting at the desk. He was probably thinking the same thing I was thinking. "How does that guy spend so many hours sitting at that desk, and even more importantly, why?"

"Frankie, nice to see you," I tried to divert his attention as I put out my hand to shake his. He took it and shook it.

"Hey kid, *ciao, come sta*?" he said while never taking his eyes off the EPS officer. He never said anything about him, but I could smell the rubber burning inside his head. It was turning high RPMs.

"Yeah, I'm good. *Sta bene*. Come on in. We gotta talk to T," I told him as I lightly touched his arm as if to turn him toward the door. I was very careful not to push him or even suggest too hard that he should turn away from the hall and go into the room. If he had other ideas, it would have taken a bigger gun than I had to get him into the room. Thankfully, he took the hint and turned toward T's room where Canevecchio was telling a joke.

"Hey kid. Why did the pervert cross the street?"

"I have no fuckin' idea," I replied.

"Because he had his dick stuck in a chicken. Har, har, har."

Everybody thought it was funny. I could even hear the EPS officer down the hall laughing because Canevecchio said it so loud everybody on the floor heard it. As the laughing subsided, I closed the door as a sign that it was time to get down to business. Frankie got the message.

"What's goin' on T?" Frankie instantly asked.

"I got a message from that guy last night. He's ready to move *now.* He wants to do the job on Saturday. He'll be there with the good, we'll finish business and he'll be on his way, all in one night."

"Whaddu mean he'll be there with the genuine?" Frankie was obviously uncomfortable with the idea this stranger would be at the printing plant.

"I mean he wants to be there and then close the deal right on the spot. *Capisce?*" T responded, signaling that it was okay with him and therefore, should be okay with Frankie, too.

"You sure that's a good idea T? I mean who the fuck is this guy? We don't know him from Adam," Frankie quickly responded, raising the level of his voice more than slightly.

"Na, it's okay. The guy comes highly recommended from friends of ours (the magic words). We did the first thing without a hitch. And besides, it's a fuckin' boatload of cash. It's better to do the job, hand it right over and run with the cash. I think it's good," T replied, being careful not to be too challenging to Frankie's concern.

Frankie looked around the room for a second or two while he rolled his lips inside his mouth against his teeth, a thinking technique for sure. We all knew for sure that no matter how enthusiastic T was about the deal, Frankie wasn't going along unless it made sense to him. I held my breath. He finally shook his head a few times up and down and said, "Okay, okay, I'll be there for ya," Frankie reluctantly agreed.

That's all Canevecchio needed. "Yeah, let's do it," he said with a jiggle.

While these guys were setting the deal up to go down in forty-eight hours, I felt like a turkey the day before Thanksgiving; I was going to get slaughtered because I had no idea how I was going to be prepared to be a printer. I had about six hours of training on how to print counterfeit in Secret Service school; I just wasn't ready. My only solution was to try and stall and hope I could come up with an answer later.

"Do we have everything we need to do this? I mean we need paper, ink, a press and how about a set of plates, to say nothing about a place to do it," I said in one long breath that left me nearly faint.

"Don't worry kid," T began. "We got it all covered. I got the plates, the press and a lead on a place. We do need some paper and ink though. My connections can get us some Double Eagle Bond, no questions asked. The black ink is already mixed with the metal flake and we can get the green for the backs, seals and serial numbers, so no fuckin' problem." T's confidence wasn't comforting to me although Frankie and Canevecchio were nodding with approval.

"I'll make a call and check out the plant site; Saturday night should be perfect," T continued.

Thankfully, T knew I was shittin' bricks and arranged it so I could separate from Frankie and Canevecchio for the rest of the day.

"So listen, you guys know who to see about the paper and ink. I'll call that guy and set it up for you this afternoon. The kid will stay with me for a while and we can go over a few last minute things about the print and he can hook up with you either at the plant or meet someplace before. Okay?" T had it all worked out.

Although I was still in a panic, I started to think it through.

"Hey listen, don't you have some tests this afternoon on your ticker?" I said to a surprised and somewhat confused T. He knew enough not to pull back and let me go with it.

"Yeah, I forgot about that," T said, making it sound a little too much like a question for comfort. But nobody picked up on it, so I went on.

"I thought the doctor said you would be upstairs in the lab most of the afternoon."

"Oh yeah, that's today? I sometimes forget I'm in da fuckin' hospital here; I'm just havin' so much fuckin' fun." T was all in now. He knew I was headed someplace with it and he was along for the ride. He closed the deal.

"Okay, you guys get goin' and I'll make the call. Between today and tomorrow we should be ready to print tomorrow night. I'll call you, *Ponte,* after I get done with the docs. Okay?"

"Okay. If I don't hear from you I'll call you tonight," Frankie said looking right at the telephone sitting on the table. "What's the number anyway?"

"Oh fuck," was all I could think of. The telephone was the line Carmine put in to loop T's home phone to the hospital room. It's the same number Miguel called on. How could we tell Frankie that it was the same number as T's house without him knowing something was wrong? So, as T just sat there completely lost, I tried to fix it.

"When you call the hospital, just ask for the room number and they'll connect you. I'm not sure how late you can call though." I was counting on TSD (technical support division) being able to get a line in there right away. We would have to figure something out for the undercover phone later.

Frankie nodded his head at my suggestion so I was relieved, feeling like we averted another calamity.

"Okay—get outta here. I gotta get ready for these prick doctors to do whatever it is they're gonna do," T commanded.

"Okay T, don't worry; we got it covered," Canevecchio reassured him in a tender voice and a pat on the shoulder.

Frankie just looked at me and said in a voice much less tender but nonetheless assuring, "We got it. *A più tarde* (See you later)." And they both walked out the door and headed for the elevator. I followed, carefully watching to see if Frankie was still checking out the EPS officer. He didn't. It all seemed cool for the moment.

When I went back into the room, T was sitting on the bed with both arms out with his palms up. "What's up with these tests and shit? You're scarin' me with all that talk. What the fuck's up?"

"Hey! I'm not ready for this print. I had to make an excuse to free you up today so we can run through it." T got a smile on his face as big as the ass on a 400-lb. hippo.

"We need a press. You gonna bring one in here?" T asked, knowing that wasn't going to happen.

"Don't get all wet on me now. I didn't say that I'm takin' you to a whorehouse. You're gonna have to work your ass off and show me how to pull off this print, or at least to start it and act like I have the foggiest idea about what I'm doin', which I don't. And don't forget, *paisan,* both our asses may depend on it. Gimme that phone. There's only one guy that's gonna pull our asses outta this fire."

CHAPTER 33

"TAKE OFF THE SUNGLASSES, JAKE."

IT WAS NEARLY 10 A.M. I was hopeful Carmine would be at the office.

"Com' on Carmine be there," I thought to myself. Then I heard his terse answer, "Perugi."

"Carmine, its Jake. I gotta talk to you."

"What's up?"

"Well, it looks like we gotta print Saturday night and the buyer insists on being there and closing the deal. Do you think I'll be able to pull this off with just a pretend print?" I asked, knowing the answer wasn't going to be what I wanted to hear.

"Not a snowball's chance in hell, not with this cat Frankie lookin' over your shoulder. He'll make you right away and close the entire caper down," he glibly responded.

Just listening to Carmine's voice usually calmed me down and gave me confidence; not this time. I felt like I was playing naked pin the tail on the donkey; I was dizzy and confused and horrified someone other than the donkey was going to get it in the ass—me. I also had a very clear feeling that Carmine knew things he wasn't telling me. I was sure he wanted this caper to succeed, but I sensed something was happening that he hadn't told me about.

"Okay, what now Batman?," I asked him, trying to keep my sense of humor and at the same time reminding him that I was now really feeling like the "Boy Wonder" and needed his help.

“Call me back in five minutes,” Carmine ordered.

“Roger.” I hung up the phone and exhaled the breath I was holding during the entire conversation. For five minutes, T and I didn’t exchange a single word. He walked to the window, which was open just a crack, and lit an unfiltered Lucky Strike. He exhaled only remotely in the direction of the open window. It was all just part of his life’s philosophy of “I don’t give a fuck about your rules.” The wait couldn’t have been any more uncomfortable if I was in the room with a constipated jackass; I knew it was only a matter of time before it got real messy. Finally, I picked up the phone and called Carmine back.

When he answered, he didn’t even say hello, but rather just barked instructions.

“Meet me at the back entrance to the Essex County Vo-Tech School on Harrison Avenue, Down-Neck. You know the place?”

”No, but I can find it. When?” I asked, trying to muster a confident sound.

”Right fuckin’ now. And bring T with you.” I wasn’t sure I heard him right, so I asked again and I got the same answer. T and I were going to take a little ride. I wasn’t sure what was happening, but because I had complete confidence in Carmine, I did what he said.

“Get dressed. We’re takin’ a ride,” I told T, who was just finishing his smoke. I thought he would be surprised, but he wasn’t. He and Carmine seemed to be receiving telepathic messages that set them both on the same course; it left me feeling like a tag along, which was okay with me for the moment. Hell, he didn’t even ask why or where we were going.

We were out the door in minutes. As soon as the EPS officer saw T step out of the door, he immediately jumped to his feet. It was the first sign of real life I saw from him. It actually made me feel like he was taking this painfully boring job seriously. I raised my right hand and just said, “Tests.” He got the message. He silently reached in his pocket, showed me a key and twisted his wrist as if he were locking the door. I nodded my head, agreeing with his suggestion and walked toward the elevator with T, knowing that his room would be locked and as far as the rest of the world was concerned, he was out getting some tests someplace else in the hospital. I came to appreciate how important the invisible cog is to the success of the machinery. I thought that kid was nobody in this and that I was a big shot. Now, the execution of his job could make the difference between success and failure of the entire caper. Especially if one of the players in this soap opera comes by looking for T.

We were down the elevator, out the emergency room door, and in the VW before T and I exchanged a word. I expected for sure that by this time T would have asked what was going on or at least where we were going. He didn't. Finally, I just had to ask.

"Aren't you interested in where we're going?" I was looking for some reaction from T.

"Listen, kid. In the end, I know full well where the fuck I'm goin', so any chance to get outta there and act like a man with a future and a life is okay with me, no matter where it is. So as long as I can get something to eat, I don't give a fuck." And then he added "So where the fuck we goin'? Go ahead, tell me."

"We're going back to school T, we're going back to school," was all I said.

"Hell, I'd rather go to jail," he responded in all seriousness.

It took us all of about twenty minutes to get Down-Neck or what some people call the Iron Bound section of Newark. It was where the Portuguese people lived. It was called the Iron Bound section because it was surrounded on all sides by railroad tracks and as a result, it developed as an insular part of the city where cops weren't especially welcome. Locals referred to it as "Down-Neck."

Inhabitants of the Iron Bound section were mostly blue-collar workers who produced a generation of Americans that moved up from their roots and took prominent positions in all professions. Literally hundreds of doctors, lawyers and business executives drove Down-Neck every Sunday to visit the family and attend the old churches. It was neighborhoods like this that produced the leaders who pulled America from the depths of the great depression, as well as the steel that freed the rest of the world from the tyranny of fascism in Europe and the Far East.

I was pretty sure that if I took McCarter Highway and then turned left onto Walnut, I would eventually run into Harrison. I was right. The only problem was, which way to go on Harrison. I turned right again and quickly learned that we were in the right place.

I had no idea there was a county school down there. But when I considered the area, it made sense to have a Vo-Tech school in a solid neighborhood like the Iron Bound section. The Essex County Vo-Tech School was located in a converted warehouse right there on Harrison Street. There were lots of buildings like this one in the area. Over the previous decades, enormous quantities of merchandise came through there on the freight trains that clogged the dozens of tracks that were its namesake. Much of the freight never made it to its final destination—hijacking was a favorite pastime of the local residents and regular visitors. It was an ingenious way for the less fortunate to share in the manufacturing might of America, without capital or a gun, during the difficult era of the twentieth century. Inevitably, a load could be had from a driver or night watchman for the mere offer of a "piece." Violence was for the drug dealers and street hoods that had neither the connections nor the imagination.

Even though there was a sign on Harrison, it wasn't clear where Carmine wanted to meet us. But, as I turned the corner on my way around the building, I saw his "G" car parked by a double, steel door entrance to the building. I pulled up, parked next to Carmine, and was about to raise him on the radio when the door to the building opened and I saw Carmine standing there. At first, I almost didn't recognize him because he was wearing a pair of jeans and a white tee-shirt. I don't think I ever saw Carmine in anything other than a suit, either before or since that day. He was a firm believer that you should always look like the quintessential Secret Service Agent.

It never dawned on me that Carmine never met T before. It was a good thing, because if it had, I would have been worried all the way over there. Carmine held the door while T and I got out of the VW, which was even more difficult for T than getting into it in the first place. Carmine nodded his head when he saw me and thereafter never took his eyes off T as we walked to the open door.

T went in first and started down the hall in front of us. Carmine grabbed me by the arm and drew me close to his face so he could whisper to me. He wanted to know why I would put T in the car without handcuffing him. I was stunned when Carmine mentioned it to me, not because I felt he was out of line or I disagreed with him. I was stunned because I actually did it and never even thought of cuffing him. I took this guy—a notorious counterfeiter and made member of the Mafia, who is facing a long prison sentence as a result of my investigation, out of the hospital alone and put him, un-cuffed, in my car, just like he was my Uncle Antonio. What was I thinking? I had no idea, but Carmine knew exactly what was happening.

Secret Service Agents are notorious for wearing dark sunglasses while on protection assignments. Whether the glasses really improve the agents ability to spot an assassin has never been established, but they do wonders for their persona. We would joke and remind each other not to forget to "wear your bullet proof sunglasses." We all knew what it meant. We were expected to take a bullet for someone else, if it came to that. Hell, while every other law enforcement organization on the planet is trained to shoot from the combat position—get low position, be a small target, set a 45-degree forward bend from the waist to create a natural ricochet angle with your rib cage, weapon out in front in your right hand and your left hand hanging between the perp and your nuts. If you take a bullet, it will at least strike your left hand and reduce your chances of becoming a gelding. But that's not what the Secret Service teaches. The Secret Service firefight position is stand tall, shoulders back, hold onto that .357 with both hands and be a human shield.

The only way you could emotionally survive in such an environment was to truly believe you were bullet proof, immortal, or just plain lucky. Sometimes that persona invaded other aspects of our work and even our private life. I never considered the possibility that I might be crushed to death in a head on with a tractor-trailer on the New Jersey Turnpike while driving a VW with the speedometer needle buried well past its top end. It wasn't even a matter of disregarding the danger—it just never occurred to me. Nor did I ever think that T would crush my skull with one of those bowling-ball fists of his and head for the old country rather than face a federal prison. I always had my Secret Service Sunglasses with me. They were either in the breast pocket of my suit, hanging from a little clip on the sun visor of the VW, or perched on top of my head even on a cloudy or rainy day when there wasn't a reason to use them as sun shades. And that day was no different.

"Take off the sunglasses, Jake." When Carmine uttered those words, I knew what I had done, and even began to understand why. I was learning so much during those days. So I took them off, but rested them on the top of my head, just in case. Hey, you never know.

CHAPTER 34

THE SECRET SERVICE GETS HIP

His point made, Carmine led the way from the old, steel, double doors down the hall to a large open room that looked like a myriad of machine shops found in so many factories in America during the early part of the twentieth century. The room was divided into sections with workbenches, tool chests and various projects, set in groupings around the room. In the far back section was a set of overhead garage doors in an area set up like a local auto repair shop, overhead hydraulic lift and all. Two '40s era cars were sitting there in different stages of disassembly. There was a tool and die area, a carpentry and electrical and plumbing section, and even a large ceramic press and kiln. Being a virile young man in America, I was immediately attracted to the automobile section. I took two steps in that direction and quickly learned I was alone in my curiosity. When I turned to see where T and Carmine were, I discovered why we were there in the first place.

In a far corner on the left side of the room was a behemoth of a machine. It was easily the largest piece of equipment in the room, it was even bigger and substantially heavier than the cars in the back. T was immediately attracted to it as Carmine hung back by the entrance obviously waiting for something. Once I realized it was there, I walked in its direction, not taking my eyes off it for a second. It's a wonder I didn't trip and fall on some of the tools left on the floor, but I just had to watch the machine carefully. I was actually afraid it would jump to life and devour us all—it looked so menacing.

T slowly and ponderously walked around the monster as if he were stalking it for the kill. Because it was genuinely huge, there was actually a wooden step and platform so you could stand next to it and operate the controls. "MEIHLE, 1950" was stamped in bold raised letters on the side. It didn't say "printing press" anywhere on it, but it didn't have to for T; he obviously recognized it immediately. Eventually I figured out what it was, but the education was just beginning.

"Dig it. Daddy-0. Ever see anything like her?"

A deep voice echoed around the room. I looked up, only half sure I heard the English language spoken when I saw a tall, lanky guy standing next to Carmine. He had to be 6 feet, 5 inches and couldn't have weighed more than 150 pounds. While his stature was somewhat unique, his overall appearance was, in that time and place, positively jolting. He sported a black beret perfectly cocked on the side of his long, thin head. A pair of black, square-framed glasses hung from his generous nose, while a perfectly trimmed, three-point goatee covered his weak, shallow chin. All this topped off a long-sleeved, black, turtleneck shirt that hung from his virtually shoulder-less torso, with a pair of black stovepipe pants that over stated his skinny legs and made his huge sandal-clad feet appear like caricatures. His overall appearance, although odd, was not unattractive. He, however, did have an unfiltered cigarette, probably a Chesterfield, hanging from the right side of his lips, which was the certain cause of the black-spotted teeth that overfilled his mouth. If his appearance didn't shout out "Beatnik," it became undeniable when he spoke.

"Carmine, you're the cat's meow, fuzz man, but who are these cool cats, Daddy-0?"

While this strange guy was doing the talking, Carmine was making all the faces. He looked directly at both T and I for the express purpose of seeing our reaction. And frankly, while I had heard of the "Beat" generation, I never actually met a full-fledged member before. I was also certain guys like this had no place in T's universe. Carmine, with a wide smile on his face, did the introductions.

"Fellas, this is Abe, Abe Leibman. He's the Vo-Tech teacher here and he's gonna help us get Jake ready for this print."

"Christ, he's a fuckin Heeb. What the fuck can he know?" T said in a voice that certainly wasn't intended to avoid insulting our new Jewish, beatnik friend, who was, however, clearly able to hold his own with T.

"Well, even though JC was a real cool cat man, you need a hipster whose bag is printing, baby, and I don't mean that dullsville day rag and magazine stuff. You gotta be in the groove to print Green, Daddy-0...know what I mean, jelly bean?" And he recited all this to the rhythmic snapping of his right thumb and forefinger. In between snaps, he was taking such huge drags on his Chesterfield that he had to close his right eye to keep the smoke from blinding him.

"Just who the fuck are you?" T asked in a condescending tone that made it abundantly clear this was now a personal challenge. Carmine stepped in to settle the score.

"Guys, like I told you, this is Abraham Saul Leibman," Carmine began, but was interrupted for clarification.

"That's right Daddy-0, but you fuzz can call me Ron Ron,"

Carmine continued, "That's right and just between us Fuzz, Ron Ron here is amply qualified to help us do this. If ever asked about this conversation, I will certainly deny it. But 'His Coolness' here was single-handedly responsible for the c.3663 note," Carmine said, with a very serious look on his face. He knew the significance of his statement, as did both T and I.

The 3663 note was the most infamous Federal Reserve Note ever counterfeited. Every agent as well as every would-be counterfeiter was thoroughly familiar with it. The c.3663 note was a quantum leap in the counterfeiting of US currency by a private, nongovernmental entity. It had been printed on commercial Double Eagle Bonded Paper from photo engraved plates, on a commercial offset printing press, much like the Meihle menacing us that day. The basic black front was printed in the appropriate metal-flake black ink and the basic back was printed in customary green ink.

There were, however, two dramatic distinctions between the c.3663 and all other counterfeit notes, printed either before or even after the c.3663. The genius who printed the c.3663 ran the paper through the press two extra times before he began the basic front and back print. The first print imposed very small red lines on the paper while the second pass complimented the red lines with blue ones, all-in-all, a very successful imitation of the red and blue fibers found in authentic currency paper. The second distinction involved more work.

Most counterfeits are made with only one serial number. That's because it takes time and enormous talent to print the green serial number over the black basic front of the note and cut it in over the black Treasury Seal so it doesn't look muddled and amateurish. The c.3663 had more than 100 separate and distinct serial numbers. The counterfeiter successfully burned 100 different serial number plates which he printed and expertly cut in over the black Treasury Seal, such that bank teller after bank teller swore the notes were genuine. It was a masterpiece of deception and craft. To top it all off, he put the notes through an aging process that made them virtually impossible to distinguish from genuine. The process was so convincing that it was never disclosed to anyone by the Secret Service.

The Secret Service never claimed to catch the c.3663 printer. It just stopped showing up in circulation one day. Rumors were that it was an inside job; either a Secret Service Agent or someone at The Bureau of Printing and Engraving was the printer. That's why when Carmine said Beatnik Ron Ron here was responsible for the c.3663, both T and I were all ears. While we were recovering from the shocking revelation, Carmine decided that he needed to get us refocused on why we were all there.

"Listen, we don't have a lot of time, so there's some ink and a set of offset plates here on the table," pointing to a cardboard box sitting on a metal table next to the press. "Why don't you two guys," pointing to Ron Ron and T, "get acquainted and figure out how you can prepare Jake in the next four hours to pull this caper off. And also, do it without making me put a bullet in both your asses. Can you two guys do that for me? I need to talk to Jake for just a couple of minutes. Okay?"

There was no response from T. He was still staring at Ron Ron in utter amazement.

"Smokin,' Daddy-0, smokin'," Ron Ron said as he dropped his cigarette on the cement floor just ahead of his size 13 sandals, crushing what little was left of it as he headed for the cardboard box.

Carmine gave me a little nod of the head and I followed him into a small office that adjoined the shop room. There was a large stationary window in the wall between the office and the shop so we could talk without being heard by T and Ron Ron but we could also keep an eye on them just in case a war of the worlds broke out.

Before I settled in the conversation, I watched the interaction between T and Ron Ron. Their progress was initially slow, but they became more engaged as they opened the box and examined T's plates. It was like being at the zoo and watching a tiger and an antelope together, hoping they would mate and make a tigerlope. You had to just keep watching and try to visualize how it would happen, while hoping for the best no matter how unlikely the outcome.

The office was just big enough to hold a bookshelf and an honest to goodness teacher's desk, just like the ones I remembered sitting in front of throughout my grade school years. This one had seen lots of school days. It was covered with scratched-in initials and little hearts forever holding young love dear. There were, however, a couple of things I never saw on any of my teachers' desk.

"Hey Carmine, what are these doing here?" I asked, as I picked up a set of drumsticks that were sitting on the top of the desk. They were really beat up and scarred about one-third up each stick from hard shots to the steel rim around the snare drum head.

"Ron Ron's a jazz drummer," Carmine said without even looking up. I just rolled my eyes because the entire experience was getting weirder by the minute.

I was dying to hear more about Ron Ron and his involvement

in the c.3663 note; it was a major topic of conversation in Secret Service training. They told us that the counterfeiter was never identified and that the note just disappeared. How could this be if the counterfeiter is in the next room wearing a beret? And why isn't he in jail? It made no sense to me. I needed an explanation from Carmine, so I asked. "Hey Carmine, is that ditz really responsible for the c.3663?"

"He certainly is and by the way that's not for publication anyplace else," Carmine replied.

"I don't get it. Why isn't he in jail, and why did headquarters tell us in training that the 3663 printer was never identified?"

"Look, when we finally caught up to him and found out he was a Vo-Tech teacher as well as an honest to God beatnik, we had a couple of choices we didn't have with a mob guy. Ron Ron is a genuine genius, no shit. He could really care less about the money. He was in it for the action, the challenge and the ability to laugh right out loud at the big bad government and all the 'squares' out there spending their lives chasing his buck."

Carmine was laying it out, but I still didn't understand why this numb-nut wasn't in the slammer. I let him continue hoping it would make sense to me in the end.

"We finally got a break in the case when Ron Ron just couldn't keep his mouth shut at some Greenwich Village pot fest. He had to tell somebody and lucky for us he told some chic who told her brother who then thought he could make a few bucks with a reward from Uncle Sam. He did, and we caught Ron Ron green handed as we say." Carmine obviously wasn't finished, so I kept my mouth shut and continued to listen.

"So, when we got him, we decided we could either prosecute him and put him in jail—criminal university—where he would probably make all the contacts he needed to become a better counterfeiter, but even worse, hold class for all the wannabes in the joint. Or we could just hold the hammer over his head and make him work for us. So we put him on the payroll. Now he's like an independent consultant who helps us with new notes at times like this. It's worked out pretty well, but only a few of us even know about him. Not even the US Attorney knows."

"Wow," was all I could say. I was really impressed that an organization like the Secret Service could think out of the box like that and really make a smart play. While I was really interested in Ron Ron's story, I could tell that Carmine brought me into that room for some other reason. He was carrying a closed manila folder under his arm that he slapped onto the desktop. A new conversation began.

"What's up Carmine? How we doin'?"

"Well, I guess we're doin' okay, considering."

"Considering what?" I asked, getting a little nervous that I fucked up again.

"You ready for this print?" he asked. I somehow knew he wasn't looking for a confident, "yes."

"I feel okay. I guess I'll be better prepared after frick and frack out there do their magic."

"Do you think you know enough about T and his guys to hunker down in a room someplace with them, a few million dollars in counterfeit, and nearly a million in good for sixteen hours or so and come outta there alive...and make the bust?"

I felt like a waitress who had just been called to a diner's table and saw half-chewed apple pie spit up all over the table. I knew I was about to get an ear-full, and I was pretty sure it wasn't going to be complimentary. So I braced my ego.

"What's wrong, Carmine?"

"We didn't do enough homework. What do you know about these guys—Frankie and Canevecchio?

When he asked the same question for a second time, I knew why there was pie all over the table. It didn't taste right to Carmine's experienced pallet. I could only try to learn what he was feeling.

"Not much Carmine. I guess not enough, huh?"

"We both dropped the ball here, kid. I was so wrapped up in the intrigue of it all that I didn't look at these guys close enough either. After all, I'm the counterfeit squad leader, but, I did try to catch up," he said apologetically and continued.

"This guy Canevecchio is an old timer. He made his bones thirty years ago as a kid running numbers and working prostitution. A fairly-square wise guy, if you know what I mean. Not dangerous—at least not anymore, kind of semi-retired. He's like an older brother to this guy Frankie—Francesco Battistini. He's the problem." Carmine paused and dug into his envelope.

"Is this Canevecchio?" he asked as he dropped a classic 8" x 10" black and white mug shot of Canevecchio on the table, numbers across the chest and all.

"Yup. That's him, a lot younger and a whole lot thinner, but that's him." I could see the mug shot was nearly twenty-five years old. "Was that his last pop?" I asked, a little surprised his last run-in with the law was so long ago.

"Yup. How about this guy? Is this Frankie?" Carmine casually inquired as he dropped a hand grenade on the desk.

In reality, it was an 8" X 10" photograph of Frankie that might as well have been a hand grenade. The photo was about twenty years old, based on his youthful look. He was a real heartthrob. He could have been competition for Sinatra with all those Jersey girls in the Hoboken neighborhood. But it wasn't his chiseled face and engaging smile that was incendiary.

"What is this Carmine?" I was asking the obvious, but I needed to start someplace.

"Well, it's an official press picture of our guy in 1945," he said.

"So I guess he was in the military," I stated more than asked, because the picture was obviously of Frankie in a US Army uniform. I recognized that easily enough. But it was the circumstances of his service that needed clarifying. So, I just kept asking stupid questions.

"Talk to me Carmine. I don't seem to be getting it and what do you mean, 'press photo'?" As Carmine began to unravel the tale, I struggled to find oxygen in the room.

"See these ribbons on his chest? They're campaign combat ribbons from World War II," Carmine began at a slow deliberate pace.

There were only a few, so I wasn't overly impressed, at least not then—that was yet to come

"This guy was there on D-Day. Not only was he there, but he was there before everybody else was there," he continued as he began to ramp it up.

I was listening closer and breathing deeper.

"Before our troops landed on the beaches in Normandy, the

paratrooper units jumped behind the German lines to cut off reinforcements to the beachheads. You know, blow up bridges, cut telephone lines, derail trains—stuff like that. Well, even before the paratroopers jumped, an elite group of 'Pathfinders' jumped into France all by themselves. It was their job to connect with the French resistance, light up the drop zones and be there when the main force of paratroopers jumped. That's why he's wearing a Bronze Star on the jump wings pinned on his chest," Carmine explained in an excited voice while pointing to the medal on Frankie's chest.

"There are two Bronze Stars on his jump wings and by the way—what's that thing around his neck?" I asked, sensing there was more to the story. I thought I was sufficiently impressed, until Carmine went on.

"The second Bronze Star is there because he made a second combat jump. That's where it all began. In September 1944, he jumped again with the 101st Airborne Division—the Screaming Eagles. This time into Holland, as part of a hare-brained scheme called Operation Market Garden. Their orders were to capture a bridge at a place in Holland called Eindhoven. The fighting was insane. The Krauts knew the allies were closing in. The bridge was wired with explosives and a lot of American boys were gonna die unless some extremely brave souls went out onto the bridge and deactivated the charges. Our guy took the lead, so the story goes, and was almost single-handedly responsible for securing the bridge and saving a shit load of American lives."

I interrupted Carmine as he was telling the story, while never taking his eyes off the photograph of Frankie. "How is it that you know so much about all this, Carmine?"

"It's history kid and it's not often that you get to meet one of these guys," he replied.

"What guys? What are you talking about?" I didn't understand what it all meant, especially to a member of the World War II generation like Carmine.

Carmine looked up from the photograph. While softly placing two fingers of his right hand on the photo as if trying to keep the connection, he lifted his head, raised his eyebrows and completed the story.

"Jake, that thing around his neck is the CMH—the Congressional Medal of Honor. It was given to him personally, by President Truman."

I had no response. I just looked down at the photograph and stared at the ribbon—13 white stars on a blue field, with a large, five-point gold star hanging below. I actually looked over my shoulder for a place to sit because I felt weak in the knees, but there wasn't a chair in the room. I tried to focus on what Carmine said and understand what it meant to the caper and us. Some things became clearer; some didn't.

"Holy Shit. That explains a lot. That's why they call him *Ponte*. *Ponte* is 'bridge' in Italian and that's why every man in the bar wanted to shake his hand and buy him a drink. Jesus Carmine, how do we arrest a guy like this? Jesus."

"I don't know Jake. I just don't know."

"And why would a hero like this even be involved in a counterfeiting caper? It doesn't make sense. He's a patriot. He risked his life for his country and now he's involved in this, with these guys. I just don't understand...I just don't understand." It was all beginning to settle in and I was becoming anxious for answers.

Carmine seemed unable to take his eyes off the picture. In fact, as he sat on the corner of the desk, he spread out both of them, Frankie's and Canevecchio's, as if he were going to interrogate them and get some answers. In reality, he was searching his own heart and soul trying to arrive at a solution. I didn't interrupt him. He just looked at the pictures, moved them around a bit and reviewed some papers he had in the folder.

My own mind was frantic, rethinking every move, look and word I got from Frankie since the first time I laid eyes on him. It just confirmed to me why I always felt there was something special about him, something different from T and Canevecchio; everybody else who knew him felt it also. However, I needed help with the "why" part of the mystery. Carmine knew it all along, in his heart, and he was trying to figure out how to articulate it to me. It wasn't long before he looked up and shared his thoughts.

"Ya know, Jake, I think you're wrong about this guy. He's not a patriot in the sense you're thinking, because he never risked his life for his country. I don't think that's the way it was."

"Why would you say that? How can you say he didn't risk his life for his country? Look at what he did," I responded, because I was now really confused. Carmine tried to put it in words I would understand.

"I'm sure this guy risked his life without even a thought about his country. He wouldn't think in terms like that. He risked his life to protect the men to his left and right. The men he bled with and crawled through the mud with. His world revolves in a very tight spiral, like a well-thrown touchdown pass. He's not concerned with the big picture. He could care less—he's concerned for his *paisani*, the men he considers his brothers. There was no fuckin' way he was going to let those guys die on that bridge if he had anything to say about it. I'll also bet dollars-to-donuts that this is the only day he ever wore this medal. The respect of his *paisani* is all he wanted. God, I bet he sleeps great at night."

The words came out of Carmine's mouth like drops of rain on a spring day. The truth of his words was unavoidable. I stood silent, remembering the way Canevecchio looks at Frankie and always defers to him. It also explains why Frankie looks after Canevecchio. He's a God to all of them, including T. It also finally answered the big question.

"And that's why he's involved in this caper. His boys need his help and he's there for them. I'll bet he could give a shit about the money. Jesus, no wonder this is so hard for T." I finally got it.

"Yup," was all Carmine said, now holding the photograph in his hand.

"What now Carmine?" I asked, now emotionally drained and confused.

"We forge ahead kid. Remember we took an oath of our own. And there's this guy Miguel out there who just ordered up a huge counterfeit print. We can be sure he's up to no fuckin' good and it's our job to stop him no matter where it takes us. If our *paisani* here get into bed with this guy, it's at their peril."

There just wasn't anything more to say, and we still had frick and frack in the next room to deal with. We also had to get me back on track and get ready for the pending print. Carmine carefully put the photographs back in the folder and we both went out into the shop to see if T and Ron Ron had come to blows yet.

Much to our astonishment, we found the two of them happily tinkering with the press. Not only were they not fighting, they were now fast friends. Evidently, they each discovered that the other had something unique to contribute to my education. They had already inked the press wheel, installed the back plate and were preparing to start the run. Carmine had to remind them that it was important to teach me how to run the press from the very beginning. They realized that they had rushed ahead, so they needed to start again, right from mixing the ink. Ron Ron developed a little hardener additive that he assured us would help the commercial ink we used match spot-on with the color of the ink The Bureau of Printing and Engraving used. He gave me a jar and insisted that I be sure to mix two heaping tablespoons into the ink mix on every run.

For the next six hours we all worked together to get me up to speed. In the end, with my hands covered in black and green ink, I was gaining confidence because I knew I was being schooled by two of the best counterfeiters in the world. And while I was still very much conflicted and confused over what I learned that day about Frankie, I was as ready as I would ever be to pull off the caper.

It was a very long and emotionally challenging day. We all bid farewell to Ron Ron, thanking him and reassuring him that he was real groovy. Carmine offered to take T back to the hospital; I knew it was much more than an offer. I happily declared my exhaustion and let him take him. As I drove away, I saw him cuffing T before putting him in the car. While I was a good half-a-block away, I thought I could still hear T say, “Ahh, what the fuck” as the cuffs twinkled in the streetlights just coming on. I went home to try to get some sleep and just put the entire day out of my mind for a while. Not for a second was I successful.

CHAPTER 35

"HOW ABOUT IT HAR, CAN YOU HELP THIS OLD DOG HUNT?"

"Al Whitaker from The FBI is on the telephone, Mr. O'Malley," the small intercom box sitting on the corner of the desk said in a soft gentle voice that was difficult to associate with the flat, curve-less cube.

Harry O'Malley was sitting in a relatively small office with a beautiful view of perfectly straight rows of newly planted Sunset Maple Trees. He could see several of them in various stages of autumn rapture just outside the large window in his office. The still-green lawn was littered with orange and red casualties of the Fall chill. It wasn't surprising that he had a view like that, inasmuch as his modest-sized office was located in one of the most beautiful and now famous small Virginia suburbs of Washington, DC. It was a comfortable setting in a building barely two years old, intentionally located in a college campus-like setting by the former DCI (Director of Central Intelligence) Allen Dulles.

Harry enjoyed the view; it helped make the seventy-hour workweeks more tolerable. Calls like the one he was about to take from a colleague whose friendship and trust he valued were often the highlight of an otherwise remorseful day. He took one long, last drag on his filtered Marlboro and put it out in the cluttered ashtray on his desk. He was been a chain smoker for as long as he could remember; it helped him cope with the long, sedentary hours spent at his desk poring over intelligence reports.

Reaching for the phone, Harry knew he could talk to his friend and colleague on this line because it was electronically scrambled and therefore secure for classified conversations. The line was set up in Harry's office because he was Special Liaison Officer between CIA and The FBI. He was "in the know" on all concurrent matters between the agencies and then some. The "then some" meant that it was Harry's job to spy on The FBI and protect CIA from any embarrassing entanglements. He did, however, like and respect Al Whitaker, even though he was a "cop." He would have made a great intelligence officer if The Bureau hadn't gotten him first. Harry was always eager to help his friend of over the past twenty years.

"Alfonso, how are you? I haven't heard from you in a couple of weeks. You takin' me to lunch or is it that your tired old career of playing cops and robbers needs a jump start?"

"You know, that's why I love calling you. I forgot. Tell me again. Why is it that I love calling?" Whitaker responded.

The banter between the two of them usually continued until one of them decided that it was time to get serious because there was an important reason for the call in the first place. This time it was Whitaker who turned the conversation serious.

"Hey Har,' what do you know about a Cuban in the States working a Hungarian family in New Jersey along with a connection to a new counterfeit $100 FRN that just broke in Las Vegas?"

A lot of the information Al was sharing with Harry was completely unverified. The specific information about the counterfeit note and the Las Vegas connection was only whispered in his ear by a member of the "mini-skirt telegraph"—the most reliable inside information network in The FBI—that Al Whitaker didn't hesitate to use in a pinch.

Since Whitaker was handed 23 Foxtrot's commission book, he couldn't rest until he had all the poop on the operation. He knew that trying to get the straight scoop from regular Bureau channels was like trying to watch the World Series in Washington, while it was being played in New York, by sticking your head out your window and squinting real hard. All you'd get would be a bad headache, with no chance of catching a foul ball. That's why Al went to Grace, Ritter's secretary, when he wanted the skinny. Now he was on the phone with Harry for the real deal.

There was a large contingent of women like Grace who had been working at The Bureau for decades. Some of them even started with The Director himself. They genuinely believed that responsibility for the health of The Bureau belonged to them as much as to the Bureaucratic sycophants; they were the den mothers who looked after them all. That's why when Whitaker told Grace that he smelled a rat in the 23 Foxtrot operation, she knew exactly where to go. Experience taught that a firm figure and a well-placed mini-skirt beat the hell out of a rubber hose any day. The "mini-skirt telegraph" was truly the world's first wireless network. It was connected to every floor and office in The Bureau, from the mailroom to The Director's office. In just a day or two, Grace had parlayed with all her sister stations and had reported the straight scoop back to Whitaker.

This was how Whitaker knew there was a Cuban connected to a Hungarian connected to a new counterfeit note connected to Las Vegas. He had lots of who's and what's, but none of the why's or how's. It was like having all the nouns of a novel, but without any of the verbs or adjectives. Even the mini-skirt *telegraph* couldn't ferret out those answers, but Whitaker was willing to bet that his friend Harry O'Malley at CIA could.

"What's the matter Al, you kids at The Bureau not playing nice again; not want to share and share alike?" O'Malley said, just unable help himself from breaking Whitaker's balls.

The truth was, that even though O'Malley and Whitaker got along famously, there was no love lost, or even misplaced for that matter, between The FBI and CIA. CIA never got over the fact that those wimps in Congress gave the responsibility for conducting foreign counter intelligence, within the borders of the United States, to The FBI. Having sprung from the head of General "Wild Bill" Donovan and the OSS at the end of the Second World War—like Athena the goddess of wisdom and battle, sprung from the head of

Zeus—CIA was the expected choice for the assignment. Problem was, the OSS did too good a job of spying on everybody, including our allies, and even ourselves. Congress felt much safer giving the domestic surveillance job to the fledgling FBI, a decision almost everyone in the country came to regret.

"How about it Har', can you help this old dog hunt?" Whitaker asked without letting him know how serious it was. But O'Malley knew just by the tone of his voice, let alone the subject matter of the inquiry.

"I can tell you this, my friend: there's no Hungarian-Cuban pair on the dance floor, never has been, that we know of. They're just not a likely couple, if you know what I mean," O'Malley began.

Whitaker could hear O'Malley lighting up and dragging on a fresh new cigarette. He just waited and hoped for more, and there was.

"We've heard of the new note coming out of Las Vegas though. The Secret Service is on it," Harry continued.

"That's it? Nothing happening with the Cubans?" Whitaker was getting fidgety now. There was a long pause, even without O'Malley taking a drag on his cigarette. He crushed the butt in the ashtray along with his reluctance to tell it all to Whitaker.

"Okay, listen. A Castro bullet shot through Key West a couple of weeks or so ago. The source hasn't been posted, but we believe he's high octane. And we know this for sure—this bullet is no counterfeiter. He's a real deal 'Jerry Lee.' Got it?"

It always annoyed Whitaker that you practically needed a codebook to understand the spooks at CIA. He knew enough about the lingo, however, to understand that O'Malley was confirming CIA had what they thought was first-rate information about a Cuban agent recently coming into the States through Key West. Describing this agent as a real deal "Jerry Lee" was a reference to the rock and roller Jerry Lee Lewis. His nickname in the music world is "The Killer." O'Malley was telling Whitaker that they were sure this agent wasn't a counterfeiter, but rather an assassin.

O'Malley continued, "Al, listen to me. This guy is a very dangerous player, who, as far as we can tell, is on a very special mission. Frankly, we have never seen this kind of play come from Cuba before. It's a rare move, even for Castro. I don't know what you guys have on the stove, but if you have a source in close, be very careful. You might even consider pulling your agent out until you're sure he's not burned or at least we know what that fuck Castro is up to."

"Thanks, Har'." Whitaker was short with his goodbye. He knew who his next conversation was going to be with.

CHAPTER 36

23 FOXTROT, NINER, NINER, ECHO GETS A GUARDIAN ANGEL

Al Whitaker was standing and heading for the door even before he hung up the phone with Harry O'Malley at CIA. Normally, he would call upstairs and see if The Director was available to see him—not this morning. This morning, Al Whitaker was having a very serious conversation with The Director whether he liked it or not. It was at times like this that Al's long-standing relationship with The Director paid off. It literally opened the door to his office. Not only did both men go back decades together—they both had a clear understanding of who they were, how their relationship fit together, and that they both possessed undying dedication to The FBI.

The Director was the man with the actual power and authority. And while there were agents and possibly Congressmen who were intimidated and even fearful of him, Whitaker wasn't. And The Director knew it. It's for this reason that Al Whitaker didn't even stop at the secretary's desk to be announced. He literally burst into The Director's office like the building was on fire and he was the fire chief. The secretary outside didn't even try to stop him. She knew all too well that she would have had better luck stopping an 18-wheeler by dragging her high heels on the carpet. Al was also prepared for his invasion, because he knew exactly what The

Director would be doing and with whom he would be doing it with at that time of the morning.

"We have to talk," was all he said, as he threw open the double, mahogany doors to the inner office and practically galloped across the huge room where he plopped himself in one of the two overstuffed leather chairs in front of The Director's desk. He never even acknowledged the Assistant Director, who was perched in the matching chair sipping on a delicate cup of chamomile tea.

Unfazed by Whitaker's actions, AD gave him a very sarcastic "Well, good morning Senior Special Agent Whitaker," without even looking at him and certainly not expecting a cordial response.

Whitaker knew that AD would be there having morning tea with The Director, but he just didn't care. He also knew exactly how The Director would respond to his intrusion, and he did just that. He said absolutely nothing. He didn't even flinch when the doors were thrown open with a bang. He just continued to sip his tea looking deeply into his Lenox cup.

"Good morning Al, how's the family?" The Director asked in a very calm, steady voice. Whitaker just forged ahead.

"23 Foxtrot, Niner, Niner, Echo," was all Whitaker responded.

AD replaced his cup onto the saucer with a clank. The Director, while not as hostile was obviously surprised at the subject matter of the visit.

"Jesus Christ, why the fuck is everybody so interested in this 23 Foxtrot all of a sudden?" he asked with a serious edge to his tone.

The Director's response absolutely astounded Whitaker and was equally as alarming to AD, who was also a very special friend to The Director. The response itself told Whitaker that it was a good thing he made the trip that day. There was obviously something very hot on the stove and Whitaker had not been invited into the kitchen. Now he wanted to know who the cook was and where did the recipe come from. AD, on the other hand, was apoplectic that The Director would be the smoke alarm and might tell Whitaker that there was a fire in the kitchen. Whitaker did not respond. He just waited for The Director to continue; he knew he would.

"Well?" The Director sang in the direction of his Assistant.

"The file is on your desk," AD said, knowing full well what The Director wanted, simply from the tone of his voice.

But that wasn't good enough for The Director. AD was expected to get up, find the file, put in his hand, and he did just that. He didn't sit back down, but rather moved to the side of The Director's desk and stood quietly where he could eyeball both The Director and Whitaker simultaneously.

The Director opened the file. Whitaker recognized the file as a personnel file, which contained a photo of the agent on the left and personnel and assignment information on the right. The Director initially looked at the photo and without going any further, said in a strong, demanding tone aimed squarely at AD, "What the hell is this?"

"We thought it was necessary," was his timid response.

"WE thought?"

"I thought it would be best in this situation," AD responded ignoring the sarcasm.

"Christ All Mighty—look at the hair—everywhere. You're not going to tell me that's regulation in the new FBI that you're building behind my back, is it?

There was no response because AD knew The Director wasn't asking a question. If he wanted to know more, he would ask him later when no one else was present. Whitaker, feeling like he was in the middle of a lover's quarrel, which he was, knew that too. So he ignored both of their statements and focused the discussion on the real reason he burst through the doors in the first place.

"Director, regardless of the details, I have good reason to believe this undercover agent is in harm's way," Whitaker said, while looking for a reaction from either of them, especially AD, which he got as expected.

"You have not been invited into the kitchen of this operation, Senior Special Agent Whitaker," AD retorted as he now breathlessly continued looking directly at The Director. "We discussed this. I just learned that 23 Foxtrot has made contact with the Cuban Rabbit..."

"Cuban Rabbit!" Whitaker leapt to his feet, interrupting him in mid-sentence. "He's no fuckin' Rabbit. He's a fuckin' cold blooded 'Jerry Lee.'"

The Director, while keeping his eyes on 23 Foxtrot's file, extended the forefinger of his right hand at Whitaker and then at the leather chair he just shot out of. He then did the same to AD, pointing to the other chair in front of his desk. Both men took their seats.

Looking at Whitaker, The Director asked, "Are you sure about this Al? How good is your source?"

"Good enough to come up here. Why is a top level FCI dish on the stove without me in the kitchen? Who's cooking this meal?" Whitaker asked already knowing the answer.

The Director didn't respond. He flashed a look at AD who did not appear surprised at Whitaker's revelations.

"Jesus...," Whitaker stopped just short of referring to The Director by his given name—something he never did when discussing official business—although in reality he knew The Director longer than nearly anyone in The Bureau, including AD. But he also knew AD was the only person in The FBI that called him by his given name. Their very special relationship was no secret in headquarters.

"Look...AD is a cock sucker. That's why he's here," Whitaker bellowed while pointing across the small round table at the chair next to him. "He's not equipped to run an operation with a Cuban 'Jerry Lee.' That's why I'm here."

The Director smiled wide at the cocksucker remark. He considered Whitaker a friend and took no offense. AD on the other hand, wasn't at all amused.

"Yes he is Al, yes he is," The Director responded, not saying whether he was responding to AD's status as a cocksucker or his qualifications to run the case. Whitaker didn't care; he was still charging straight ahead.

"We need to immediately reassess this hunt and see if we need to get this agent out, or at least change the recipe, even add some salt and pepper (additional agents to the case)," Whitaker said with authority.

"What makes you think we haven't done that already, Senior Special Agent Whitaker?" responded AD, in a condescending tone, after which he turned his attention back to The Director.

"I told you we have just made contact with the Cuban agent, whatever he is. We know Castro is trying to raise him through the KGB, only they aren't sure where he is at the moment. We have the message and we are making a move to get it delivered and turn up the heat on the Cuban. We're driving the bus right now. As far as 23 Foxtrot is concerned, we can assess that situation at a later time."

"When later? When we have a dead agent to explain? And for what? What the fuck are we cookin' with a Cuban 'Jerry Lee'? And what's the message we're delivering to this fuckin' killer? Since when are we mailmen for that fuckin' commie prick Castro?" Whitaker kept asking, while not waiting for an answer to any of his questions.

The Director slightly nodded his head authorizing AD to tell Whitaker the message. Even though he didn't visibly disagree with the order, AD didn't want to tell Whitaker because, unlike The Director, he did not want to bring Whitaker into the fold. However, he reluctantly told Whitaker—confident it would mean nothing to him without the background only AD knew.

"Castro wants his agent to drop the counterfeiting operation and go to New Orleans to connect with a group of pro-Castro organizers. For what, we don't know yet," he said while looking up from his tea cup.

Whitaker thought for a second and responded, "How do we know that wasn't Castro's plan all along? He could have enticed the agent's enthusiasm into the deal with the promise of a big payoff intending to divert him at the last minute to a killing field. That would also keep all of us off guard, including the Secret Service, who thinks they're just working a run-of-the-mill counterfeiting caper."

Now, looking straight at The Director, Al continued; "This could be a very serious move. We need to climb all over this right away."

At that point, The Director didn't know himself what was happening, although he did suspect that AD wasn't giving him the entire recipe. And, although he trusted him and didn't believe he would ever do anything to damage The Bureau, he decided to open the kitchen door and let Whitaker see what was cooking.

"Okay, here's what's gonna happen. I want both of you two to cook this up. I don't know what's going on. I think you're both right. I think we've got a pretty good handle on it, but I don't like how it smells and I think that we can't afford to lose 23 Foxtrot, especially after we made this move in the first place. So, you keep cooking this thing, but I want Al in the kitchen, especially to look after 23 Foxtrot. If things get too smoky, Al, you can be the hero and do a fireman's carry and get 23 Foxtrot outta there. I also don't want any sniveling about who's in charge. Work it out. Understand?"

Both men, knowing The Director had made his decision and the matter was now settled, said nothing.

"Now both of you get the fuck-outta here. I'm fuckin' exhausted," The Director ordered with a knuckles-up wave of the hand toward the door.

CHAPTER 37

TOMATO PIE, BASEBALL AND THE FBI

The door buzzer to Miguel's apartment was about as annoying as a drunken old aunt at Easter dinner with the in-laws, but the message it carried was warm and wonderful.

Miguel dropped Azzimie off at his apartment after their visit to the bowling alley and told him he would see him first thing in the morning. He figured he had him both scared enough and enticed enough to stay close, at least until he knew where this was all going. Miguel never explained to him about the timing of the print. He knew that Azzimie thought there was just a single print and that Miguel was sitting on another stash of product, hidden someplace else other than in Marilyn. It was both the fear and the greed that enabled Miguel to play him real hard. But right now, Miguel was just tired and he knew, after his short telephone conversation with T that he had a very busy weekend ahead of him.

Even though he had a few beers at the bowling alley, Miguel now wanted what he knew he would soon have to do without—a New Jersey Tomato Pie. Not that run of the mill pizza slop you can get just anywhere, but that special Jersey blend of fresh tomato sauce, cheese and extra thin crust. There are important and significant differences between pizza and tomato pie. First, the sauce is completely different. The sauce on a pizza is really only half-a-step above ketchup, while the sauce on a tomato pie is made with fresh chopped tomatoes that are lightly marinated with olive oil and garlic, so the rich, wholesome taste of the Jersey tomato emerges. And the crust? The crust on a tomato pie is as thin as the maker can pull it. It's cooked in an extremely hot oven until it's golden brown and crispy. If properly made, it's so thin and crispy you can eat three times more tomato pie than doughy pizza.

Miguel already had the money in his hand as he quick-stepped to the front door in response to the buzzer. He could almost smell the fresh, hot tomato pie on the other side of the door. And sure enough—when he opened the door, without even peeping to see who it was—he wasn't disappointed. Although the young man standing at his door was a complete stranger, Miguel's anticipation could not have been any greater if it were a beautiful woman in a negligee. He always loved tomato pie and one of the few places on the planet to get the genuine real deal is in New Jersey. Miguel knew that in a couple of days his entire life would change, and the chances of him returning to Jersey in the near future were slim-to-none. Therefore, this tomato pie was going to be very special. He had no idea how right he was.

The switch of the cash for the pie was so quick it could have been a drug deal. Miguel never even looked at the delivery boy, something in just a few short minutes he would deeply regret. He carefully carried the pie with two hands, trying to avoid burning them on the bottom of the generic cardboard box, and set it on the kitchen table. He pulled the top of the box off and it flopped over the side of the table so it hung perpendicular to the linoleum floor.

It's always a thrill to watch the first piece of a tomato pie separate from the remaining seven slices, and so it was for Miguel. There's always some sauce and cheese that clings to the piece being removed so you have to turn and dip your head under the pointed end of the slice to surround the dangling morsels and steer them into your mouth. The first slice is always the best; it's the hottest and the most coveted.

Only after he devoured the first slice did he move away from the table and look in the refrigerator for a cold beer to compliment the hot and sticky sauce and cheese of the pie. When he turned back to the table with that cold bottle of beer in one hand, a sliver of crispy crust in the other and mozzarella and tomato sauce stuck in his teeth, life suddenly went from perfect to petrifying. He shakily tried to set the beer on the kitchen counter next to the sink, but couldn't take his eyes off his discovery to negotiate the maneuver. The bottle of beer hit the floor with a thud, covering the linoleum with foam and fizzle. He hardly even noticed, because it was then that he realized he wasn't going to be eating or drinking anymore that night.

Miguel stuck the piece of crust in his mouth and held it in his teeth, not chewing at all. He stepped up to the table, twisted his torso over the top and crooked his neck so his head was practically upside down. He could have lifted the top of the tomato pie box, but he thought that if he didn't touch it and concede that it was real, the writing on it might just evaporate and he could go back to his tomato pie and beer—no such luck. As he peered over the side of the table and confirmed that, in fact, there was a message written on the inside of the top of the box as well as an envelope scotch taped next to the message, he nearly collapsed into the chair next to the table. The perfect crust he so longed for only minutes earlier dropped from his teeth to the floor and curled in the beer.

"What did that kid look like? Did he give me a sign that I missed?" Miguel just kept repeating in his mind.

The message was not unfamiliar to Miguel. More importantly, he knew exactly who sent it. It was a coded message arranged between himself and Castro. The kid who delivered it was probably nobody. It was more likely that the KGB found him and set up the communication. He still didn't know what it meant, other than he already knew it was confirmed and authorized by Castro. The note was written in bold black letters resembling the work of a child:

"It's the bottom of the 8th, the score is tied 3, 3. There are men on first and third with one out."

One third of the code was there. He didn't even have to open the envelope to know what it contained, but he did anyway. With a slight tremble in his hand, he tore the end of the sealed letter envelope, confident that its contents were safely at the other end. He pulled out the single ticket and then looked at his watch.

It was 6:30. He had just enough time to shower, dress and get to the Bronx—The New York Yankees v. The Boston Red Sox—"good game," he thought, but he knew he wouldn't get to see much of it. He dropped the ticket on the table and headed for the shower. The beer and the tomato pie were forever orphaned; none of them, including Miguel, would ever be the same.

Driving a new Vette into the Bronx was like taking the prom queen to a Hells Angels party; everybody who saw her wanted to take her for a ride. But Miguel had no choice since he didn't have any other wheels. Besides, he resigned himself to the fact that he was going to leave this meeting with bad, maybe even very bad news, and the drive home in Marilyn would cheer him up.

Weekend games are always tough on parking, but if money doesn't matter, a spot is always available. A crisp $10 bill usually takes care of it. The Yankee Stadium attendant gave Marilyn a special spot where he could keep a watchful eye on her with another $10 in the deal when Miguel returned and Marilyn was unmolested.

The walk up the interior ramp of the stadium was a considerable workout. The ticket was for a seat in the nose-bleed section in the right field grandstand. The outfield sections of Yankee Stadium are still good seats; they wrap around the foul poles and provide for a nice look into home plate. Naturally all those lefty hitters on the Yankees make for more action in right field than in most other major league parks.

Miguel found a good seat and waited. He got there early hoping to eyeball somebody, but as the seats around him filled up, including the seats on both sides of him, he was still unapproached. The game started and, as always, he had to get a dog or it just wasn't worth the trip, especially since he only got one slice of the tomato pie he left on the kitchen table.

There were about four guys in front of him at the "red hots" stand located just inside the interior hall, adjacent to the seats. Miguel could never understand how Americans were so calm and obedient when it came to standing in line. It never made sense to him. In Cuba, no one stands in line; they just crunch and push forward until they get what they want. Maybe Americans don't mind waiting in line because they all bathe every day and generally smell pretty good; unlike in Cuba, where the stench of a group of men is like being at the zoo the day before the semi-annual cleaning of the cages.

"Two red hots with the works and a Bud," Miguel demanded like a true New Yorker.

It took the kid at the counter all of ten seconds to throw the "red hots" and a beer at Miguel. He fought his way back through the line to a long counter against an open wall where he could stand and eat his "red hots" and still see the game.

"What Neanderthals," he thought.

In Cuba, you would never even consider standing and eating. Everyone sits like human beings and converse while they dine, even if they only had a boiled potato to eat. Miguel, enjoying the first "red hot" with tangy mustard and green relish all over it and his fingers, almost forgot why he was there. He gave no thought to the guy standing next to him—he was obviously a clean-cut gringo with very little hair—probably some Wall Streeter out for the night. But then again, this evening was going to be full of surprises.

"How many outs?" the gringo casually asked in Miguel's direction.

Initially Miguel looked up at the scoreboard. For a second he was confused, but that passed and he knew what the answer had to be.

"One out. He'll probably throw a knuckle ball," Miguel responded in a near whisper.

"That's too bad. The batter will probably hit a pop-up invoking the infield fly rule and he'll be out; the runners will have to hold," the gringo responded as if it were actually happening on the field.

The question had been asked, and both men gave the correct answer. Now they both knew who the other was, at least they thought so. Now they could get down to business. Miguel started.

"Why am I here?"

"There has been a change of plans," the gringo responded.

"Who changed the plan?" Miguel asked, knowing there was only one plan changer in this operation; he got the expected answer.

"*El Presidente.*"

"What's the change?" Miguel was now clearly agitated.

"You are to immediately drop what you are doing and go directly to New Orleans. Check into La Pavillion Hotel under the name of Michael Charles, and wait for contact."

This made no sense to Miguel. The counterfeiting operation was at the top of El Presidente's hit list. While he was originally confident he was coming to a meeting with a *compadre*, because they had the complete contact code, he wasn't so sure anymore. Something was awry. This gringo was exactly that, a gringo, and now he had Miguel right where he wanted him. His shorts and shoes started to feel tight; he couldn't just stand there, nor could he walk away.

"Who is this guy and where did he get the code?" was the question he couldn't answer. Miguel's hesitation signaled the gringo that he should start to reel him in a little and see if he would take the bait, so he continued.

"Listen, these orders require you to walk away from a very hot hand. If you prefer, you can play that hand and stay in the game. You have friends," he precisely stated.

Miguel knew then that he was dancing with an alligator. Either he was going to ride him to shore and make friends, or he was going to fall off and get eaten. It was a decision he had to make right then. If he only had a better feel for whom this guy was, the decision might be more apparent.

"This gringo could be a test from Havana—having the code made it very likely. He could also be the KGB trying to double down on Havana, or a Chinese agent or almost any other intelligence service; they all operate in the States. Hell, this guy could even be CIA or FBI lookin' to roll me over," Miguel thought to himself.

The gringo was holding all the cards; Miguel decided to ante up.

"New friends?" he asked in a tone of mild interest.

"Yes. But you don't have to give up your old ones," the gringo told him with high confidence.

Miguel knew the hand was still undecided. His last draw from the deck could be either very good or very deadly. If it was a legitimate offer from strangers, he understood they wanted him to deal from the bottom of the deck and keep Havana on a string. He needed to know more, especially what was in it for him. Walking away from the counterfeiting plot would cost him dearly. While he could only suspect why he was being sent to New Orleans, Miguel certainly wasn't happy about the order. He felt he had paid his dues to the revolution by enthusiastically providing a very specific and dangerous service to Castro and the cause. With the opportunity to participate in the counterfeiting operation, he hoped to change all of that. At that moment, however, it occurred to him that maybe Castro had played him from the very start? Did Castro just entice him into carrying the ball this far, planning to then steer him off to a new assignment in the same vein as his prior service? Miguel was no longer interested in being a "trigger finger." He decided to see one more card in what was turning out to be a real game of chance for Miguel.

"Friends don't have secrets. Tell me yours." This was the safest tack for Miguel. If it's Havana trying to steel him, then he's still safe because he hasn't agreed to anything yet. If it's the KGB, CIA or FBI, then it's time for them to show their cards. If he hears the details, maybe it would help him make the right choice; he was all ears.

"Just follow the new instructions, but finish your meal first. We'll be sure you have leftovers to take home for lunch another day. We'll cover the timing. Havana will just think you didn't get the message in time. No one will ever know of this conversation, but you will have to move fast."

Miguel understood perfectly. They were offering him a piece of the counterfeiting print, assuming they had the right scoop. He would go to New Orleans after and tell Havana that he followed instructions and there was no print, returning the genuine they gave him to pay for the counterfeit. Since, as far as Havana knew, there was no print, Miguel, according to his new friends, could put a large slice of the counterfeit away to take to market on some future rainy day. So far so good. Now all he needed to know was what he had to give in return and who was he giving it to.

"That's a good friend, and in return?" he asked.

"We just want to be your friend. We will pay you a discreet

visit every now and again to reminisce about old times and new times alike."

"And who are my new friends?" Miguel asked, knowing the response would certainly be circumspect

"Does it matter?"

"It might. Do we have mutual friends?" Miguel responded in a more demanding tone.

"We have no friends—only business associates—in Havana, Washington, Moscow and other places. We would like you to join us."

Miguel looked hard at the gringo and was satisfied that he correctly made him when he first saw him The fact that they had the correct code also told him that they had a reliable source very close to Castro himself. Only a small number of inner circle members would have access to the code information and only very few "business" organizations have the muscle to get it. Miguel was betting on the Americans. He was betting his life on The FBI.

Miguel quickly realized he had few choices. If he turned them down after they showed their hand, they couldn't risk him running back to Havana and blowing their cover and most likely their valuable source. Even if they didn't kill him, he was still going to be left with no future independent of Castro. He would have to dutifully drop the counterfeit operation, scamper to New Orleans and fulfill whatever psychotic delusion Castro had developed in his absence. He had no choice other than to continue to play the hand he was dealt.

"Everyone comes to America to do business, don't they?. You know where to find me when you need to. I have a busy day ahead of me," Miguel said as he set his nearly empty Bud down on the counter and walked toward the exit ramp.

As he walked away, he turned for a last look at the gringo.

"Enjoy the game, root for the Yanks. I always do," Miguel quipped with a sarcastic smile.

"By the way, when you come calling, how will I know it's you?" Miguel added.

"We'll ask for the name of the best hurler in New York."

"Whitey Ford?" Miguel suggested.

"Y.A. Tittle," replied the gringo, not revealing whether or not he knew that Y.A. Tittle was the quarterback for the New York Giants football team.

"Stupid fuckin' gringo; they think it's their game," Miguel said to himself as he took one more look at the famous Yankee Stadium outfield façade and headed down the ramp.

Tom Ritter dropped his barely eaten "red hot" on the counter and expelled a deep breath followed by a long gasp of air. He felt like he had been holding his breath since AD walked into his office and gave him this assignment over twelve hours ago. This was the first real undercover meet Ritter ever had and he didn't like it. He was much more secure within the walls of his dull, drab, headquarters office. It wasn't very stimulating, but he felt much safer and in control—a necessity for his continued wellbeing. All-and- all, he thought it went well. AD gave him only one unbreakable rule: "Never mention the FBI ." He didn't have to.

Ritter had no interest in the ball game. After waiting a safe time, he headed for the exit ramp. He did what he was ordered to do, although he had no idea what he was getting himself and The Bureau into. He recognized that he probably had much more confidence in AD than he should have had. Even a bureaucratic self-preservationist like Ritter would have stutter stepped if he had any idea where this liaison was taking him, The FBI and literally the entire planet.

CHAPTER 38

DETAILS, PRECAUTIONS AND REGRETS

IT WAS 6:00 A.M. ON Saturday morning—day of all days. I woke up slowly over nearly an hour. I have always been a difficult sleeper. In fact, I'm known as a "time stalker." The first thing I do every single day upon opening my eyes is look at the clock. This happens no matter where I am. In fact, if I wake up in the middle of the night in a completely darkened room, I will struggle with all obstacles, including an occasional sultry overnight guest, to find out the time of day. I'll stop at nothing. If I can't find my watch, and by the way I won't even consider any watch without that radioactive green glow in the dark stuff on the dial, I'll scour the room for a clock. No clock? Then it's the radio or television, immediately, without any concern for the calm tranquility of the darkened room or its other occupants. Indeed, sometimes the radio or television is just too slow. They tell you the time when they want to tell you the time. I need to know it immediately. My entire life cycle is off balance without time regulation. I actually tremble and my heart goes arrhythmic. I have never learned what I am afraid of; all I know is that it's real terror.

If I'm staying in a hotel, a firm tug on the drapes will often help. Even if it's still dark outside, an experienced "time investigator" can quickly analyze the subtleties of the night. Initially, I instinctively search for any glimmer of the emergence of the sun, although often fruitless. If I can see the hotel entrance, I'm sometimes able to analyze the direction of the movement of people on the ground. People entering the hotel usually mean its late night or very early morning, especially if they were traveling in groups or clinging couples without luggage and displaying a well-defined stagger. Taxicabs loading "suits" with bags are a sure sign of a new day soon to dawn.

If there's nothing to see, I'll just listen. The sounds of the night often tell me as much, or even more, than the sights. Cheerful voices laced with the tone of anticipated sex, or even the sound of a cheerful "good night" means that the dawn was still hours away. A steady rising whine of traffic usually foretells dawn is close at hand. A dead giveaway of an impending sunrise is the grind of accelerating delivery trucks or the rattle of empty garbage cans hitting the pavement after being relieved of their contents. I have no hope of returning to sleep unless I was successful in my quest.

If it wasn't for the ink still on my hands, I would have been sure I dreamt the entire meeting with Ron Ron as well as the Medal of Honor discussion with Carmine. As my head cleared of sleep, I realized that it was all true. I just couldn't help but smile at the thought of Ron Ron.

"Cool Daddy-0," I kept saying out loud as I tried to drag my ass to the edge of the bed.

I felt a sense of uncertainty about the caper that I hadn't felt since it all began. I knew that in just a few short hours, I would be with Frankie and Canevecchio, printing several million dollars of counterfeit $100 bills, all at a location I still didn't know. I was confident now that I could pull it off—that part didn't bother me anymore. I was much more upset about the fact that at some point in the next twenty-four hours, both Frankie and Canevecchio were going to get arrested and thrown into jail. Knowing this was going to happen to them, while they were at the same time making plans for their future, made me feel like a soothsayer. I, unlike either of them, knew this catastrophe was about to befall them and I was the catalyst about to put it all in motion. I was much more uncertain how I would react when the time came to arrest them than I was about setting up and completing the print.

I finally made it to the sitting position on the edge of the bed and eventually dragged myself up and into the shower. Bookie and Ava were still sleeping, so I was able to shower, get dressed and slip out of the apartment without any distractions.

The VW was parked downstairs in the same spot I always parked it. It was amazing to me how much comfort that little bug gave me. It helped me keep in touch with who I really was because although I respected its mission, my spirit just didn't fit the mold of a Secret Service Agent. The car kept me feeling like a kid, full of adventure and enthusiasm. I often had to remind myself I really wasn't that old yet and life didn't have to be full-throttle serious, even though I was involved in a very serious profession. One thing I did do, without the office even knowing, was to change out the cheap radio and cardboard speakers in the VW with a super Blaupunkt radio and kick-ass speakers. The faster I drove that little terror, the louder I would play the music. Both seemed to steady my nerves and inspire my imagination.

On this Saturday morning, the radio volume was on "10" as I drove to the hospital to see T. It seemed to be working because my nerves seemed to bottom out. That is until the Secret Service radio in the glove box began to squawk and call out my name. It was Carmine on his car radio trying to raise me on mine. I didn't think I would hear from Carmine so early this morning and I became a little troubled that something had gone wrong while I overslept.

"Go ahead Carmine, this is Jake." I was able to answer him only after he tried to get me four times because I had to get the radio mike out of the glove box, turn down the music, drive and worry all at the same time.

"What's your present location? Over." Carmine always obeyed perfect radio etiquette.

"I'm on Broad Street en route to meet our guy." You always had to be careful never to give too much information out over the radio. You never knew who was listening.

"Meet me at location Blue, directly. Copy?"

It was a short statement, but it contained a lot of information and instructions. Because we never knew who was listening, or even watching us, we had a list of meeting locations that were identified over the radio only by their color code. Location Blue was an old abandoned gas station on McCarter Highway in Newark. Carmine wanted me to meet him there immediately and he wanted me to confirm that I fully understood the request and would be able to comply. I did and I could, and so I told him:

"Roger," said it all.

Just minutes later, I pulled into the abandoned gas station and drove around back, off the road. Carmine was already there, having driven his 1958 Buick Roadmaster, the last one they made. That car was huge, even bigger than the Cadillacs the dagos drove. The guys in the office called it the "Jewmaster" because it was seized from an old Jewish bank president that Carmine arrested a few years earlier. The old guy had a great scam. He would go to his loan officer and arrange a loan for one of his cronies for a couple of hundred thousand dollars. The bank was happy to give the loan because it was well secured by a $250,000 US Treasury Bill. These bills, while fairly rare, were like large US Savings Bonds. They were fully insured by Uncle Sam, good as gold. Our banker pal would then take the money he got on the Treasury Bill and make either a very good short term investment or loan it out to his tribesmen for some heavy *vig* (vigorous, a wise guy term for interest). After the money earned him a handsome profit, he would return it to the bank and they would give him back the Treasury Bill. This worked perfectly for the first three times he did it.

However, on the fourth go-round, a young teller was sent to the vault to retrieve the Treasury Bill. The kid never saw anything like it before, so he took it out of its plastic protective sleeve and examined it closely. The kid nearly had a stroke when he saw that the ink on the bill was smudged. He immediately panicked, thinking he did it when he pulled it out. Not being a complete idiot, he tried to cover it up by sliding the bill back into the sleeve, which only made the smudges worse. Finally, he had no alternative and told the loan officer. Well, the loan officer had never seen a US Treasury Bill before and actually thought the smudge was an imperfection in the printing by the Treasury Department. Wanting to stay on the good side of the bank president, he decided to get it straightened out, so he called the Treasury Department in Washington. Even the clerk who answered the phone at the help desk knew it was highly unlikely that a $250,000 Treasury Bill would be issued with such an imperfection. He called us to check it out.

Carmine got the call and took a ride over to the bank and sure enough, the Treasury Bill was counterfeit. Our tribesman banker, who made a ton of money getting uncollateralized loans and turning profits with the money, insisted that it was genuine and that the US Treasury owed him $250,000 for giving him a bad Treasury Bill. Carmine said it was comical to watch him try to make that argument. The IRS took everything the guy owned or would ever own. And so now, Carmine drives the guy's car. When he got out of jail, he unknowingly moved into a house in South Orange, just around the block from Carmine. As a result, Carmine drives the car past his house almost every day. If the old guy is outside and sees him, he defiantly flips Carmine the finger as he drives by. Carmine just toots the horn.

I squeezed out of the VW and practically rolled into the passenger seat of the Roadmaster. It felt like there should be a terry cloth robe hanging over the seat and a hot toddy on the dash. What a great car for a hot date. There was more room in that car than in most motel rooms I've stayed in.

"All set kid?" Carmine asked.

"Yeah. No problem Why?"

"Did T get the plant location from Frankie yet?" Carmine continued.

"I don't know. I figured I'd find out when I saw him this morning. I'm on my way to the hospital now."

"Okay. As soon as you find out, you gotta call me. We got a lot of work to do." I could feel Carmine's tension.

"Sure. What's the plan?" I realized that there were lots of angles to closing this caper that I hadn't thought about yet. Thank God for Carmine being there. He had it all planned out for me like a First Communion party. He laid it out for me:

"First of all, we gotta get an eyeball on the place. Hopefully, it's a place we can get into before tonight. The best cover would be to get a wire in the place so we can hear what's goin' on, but we won't be able to count on it. The press will be running most of the time you're in there and it will kill any chance to hear what's happening. We're gonna have to rely on you to keep us posted. Remember that. We won't be far away, but we can't help if you don't let us know you need it."

"Jeez, don't make me nervous, Carmine. What could go wrong?" I asked.

Carmine flashed me a look I had never seen before. It was like an ice cold shower that let me know to take this thing very seriously. "Always remember that in the end, if we win, all of these guys are gonna get hard time. Do not underestimate how far they'll go to beat that rap," Carmine reminded me.

"I got it."

"Okay. So, here's the deal. Remember this. TSD will put a wire in the cellar. When you turn off the press, we'll be listening to every word that comes outta there. When it's time to take everybody down, you just turn that fuckin' press off and very clearly say the code word. We'll be bustin' through the doors and windows in minutes. Don't worry—we'll come down the fuckin' chimney or up through the toilet if we have to. We're not gonna leave you out there hangin' by yourself."

"Well, gee, Carmine, that's good to know," I said only half kidding, and seriously letting him know that I appreciated it. "What's the code word?"

"That's the trick, kid. We gotta pick a word that there's no chance will get said accidentally. So...how about, 'Mississippi? I figure there's little chance these guys will be talking about the great southern state of Mississippi. Okay? Remember, even if the print isn't where you want it, if the shit hits the fan and things start to go sideways, just turn the press off and yell 'Mississippi.' We'll be listening. Got it kid?"

"Got it," I assured him again.

"And, no matter what you think of these guys, you're gonna be out-numbered in there. We figure it's gonna be Frankie, Canevecchio and this mutt Miguel, at best. That's three to one. It could even get worse if Miguel shows up with somebody else, which could happen. He knows he's walkin' into 'Casa Dago' with a lot of cash. It wouldn't be totally crazy for him to bring a gun or two to be sure this deal goes down according to Hoyle. So be careful."

Carmine just kept pourin' it on and my dick just kept getting smaller and smaller, like a turtle takin' cover in its shell. I decided now was the time to bring up something that was on my mind.

"Hey, Carmine, what about my piece?" I shyly asked.

"Fugetaboutit. Your commission book, too. Nothin' goes in there except you and your wits." Carmine was as serious as I'd ever seen him.

All the time I met with T and Frankie, I always carried my .357 in my left boot. I wasn't sure I would ever need it, but it was like having a rubber in my wallet on a first date with a hot chic—better to have it if I needed it than need it and not have it. I understood why Carmine said not to take it and I was okay with that. I knew there would be a small army of agents in the neighborhood and I really had no concerns about Frankie and Canevecchio. I didn't, however, know anything about this guy Miguel and I did have a nice, small, five-shot, stainless Colt .38 Detective Special that would make me feel very warm and cozy if stuck in my left boot. But I trusted Carmine's judgment, so I let it go.

"What about the size of the print? I'm not sure how much ink and paper Frankie and Canevecchio got. Do we let it run and print it all?" When I asked that question, it was the first time in the entire conversation that Carmine smiled.

"You bet bucko. Unless there's a problem in there, let them print it all up. It's one thing to get them on a conspiracy to print a shit load of queer; it's another thing to actually get them holding it. You got Ron Ron's hardener. Don't forget to mix it into the ink on every run. It's a critical ingredient."

"Yeah, okay, I got it. I guess I'll head to the hospital. I'll give you a call as soon as I hear about the place." I had heard enough. It was time for me to get to work, but Carmine had one last comment.

"Good idea. Listen kid, I know what you're thinking."

As soon as I heard Carmine begin the sentence, I knew where he was going and I felt like a sad, old song had just come on the radio and was about to make me cry. He continued and I listened.

"It's not our job to judge these guys. Twelve people on a jury will do that later. We took an oath to protect and defend the Constitution and the people of this country. That's what we do. I have to tell you though...I do understand your quandary. I read every single word of this guy's military file—it is remarkable. Thirty guys gave testimony in support of his nomination for the CMH, when usually there's only one or two. You know what virtually every one of them said?"

"No, what?" I asked even though I wasn't sure I wanted to know anything that was going to make my job any more difficult than it already was.

"They said that one Medal of Honor wasn't enough. They said that what he did on that bridge, he did for those guys day in and day out throughout the invasion. He consistently put his life on the line to protect his fellow paratroopers.

"And I'll tell you something else. You remember that Breitling watch you told me he wears, a Navitimer? That watch was given to him by the Mercury 7 astronauts in recognition of his courage. One of the guys he saved is a brother of one of the astronauts. You can't fuckin' make this shit up."

"What do you think that's all about Carmine?" I asked because what he was telling me wasn't making my job in this caper any easier, but I wanted his insight.

"I don't know for sure. Most guys that behave like that, hero or not, have a death wish or at least place a low value on human life, including their own. They just find themselves in that situation and they react accordingly, and someone happens to call them a hero. Frankie wasn't much older than most of the guys in his platoon. Hell, they were all just kids, but he assumed the protector, older-brother role. I think he valued his own life, but it was more important for him to defend his brothers than ensure his own survival. I think we have to remember this and watch that he doesn't do something like that here when the bust goes down. Remember kid, this guy, uniform or not, has taken life before, lots of lives to protect his *paisani*."

I never, even for a second, thought of it that way before. I started to think that maybe Carmine was right. It was then that I decided I needed to make my own decisions, just in case my soft thoughts about these guys were off base.

"I better get going," was the only response I had. My head and heart were reeling.

I rolled out of the Roadmaster and squeezed back into the VW. I was only a few minutes from the hospital.

CHAPTER 39

JUST A FEW FINAL WORDS WITH T

THE TRIP TO THE HOSPITAL had become all too familiar. I could also tell that the EPS officer in the hall was getting pretty tired of the drill. As I got off the elevator and approached T's room, he just rolled his eyes at me as if to say, "Please, can I get the fuck outta this hall and back to some real police work." I just gave him a little sympathetic smile as I pushed open the door to T's room.

Considering the cast of characters in this caper, I shouldn't have been surprised by anything, but for some reason I was. I guess I figured that because the last time I walked in on T unexpectedly I found him cock chokin' the night nurse. What could happen in the middle of the morning? Well, I quickly found out when I opened the door and smelled the stogie.

There he was, sitting up in the bed with the *Star Ledger* held full-open, high in the air. He sported a pair of black reading glasses down on the end of his nose and an enormous cigar in his mouth. I don't know how everybody on the floor didn't smell it; it was really strong and completely filled the room with smoke. I figured telling him he was in a hospital and smoking a rope wasn't acceptable behavior just wouldn't cut it. So I decided I would just ruin his appetite for the smoke.

"Nice rope, T. Do you have them made special on the Avenue to smell particularly bad? By the way, you know what they call those things in the joint, don't you?"

"Nope. What the fuck do they call 'em?" he quipped with a sarcastic, cocky tone. So, I told him.

"Nigger Dicks."

He lowered the paper as the cigar drooped in his lips, so I told him again.

"Yup, that's what they call 'em...'Nigger Dicks'. Ya wanna know why?" I knew the last part would really get him.

"Go fuck yourself you little prick," he said as he threw the lighted cigar in my direction. As it hit the linoleum floor, it caused a burst of red ashes to detonate. I quickly covered it with my boot, unable to hold back an ear-to-ear grin. Then I gave him the bad news.

"You know, you should try to leave the place nice and neat." After he looked at me with his mouth open and eyebrows arched, I continued.

"You realize this is gonna be your last night here, right? If this goes down like we plan, you'll be back in the slammer tomorrow. I can't help you. I don't have a choice in the matter."

"Fuck," was all he could say. I tried to allay his fears of the worst. I actually felt bad for breaking his balls over having to go back behind the wall, but it was completely out of my hands.

"T, don't get your shorts in a knot. I won't forget what you've done here. Okay? So tell me about what's going down tonight. Let's start with where," I asked, getting back to business.

I was actually surprised how quickly T shook it off and got back to what we were doing. It was almost as if it didn't matter where he went from here. He had lots of news for me.

"I spoke to Frankie just a little while ago. They got the press and they're deliverin' it to the plant."

"Where T...where?" That's all I wanted to know for the moment. I knew Carmine and the TSD boys were waiting to wire the place.

"The only place that can keep jumpin' all Saturday night and nobody gets suspicious," he quipped.

He was intentionally breaking my balls back just a little; I couldn't blame him. I just looked at him, nodded my head, lifted both of my hands palms up, raised my eyebrows and waited. Eventually he told me.

"A bakery, *stupido.*"

"A bakery, what bakery? Where?" I acted incredulous, but I knew it was actually ingenious.

"They moved the press into the cellar of La Ragazza Bakery on Freemont Street in Belleville. They picked up the same press I used for the first print and dropped it off in the basement over there this afternoon. The place is closed now, but it'll be hummin' by 8:00 tonight and we can move in and *finito a collazione* (finish by breakfast)."

"It's closed now?" I wanted to confirm so I could tell Carmine. I didn't tell T that we were going to wire the place. He didn't need to know that.

"Yeah. They gotta sleep sometimes. Don't worry. They'll open up by 8 p.m. and nobody'll ask any questions. Hell, I don't think any of those wops even speak English. It's taken care of," he said, trying to reassure me and missing the point completely, I thought.

I reached for the telephone and called Carmine. I told him what I learned from T; he knew the place immediately.

"Shit, that's a great bakery. My mother-in-law stops there every Sunday after Mass. It's gonna be a shame to close that place," Carmine lamented.

He assured me not to worry—the TSD guys would be able to slip into the place this afternoon before the joint opened and all would be as he promised. He sounded like a wedding planner or even worse, a mortician; I only hoped it wasn't my funeral he was planning.

I hung up with Carmine and refocused my attention on T. I was confident that he didn't catch on to my conversation with Carmine.

"So you're gonna bug the place, huh?" was the first thing out of his mouth.

"Jeez T, just be cool, will ya? Let us handle this, okay? Where's Frankie and Canevecchio?" I asked, trying to change the subject.

"Sleepin', like you should be doin'. It's gonna be a long night, kid."

I ignored him.

"Tell me about the press. It's not going to be like the one at Ron Ron's is it?" I asked.

"Hell no, this is an American press. It's one-fifth the size of that whore at Ron Ron's, but it'll do just as good a job. She's just like a chic though—you gotta pay her lots of attention—keep her lubed up and she'll cum for you all night long. Get it, kid?"

"Yeah, yeah, yeah, I got it. I got it." I guess I just wasn't in the mood to listen to that kind of talk. It had been a very long time since I spent a night like that.

I handed T back his cigar. He cut both ends and relit it so he could finish it in the chair by the window—the same chair that Frankie was sitting in when I first laid eyes on him. Maybe that's what made me decide to sit on the corner of the bed next to T and have a little heart-to-heart with him. I wasn't sure how he was going to react, but I needed to do it, for me.

"Hey T...why didn't you tell me about Frankie?"

"I dunno. I didn't think it was something you wanted to know until you was ready. I mean you guys are the fuckin' Secret Service, right? I figured you'd find out soon enough. Actually, I'm surprised it took you so long." T immediately knew what I was talking about.

"Ya know, when we went to eat that night, every guy in the place had to shake his hand and pat him on the back before he could leave. Is that because of the Medal of Honor?" I was trying to understand the dynamics of the relationships.

"Fuck no. Do you think those wops at Lapanto's give a shit about your fuckin' Medal of Honor? Hell, halfa dose guys were in the fucking Italian army; they came here after the war was over. Most of them don't even know about it."

It was fascinating to watch T at that moment because his gruff façade softened when talking about Frankie like that. I wanted to know more; it was also a good diversion because I was already getting nervous about the impending night.

"But isn't that why everybody calls him *Ponte*—because of the bridge at Eindhoven?"

"Listen, kid. Guys like us ain't impressed because some hot shot in Washington pins a medal on a guy. That don't feed our families. All we know is who the guy is in the neighborhood, *capisce?* I mean maybe alotta' guys know about the Medal, or at least heard about it. But nobody would ever ask him about it. Hell, I'm one of the few guys who've actually seen it and that's only because his mother showed it to me years ago, before she died. We call him *Ponte* for a much more important reason. We call him *Ponte* because he helps guys navigate *aqua pericolose*." I understood the literal meaning of *aqua pericolose*—perilous waters. But I didn't really get the drift of where he was going, so I asked.

"Whadda you mean, T?"

He began to explain.

"You gotta remember that we're all just a bunch of swingin' dicks and most of us have no social skills to speak of. When trouble starts, alotta guys do things the old way; they just whack a guy and finish business. It's quick and permanent, but it also brings heat on all of us and sometimes it's just wrong."

"Frankie, on the other hand, is a smart guy. He's saved alotta guys from getting it in the back-a-da-head. He's the guy everybody goes to, to make peace, to help explain some stupid move they made, or even to just beg for forgiveness. Sometimes these things happen between families or even inside the same family. That's why everybody wants to shake his hand. There probably wasn't a guy in Lapanto's who hasn't gone to him for help or knows that they will go to him for help someday in the future."

"Why Frankie, T? Why him?" I still didn't get it.

"That's just the way it always was. Even in the schoolyard, Frankie was the peacemaker. He was also the guy nobody wanted to fuck with, either. He always looked after everybody. Hell, look at Canevecchio. Nobody has a place for him anymore. He just ain't the same guy he was when he was a kid. Nobody really knows what happened, but he just can't earn no more. But Frankie has never abandoned him. He takes care of him just like his name says—he's an old dog that can't hunt no more. But Frankie is still there for him. Ya know what I mean?"

It all started to make more sense to me. It didn't make me feel any better, but I really had no choice. It was just as Carmine said—I had my own oath and responsibilities to live up to, and somebody else will have to decide how to handle it after I finish my job.

Intellectually I knew all that, but it still left me feeling empty and a little sick inside. I needed to refocus on getting through the print.

"Okay T, so now what?"

"Now nothin' kid. Show up at 8:00 at the back door of the bakery and the guys and the press will be ready to go. And don't forget to try the *cannoli*."

"What about the buyer, this guy Miguel?" I asked.

"Well, whadda you want me to do? I expect him to call any minute and he'll wanna know where the plant is. And, remember he still has no idea about you bein' the printer."

"Shit!" I thought to myself. I completely forgot about that little twist. I figured that we just had to stick to Carmine's plan. So I went over it one more time with T.

"Okay. When he calls, just tell him where the plant is and to be there at 9:00. That'll give me time to get set up so when he gets there he'll see we mean business. Don't tell him anything about me; just leave him with a hard-on. I'll take care of it when he arrives at the plant. I'll give him the same cover story I gave the guys. I'll invite him to call you here through the hospital switchboard, but he won't be able to get you though. Hopefully he'll figure that he's already there with the good and we're already printin', so he'll close the deal. If he decides to walk, we'll just have to improvise."

I knew that improvise meant that we would just have to take it all down sooner rather than later. There was no way Carmine was gonna let this guy get away; we had way too many questions.

"Got it, T?"

"Yeah, I got it," he answered in the saddest tone I had ever heard from him.

"Listen kid," he continued. "Be careful, for everybody's sake. I know I'm gonna rot in fuckin' hell for what I'm doin' here. So don't make it worse by letting my guys get hurt. Okay?"

"Don't sweat it, T. Nobody's gonna get hurt. It'll go down like a prom queen after the dance and a pint of vodka. Relax. I'll stop by tomorrow and see ya."

T just looked at the floor and nodded as I headed for the door.

I went downstairs, got into the VW and just sat there because I really had no place to go until 8 p.m. I just kept thinking about what Carmine said about Frankie being a life-taker and God knows what this Miguel character is. I started the VW and drove around aimlessly for a while; I just couldn't get the worry out of my mind. I decided to take a spin past the apartment since it wasn't far from the plant site. I didn't see Bookie or Ava's car, so I figured no one was there. I was right. I only stayed a few minutes; there was only one thing I needed.

When I got back to the car, I drove around some more and decided to stop and get something to eat. I started to feel better and more relaxed. The 5-shot, .38 Detective Special that was now inside my left boot may have had something to do with my renewed confidence. I knew it was against Carmine's instructions, but every undercover agent has to make up his own mind about carrying a gun when working under cover. I just made my decision and now all I had to do was wait.

T, back at the hospital, was attending to some final details.

Later that evening

T sat on the hospital bed and just listened to the telephone ring. He didn't have to answer it to know who it was; he was certain it was the same guy calling every thirty minutes since I left. Third ring, fourth ring, as T looked at his watch.

"6:15," he thought to himself. "It's about the right time," he decided.

"*Pronto*," he said in an intentionally exhausted tone, trying to set the mood for what he was about to do, just in case Miguel thought about it later when he showed up at the plant.

"T, it's Miguel. Where the fuck have you been? I've been callin' all fuckin' day."

"I guess I fell asleep. I'm feeling *stanco*, tired," T said, correcting his Italian to English.

"Tired? Get the fuck up; it's a big night, *paisan*." Miguel liked to throw around an Italian word or phrase occasionally, just to show how cosmopolitan a Cuban could be. He always butchered the pronunciation by cutting off the vowels that are the essence of the Italian language.

"Are we set?" Miguel asked.

"Yeah, we're all set." T decided to force him to pull the location out of him.

"Where and when?

"They'll be set and running at 9:00 in the basement of La Ragazza Bakery on Freemont Street in Belleville. You know where it's at?"

"I'll find it. See you there." And he hung up.

T softly put the receiver down on the telephone and laid his head back on the pillow. He knew there was nothing he could do now for anybody, including himself. He was ready to fall asleep early that night. He was happy he enjoyed a cigar and had that little conversation about Frankie. He knew he should call Lucille, but he decided it was better that he didn't. There was so much he wanted to tell her, but he knew he would never be able to find the words. The hospital bed was more comfortable than he remembered. He hoped all would be well for the guys when the sun came up. He prayed for their forgiveness.

I wish I had stayed with him a little longer that night.

CHAPTER 40

"WHY ARE YOU LETTING THAT BARBARIAN HOLD YOU ON A LEASH?"

MIGUEL HUNG UP THE TELEPHONE in his apartment and headed for the door. On his way out, he grabbed his dark green, London Fog jacket. It fit just to his waist and when he zipped it, even half-way up, it nicely covered the Mauser tucked in his waistband. As he headed downstairs to get Azzimie, he decided he was going to keep him in his sights until this thing was over, and then he would blow a hole in his head. He relished the thought.

Miguel had a good idea where the bakery was located. He knew it was going to be a long night and, if he learned only one thing from being a revolutionary soldier, that was to eat when you can. You never know when you'll get the chance again. So he decided they would grab something to eat and then go by the bakery and check it out. Azzimie had other plans.

Just minutes later, Miguel was rapping on Azzimie's door. Azzimie had no reason to expect Miguel. In fact, considering what happened at their last meeting, he hoped he would never have to face him ever again. But there he was, just on the other side of the rap. Azzimie wasn't courageous enough not to answer.

"Get your jacket. We're goin' for a ride." Probably the very last words Azzimie wanted to hear, especially from Miguel.

"Where we goin'?"

"What's the difference...just get your coat," Miguel commanded again.

"Let's get a drink and see the girls," Azzimie suggested, hoping that if anything could distract Miguel from whatever he had planned, seeing LJ and Julia could do it. Thankfully, Miguel took the bait. In fact, he never even saw the hook.

"Are they working tonight?" Miguel quickly responded.

Azzimie hit on Miguel's greatest weakness—he could never resist the challenge of hard-to-get ass. If a chic wanted to trap him, all she had to do was wiggle her ass and then walk away as if she just didn't give a shit. Miguel, the predator, couldn't resist the chase, which is exactly how he felt about LJ. He was hungry anyway, so Miguel thought it wasn't such a bad idea to eat at the bowling alley while leering at LJ and Julia and then go to the bakery. It was going to be a long night and he didn't think he needed to be there right at 9:00 anyway.

"I don't see why not. I'll call over and check," Azzimie said as he headed for the telephone in the kitchen, leaving Miguel standing by the door.

Azzimie was on the telephone no more than two minutes. He returned to the front door with a little more spring in his step and assured Miguel that the girls were working. Miguel went for it and just a few, short minutes later he was behind the wheel of Marilyn, with Azzimie next to him, on their way to the bowling alley. Miguel mistakenly thought he was the only one that knew it was the last trip either of them would take to the bowling alley. He had no idea Azzimie had his own plans for the evening and for both of their futures.

While Miguel and Azzimie were both in the same car driving to the same place, they were about as far apart as two bodies could be and still be orbiting around the same sun. Miguel knew that shortly after 9:00, he would be arriving at La Ragazza Bakery, with Azzimie in tow. He was also sure that sometime later, probably early the next morning, just about the time Azzimie was convinced he was going to strike it rich, Miguel would put one of the .380 caliber Mauser rounds in the back of his head, and enjoy watching his brains ooze out onto the floor.

Miguel didn't know why he was going to enjoy killing Azzimie, but he was certain he would. He felt Azzimie deserved to die a violent and impertinent death. Maybe it was because Miguel, although nothing more than a hired gun with no education or class status in his own right, was indeed an elitist. He saw himself as deserving of a higher station in life, not as a result of birth or achievement, but rather simply by way of entitlement—entitlement through ultimatum. Miguel believed that "he with the biggest balls won. If you want it, take it all and give nothing back." He saw no reason why that smelly, scrawny Azzimie should live as well as he did, or in fact, live at all. He was a member of a mongrel race with no historical significance—unlike even the poorest Cuban peasant who was part of a chronicled lineage dating back to the dawn of civilization. It also bothered Miguel that girls as stunning as LJ and Julia would even associate with a despicable swine like Azzimie. He actually fantasized about killing him before their very eyes so they could see what a powerful alpha male he was and then fall to their knees at his feet.

It sickened Miguel to have Azzimie even ride in his Marilyn. He felt that he deserved to die just for driving her without his permission while he was in Cuba. She was soiled, like a woman raped by a criminal. It may not have been her fault, but no self-respecting Cuban male would touch her after such despoliation. But Miguel couldn't see Marilyn in those terms. Even considering her uncleanliness, Miguel decided he wasn't going to abandon her, but rather drive her to New Orleans and assume his new double agent role in style. It was ironic to him that now he would be working for the Americans and driving The Great American Sports Car. "I deserve it," he thought to himself.

Miguel had worked and reworked his escape plan, over and over in his head, ever since his meeting at Yankee Stadium. He was confident his new business associates at The FBI would allow the print to continue to complete fruition. But in the end, Miguel would certainly walk away with $2 million, maybe $3 million dollars in prime, counterfeit $100 bills. He would also report to Castro's contact in New Orleans with the original genuine notes he was supposed to use to pay the counterfeiters, and thereby be in good stead with *El Presidente*. He would then play ball with the Americans until the right door opened and he could make his exit and his own future.

As he drove Marilyn to the bowling alley for one last visit with LJ and Julia, with Azzimie in the dead man's seat, his instincts were dulled by thoughts of his prosperous future. Maybe that's why Miguel missed all the signs from Azzimie that he had a different future of his own in mind. And that future didn't include a Mauser round in the back of the head; at least not his head anyway.

While Miguel was concentrating on his long-term future, he neglected to care for the details of his immediate security. He simply assumed that he would be able to lure Azzimie to the plant, hold his interest there all night on the hope he would get a piece of the print and then kill him in the morning. Actually, it might not have been such a bad plan if there wasn't another chef in the kitchen preparing a meal of his own. Brus had been stirring the pot, hoping to throw Miguel in the hot broth ever since the minute he suspected Miguel was the source of the Las Vegas notes. The day Azzimie got that Mauser screwed in his ear was the day he decided he would hold the pot and help Brus scald Miguel.

What Miguel didn't know was that earlier that week, after Azzimie left the bowling alley with Miguel and went home, Brus showed up at about 3 a.m., pounding on Azzimie's apartment door. Azzimie at first thought Miguel was returning to finish the job he started earlier that night. He fully expected to open the door and catch a round from that Mauser right between the eyes. Needless to say, Azzimie was both shocked and relieved to see Brus at his door. He didn't know he even knew where he lived. Brus, like the mumps or the measles, didn't wait for an invitation to come into Azzimie's apartment and life. He stepped over the threshold that night and instantly announced his intentions.

"Why are you letting that barbarian hold you on a leash? The money could be ours and we don't have to kiss his Cuban ass for it." Brus, of German descent and wearing a mustache last worn by possibly the most evil person in the history of the planet, had complete disdain for Miguel and his Cuban heritage.

Azzimie was immediately suspicious of Brus. He even considered the possibility that he was sent by Miguel to test him. After all, Azzimie was most vulnerable; he could still feel the barrel of that Mauser pushing against the back of his head as he waited to see his brains come spilling out of his forehead and onto the floor, in what he was sure would be his last earthly glimpse. However, while Azzimie always thought Brus was more than just a tad strange, he also felt an undeniable connection to his persona. So as Brus began to unravel his twisted plan, Azzimie actually thought there might be some sense in it. He elected to say nothing, but instead walked to the kitchen and sat on a chair at the table and listened.

"We can do this," he said. "We sweat the location of the counterfeit out of him and then waste him—easy as that. I got a friend that works at the GM plant in Harrison. He's in charge of the boiler room. We can take him there and 'poof', he's up in smoke."

Azzimie and Brus had no idea who or what Miguel was about or who he worked for. As far as the two of them knew, Miguel was just sitting on a stash of counterfeit notes. It never dawned on either of them that there was a second print in the works or that there was a conspiracy of historical proportion brewing.

As a result, on that Saturday night when Miguel came rapping at Azzimie's door, Azzimie decided it was the time to muscle up with Brus and take a stab, literally, at Miguel's fortune. All he had to do was get word to Brus that he and Miguel were heading to the bowling alley. The easiest way to do that was to call him on the telephone. And since Azzimie had spoken to Julia earlier that afternoon and knew she and LJ were working that night, he calmly walked to the kitchen wall phone and called Brus while Miguel was convinced he was calling the girls at the bowling alley. Brus instantly caught on and assured Azzimie he would be there to cover his back. Neither of them had a specific plan for that night, but Azzimie, terrified his days were numbered, knew that if they were going to move on Miguel, it had to be very soon.

So as Miguel and Azzimie rode in Marilyn to the bowling alley that Saturday night, each of them had big plans for their own future that also included a lone, dark, destination for the other. Brus, on a perpendicular course destined to collide with both of them, rushed from his apartment to the bowling alley. None of them knew how it would all turn out, each of them failing to recognize there were opposing forces in the universe that would undermine their best-laid plans. Only history and a long, long, look back would reveal the consequences.

CHAPTER 41

MAYBE I CAN EVEN GET 'EM TO WASTE THAT LITTLE NAZI.

MIGUEL WAS SADDENED WHEN HE pulled Marilyn into the bowling alley parking lot. At first he had no idea whatsoever why he felt that way; he seldom felt that emotion. There was no apparent reason for his anguish. He certainly didn't give a shit about Azzimie. One more pile of bones on his head was of no concern to him. However, he found himself confronted with issues he never faced before.

Miguel actually liked the life he established for himself in the States. It certainly wasn't what he envisioned, nor was it the style he intended. But it did provide a certain amount of stability that offered comfort and happiness to his hectic existence, like ballast that kept a sailboat from capsizing and sinking in rough waters. He was able to navigate difficult days knowing he would return to his apartment and Marilyn at night or even to the bowling alley for comfort food and familiarity. It was a life style never achieved before, no matter how long he stayed in a place, yet he was able to develop such feelings while being in the States for only a very short time. There wasn't even a woman involved. "I'm not even getting any pussy," he said to himself.

But then he started to reflect on that missing woman, and for the first time, he recognized that maybe pussy wasn't the measuring stick of intimacy with a woman. Maybe a woman was involved in his life even though there wasn't any sex. He recalled how he feels every time he drives to that stupid bowling alley, supposedly just to get something to eat, but really to look at LJ and spend some time actually talking to her. Where he came from, women weren't for talking to unless, of course, they were naked and you were on top of them. Then you could say whatever was required and not be accountable for it.

These thoughts ran through Miguel's head as he drove through the parking lot and pulled up in front of the red "lounge" sign. He turned the rumble of the side pipes off and sat there in silence for a few seconds before Azzimie pushed open the passenger door and broke Miguel's concentration. It was alright though. He snapped to and jumped "off" of Marilyn, as he liked to think of it. He practically lunged though the lounge door, knowing he was there for only a short time because he had a destiny to fulfill in a bakery in Belleville at 9:00.

They sat at Miguel's favorite table in the corner, with a clear view of the bar and the girls as they wiggled their way around the room. LJ came right up to them and gave them an extra special hello. She put the palms of both her hands on her knees and bent all the way forward. Her perfect boobs spilled out over the top of her t-shirt all the way to the tan line just above her nipples. The maneuver was certainly a tip builder and just couldn't happen by accident.

"What can I get you boys?" The answer was obvious, but both Miguel and Azzimie were sure it wasn't on the menu, so they both ordered the usual—a couple of cheese steaks and two draft beers.

Miguel's mind was fully occupied, moving from fantasizing about LJ to wondering about the print to the future uncertainty of life with his new friends. As a result, he failed to notice that when Azzimie left the table to go to the bathroom, he went out the kitchen door instead. In a less distracted state, Miguel would have never missed it. But on that night, he did. Brus was already waiting around back.

"What's happening here?" Brus asked as he pulled a Lucky Strike from beneath his toothbrush upper lip.

Azzimie was so electrified he could hardly speak. Brus offered him a smoke, hoping to calm him down—he had to hold Azzimie's trembling hand and light the cigarette for him. After taking a bottomless breath that swelled his concave chest to nearly normal dimensions, Azzimie was prepared to discuss the situation.

"Talk to me," Brus whispered as he cocked his head and moved close to Azzimie's face so he could look him in the eyes.

"I don't fuckin' know, but something's up. He came rappin' at my door and when I told him we should come see the girls, he looked at his watch before he said, 'okay.' Something's goin' on. I think he's gonna try to kill me tonight. I just got that feelin'."

Brus displayed no reaction at all. He didn't even un-cock his head. He just kept sucking on the Lucky Strike while holding it between the thumb and forefinger of his left hand, palm up, European style. Brus's chilled demeanor didn't reassure Azzimie, so he continued his call for action.

"We gotta move on this motherfucker now, tonight, before he whacks me."

Brus finally dropped the cigarette and crushed it with his right foot, clad in a black, army jump-boot laced only half way up and in desperate need of a shine. He was trying to slow Azzimie down.

"How do we know his next move ain't a cash move? We should stay close and see where it goes. He's a dead man no matter what. If we can score before we waste him, then why not wait? We just gotta be sure he keeps you in the loop for now and decides to kill you after and not before it goes down. See what I mean?"

"Yeah, sure, I gotcha. I'm gonna get fuckin' dead and you're gonna be right behind me! What, you gonna bring the shovel to dig the fuckin' hole?" Azzimie was now talking and jumping up and down in cadence with every word.

"Relax. When you leave here, I'll be on your tail. We'll see what's up and take it from there."

"In what...that green piece-a-shit Plymouth? Everybody in town knows that car, including Miguel. You'll get burned in a fuckin' flash. And besides, the way he drives, you'll never be able to keep up with Marilyn." Azzimie was nearing hysteria now.

"Okay, okay...I'll get LJ's car. I'll be there. You just go the fuck back in there and stay with him until he makes his move." Brus was still trying to calm Azzimie down, but with little success.

Azzimie wasn't happy with the arrangement, but he knew it was the only plan they had. He was certain in his heart that Miguel was going to kill him, sooner or later. So, he grabbed another Lucky Strike from Brus and lit it as he headed back inside.

When he arrived back at the table, the cheese steaks and beers were already there. Miguel was deep in thought and barely even looked up at Azzimie when he sat down. It was times like that, when Miguel didn't even acknowledge that he existed, that Azzimie feared for his life the most. He had no idea what the experts called his affliction; he only knew that Miguel thought he was the absolute center of the universe and everybody else was there merely to keep the planets revolving around him. No person or thing had any purpose to exist if not to serve or accommodate Miguel. That's why Azzimie knew it was only a matter of convenience for Miguel that he was still alive, and Miguel would certainly kill him at almost any time.

Miguel ate his cheese steak without uttering a single word, never taking his eyes off LJ. He was obsessed with her. They sat there longer than usual, quietly drinking several beers. Then, all of a sudden, just as Azzimie was starting to relax a little, Miguel jumped up and said, "com' on, we gotta go."

"Go where?" As soon as the question rolled off his lips, Azzimie knew it was the wrong response.

For good measure, Miguel gave him a look that would have caused a terminal brain hemorrhage in a more sensitive man. There was nothing more to say. Azzimie just got up and followed him to the door. Without looking too obvious, he tried to scan the room to be sure Brus knew what was happening. Thankfully, he caught a glimpse of him in the doorway between the bar and the kitchen. He must have seen what was going on because he was working LJ real hard.

"Com' on give him the fuckin' keys," Azzimie said to himself, trying to communicate telepathically with LJ.

The last thing he saw was LJ heading for the ladies room and Brus scampering toward the back door. Brus flashed him a nod letting him know it was all set. Azzimie knew that if Brus couldn't con those keys from LJ he would be suckin' on the barrel-end of that Mauser before the night was through.

Miguel and Azzimie got back into Marilyn, with Miguel not saying another word. Azzimie decided it was about time he started asking questions to try and figure out what was happening. For all he knew, he might be on his own for the rest of the night and if he was going to talk himself out of a bullet in the head, he might as well start now.

"Okay, Migs, what's going on? Where we goin'?"

"We're going to finish the job." Miguel had no hesitation in telling Azzimie what was happening, to a point. He decided to tell him about the print because it would make things a lot easier throughout the night. It was also much more amusing to Miguel to see Azzimie all excited, thinking he was going to strike it rich, only to finally realize he was going to get capped in the morning instead. So, without Azzimie even asking what job Miguel was referring to, he laid it all out for him.

"We're going finish printing the counterfeit. You remember the counterfeit, don't you?" Miguel said in a sarcastic tone laced with the twinge of violence that Azzimie was all too familiar with.

"Finish?" Azzimie asked, fearing that 'finish' meant there wasn't any more counterfeit left and unless they followed Brus's hunch and let Miguel finish business, there would be no pay-off in it for them. Still not sure how all this was going to happen, he tried to nonchalantly check the passenger side, rear view mirror to see if Brus was back there. He would have been happy to see either car, at that point, but there was no sign of him.

Then Miguel continued. "That's right, amigo. You and that half-breed gang of misfits blew the entire initial print. Now we have to print more and change the serial numbers before they can be distributed."

Miguel told that story to Azzimie, knowing only a portion of it was true. He wanted him to think there was going to be a major distribution of the notes so he would angle throughout the night to get a spot in the chain. He figured that would keep him occupied, compliant, and maybe even useful, although he doubted the last.

Azzimie was going for it—hook, line and sinker. He even started to think that maybe he was wrong about Miguel's plans and maybe there was a future for him in this escapade. He was already beginning to connive how he could distribute the queer through his many and various contacts in Newark, Irvington and East Orange. He figured a thirty point spread with five to the street punks, fifteen to Miguel—leaving an easy ten points for him. He could see himself moving out of that basement apartment and maybe even getting a Vette like Marilyn. He did have one problem though, and that might or might not be in a car somewhere behind them.

Somehow, Azzimie had to get the message to Brus that he was right and they had to let Miguel finish the print before they moved on him—or maybe not move on him at all if there was more to be made. Azzimie knew Brus would like that because being told he's right puckers his little mustache and makes him very happy. Simultaneously, he was already trying to scheme a way to cut Brus out of the entire deal. If Miguel wasn't going to kill him, he didn't need Brus anymore.

"Maybe I can even get 'im to waste that little Nazi," Azzimie thought to himself.

Just as he held that thought, Azzimie looked in the mirror and there it was—a pale blue Chevy Bel Air. It was about three car-lengths back. He could see the shadow of LJ's hair in the driver's seat and just the shadow of what had to be the top of Brus's head in the passenger seat.

"I should have known she would never let that wimp take her car. Now what am I gonna do with her?" Azzimie thought to himself, no longer looking in the mirror so as not to tip off Miguel.

Azzimie was at a complete loss. He had no idea how to handle the situation. In the last ten minutes, he went from being certain Miguel was going to kill him that very night and Brus was his knight in shining armor, through a complete reversal. He was now convinced that Miguel is on the verge of a tremendous score and he's right there to get cut in. But what does he do with the car lurking in the shadows behind them? While he was feeling safer with Miguel, he knew if he got even a hint that Azzimie and Brus were in cahoots, Miguel would for sure waste both of them. But there wasn't much Azzimie could do about it now. All he could do was let Brus and LJ follow them to wherever they were going and then look for an opportunity to slip away and call Brus off the hunt.

Azzimie was gullible enough to think he could convince Brus to give it up and go home so he could make the biggest score of his life while flying solo, while cutting Brus out like a puss-laden splinter—never happen. What's more, he never even gave a thought to what LJ being there added to the blend. That's like not realizing what chips of chocolate did to plain old vanilla ice cream. But Azzimie pressed ahead anyway.

"Okay, so where to?" Azzimie asked.

"You like Italian bread?"

"Sure, so what?"

"We're goin' to a bakery," Miguel finally revealed.

"Oh yeah? Where's it at?" Azzimie asked, not yet realizing he was never going to get an answer, and he didn't. So he tried another approach.

"How long we gonna be there?"

"As long as it takes." Now Azzimie was getting somewhere. He figured that meant they were there for the night and, it also meant they were printing up a new batch.

"Yes!" he said triumphantly to himself.

It wasn't but a few minutes later that they rode past La Ragazza Bakery in Belleville. Azzimie knew the place; it was perfect. There was nothing suspicious about the lights being on in a bakery all Saturday night. After all, Sunday morning after church was the biggest day of the week. The baker had to work all night to fill his shelves for the morning rush. Only thing, on this night there was gonna be a lot of shakin' to go along with the bakin'.

CHAPTER 42

"YOU WANT SOME FRESH BAKED BREAD, DOLLY?"

MIGUEL PARKED MARILYN ON A quiet street around the corner where he thought she would be safe from the local dagos. He could tell it was an Italian neighborhood by the number of Madonnas—affectionately known as "Mary on a half shell"—on the front lawns.

Young dagos were crazy about Vettes. They wouldn't piss on the tires of a Mercedes costing three times as much, but park a Vette in the neighborhood and every dago dude gets a hard on until he steals it. Miguel believed that Marilyn wasn't safe on any street that collectively bought more than two quarts of olive oil a month. On that night, however, he had little choice other than to leave his beloved Marilyn, unchaperoned, in a neighborhood he knew was full of fiberglass predators. So he put her under a nice, bright, streetlight. And for added security, he popped the hood, took the number one spark plug wire off the engine and put it in his pocket.

Azzimie, who silently stood by as Miguel prepared Marilyn for her wait, followed Miguel down the block and around the corner. La Ragazza bakery was in the next block, on the corner. A small, dimly-lit, homemade sign hung on the front of the building. While the neighborhood was primarily residential, it wasn't unusual to find a family-run restaurant, bakery or even *una cantina* (a cool basement where salami, prosciutto, cappicola and provolone were stored) being operated out of a family home.

Most of the homes on the street were "row" houses, all attached in a long row down the street. Luckily, La Ragazza was the last house on the block, but more importantly, it was a free standing building, surrounded by remnant trees and bushes from before the neighborhood emerged from the woods. It's hard to imagine, but it wasn't too long ago, before Newark began its sprawl, that places like Belleville and Bloomfield were park-like suburban communities.

The red brick building, originally designed as a house, had only two, modest-sized windows in the front, and two similar windows on each side of the building. As a result, the interior activity was somewhat concealed from public view. Although it was obvious that the lights were on inside and something was going on in the building, no telltale signs of any conduct not wholly consistent with the operation of a bakery on a Saturday night were visible.

Miguel, with Azzimie still following like a dutiful puppy, walked past the front of the building and around the corner to the rear. A small stoup with three steps, on the back of the building, led to the back door. Miguel walked directly to the six panel, traditional wooden back door, and twisted the unlocked, old brass knob. Miguel wasn't surprised, nor did he hesitate, as he confidently pushed it open. Once inside, he descended the cellar steps immediately to his right as if his arrival was expected. Azzimie correctly deduced that this was the location of the plant and followed closely behind like a six-year-old with mom at the A&P.

The door wasn't unlocked by accident, nor was it unattended. From a small clump of birch trees near the back property line came the telltale pant of a mammoth biped, whose lungs struggled to oxygenate enough blood to fill a 50-gallon Jack Daniels cask just to keep the creature upright. Canevecchio, simultaneously sucking on a Benson and Hedges, watched the prowlers from the time they first approached the building. He concluded they must be the guys Frankie told him would be showing up when he sent him out there about a half-hour ago to keep an eye on things. Although he only expected one, they looked right, and the fact that nobody plugged either of them when they went inside was a good sign they were expected.

Canevecchio waited a few minutes to finish his smoke and to be sure all was well. Then, just as he crushed out his cigarette, he was surprised by two more guys heading for the same door. He held his ground and soon found that things were even more unusual than he could have imagined.

"Fuck, those ain't guys," he said to himself. "One's a chic for sure," he concluded with amazing alacrity, considering one of them was bare legged and wearing a mini- skirt. He was equally certain that these next two looked wrong—all wrong. While both of them stopped at the bakery's back porch, the chic stood on her tippy toes to peer thru one of the two top windowpanes of the door. She even opened the door slightly to eavesdrop on what was happening. While Canevecchio wasn't sure what to do, and Frankie wasn't there to tell him, he knew he had to do something. His first thought was to whack both of them, although he didn't have a gun, because he never carried one; he really never needed one anymore. He could just grab each of them and break their scrawny necks, but he was unexplainably reluctant to do so. He knew that Frankie wouldn't approve of just killing them, so he did the only other thing he could think to do. Moving in surprisingly smooth and swift strides, he approached the unexpected guests and grabbed both of them by the scruff of their necks.

"Hey pal, watch it," was Brus's reaction, while LJ reached up with her elbows high so she could grab his forearm with both hands. At that point, it wasn't clear who had who, even though Canevecchio was three times her size. Canevecchio might have had this little girl by the scruff of the neck, but he knew it wasn't the size of the dog in the fight, but rather the size of the fight in the dog that mattered. He was careful. He didn't want to have to kill her. Brus, on the other hand, had no fight in him at all; he tried to talk his way out of the behemoth's grip. The more he yelped, the higher Canevecchio lifted him up off the ground. LJ was holding onto Canevecchio's huge arm to take the weight and pressure off her throat and windpipe. She was ready to let him have it with one of her CFM's right in the nuts, but she thought better of it. LJ actually feared Canevecchio was going to hang Brus, so she stopped struggling, hoping to calm the situation down a tad. Even though she knew this was a very dangerous beast, she felt he wouldn't actually hurt them unless provoked. She was half right.

The door to the bakery was already ajar. Canevecchio, not being certain what to do with the two vermin he had in his grip, pushed them through the doorway. When they crossed the threshold of the outside door, he let them both go with just a tiny shove. Inasmuch as they were already on their tippy toes on the landing to the cellar steps, it was more than sufficient. They both tumbled ass-over-elbows down the steps, spilling out on the cellar floor like two broken sacks of potatoes. Miguel, standing at the bottom of the steps, still making his own introduction, was startled and actually started to reach for the Mauser. I, on the other hand, thought it was Christmas morning when I saw that red and strawberry blonde hair splash all over the cellar floor like a fine cabernet overflowing a beautifully sculptured crystal goblet. When LJ came to a rest, she tossed her *testarossa* back hard to get the hair out of her eyes; I immediately recognized her. It took me a bit longer—maybe because I couldn't take my eyes off of LJ—but I eventually suspected Brus as another Las Vegas player.

Frankie and I were just beginning to work out who Miguel and Azzimie were when these two literally dropped in. I was standing behind the press, starting to attach the back plate and mix the green ink onto the roller wheel, while Frankie was on the other side of the press, closer to the door, laying out some ground rules to Miguel and Azzimie. No sooner had all that happened when the stairway begin to quake as Canevecchio sashayed down the steps like Cassius Clay after he beat that Polack Zigzy something-or-other in the Olympics. Frankie was really pissed off. I was lucky he was focused on Canevecchio. He didn't notice I was completely captivated by LJ, who was so elusive in Las Vegas but was now spread out on the floor at my feet. Jesus, she was the most beautiful thing I had ever seen. Too bad she was a perp who obviously kept very bad company.

"Cane', Cane'. What the fuck are you doin'? Who the fuck are these guys?" Frankie said in a tone I had never heard him use to Canevecchio before. Actually, I don't think he even noticed that one of "these guys" was a chic.

"That one's a chic," Canevecchio pointed out in a serious but almost comical tone.

"No shit. Whadda you know? I got eyes. I know that's a chic, but what's she doin' here on the plant floor?"

"Ponte! They came right after deese guys and dey were lookin' in da windows. I figured it was a set up. I woulda whacked'em, but I thought you would be pissed?"

If there was ever such a thing as a gorilla with a puppy dog face, Canevecchio was it that night. Frankie just couldn't stay angry at him, but he did make a suggestion or two.

"I'm gonna get your fuckin' head examined as soon as we finish this job. Did you ever think they could be cops? Are they packin'?" Frankie was obviously still agitated.

The puppy dog face disappeared as Canevecchio terrified even me, and there was a thousand pound printing press between us. He grabbed Brus and lifted him completely up off the ground in one motion.

"You a cop? You packin' heat?"

"No, No. We're not the fuckin' law. Ask them," Brus pled without being able to identify who the "them" was. It didn't make a difference though. Miguel immediately turned to Azzimie, now certain he made a mistake in not killing him a week ago.

"They must have followed us here. Isn't that right, Azzimie?" Miguel said, looking at Azzimie, but clearly speaking to the rest of the room. Miguel continued.

"It appears that you and your amigos here had a plan of your own. Too bad, too bad," he said, now looking Azzimie right in the eyes.

Frankie didn't care about a response or an explanation. It was clear that he felt T made him responsible to see to it that the print went smoothly. He had lots of questions, especially since no one bothered to tell him about the debacle in Las Vegas. He had absolutely no reason to know where all these other guys fit into the caper. I, on the other hand, had some of those answers. But I knew enough to keep my mouth shut and just keep mixing the ink with the special hardener my new beatnik friend Ron Ron said was essential to a successful print.

"Who are these guys and why are they here?" Frankie barked in Miguel's face. "T never told me about anybody else other than the buyer and that's you. Right, amigo?" Frankie said, looking at Miguel with a tone and stance that made Canevecchio appear like a lap dog.

Azzimie had the poor judgment to begin to respond, not realizing Frankie wasn't interested in any response he could offer. Miguel, a street animal with plenty of moxie, took the cue.

"That's correct," he said using his best English, deciding it was safer to begin his response on a positive note. He knew he had the Mauser in his waistband, but he also realized he would most likely need a Howitzer Cannon to stop the likes of Frankie and Canevecchio. At that point, he had no idea who I was—he was still expecting to see T there. And things were happening so fast, we didn't get the chance to tell him T wasn't coming and that I was the printer. Miguel, a historian of violence, knew that it's never smart to take sides too early in a fight. It's always better to see who grabs the broken beer bottle first. He continued his sell.

"I'm the buyer. These people are nobody. Do what you want with them."

At first Azzimie looked like a kid who just found out there was no Santa Claus. When he realized what Miguel's disclaimer meant to his immediate well-being, he just collapsed on the floor sobbing. LJ stood up straight as if to say, "Hey, I'm not with these guys," and Brus gave him the "You can't do this to me...Don't you know who I am?" look.

"Where's the genuine?" Frankie demanded, ignoring all the other histrionics in the room.

"In the car," which explained why Miguel had the spark plug wire in his pocket.

"Go get it, now!"

"Hold on a minute. How do I know this is all on the level? Let me see the product first and then I'll show the genuine." Miguel knew that approach wasn't going to work, but he had to give it a try. His instincts were right—it didn't.

Frankie didn't respond, at least not verbally anyway. The silence was homicidal. He didn't move a muscle in his body except for a very subtle "eyes right" that even Ray Charles would have been able to see as a wakeup call to the 350-lb. gorilla in the room. Canevecchio caught it; so did Miguel. He didn't need to wait for the gorilla to react.

"Okay, just to prove I'm on the level, I'll get the genuine," Miguel volunteered.

Frankie still didn't move a muscle. Miguel scampered up the steps and out the back door. By this time, the bakers upstairs started to work and the place started to fill with a bouquet of fresh baked bread. It was absolutely tantalizing. Once the door shut behind Miguel, Frankie turned his attention to LJ and Brus. I continued to keep busy getting ready to print the back of the $100 notes.

"You two sit on the floor over there," Frankie told them as he pointed to a section of the cellar, where a steel column was cemented into the floor and extended vertically, and was nailed to the wooden floor joists above. Frankie made them sit on the floor, back-to-back, with the pole between them. He went to his bag and, to my amazement, pulled out two pairs of handcuffs. He handcuffed LJ's left hand to Brus's right and her right hand to Brus's left so they were cuffed together, back-to-back with the column between them. They both started to look scared and less brash.

It wasn't but a minute or two when Miguel came back down the stairs with a large, fully stuffed duffel bag over his shoulder. He plopped it down on the floor just at the bottom of the steps and asked the question I had been anticipating for days.

"Where the fuck is T, and who the fuck is that guy?" Miguel spewed, accentuating his concern with a seldom-used vulgarity, while pointing menacingly at me.

As I opened my mouth to answer, Frankie once again established that he was in charge.

"T's in the hospital. That's his godson. He's got T's plates and he's gonna finish the print. He's a helluva printer. You got a problem with that?"

"Jeeesus, Frankie. Why don't you just set this guy on fire," I thought to myself. It was like the Guatemalan Gardner who got caught in the sack with the boss's wife and then demands that the cuckold husband mix him a drink. I was ready for the entire caper to crash. I also figured that this guy was packin' heat, while I was confident that Frankie and Canevecchio weren't. I had a wrench in my hand that I used to tighten down the plate and I softly set it on the side of the printer. I slowly raised my left leg and propped my left foot against a bar on my side of the printer. It was the first time that night that I was glad I didn't take Carmine's advice. The 5-shot-Detective-Special in my left boot was like having a 100-mile-an-hour southpaw relief pitcher in the bullpen; if needed, I could call him in to mow down the opposition. I kept inching my right hand closer to the boot, hoping that if the shit hit the fan I would be able to draw and fire with a nice 1000-lb. press between me and Miguel.

Then, to my complete astonishment and relief, it was all over in an instant. Miguel simply said, "Okay. We're still gonna finish business tonight and be on our way, right?"

"Absolutely," was all Frankie needed to say.

Miguel just nodded his head slowly. He picked up the bag with the genuine and walked over to an old, metal, kitchen table and chairs on the other side of the room. Looking back on it, Miguel took the only play he had. He knew he was being covered by his new associates at The FBI and his immediate payoff would be the results of the print. If he made a stink about T not being there, all he would get would be a busted print and everybody would go home with what they came with. That was a stone-cold loser for Miguel. So he decided to play his hand light, let us print and wait for the cavalry to rescue him and his cut of the queer.

"Hey, anybody hungry?" Canevecchio cheerfully inquired as if there was nothing more important going on.

Frankie just rolled his eyes and shook his head. By this time, I had successfully buttered the print roller with the mixed green ink and Ron Ron's hardener, and the press was humming away, rolling out sheets of partially completed $100 bills. If T was right, I had about thirty minutes before I needed to re-ink the roller. Naturally, I already knew how I wanted to spend my time. I wanted to try to get to know LJ better before I had her hauled off to jail. Frankie was with Miguel, looking at the genuine in the duffle bag. Then all of a sudden, Canevecchio, who I guess felt bad for roughin' up LJ, walked across the room and knelt down next to her.

"You want some fresh baked bread, dolly?" he asked in his best suave and debonair tone.

At first, she looked at him like he was completely insane, but then she changed her tune. I kept a watch from behind the press like a voyeur. LJ nodded her head. Then, as Canevecchio went upstairs to get the bread, I walked around the press and approached her.

"Have we met before?" she asked as her gray eyes softened and revealed a deeper intellect than was apparent from her initial entrance into the room. Her look refreshed my memory of her from that day in Las Vegas when she not only outran me, but outsmarted me as well. I immediately started to connive how I could drag this night out so I could get to know her better. Then reality bit.

"Hey, kid, I wanna talk to you." Frankie had that, "let's get down to business look." He was right. You would have thought that he was the agent; he's checking the genuine, while I'm flirting with a perp. In the meantime, there were probably a dozen Secret Service Agents cruising the neighborhood, waiting for the signal to take this caper down and ruin everybody's day, or even worse. Little did I know, that the bad guys on the inside were the least of my impending problems. It was the bad guys on the outside, who were about to crash the party, that were going to get us all nearly killed .

CHAPTER 43

IT WASN'T LONG BEFORE HE PUT HIS NEW PARTNERS TO THE TEST.

WHILE ALL HELL WAS BREAKING loose in the cellar, Carmine and the raid team were trying to settle in for a long, boring night. It was like being a fireman—when the bell rang, you had to be 100 percent. But until then, it took all your strength and imagination to stay awake, let alone alert. Every agent developed a unique ritual to get ready for a siege like this. You knew that if things went well, you would be confined to your car for nearly twelve hours. Everyone had his own priorities. For some it was food, some music and still others comfort. But everybody had to be prepared to outsmart the perps.

It was expected that any perp in a counterfeiting case, big enough to involve the Secret Service, had to have an organization operating with him. That meant co-conspirators with distinct specialties, one of which was counter-surveillance. Being able to beat a wire on a telephone, in a room or a car was essential to a successful new-age print and distribution. Before the age of electronic surveillance, all a good agent had to rely on was his wits, a hunch and two clever disguises—the entire caper turned on the agent's ability to maintain a good physical surveillance. If you wanted to know where the perp lived, you followed him. If you wanted to know who he hung with, where he hung and what he did, you followed him. The only pathway to answer almost any question that might arise in the investigation was physical surveillance. To succeed, you needed a good, reliable car and a couple of disguises; a second agent to take some of the heat off would also help.

However, in a quasi-new-age caper like this, the Secret Service tried to combine their surveillance options with an undercover inside, a wire in the room and a four-car moving surveillance team to keep an eyeball on any moving target. A well-armed raid team ready to go bang, bang, splat, splat all over the neighborhood was the final solution. The perps were fully aware of this and, as a result, developed their own style of bursting a bust. On that night, Carmine had six cars ready to roll. He had four undercover cars with one agent in each to do the moving surveillance and stay close to the bakery in a revolving pattern. He had to keep them on the move because a stationary surveillance would certainly attract the attention of the Belleville police, and that would only make the situation more dangerous. If they showed up at the raid, there would be a better-than-even chance they would shoot one of our guys. He also had two traditional Ford Crown Vics, with four agents each, ready to pounce when the signal was given.

Even with all six cars constantly on the move, there had to be some small intervals where there wasn't an eyeball on the bakery. That was tolerable to Carmine because he had the joint wired. As he promised, the TSD guys were able to get into the bakery cellar and wire the basement. But, as he predicted, the wire in the cellar was virtually useless when the printing press was running. Luckily, between a few quick surveillances of the back door and monitoring pieces of conversation from the wire in the cellar, Carmine wasn't completely in the dark. He knew a couple of unexpected players were on the scene, but other than that, the caper was on track. He figured I could sort it out and hold it all together. If things got too far off track, he knew I could just turn off the press, give the code word and they would move in. As far as I knew, he was right.

It was approaching midnight; the press had been running for about three hours with only some minor adjustments. I finished printing all the backs of the notes, switched out the plates and filled the press with a perfect, black ink mixture to start the basic front, being sure to mix in the hardener Ron Ron insisted I use. Since the press was off, and I knew Carmine was listening intently, I tried to give him an update without telling everybody in the cellar that I was talking to the Secret Service who was waiting outside to arrest them all. It wasn't difficult because most of the players were in various stages of slumber. Canevecchio and Brus were pretty much out. Actually, Canevecchio's snoring was almost as loud as the press, which made me wonder if Carmine was getting anything at all from the wire. Miguel was in the far corner, still sitting with his money and very much awake. So was Frankie. He was sitting in an old stuffed chair just on the other side of the press. He had discovered an old baseball glove and baseball on a shelf and was passing the time by tossing the ball into the glove, which made a slapping sound with each throw. I called Frankie over to the press, showed him the product that was completed and explained the next step. I figured that Carmine could hear the conversation and would know the print was proceeding as planned. While Frankie listened politely, he was almost entirely focused on Miguel, never taking his eyes off him, which was probably a break for me.

While we in New Jersey all thought we were very clever and surreptitious, The FBI in Washington had our number since the minute we started the print. By 9:00 that night, AD was putting into effect The FBI's own brand of justice, right from his overstuffed leather chair in the Assistant Director's office.

Ritter—with no other life to go to—was still at work. Having no family, or even friends, made it a simple choice for him to stay at his desk in the only place he really felt he was wanted. Lots of The FBI Headquarters staff worked late into the night—a byproduct of the paranoia that consumed nearly every personality in the building. Most of the high level supervisors were too insecure to leave the building or even consider going home—while The Director and his henchmen were still on the prowl—let alone close their eyes and sleep. So on that night, just as Tom Ritter began to think about going home, his inside line rang. His immediate reaction was relief that he was in his office to answer it.

"Ritter? This is AD. One of our surveillance teams in Jersey just confirmed that 23 Foxtrot and all the players are hunkered down in some Guinea bakery. You better get up there. I want that Cuban nurtured and sent on his way to New Orleans. Got it?"

"I'll get right on it," Ritter dutifully replied, knowing what was required of him even before AD continued.

"And take Whitaker. Let him grab 23 Foxtrot for debriefing. It'll make him feel useful, and you can see to it that the Cuban gets on the right track. The two of you can handle it—it's just a couple of dago counterfeiters. We released our surveillance team to avoid entanglement with the Secret Service who is also on the scene, so you need to re-establish contact with 23 Foxtrot when you arrive in the area. The Cuban knows what to expect—he'll be looking for us to show up. Keep a low profile but protect our new Cuban investment."

Ritter listened without uttering a single word while AD went on.

"Keep me, and only me in the loop, understand? And by the way, there's a second player in the car with 23 Foxtrot. We don't need any witnesses to this move. Let Whitaker take care of it. Do whatever you need to do. You'll be on your own, but don't fuck this up."

"What about the Secret Service? What do we tell them?" Ritter finally queried.

" Nothing. We'll tell them what we want to tell them later. This is national security—we'll pack 'em a lunch and they can eat it or go hungry and get nothing. Understand?" AD said as he hung-up the phone.

"Yes, Sir."

Ritter knew exactly what AD was telling him. No one, not even The Director, was in the loop. He was to tell Whitaker to scoop 23 Foxtrot and get out of the game, while he saw to it that the Cuban got what he needed and was safely on his way to New Orleans, where he could start cooking for The Bureau. The second player in the car with 23 Foxtrot was expendable, and headquarters would deal with the Secret Service later. "National Security" was a trump card that The Bureau played to call everybody off. The Secret Service would have no alternative other than just let it go. He wrote down the name and address of the bakery, and hung up the already dead telephone line.

"La Ragazza. I wonder what that means," Ritter thought to himself as he stared at the note he had just written and reflected on what just happened.

When the phone had first rung, Ritter's hands started to tremble because he knew it had to be something relatively important to get an inside call that late; he never expected the call he got. Ever since his little pow-wow with Miguel at Yankee Stadium, he knew something would eventually develop; he had no idea it would turn so quickly.

Ritter was nearly paralyzed with anticipation. Going out to parlay with this guy was one thing; actually making a move on him in the field was something else. It's not that Ritter was a coward—he wasn't nearly as afraid of getting hurt or killed as he was of failure. His entire being was wrapped up in a very tight little bow around his position at The Bureau. Without it, he was nothing at all. At this stage in his life, he would have probably worked at The Bureau for nothing and lived in a cardboard box in the park. He pulled his .38 Smith & Wesson revolver from his desk drawer, blew off the dust, slipped it into his waistband holster and headed for the door.

It was a five-hour drive to Newark, maybe less, if one drove like a cop. Ritter called Whitaker at home and told him the parts of the plan he needed to know. Whitaker lived in Maryland, north of DC, so he took his "G" car and got directly on I-95, heading for the Delaware Memorial Bridge and the New Jersey Turnpike to Newark. Ritter was about twenty minutes behind him. They both had Bureau radios in their cars, so they planned to hook up at The FBI Field Office in the Federal Building, on Broad Street, in Newark.

As it turned out, the drive typically took longer than planned. Due to an unanticipated scenic tour of Belleville while trying to find the obscure La Raggaza bakery, Ritter and Whitaker wound up at the plant around 3:30 a.m. Not knowing how to get in touch with either the Cuban or 23 Foxtrot, Ritter decided to park his "G" car around the corner and walked through the tree line to the rear of the bakery. After settling under a tree with a portable radio, Ritter let Whitaker—still in his car about three blocks away—know what was happening. He hoped that Miguel would surmise they were there to make good on their bargain and would eventually make whatever move was needed to establish contact with them. Neither Ritter nor Whitaker gave any thought to the possibility that the Secret Service could be looming around the neighborhood—good thing.

Miguel's intuitive survival instincts didn't disappoint. It wasn't long before he decided to put his new partners to the test.

CHAPTER 44

"IT ONLY TOOK YOU SO LONG BECAUSE YOU DON'T HAVE OVARIES, SILLY BOY."

IT WAS ABOUT 4 A.M. and I had completed nearly $15 million in what, I had to admit, were pretty good looking counterfeit $100 Federal Reserve Notes. Everything was going smoothly. The printing pretty much took care of itself once I got the press rolling. All the basic backs and fronts were complete. I was continuing to run the bills through the press a third time to insert the green Treasury Seal and serial numbers. It was a good plan. It required about an hour to complete each run. I had three to go. I figured I would finish right on target, between 7 a.m. and 8 a.m.

I had just started the third run when I noticed that LJ was awake. Her feet were flat on the floor, her knees bent. With her long legs pressed together, she could rest her head on the flat spot where her knees and thighs joined. Although her eyes were closed, I was certain she wasn't sleeping. I also knew this was probably the last chance I would have to talk to her. Even though I wasn't sure it was a good idea, I decided to go for it. There was a refrigerator along the wall behind the press that had some cold cokes in it—I grabbed two and made my approach.

"So, what's a girl like you doin' in a nice place like this?" I asked with a smile on my face and a coke outstretched in my hand, forgetting that she was still handcuffed to Brus and the pole.

With her knees bent vertical, her skirt was pulled tight against the outside of her well-defined, rock hard thighs. When I looked more carefully, she appeared much more of an athlete than a waitress. Her shoulders and arms were also well-defined. And her hands—covered with silky, smooth skin that was as inviting as a soft, white cotton quilt to a nap on a wintry Sunday afternoon—looked strong and purposeful. The contrast with the hot pink nail polish over a perfect manicure, together with a complimentary pedicure and toenail polish, was a bit incongruous. Naturally, it took discipline to notice these attributes. I first had to get past her black silk t-shirt with its plunging neckline that revealed a perfect set of full round, softball-like, 35 Ds. It was difficult not to have a delightful fantasy looking down at them as she sat on the floor. All-in-all, she was a passionate package. But there was more.

Her most alluring feature was her eyes. And it wasn't the gray-green color enhanced by exquisitely applied makeup; it was their warm radiance. They were positively radioactive. When she flashed them at me, I felt like I was baking under a burning tropical sun. The flesh on my face actually started to heat up and pulled tight against my bones. My mouth and lips dried as my tongue thickened. While my survival instinct told me to shield myself, my venereal instincts drew me closer. I was nearly transfixed and wanted to put my hand in the fire no matter how badly I would get burned.

"Thanks," she whispered with a kindly smile at my pathetic joke. I realized she couldn't hold the coke, so I held it to her lips at a slight angle so she could suck a little from the top of the bottle. I knelt down next to her before I collapsed from overstimulation. I had a thousand questions, but she seized the conversation instantly. Suddenly I was on the defensive.

"What's your name?"

"Jake. What's yours?" As if I didn't know.

"They call me LJ."

"LJ, what's that stand for?" I'd been waiting for an answer to that question for a long time.

"Nothing really, just LJ. So you're the printer, huh?" She didn't want to tell me what it really meant. I had to wait until later for that.

"Just the fill-in. My Godfather,T, is in the hospital, and he asked me to finish this job."

"You didn't make the first batch?" she asked, using a term better suited for cookies. How cute, I thought. It was also my chance to take the offensive.

"No. I hope I do as good a job as T did. Did you see the first notes?"

"Yes, uh huh. I went to Las Vegas with them."

"I heard about that trip. The cops busted you guys?"

"No, not me. I got chased by some old, outta shape cop. He was really pretty pathetic. It wasn't even that he was old and tired, but he wasn't very smart, either. He was really pretty stupid. I gave him the slip in a casino. Actually, I felt bad. I hope he didn't get fired or anything."

I was never so mortified in my life, before or since that day. I didn't know whether to throw my coke on her or take the cuffs off and challenge her to a fist fight. I kept my cool though and decided to defend my honor some other time.

"That's pretty funny. So the notes were good in the slots, huh?"

"Yup. They worked almost every time. Every once in a while you had to run them through twice, but most of the time you got a hundred credits first try. Those idiots at the casino just let you cash them out without even having to play at all. We made a boatload of money that trip. Too bad we lost it all."

It was a perfect admission from a perp, but I was disappointed to hear her say it. I guess I was hoping that somehow she had been kidnapped and taken to Las Vegas against her will. But that was only fantasy. She was in this up to her gold hoop earrings, which, by the way, I still wanted desperately to suck right off her ears.

"I'll tell T. He'll be glad to hear that."

That was all I could say. We lapsed into silence while I helped her sip a little more coke and I just stared at her. I was thoroughly confused. While she talked like a perp, there was something high-quality about her. It was like using a Rolex to hammer a nail; it'll do the job, but you just knew it was meant for something much better. I was actually thinking that maybe we could have dinner or something when she got out of jail. What a jerk I was.

"You seem familiar," she said, still licking the top of the coke bottle and running her tongue over her lips. The subliminal message was nearly disabling.

"Really, I look familiar to you? I can't imagine why."

"It's not exactly the way you look. You just seem familiar."

I was sure that topic was going nowhere good, so I changed the subject.

"So what are you doing here?"

"That creep Brus wanted my car. I really had no choice. If I didn't take him, he would have just taken it and I probably would've never seen it again. I can't afford to give it up, so here I am. Do you know what's going to happen here?"

"Everything will be cool. I'll finish the print in a couple of hours and everybody will be happy and be on their way. No sweat," I said, trying to console her. She did, however, have some questions of her own.

"So what's a nice guy like you doing in a cellar like this, with a cast of characters like these guys?" she asked, catching me completely by surprise. I wasn't able to create a new story on the spot, so I fed her the party line.

"I told you. T was the original printer, but he's in the hospital, so I told him I would finish the job." My explanation seemed okay to me, though not to her. Her response was direct.

"Why?"

"Whadda you mean—why?" I responded, while trying to analyze where she was going.

"Why? Why would you put yourself in a position to go to jail or even worse? What's the motivation? I mean what's in it for you?"

"Because T asked me to cover for him, help him out. Why wouldn't I do that?"

"Why would you?" She continued.

"Because he's family; it's about blood and dedication and commitment. Sometimes you put the well-being of others before yourself for reasons you can't explain. It's a human family phenomenon. Haven't you ever experienced that feeling? The feeling that you would jump in front of a train for someone or fall on a hand grenade or run out onto a bridge filled with Nazis to save a combat brother?" As I listened to the words come out of my mouth, I turned my head to see who was talking because I didn't recognize them as my own.

I looked at LJ for some recognition of understanding. She caught me looking.

"Oh, you think I don't get it. Let me guess—you just figured this out. It came to you in some revelation. It only took you this long because you don't have ovaries, silly boy."

I was beginning to wonder what it was that I liked about her, when she continued on.

"This is some macho guy thing you're trying to run by me, right? You guys think that if you show you give a shit about somebody else, then you're a fuckin' hero. That's only in the eyes of the other guys. Women don't see it like that," she said.

Having been male all my life, I never considered what she was about to tell me. But when I heard it, a page turned in my book of life's understandings. She continued.

"Women are life givers. We fully understand what it means to give life, protect life, nurture and grow life. We don't start wars; we talk. When's the last time you heard of a female serial killer? Never. Listen, *hombre*—a woman spends her entire youth struggling to look good in a bikini and be alluring to guys like you and your *paisani*, and then throws it all away to conceive, grow and give life to another. And in many cases, do it over and over again. We often do it all alone, with some guy like you in a local gin joint, smoking a stogie and braggin' about what he did."

"Woman," she went on, referring to the entire gender, "doesn't have to fall on a fuckin' hand grenade to prove she's willing to sacrifice for another; we spend a lifetime of sacrifice for the species. That's also why the woman is usually the faithful one in a relationship, while you pigs are always on the make. It hurts a woman to be unfaithful, dishonest and hurtful to the one she loves. Understand?"

Although I had never before been lectured about the virtues of women—at least not by one I was on fire for and desperately wanted to fuck—I did understand about the basic differences in the genders.

"So tell me, are you a hero?" she asked, without waiting for a response to her mini-lecture.

"No, but I do know a guy or two that might qualify."

"Well, if you do, you should shelter a guy like that and hope some of what he has will rub off on the rest of you slugs. Remember—the human condition is like old-time TV. It's not just black and white; there are a thousand shades of gray that complete the picture. So even if you're here and you fuck up a little, keep in mind that sometimes good people do bad things, but that doesn't make them bad people. At least that's what my mother always told me whenever I was too hard on my friends, and especially my kid brother, who was male all the way."

"So, are you telling me that even though I'm here in this cellar runnin' that press, I can still be a hero someday?" I said with a soft smile on my face.

"That's what I'm telling you. You have to protect your own self-image and know that even if you make some wrong decisions, they're just wrong decisions and not a verdict on your value as a friend, family member or even a *paisan*, as you guys call it. There's always time in life to make it all right."

As we ended the conversation, I realized how much more I understood about my feelings for Frankie and Canevecchio, and even T. For the first time, I realized the excruciating pain T must be suffering because of his cooperation with the Secret Service. I couldn't wait to get the print over so I could talk to him and let him know that I understood.

CHAPTER 45

"AS SOON AS I TWISTED THE KEY, I REALIZED WHAT I HAD DONE."

LJ AND I WERE STILL huddled together on the floor, talking. I was focused on what it was that I immediately liked about her, even when I was chasing her through the casinos. Soon, however, I realized that we weren't having a private conversation. I was so focused on her that I had completely forgotten that she was handcuffed to Brus, who was just on the other side of the pole. When I took my eyes off LJ for just a second, I caught Brus looking at me with his cold dark eyes. I immediately felt vulnerable because I knew he was listening to the tender conversation I was having with LJ, and he was calculating how he could use my apparently soft, vulnerable side against me—and her—for that matter. It was clear to me that Brus was the only species of his kind in the room, and that was just how he liked it. He would take everybody out if it suited his purpose and never give it a second thought.

At that moment Miguel broke the looming tension in the room by standing and telling everyone he needed a smoke and some fresh air. He had been doing it nearly every hour since midnight. It seemed a little incongruous to me, but not atypical of smokers. This trip he tried something a little different. He picked up the duffle bag of genuine, which he was never far from, and walked toward the stairs leading up to the back door. This precipitated the first of several confrontations that night which literally rattled the rafters.

"Leave the genuine," Frankie told Miguel, as he stepped forward blocking his route up the stairs.

"We've come too far for the genuine to disappear now! It stays here," Frankie said in a firm unwavering tone.

He stood at the stairway entrance with his feet wide apart, both arms up, chest high, fingers pointing up and both palms set firmly against Miguel's chest. I don't think any of us knew, at that moment, that while Miguel was holding the duffle bag in his left hand, he had his right hand on the Mauser tucked in his waistband just under his shirt.

Miguel put up surprisingly little resistance. It felt all wrong that he would have just dropped the bag at Frankie's feet and headed up the stairs without so much as a Neanderthal grunt. However, while it didn't dawn on me at the moment, because I was fully enthralled with LJ, it became horrifyingly clear when he came back down the stairs a few minutes later.

Everyone in the room believed Miguel was going out for a smoke. No one, including me, ever suspected that he was going out in the back yard to plan a coup with The FBI, who was hiding in the bushes. I went about my printing responsibilities and wooing the new girl in my life, even if it was only for a short time more.

"Excuse me. Is it possible that I can use the bathroom?" LJ asked, directing her request at me.

It was easy to completely ignore whatever was happening between Miguel and Frankie and attend to her request. She had been sitting on the cold cellar floor for several hours, and it wasn't surprising that she needed to go. I looked over at Frankie, who was still focused on Miguel, who was just reaching the top of the stairs, heading for the back door. Frankie looked over at me, clearly not having heard the request from LJ. Realizing that I couldn't get her loose from Brus, I repeated her request.

"She needs to go to the bathroom. You have the key to the cuffs?"

Frankie, with his mind still on Miguel, clearly perplexed that he gave up the genuine so easily, dug into his pocket and tossed me the key, with little or no thought. I caught the key cleanly and turned toward LJ, intending to set her free from the pole and Brus, knowing that she detested both of them in equal proportion. She smiled and leaned forward as I knelt down to unlock the handcuffs encircling the pole.

I inserted the key into the cuff on her left hand and twisted left. When it failed to release, I realized the cuff was double-locked. When handcuffs are put on someone, the object is to insert the notched end of the cuff far enough into the receiving end so the person's hand cannot pass through the opening. The problem is, once they're on, the notched end will continue to click through the receiving end, closing the opening down until it lodges tightly against the wrist and cuts off circulation; obviously a very dangerous situation. There is, however, a way to prevent this from happening. On the bottom-side of each cuff is a small push button. Correspondingly, on the back-end of a handcuff key is a small pin-like protrusion that fits perfectly into that push button. If the button is pushed while the notched end of the cuff is inserted into the receiving end, the notched end will be held in place so it can no longer continue to tighten down on the wrist. The cuff-size opening will not decrease nor will it increase; the handcuffs become "double-locked."

Frankie knew enough to double-lock the cuffs when he put them on LJ. He evidently had some personal experience with the device. A kid printer like T's godson, who had never been in trouble before, would have no idea of the "double lock" phenomenon, let alone what it's called or how to defeat it.

"Hold still, they're double-locked, give me a second," I said to LJ as I twisted the tiny key in the cuff, first left, then right, to release the double lock. But to Frankie, it was as if I said, "Hi, I'm Jake from the Secret Service. Mind if I arrest you and your friends today and ruin the rest of your fuckin' lives?"

Still focused on LJ and completely ignorant of what I had just done, I didn't notice Frankie take two very soft steps toward me and LJ.

"They're double-locked," he said, repeating what I just told LJ.

"I think I got it," I obliviously said, confirming the treachery and deceit of not only myself but also of T.

I can only imagine the absolute horror and heart break that washed over Frankie when he realized not only who I was and what T had done, but also that the life he lived and loved was over. It was probably just what he felt on that bridge in Holland in 1944. They say the secret to heroism in combat is the realization that you're already dead, and so, there's no anxiety over the future. I'm sure, at that moment, Frankie believed his life was as worthless in that cellar in Belleville as it was on that bridge in Holland.

Frankie stood silently and watched as I pulled the receiver from the cuff to release LJ's left wrist. His suspicion was confirmed; he didn't need to see or hear anymore. I didn't realize what had happened until I looked up and saw the despair on Frankie's face. There wasn't even the slightest hint of anger, just nearly-haunting sadness; I would have preferred anger. I didn't know what to do or say. I just turned away and continued releasing LJ. I figured I would let it lay; the next move would be his. It wasn't until later that morning that I learned how Frankie would react to this discovery, together with a firsthand definition of "Hero."

I had successfully freed LJ's left hand from Brus's right. As a result, she was no longer confined to the column, although her right hand was still cuffed to Brus's left. Nevertheless, the instant her left hand was free, she bounced to her feet in a single bound. Brus, still half asleep, was jerked so hard to one side that the neighbors across the street probably heard his head bang against that metal column. It's a miracle he was still conscious.

"Easy, easy," I said, trying to get her to stay still while I attempted to un-cuff her right hand from Brus, who was slowly being pulled by the arm, up and around the pole, as LJ became more animated and mobile.

Just as I got the key in the second handcuff, everything suddenly ground to a halt. I heard LJ, who had mysteriously stopped wiggling, whisper, "Oh shit." When I looked up, pulling the handcuff key from the lock, I echoed her sentiment.

CHAPTER 46

A ONCE AND FUTURE HERO

YOU WOULD HAVE THOUGHT IT was the day the earth stood still, and Klaatu with his roboton sidekick Gort walked down those cellar steps. But it wasn't a couple of sci-fi characters. It was Miguel, followed closely behind by Special Agent Ritter, who was, at the time, a complete mystery to all of us. He did, however, heighten my suspicions about why he was there when he pulled what was clear to me to be an FBI issue .38 caliber, S&W revolver. It was a standard blue combat revolver with a 4-inch barrel. As soon as I saw the gun, his butchered haircut, close shave and cheap suit, I began to become suspicious. No self-respecting big city detective or hood would ever carry such a copper gat, nor project such a flat persona.

The Mauser in Miguel's hand was, however, a completely different matter. Interestingly, Ritter's surprise at the sight of the Mauser was second to no one else's in the room. It clearly wasn't part of his game plan, although he didn't protest when Miguel walked directly to the duffle bag of genuine currency, picked it up and tossed it to Ritter. He then turned his attention to me.

"Bring me that box of counterfeit," Miguel said, waving the Mauser toward the clattering printing press, which was still pumping out finished product.

While I eased my way back behind the press, contemplating

as many options as I could think of—which weren't many—Miguel ordered Azzimie and the still-tethered Brus and LJ against the far wall. Canevecchio was now standing near the front wall, closer to the stairs, trying to wake up, while Frankie took a step back and stood next to the stuffed chair where he kept the baseball glove with the baseball wrapped in its pocket. Miguel quickly realized that I was stalling, so he stopped waving the Mauser and started to point it with more intention and menace.

"Let's go. Move it," he said

"What? I can't hear you. Let me turn this press off," I said as I slowly moved to the front of the press where the on/off switch was. It was all I could think of. I figured if I turned the press off, I could give the signal and let Carmine and the raid team come to the rescue.

Then, just when I thought I found a solution and continued to inch closer to the on/off switch, all hell broke loose. Even over the clatter of the press, I could hear the back door to the bakery slam and the rhythmic gallop of more trouble descending the wooden stairs as they vibrated and shook. I remember thinking that whoever it is sure isn't concerned about announcing his presence. At first I was actually fearful it was Carmine and the raid team and we were all about to break out into a Hollywood-style gunfight. But it turned out to be just another blue, S&W, 4-inch .38, this time attached to Senior Special Agent Al Whitaker. He burst into the room so suddenly that most of us hardly knew how to react, including Miguel, who was still pointing that Mauser at me. But Ritter wasn't the least bit confused; he knew exactly why Whitaker was there. Without so much as even a pithy salutation to or from Ritter, Whitaker walked directly over to Brus and LJ and started barking orders at them that made as much sense to me as a raincoat on a furry farm animal on a sunny July afternoon. They were still obviously cuffed together, and as a result, it was unclear which of the two Whitaker was barking orders at. He quickly became frustrated and started making demands of everybody in the room.

"Somebody un-cuff these two," Whitaker commanded.

Nobody responded. The only key in the building I knew of was in my jeans pocket. I put it there when I took it from the cuff on LJ's right wrist when the commotion started. It wasn't clear to me what this guy wanted with either LJ or Brus and I was not going to release her. Thinking back on it, maybe I should have. I figured as long as they were cuffed together whatever was happening would slow down and give me some time to come up with a move. I didn't anticipate Whitaker's next decision.

"Okay, both of you, up the stairs."

He grabbed the center chain of the handcuffs and jerked both of them toward the stairs. They stumbled and tripped and struggled to keep their balance, but in just a few seconds all three of them were up the stairs and gone.

My initial reaction was to leap over the printing press and stop them, but with four guns in the room—and three of them in the grip of the bad guys—I decided I couldn't risk a shoot-out by myself. I needed to get Carmine and the raid team in there immediately. I moved to the front of the press, once again hoping to turn it off so Carmine would be able to hear the code word and get the fuck in there. My luck was still all bad.

"Where are you going? I told you to bring me that box of queer," Miguel ordered again.

After two attempts to turn off the printing press, I finally resigned myself to the fact that so long as Miguel had that Mauser pointed at me, I was going to have to think of another idea. I was also distracted from my ultimate goal because I had no idea what was happening to LJ. I even began to question my suspicions that these two guys were really working for the government. I broke into a cold sweat when it dawned on me that it could all be a set up and they weren't the law, but were in fact bad guys like Miguel. My only hope was to get Carmine's attention and let him know what was happening, so that's what I tried to do.

"What the fuck is going on here? What are all these fuckin' guns for?" I said in a very loud voice. It was tantamount to yelling "fire" in a crowded theater; I only hoped somebody was listening. I continued anyway, hoping Carmine could hear something over the clang of the press.

"Who the fuck are you guys? What is this, a hold up?"

By this time Miguel was looking at me as if to say, "What are you doing? Don't you see this gun pointed at your fuckin' heart?" He had no idea what I was doing. It was unfortunate that Ritter correctly figured it out.

"Shut him up. Shut him up. The place is wired," Ritter told Miguel, in both an alarmed and muffled voice clearly intended to avoid interception by the wire he suspected was in the room. He was obviously shaken by his suspicions. If there was a wire in the room, then there was probably also a Secret Service Agent in the room and I was most likely that guy. However, when Ritter suggested that Miguel should shut me up, I'm not sure he intended that Miguel use the Mauser to do it.

I was still mostly behind the printing press when I decided to try once again to get Carmine's attention. I stayed there because I forgot to ask Carmine where TSD installed the wire, so standing anywhere in the room was as good as the next. When Miguel heard the order from Ritter, he almost instinctively jerked off a shot at me. It happened so fast I didn't have time to react in the slightest. He took me completely by surprise. That was the last time I let him do that.

POW. A single shot from the Mauser exploded in the small cellar. The explosion was more than just noise. The entire cellar shook from the impact of the shot and immediately filled with gun smoke. It felt like an 18-wheeler just broke through the back door and hurled down the steps. The .380 caliber round ricocheted like it was in a pinball machine—first off the printing press and then around the room. Everyone in the room dove for cover except one. Miguel moved to his right around the end of the press to get a clear shot at me for a do-over.

As he improved his angle of fire, he began to raise the Mauser to what I clearly knew was a killing position. Whenever you can see the front sight, barrel nose and trigger of a gun, all at the same time, you know you're about to get shot; this was one of those times. I surrendered any idea of Carmine coming to the rescue, so I started to reach for the detective special in my left boot—convinced it was way too late.

I instinctively lurched in anticipation of the searing pain of the gunshot wound I was certain to receive. The noise from the second shot was deafening as I raised my arms in front of my chest in what I knew was a futile attempt to protect my vital organs. At first I thought the white flash that crossed before my eyes and bounced off the walls was the result, but the piercing burn from the hot lead I surely expected was absent. When I saw Miguel holding his shoulder, writhing in agony, I realized what happened. I then knew how those guys on that bridge in Holland felt.

CHAPTER 47

"JESUS, JAKE," WAS ALL HE SAID

When Miguel moved to get a deadly bead on me, Frankie fired first, only instead of a gun, he fired the baseball he had been toying with all night. He hit Miguel square in the shoulder, which caused him to fire the second round into the ceiling joist instead of my chest. Frankie saved my life. I looked over at him to let him know that I was grateful for what he had done, but he wasn't looking at me. He never took his eyes off Miguel. He was like a heavyweight fighter coming out of the corner to finish off an opponent. His rage was electrifying as he began to move in for the kill. I fully expected a third shot from Miguel, even if his shoulder was shattered like a broken china plate. Then, like most of the night, everything went sideways.

As I looked back at Miguel, I got a sick feeling in my stomach. Miguel had turned away from me and squared off at Frankie, who was barreling down on him like the Hulk leaping right off a comic book page to pulverize a bad guy. I decided it was time to give it up. I slid my right hand into my left boot, palmed the forbidden revolver and yanked it free. With the .38 in my right hand down at my side, I began to step from behind the still cranking press to hopefully get the drop on Miguel. I was ready to plug him, when I realized that Miguel no longer had the Mauser. In a desperate attempt to defend himself, he squared off at Frankie while he was obviously looking for the .380 German equalizer. He couldn't find it. He didn't know where it was, but I knew and it didn't make me feel a whole lot better.

Evidently, when Miguel was nailed in the shoulder by the baseball, the Mauser went flying. I couldn't tell you its trajectory, but somehow it landed at Azzimie's feet, who joyfully picked it up like it was Excalibur itself. His persona was transformed in an instant. I was convinced it meant bad news for me, and probably Frankie as well. I fully expected Azzimie to hand the gun back to Miguel, but once again I was wrong. I woefully underestimated the thrill of revenge harbored in a heart abused. At the time, I had no idea of the abuse that Miguel and his trusty Mauser had heaped upon Azzimie. Now it was Azzimie's turn.

Holding the Detective Special made me feel less vulnerable, even though I was invisible to everyone else in the room. They all had their eyes glued on the ensuing showdown between Azzimie and Miguel. Frankie stopped dead in his tracks when he realized where the Mauser was. Ritter stood frozen with fear and indecision, even though he was the third gun in the room. I held the Detective Special down at my side, still partly protected by the printing press, hoping no one in the room even noticed I had it.

With Azzimie holding the Mauser on Miguel, you would have thought Miguel would have played it smart and tried to "will" the gun away from the simple-minded Azzimie. That just wasn't his style. Instead, Miguel ordered him to give him the gun and when Azzimie didn't immediately comply, he launched a barrage of insults and attacks. Miguel simultaneously walked toward him with his right arm outstretched reaching for the Mauser. Azzimie, shaking his head left and right, took a step back and told Miguel in a loud, almost tearful voice, "No!" Miguel halted his pursuit for only a second or so and then began yelling at him in Spanish, while closing the distance between them to only a few feet. Azzimie responded by taking another step back, only this time he raised the Mauser to near-shoulder height and said in a loud cry, "Die Motherfucker!" At that instant, a shot rang out and I, along with almost everybody else in the room expected Miguel to fall over dead. Not so.

I was looking almost square at Azzimie from behind the printing press. Miguel had his back to me as he was pursuing him. When the Mauser erupted, there was no recoil or smoke. It was only when I saw the sunburst of red appear on the front of Azzimie's white shirt, like the rising sun on a hot summer morning at the Jersey Shore, that I put two and two together—I didn't see any reaction from the Mauser because it wasn't the Mauser that fired. Before Azzimie could take his revenge and kill Miguel, Ritter fired one shot from his .38 and hit Azzimie, square in the middle of the back, which I'm sure pulverized his heart and killed him dead before he realized what had happened. He melted into a clump of cotton, blood and sneakers that soon were completely scarlet-colored.

Miguel, who seemed completely unfazed by the death of Azzimie right before his very eyes, wasted no time in retrieving the Mauser. He quickly stepped up and grabbed it almost before Azzimie hit the floor. I guess he thought he had won the duel of mouth, wits and hardware, but he overlooked one thing—Frankie. Frankie, who was accustomed to death, immediately pushed forward. He caught Miguel just after he grabbed the Mauser but before he was able to straighten up, gun or no gun, Frankie was going to finish what he started with the baseball.

Frankie grabbed Miguel by the front of the shirt with such force that his eyes rolled back into his head from the trauma. Miguel dropped the Mauser and Frankie kicked it against the wall under a small chair. He then hit Miguel so hard, square in the jaw with a right-cross, that I thought he killed him. Frankie followed after Miguel's flailing body like a cat would follow a wounded rat.

As I watched the fight erupt between Frankie and Miguel, I was still stunned by the reality that Ritter, who I was convinced was either FBI or CIA, had just drilled Azzimie. I then realized Ritter was there that night to accomplish something that was important enough to kill for. The corollary of that still left the unanswered questions of where he would stop and if anyone was immune from his apparent license to kill.

While Frankie was about to unload on Miguel again, I had mixed feelings as I realized Frankie was set to kill him—something

I didn't want to happen because I was already going to catch shit for Azzimie bleeding all over the fuckin' floor. And then it happened. It was like all the forces in the room—good, evil and otherwise—just decided it was time to rumble and put an end to all the shenanigans, all in about ten seconds.

Frankie held Miguel with his left hand while he drew back his right fist, even with his right ear. He was poised to launch a skull-crushing roundhouse on Miguel. Canevecchio knew what I failed to pick up earlier—Ritter was there to protect Miguel and he would kill Frankie if he got in the way. And he was certainly very much in the way.

Convinced of the danger, Canevecchio, who up until that time was a spectator, quickly moved in on Ritter. Like a 350-lb. Gorilla in the room, it was impossible for Ritter not to see the danger as Canevecchio lumbered toward him. With surprising agility, Canevecchio closed in on Ritter much more quickly than Ritter predicted. However, he did have the equalizer. Canevecchio closed within six feet of Ritter and attempted to grab his arm holding the .38. But Ritter would not be deterred. He snapped both arms free from Canevecchio's grasp and simultaneously cranked off a round, shooting Canevecchio. I couldn't see where he was hit, but he went down like a brick shithouse and lay lifeless on the floor. This certainly got Frankie's attention. While still holding Miguel by the throat, Frankie now squared off against Ritter completely oblivious to the reality that Ritter had a man-killer in his hand and was prepared to use it. Miguel looked like he just couldn't take another haymaker and Ritter wasn't going to let that happen anyway.

Ritter, only about seven feet from Frankie, raised the .38. I could see him stiffen his body in anticipation of the recoil from the revolver as he strangled the pistol grip so ferociously that the blood began to drain from his hand. There was no doubt in my mind that he was already squeezing the trigger and was about to unleash the cold blue steel revolver's burning hot slug on Frankie. I was horrified by each passing second as the six shot cylinder of the revolver began to rotate in cadence with the retreating hammer and squeeze of the trigger.

POW. The detonation of a .38 loaded with Super Vel Hollow Point Ammunition is unmistakable, as is the effect. Flesh and bone is no match for the scalding hot lead projectile that splinters into shards, designed to rip and tear thru vital organs and kill with impunity. And it did, just as Ritter calculated. To his surprise, however, Frankie did not immediately collapse to the floor in total capitulation to the deadly blow. I could see the confusion in Ritter's squinting eyes and slightly cocked head as he began to realize it wasn't his .38 that unleashed the mayhem.

As I watched the confrontation evolve, I became convinced the outcome would be certain and unbearable. So it was at that instant that my life turned on a dime, and has never turned back since. The reality evolving before me was just not acceptable. I just couldn't stand there and allow it to happen. So as Ritter squeezed the trigger on his .38, like any well-trained FBI Agent, so as not to jerk the gun and therefore get a clean kill, I yanked and drew that Detective Special like only a man wearing a pair of cowboy boots could. I slammed my finger on the trigger, holding down the recoil from the gun with pure adrenaline.

Ritter was still squeezing when the Super Vel load in my Detective Special fired, shaking the dust from the rafters and even drowning out the pounding of that fuckin' press. When Ritter heard the detonation, he surely thought he was at the end of his long controlled squeeze, but he was wrong-dead wrong. I killed Ritter fuckin' dead that night and don't regret it for a minute. He fell to the floor in a heap, still clutching the .38, waiting for it to go off, as his heart stopped beating. I wasn't sure if Frankie realized what had happened; he never turned to see. He went directly to Canevecchio.

Smoke and soot fogged the cellar while the printing press continued to bang away without missing a beat. It was almost surreal. The press just kept birthing counterfeit, undeterred by the death and destruction that filled the room. While I, too, was concerned for Canevecchio, I had other responsibilities. Azzimie was down and from the looks of it probably dead as a door nail, as was Ritter. I still didn't know what happened to LJ, or even Brus for that matter. And I just had to stop that damn press from clanging in my ear anymore. And, oh yeah, where the fuck was Carmine?

First I checked Azzimie for a pulse; he was very dead. While I was doing that, I looked over at Canevecchio and was relieved to see him talking to Frankie, who was holding his watermelon-like head in his arms. His breathing was labored, but his eyes were clear and the blood didn't seem too bad. Frankie looked up with tears welling in his eyes like a small boy holding a crushed cocker spaniel in the middle of the street. He said nothing to me, but rather looked back at Canevecchio.

"It's gonna be okay, ya hear me? We're all gonna get pinched and you'll get a good Scorp doctor, understand? The kid'll take care of it."

Frankie looked back at me for a sign that it was true. I couldn't look him in the eye, but I nodded my head as reassuringly as I could. I then got up, turned the press off and yelled for Carmine.

"Mississippi, Mississippi. Fuckin' Mississippi. Carmine, get the fuck in here and get an ambulance," I yelled at the ceiling while walking around in a circle because I still didn't know where the fucking wire was.

I then stood over Ritter, thinking to myself, "God, I hope this guy's not really FBI. I'm gonna be in deep shit if I just killed an Agent to protect a perp."

Even though I knew I was in a world of hurt, I had no regrets. Then I got that familiar sick feeling in my stomach when I realized that in all the commotion after the shooting, I didn't see what happened to Miguel. I half expected to find him collapsed in a corner somewhere, beaten to a pulp after getting clocked by Frankie. But he wasn't. To my horror, he was gone. The box that was catching the sheets of counterfeit $100 bills as they were spewing from the press was still there untouched. I was surprised to see that. I couldn't figure out what happened because I was sure Miguel wouldn't try to make a run for it without something to show for the effort. Then it became clear—the duffle bag with the genuine was gone. Miguel must have slipped away while we were all concerned with issues of life and death. He grabbed the genuine and busted up the steps. I could only hope that Carmine grabbed him, but somehow I didn't think so.

Two minutes later, Carmine and the raid team plowed through the back door and poured down the wooden steps. I'll never forget the horrified look on Carmine's face when he saw the carnage in the cellar. "Jesus, Jake," was all he said.

"Miguel is gone. He took the genuine and bolted during the shootout. You guys didn't get him, did you?" was my first comment.

"No, never saw him. Don't worry, he'll turn up." I could tell Carmine was trying to be calming. That wasn't easy in light of two dead bodies, nearly $1 million of buy money missing along with three perps. I felt the need to fill in the details, although it didn't appear that Carmine was all that interested.

"There were two other players—the chic from Vegas and another guy. They were both dragged outta here by a guy working with the dead guy over there. I gotta tell you, Carmine, I think those two guys were..." Carmine stopped me cold just as I was about to give him my theory on what happened. He took me by the bicep and, with a very firm grip, turned me toward the stairs.

"Listen kid, don't worry about it now. Take my car and go home. We'll clean up and we can talk when you're ready."

When I hesitated, he gave me that "don't fuck with me" look. I took the hint and turned toward the stairs. Carmine was right. I had no stomach for the arrests of Frankie and Canevecchio nor the handshakes and backslaps from the other agents. I just wanted to leave, go home and put my head under the covers like when I was six. And that's exactly what I did.

CHAPTER 48

YEAH, SURE, I HAD IT ALL UNDER CONTROL, COULDN'T YOU TELL?

I HAVE NO RECOLLECTION OF EVER sleeping so long, before or since that day. I don't even remember driving Carmine's car to the apartment or getting into bed for that matter. When I awoke, a fog seemed to cover me like a blanket. Luckily, Bookie and Ava were out of town, so I didn't have to talk to anybody. When I finally got out of bed, I did notice, however, that there was some food in the kitchen and a note. Liz, a career secretary at the office who was a mother to us all, had sent it over. She filled the refrigerator with my favorites: hard Genoa salami, imported provolone and nice *cappicola*. A baguette of fresh semolina bread topped it all off. From the looks of the kitchen, I must have eaten some of it, but Christ, I couldn't remember.

I finally got the energy to take a shower, brush my teeth and put on some jeans. There were so many questions bouncing around in my head. I had to get some answers and as far as I knew, there was only one place to get them. So, after I cleaned up and began to think a little, I picked up the telephone and started the trek back to reality.

"Yo, Carmine," I said relieved to hear his steady, fortifying voice.

"Hey, kid. How ya feeling?"

"I'm okay. I'm gonna come into the office, but first I thought

I would stop by the hospital to see T before they move him to the detention center."

"He's not there," was all Carmine said.

"Oh. I guess he's back at the FDC. I'll see him later then."

"Yeah. Come to the office. I'm here."

"Okay. See ya in a few." I hung up and began to look for the keys to the VW. I looked, on the verge of hysteria, until I remembered that I didn't have them. I drove Carmine's car home, which explained the unfamiliar key on the dresser that I passed by a dozen times.

I finally succeeded in getting my ass out the door and into the car. I was actually relieved to see that the world seemed like it continued to spin, even while I was otherwise occupied somewhere else for a while. It was a clear, cool but not cold November day—football and turkey weather. As I maneuvered that big boat of a car down Clinton Avenue toward Broad Street, questions and suspicions began to clutter my mind. I had both questions and answers, but couldn't get the two to correlate and make any sense. Eventually, I was able to get some of the answers to go with some of the questions. The remainder were just random thoughts that fluttered in my head, not seeming to fit in anywhere at all. I hoped Carmine could clear some of the muck from my memory of what happened.

When I arrived at the Federal Building, I pulled into the underground garage and parked in the spot assigned to Carmine. As I jostled in the seat, I realized I wasn't carrying my issued .357. I left it at the apartment and instead, by reflex I guess, stuck the Detective Special in the inside of my left boot. I could also feel my creds inside the other boot. I remember thinking that I didn't know how they got there that morning. Nonetheless, after I parked the car, I drew the Detective Special from my boot and just looked at it. It was dirty with the residue from being fired. The Super Vel rounds were a very hot load, which is why they are so destructive. I had never killed anyone before and here I was, holding the instrumentality of that death. But, as I decided that night, I knew the consequences of my failure to act and I still didn't regret what I did. The choices were even clearer to me then than they were that night.

I got out of the car and meandered into the elevator that took me to the second floor of the Federal Building and the Secret Service Newark Field Office. I just didn't have the stamina for any of the reactions I would get from the bosses and other agents, so I went to the back door and let myself in with a security key that I wasn't supposed to have, but had anyway—a concise verdict of my Secret Service career. I went directly to Carmine's office without a word to anyone and closed the door. Carmine, looking worn and older than I remembered, was sitting at his desk.

"Hey," I said in a low voice as I flopped into the straight-backed, barely-padded, steel GSA chair that stood in front of his desk.

"Jesus Jake, you don't look like a guy who just slept for two days.

"Two days, what are you talking about? What's today?"

"It's Wednesday the 20th." Carmine might as well have told me we were on the moon. I couldn't believe it. The last thing I remembered was Sunday night, early Monday morning. I looked at the calendar on his desk to confirm that it indeed was November 20th, 1963.

"I'm sorry Carmine. How bad did I fuck it up? What's the fallout?"

"No fallout kid. In fact, we just made the biggest recovery of counterfeit $100 Federal Reserve Notes in the history of the Service. Nobody asked, by the way, who printed it. Headquarters just assumed that the bad guys did."

"Really! What bad guys is that?"

"Well actually, the two who got dead, that's who."

"What?" I was in a state of disbelief.

"It's a case of living history—he who lives, gets to write the fuckin' history," Carmine matter-of-factly declared.

I got up out of the chair and walked to the back of the small office. I just couldn't sit still any longer. I put both of my hands in the back pockets of my jeans with my palms facing forward, double cupping my ass, trying instinctively to cover it. I had a long list of questions and I was having a hard time determining where to begin. I decided I would begin with the easy ones and work up to the harder ones, hoping that during the process I would be able to clarify my thoughts and articulate how I felt. Once again, I was completely wrong. My first question and answer weakened my knees. The ones that followed only got worse.

"So, did you talk to T since it all went down?"

"No."

"What, you sent him back to the FDC without telling him how we did?"

"No."

"Well what? He's back at the FDC, right?"

"No kid, he's not."

When Carmine gave me that third "no" in a row, I knew it was time to sit back down again. I took my hands out of my pockets just in case I needed them to break my fall and returned to the chair. It was a good decision.

"He's dead kid," Carmine told me in a voice I never heard him use before. It was soft, yet strong and supportive. It was a Kevlar voice, not one of steel, but just as strong and life-saving.

"How?" was the only word I could articulate.

"As near as we could figure, he took the call from Miguel and sent him over to the bakery. He got all cleaned up and climbed into bed. About midnight, his little nurse *goom* went in, probably for a little night pok-er, and he was dead. The docs said there was no apparent reason for his death other than he just stopped breathing. He just fuckin' stopped breathing, that's all."

I wasn't there, but I knew exactly what happened. T just didn't want to live any more. He wasn't able to face the shame of ratting out his guys and he just gave it up. I felt responsible and sick to my stomach. For the first time in my career, I regretted becoming an agent. I took that fuckin' job to be a good guy, not ruin good people's lives, no matter how badly they may have behaved. I just sat there looking at the ink stains still on my hands. The color was green, but the stains were red, blood red. Carmine wasn't finished though. What followed, while not nearly as devastating personally, was in the long run, universally more catastrophic.

"There's more we should talk about," Carmine said.

"Okay, but I have a few questions first," I insisted.

"Shoot," he said.

"How the fuck did those two guys ever get in that cellar without you guys makin' 'em? Riddle me that, Batman."

"Garbage."

"Garbage? What the fuck is that about?"

"The eyeball surveillance car got hit by a garbage truck. The impact not only totaled the car, but it shorted out the radio, so we didn't know it even happened. Billy Carter had to find a public telephone and call the switchboard, which then raised us on the radio. By the time we regrouped and it all got sorted out, we missed 'em. Just bad luck kid. We were only outta play for maybe twenty minutes."

"What about Miguel and Azzimie? Did you get my message over the wire when they arrived?

"Yeah, we got that, but when that press was crankin' we couldn't hear a thing. We figured that Miguel bein' there was right on track. We weren't too surprised to see he brought Azzimie; after all, he was the guy in Vegas. Besides, it seemed like you had it all under control. Right?"

"Yeah, sure. I had it all under control. Couldn't you tell?" I said with just the right touch of sarcasm.

Carmine continued to tell me the facts of life, like a dad talking to his teenage son about sex—the kid thought he already knew it all, but naturally had it all wrong.

"Well, we had no idea who the chic and the other guy were. That was a big surprise. But we knew that Miguel arranged for a split of the counterfeit and he wanted it all done that night. We figured he didn't worry about the plant location because he was immediately going on the lam, never to return. We had taken precautions, so I didn't worry about the distribution of the notes. I thought we had it under control and we could round them up when the dust settled. I had no idea it was gun smoke that would have to settle first."

I wasn't happy about the gun smoke comment, but I let it go. Now wasn't the time to get sensitive. There was, however, one thing Carmine said that I didn't understand.

"What precautions did you take? What are you talking about?"

Carmine blew right past that question and continued in his own order. I knew he wouldn't keep anything really important from me so I decided to be patient and just listen.

"So, I guess we should talk about the two stiffs, huh?" he suggested.

This was the part I was really nervous about. I half expected The FBI or CIA or somebody to bust in the door and arrest me for murder. I only hoped it wasn't going to be Carmine who would have to do it. I went limp in the chair and tried to keep my heart rate below 250 while I listened to Carmine spill the beans.

"The first guy, Azzimie, was a shit-um street hustler. He was connected to the family busted in Las Vegas and was probably the one who got the first batch of notes from Miguel. He was the super in the East Orange apartment complex where Miguel was holing up. My guess is that he somehow grabbed the notes without Miguel knowin' and the shit hit the fan in Las Vegas before Miguel found out. Chances are Miguel just kept him close until he was ready to rub him out. There sure as hell wasn't any way he was gonna take him on the lam with him. He was not only expendable, but Miguel probably brought him along that night in order to finish him off and be done with it.

"You wanna tell me what happened?" Carmine ended with a question.

Carmine had a pretty good grip on what was going on between Miguel and Azzimie, but I didn't know if he knew what exactly happened in that cellar and how Azzimie got dead. So, I stood back up and paced the room while I gave him every detail. Well, almost every detail—I didn't tell him I killed Ritter. I guess I wanted to see how much trouble I was really in before I copped to that mess. Other than that, I told him the good, the bad and eventually the ugly, too. I told him how I blew my cover because I had a hard on for LJ and Frankie caught the handcuffs double-lock fuck up. I also told him that there was no doubt in my mind that Frankie saved my life even after he knew I was an agent. Surprisingly, my description of how Azzimie was shot by Ritter didn't seem to faze Carmine in the least. When I was finished, I asked the big, very big question.

"Just exactly who the fuck was that guy?" I asked referring to Ritter, not entirely sure I wanted to hear the answer.

"The guy that shot Azzimie or the guy you shot?"

At first I thought Carmine was fuckin' with me, but then I realized he wasn't. At that point I just threw my hands up in the air and sat back down in the chair. I was certain that's what Carmine wanted because after he asked the question, he lowered his eyes and didn't look up again until I was settled.

"Okay, Carmine...give it to me."

He began to unravel the tale. "Well, the guy that you shot and killed, by the way, was nobody."

"Nobody...whadda you mean... nobody?"

"I mean no-fuckin'-body. The guy had no ID, his fingerprints aren't on file anyplace and the .38 he was carrying had the serial number filed off. He's a complete ghost; nobody even claimed his bones. Now the guy that shot Azzimie, on the other hand, I'm convinced was an agent, but I can't prove it."

It made no sense to me. "What the fuck are you talking about, Carmine? How's that possible? They were the same guy," I asked in a state of bewilderment.

"Look, there's no doubt that guy would have been an agent had he just popped Azzimie, pulled Miguel outta there and got him onto his next mission. That's the reason he was there in the first place. But once he crossed you and your posse in there, and got himself dead on the floor, he was disavowed and became a nobody. Anyway, that's their story and they're stickin' to it. *Capisce?*"

"Listen Carmine, you wanna hear how he got that way?" I asked, not sure he knew exactly how it happened; especially the part where all that gun smoke came from the Detective Special that I wasn't supposed to have in the first place.

"I know how it happened. But, if you wanna talk about it I'm here."

"How do you know what happened?"

"I talked to Frankie."

"He told you what happened?"

"Yup. You shot that guy with a rod that if you had listened to me, would never have been there."

"Yeah," was all I could say.

"I guess it's a good thing you can make your own decisions, huh?"

"I guess. Is there gonna be any fallout about it?"

"I told you the guy was nobody."

"Okay," I acquiesced. Several seconds passed and I continued. "By the way, what else did Frankie tell you?"

"He told me the guy had the drop on him and you plugged the guy in the nick of time to save his life. He was actually very appreciative."

"Did he tell you why?"

"Nope. He didn't have to. I figured it out just from the looks of the place and your face when we got in there."

"Carmine, Frankie saved my life, like I told you, even after I blew my cover and he knew I was an agent."

"Huh huh."

"No, listen, that's the truth. He didn't have to do that. What was I supposed to do, let that creep kill him right in front of my eyes for no good reason at all?" I was pleading my case to Carmine.

"Kid, for whatever it's worth, you did the right thing."

I could taste the relief in my throat. It meant so much to me what Carmine thought. Even if I had to face the wrath of hell and the Secret Service combined, Carmine's respect was enough to sustain my heart and courage. A full couple of minutes passed in silence while Carmine let me gather my nerves. I had more questions.

"Hey Carmine, where are those guys? Are they in the FDC? Do they know about T?" He clearly understood I was referring to Frankie and Canevecchio.

"No. I figured they would find out soon enough."

"How's that, if they're in the FDC?" I asked.

"I didn't say they were in the FDC," Carmine rapidly responded.

"Well, where are they then?" I was even more confused.

"They're at Fort Dix."

"What?" I said incredulously because Fort Dix is an Army Base in the pines of New Jersey.

"Yup. The 'old dog' is in the hospital there, doing nicely, by the way, and Frankie is by his side. The doctor said it was essential to his recovery. Who am I to quarrel with modern military medicine?" he quipped with a faint smile on his face.

I had no idea why they were not at the FDC but in an Army hospital instead. I figured, though, it was as good a time as any to see what Carmine thought about their future. I was having my own thoughts.

"So, Carmine, where are we with those two? Frankie did save my life, for whatever that's worth, and Canevecchio helped. I know they're perps, but is there anything we can do?"

"Well kid, here's where we are. We got just over $16 million in crisp, counterfeit notes and two dead guys, one of whom I'm sure was some kinda G-man. Then we have four missing players, including two perps, an honest to goodness FBI Agent, who pulled two of them outta there because you had 'em cuffed together, and some kind of mission specialist, who The FBI was prepared to kill nearly everyone, to protect.

"Now the good news is, this was the biggest counterfeit haul in Secret Service history, and lucky for us we got the pictures to prove it. Thankfully, nobody knows we did the printing, so we can still look like authentic crime stoppers. So what did you have in mind for these two *paisani*?"

I knew there was a hint in Carmine's little summation, but I wasn't yet sure what or where it was; so I asked the first question that came to mind, no matter how stupid it seemed.

"Whadda you mean, 'lucky for us we got the pictures to prove it'—we got the notes, don't we?"

"Yeah, we got'em for now, but not for long, Daddy-0, not for long."

I gave Carmine that little smile you save for when you eat something real bad, but you don't want to spit it out on the floor in front of everybody. I knew I should be able to figure this out, but I wasn't getting it. Then it hit me. Daddy-0 did it.

"We're gonna lose the notes, aren't we?" I asked without really articulating more, because I couldn't. I knew I was on the right track and that Ron Ron had something to do with it. But, I hadn't quite figured it out. I was hoping Carmine would fill in the gaps. As usual, he was glad to.

"Yup. Listen, we didn't know exactly where all these notes were going and we couldn't risk losing that many notes, especially since we were the guys who printed them. So, that's why we went to see Ron Ron. I figured we only needed the notes for a short window of opportunity to grab these guys and see where they were going. So I had Ron Ron give you the 'hardener' to mix into the ink. I didn't wanna tell you it was really a detergent dissolver that would destroy the notes in about forty-eight hours, because I thought you'd think I didn't have confidence in your ability to protect the counterfeit. That's where we are kid."

I was trying to skip ahead to figure out what it all meant. I thought it was all good news, but I had to hear it said aloud to be sure.

"Okay, so now what? Does that mean that there's a 'Daddy-O' defense out there for Frankie and Canevecchio? Just like Ron Ron?" I could barely restrain the glee in my heart.

"I guess so. In just a couple of hours from now the notes will all be gone," Carmine responded in a serious tone.

"Are you gonna take some heat for this, Carmine?"

"Nah. This ain't protection. Nobody really knows what we do anyway. We'll take credit for the seizure, blame the print on the two dead guys, then just tell everybody we destroyed the notes as SOP (Standard Operating Procedure). I may have to start a little fire in the fireplace tonight to tidy things up, but there's a chill in the air. Don't you think, kid?"

"Oh yeah, I hear it's gonna be a very chilly night," I responded as a willful co-conspirator. Carmine still had some concerns though.

"The only wrinkle here is this guy Miguel. I got a bad feeling about that rat and the rat keepers he's workin' for at The Bureau. I'm afraid they're up to something, but I just can't figure it out. They went way out on a limb for that guy. They normally only do that when a very big move is afoot. The only guy over there that probably knows, other than The Director and his twit AD is Al Whitaker, and he aint given it up, and that's the part that really worries me. I guess we'll see, won't we."

I gave Carmine a little nod and began to head for the door, thinking I got all the answers and was very satisfied with the outcome. Then, not believing I could overlook her, I remembered LJ.

"Hey Carmine, what about LJ and Brus, and by the way, what's the story with that guy who grabbed 'em?"

"Oh, that was Al Whitaker. We go back a long way. He called me that night as soon as he got a whiff that The Bureau was gonna step on our solo in the bakery. All he wanted to do was pull out their undercover who was workin' that family on some mid-eastern FCI scam. At least that's what he said I'm not entirely sure he knows what the real truth is, though. You made it difficult when you cuffed those two together. He called me the next morning to let me know it went all right, eventually. We had a good laugh because he hasn't carried a handcuff key for over a decade. He had to take them back to the field office to get them loose."

"No shit. Did you tell him I'm real fuckin' sorry? Why didn't they clue us that they had an undercover inside when we got started?"

"Now, don't be disrespectful kid. You know the drill. Besides, Whitaker's one of the good guys over there."

"Well, is he gonna hand over the chic? We can still prosecute her for the notes she passed in Vegas," I suggested, probably still pissed over the comment she made about the stupid copper she gave the slip to in the casino. Then I got it right between the eyes.

"The chic? Jesus kid, not much luck with the ladies, huh? The chic IS the undercover."

"WHAT?"

"You heard me. That LJ chic is the one they call 23 Foxtrot, Niner, Niner something or other. She was inserted into those mutts right from the top of The Bureau. She's a brand new species, the first of her kind. It's a new world kid. Someday we'll probably even have a chic Attorney General."

He continued.

"Ya know, you musta got closer to catchin' her in Las Vegas than you thought. At some point in the chase, she dumped her FBI credentials in a mailbox because she thought you had her. Al Whitaker gave me the whole story the morning after."

"Where is she, Carmine?"

"Well, when I spoke to Whitaker about thirty minutes ago, they were both in The FBI Field Office upstairs."

I didn't hear another word Carmine said. All I knew was that LJ wasn't a perp—she was an FBI Agent. For a minute, I wasn't sure which was worse. I didn't know whether to shit or go blind. I did know, however, of one thing I wanted to do for sure.

CHAPTER 49

...EVEN MORE IMPORTANTLY, SHE TOOK HER HAND OFF HER GUN

Both the Secret Service and The FBI were in the same federal office building, only three floors apart. We parked in the same garage, rode in the same elevators and often times ate in the same cafeteria. That was always one of the ironies of federal law enforcement. We were supposed to work together, but for some reason we just hated each other. I could never really figure it out. I guess we were just different. We just never felt we were on the same team. All that aside, I knew exactly where she was and what to do.

I dashed from Carmine's office down the hall to the evidence room. I knew I needed an introduction because walking up to her and saying, "Hey, I'm not really a counterfeiter," just wouldn't work. "I was the stupid cop you gave the slip to in Las Vegas," wasn't gonna do it either. But I knew what would do it and where to find it. It was in a brown paper bag, inside a locker, in the back of the evidence room. I found it and, within seconds, I was on my way. I didn't even need to open the bag.

I was out the door, in the elevator and on my way up to The FBI Field Office before it dawned on me that I had no idea what to say to her. I decided I would figure that out, if, and when, I was able to catch up to her. This was going to be my one and only chance to hook up with her. I knew that if she left town and went back to Washington, where I assumed she was assigned, she would be gobbled up by The FBI bureaucratic bullshit and be swept into another operation, and lose any hope of having a real life. I was also uncertain what I wanted from this chic. All I knew was that I wanted to be close to her. Hell, I even liked talking to her.

I leaped off the elevator and burst through The FBI outer glass doors. "Excuse me. I'm looking for..." I started to say to The FBI receptionist, when I realized that the only name I knew was LJ. I wasn't confident that was going to get me to her. So, I used the only name I was sure of.

"I'm looking for Al Whitaker. He's here from Washington with another agent. I'm from the Secret Service," I finally asked the receptionist while holding my Secret Service Commission Book in my hand, hoping it didn't smell like an old boot since that's where it was most of the time.

"I'm sorry, sir, you just missed him. He just went down the elevator."

"Where did he go?" I blurted, on the cusp of a demand.

"I don't know, sir."

"Was he alone?"

"I believe he was with a young lady, also from Washington. Can someone else help you?"

I knew I was getting nothing more from that woman, so I turned back to the elevator. I immediately realized I was on the fifth floor of a sixteen-floor building and there were only four elevators that, like most of government, weren't in a hurry to go anywhere. If I had any hope of catching them, the stairs were my only option.

I literally tumbled down the five flights of stairs and burst into the first floor lobby like my pants were on fire and I was looking for a water cooler. I immediately saw just a tassel of that red and strawberry blonde tuft go through the revolving door. I didn't even see her face, but it didn't matter anyway. Trying not to alarm the people in the lobby, I double-timed it to the door. I could then see her walking down the street toward Broad with Whitaker, the same guy who busted her out of that cellar. I literally spun the door like a roulette wheel, barely able to keep up with it and get through without falling. It only took a few giant steps and I was less than a dozen feet behind her. "Here goes," I thought to myself.

"LJ," I said, but nothing came out. My mouth and throat felt like I just drank a coke bottle of sand. I cleared my throat, mustered my courage and tried again.

"LJ," I said in a booming voice.

Both she and Whitaker spun around, obviously startled, probably by the fact that someone was using her undercover name out on the street in front of the Federal Building. I guess my tone didn't help much either. As soon as they turned around, I realized that maybe it was a mistake to confront both of them on the street. Maybe I should have asked Carmine for an introduction. I remembered that probably neither of them knew I was anything other than a wise guy counterfeiter who might not be real happy over getting pinched. This all dawned on me when they both turned and LJ began to draw down on me right in the middle of the sidewalk.

"Whoa, whoa!" I said with both hands in the air, still holding onto the paper bag in my left.

"I'm Jake."

"I know who you are. What are you doing here? Why isn't he in custody?" she said, clearly directing her last observation to Whitaker.

Whitaker leaned in and whispered in her ear. Carmine must have given him the low down. Her face immediately softened and even more importantly, she took her hand off her gun.

Seeing that we had something to discuss, Whitaker did the right thing.

"I'll see you back at the office, LJ. Nice meeting you, Jake. Give my best to Carmine," he said while turning up the street alone.

Unable to resist breaking my balls, LJ said, "You got any ID?"

"Yeah, it's in the inside of my right boot," I answered, in a very serious tone—still having no idea how this was going to turn out. For all I knew, she still wanted to shoot me.

"Those boots?" she asked as she diverted her eyes from mine for the first time and took a long, slow look down to my Lucccheses and back again. "Not bad." she quipped with a little twitch of her eyebrows. I wasn't sure what she was referring to, but I could only hope it wasn't the boots. I knelt down and pulled the credentials from my boot.

"Let me see those creds," she demanded, as she grabbed them from my hand.

Normally, in a situation like that, when confronted with a stranger, a well-trained agent would grab the ID and then step back to gain some defensive room. She didn't. She stayed in good and tight. She smelled really good, too.

"So, you're SS, huh? That's too bad. I kinda liked you as a bad boy perp."

"This is gonna be more difficult than I thought," I said to myself.

"I was also the old, stupid cop in Vegas you dodged quite well in the casino," I reluctantly admitted.

"Oh boy, what a loser," she sneered and then smiled sympathetically.

"What's in the bag?" she seriously inquired.

"Nothin'," I said, obviously hiding something and now toying with her.

"Oh yeah? Let's see."

"Nope. I can't. Its classified; evidence of a serious crime."

She crooked her neck and looked at me sideways with a bit of a smile, but not too much. She was still holding my commission book and pulled it away as if to put it in her pocket.

"Okay, okay. You give me my creds and I'll give you the bag."

"No, no, no. How do I know I can trust you? You give me the bag and I'll give you your creds," she quickly retorted.

"Of course you can trust me. Look at my creds," I told her with a very straight face. She flipped them open, read them to herself and then aloud:

> **The person identified herein is commissioned as a Special Agent of the United States Secret Service by the Congress of the United States of America. He is commended to those with whom he has official business as being worthy of trust and confidence.**

"Wow, very impressive. Okay," she said as she handed them back to me; I gave her the bag.

"I've been holding on to this, hoping to be able to return it to its rightful owner someday. I hope this is that day," I told her, although I was dead certain I was giving it to the right person.

She opened the bag while looking at me with an inquisitive eye. When she lowered her gaze, her face brightened and she grinned from succulent ear lobe to succulent ear lobe. She practically tore the bag apart. Finally, she pulled out the perfectly-aged and fitted Marlon Brando black leather jacket she sacrificed in that bathroom in the Flamingo Casino in order to give me the slip.

"I took the $100 counterfeit note out of the pocket, just in case you were looking for it," I added.

"I thought it was gone forever! Thank you so much," she said in a soft, creamy voice as yummy as a Dairy Queen Sundae. Then she leaned in and kissed me square on the lips; I could feel the tires on my life screech as they slid and drifted around that dime again.

"Do you have time for coffee?" I would have been crushed if she said no.

"Sure," she said as she caressed the jacket.

"We can walk up to Broad Street. There's a great deli there," I suggested.

We walked and talked for about half a block when a black Crown Victoria wheeled up. It was a Secret Service ride, the kind that's usually reserved for a protection assignment. Bill Carter, a new, energetic, enthusiastic agent, who was way smarter than most of the guys, was driving. Ray Hotchkiss and Pat Flannigan were also in the car. All three of them were in protection suits, so I immediately knew something was up. It was obvious that they saw me with a hot chic and having no idea whatsoever who she was, they just had to check her out.

"Hey Jake, what's up man," Carter yelled as he rolled down the driver's window. In fact, all the windows on our side of the car opened; I'm sure so everyone inside could sneak a peek at LJ. From the looks on their faces, I'm sure they weren't disappointed.

"Nothin'. We're just gonna get a bite. Where are you guys goin'?" I asked, not really caring in the least.

"We're headin' for the airport. There's a Presidential movement so were goin' out to do the advance preparations."

"That's great," I said, not really thinking so, because any field agent called in to help out with a Presidential movement usually gets a shit assignment—guarding a mailbox or man hole cover or some such crap.

LJ didn't say anything. She just stood close to me, maybe even holding my arm, looking like 10 million genuine. As Carter started to pull away, for some inexplicable reason, I had to ask. "Hey, where's the movement?"

"JFK is goin' to Dallas on Friday. We're gonna meet him there. It should be a one-dayer." And then he drove off.

I don't remember if I ever saw those guys again. Actually, I don't remember much at all about the days that followed.

LJ and I just stood there on the street. She suddenly shivered a little and crossed her arms over her chest, rubbing the outside of her shoulders with her open palms.

"Hey, did you feel that? Feels like there's a chill in the air," she said. I didn't immediately reply.

It was a deep chill, from the inside out. It wasn't the kind of chill you could cure with a warm jacket or a nice fire; it wasn't how you feel on a winter morning when you can't wait for the car to warm up so you could blast the heater. It was different. It was a dizzying chill, deep from the heart—the kind you get from a call at 3 a.m. telling you your 52-year-old father just died of a heart attack or your 18-year-old son was just in a motorcycle accident. I could neither explain it, nor could I shake it.

We walked to the corner of Broad and Walnut. It was a huge intersection, with an expansive view of the sky that was unusual in the city. I just stood and turned in a circle, checking for danger in every direction, like a mariner looking for a red dawn sky, warning of impending danger. We got no such warning that day. If only we had; I guess there would have been a chance that things might have turned out differently. Maybe not.

EPILOGUE

November 25, 1963,
FBI Headquarters,
Immediately Following JFK's Funeral

"SOME FUCKIN' SHOW, HUH? I liked the rider-less horse best. Great stallion," The Director quipped to AD who was standing next to him in the Director's office. "Black Jack is his name."

"Whose name?" AD snapped, obviously impatient with The Director.

"The stallion, you twit. The stallion—the rider-less horse—his name is Black Jack. Some shit, huh? He almost starts a second Civil War over civil rights in Mississippi and Alabama and they gotta find a black stallion named Black Jack to march rider-less in his funeral. What's the message here?"

AD, not at all interested in the conversation, poured a cup of tea for both of them as The Director went on.

"I'll tell you what. There are a lot of people who think this whole country is lost and leaderless—defenseless without him. If they only knew how close he brought us to the brink. We know how to protect and defend this country. We will do what needs to be done.

By this time, The Director had his tea delivered to his now trembling hand. He sat at the tea table in his office instead of at his desk. After a couple of delicate sips, The Director changed the subject. He did so, not out of idle curiosity, but because he had something very specific on his mind. From the time he awoke that morning, he intended to maneuver his way to that particular subject. He started the journey.

"So, what ever happened with that 23 Foxtrot thing?" The Director asked in a disarmingly casual tone that didn't fool AD for an instant.

"As anticipated," was AD's patented response when he wanted to irritate The Director for no reason other than he wanted to remind him that he could. The sound of The Director's next slurp of tea confirmed his success, so he decided to give him a little satisfaction.

"Whitaker pulled 23 Foxtrot out of the fray. I'm holding both of them in the New York Field Office for now."

"Well, we have to figure out what to do with her. If the cops in this country find out we have an agent like that, we'll be the laughing stock of every police department in America," The Director said in a huff.

"With that bunch of cowboys moving into the White House, I'm sure we can use an agent like that to keep tabs on all their dirty little secrets," AD said, knowing that was exactly what The Director wanted to hear.

They both sipped their tea in silence until The Director continued, still working his way to his final objective.

"I hear we have a vacancy to fill in headquarters."

"Yes, apparently Special Agent Ritter decided he needed a rest. I'm not sure he'll be back at all," AD replied, knowing exactly what unidentified grave held his body.

"We need a new Ghost," The Director simply stated.

'Yes. I have someone in mind."

Preparations like that were never made by The Director. That's why there was an AD; that was his specialty. He was always the one left to keep The Bureau tidy. In order to do that, a disposable facilitator was sometimes necessary. He knew very well, however, that a tool such as that was not one you could just call upon. You had to be prepared for its use long in advance, sometimes decades. That's why Ritter was a ghost for so many years. He was only a real person within the four walls of FBI Headquarters. Plucked from a pool of applicants over two decades earlier, he was held for just the right assignment. And, while no one expected, nor planned, that he would get killed in that cellar in Belleville, it didn't matter much to The Bureau because a ghost has no past, present or future—hence no explanations to anyone were necessary. Not only were there no official records, but there was no family, or outside friends, or even a landlord to account to. His entire existence was maintained by The Bureau for just such an occasion. But, now he was gone, and it was time to find a new ghost to live and die for The Bureau.

"Actually, we discussed this candidate earlier. I think he would be happy to assume the post," AD continued.

"Oh yes, I remember the photograph. Just make sure he gets rid of that hideous Hitler mustache. We can't have two dictators in headquarters, can we?" The Director said, only half-jokingly.

He was intentionally unclear in his reference. He was either referring to himself or did it as a dig to AD, who he often referred to as his "Little Dictator."

The Director had sufficiently warmed the waters. It was now time to get down to the subject matter he targeted when he first initiated the conversation. However, he would keep in mind that they were talking in FBI headquarters and a completely open discussion was ill-advised. "So tell me—I hear that it was confirmed there was a Cuban 'Jerry Lee' involved in that 23 Foxtrot thing?"

"Here we go," AD said to himself, just waiting for The Director to open that Pandora's box. He knew it was coming, but he was surprised it erupted so soon.

"Yup," was all The Director got.

"I hear he took off to New Orleans after that thing went down," The Director continued to pursue.

"Yup, I heard that, too." AD was still playing hardball. He knew exactly where Miguel went and why he went there. After Ritter bit the dirt cellar floor in Belleville, AD had to personally take control of Miguel and see to it that he was properly instructed and motivated. Everything was under control and he wasn't going to let The Director muck it up now. But The Director was the boss, and if he wanted the details, he wasn't easily deterred.

"So is the 'Jerry Lee' still in New Orleans?"

"No," was AD's initial response. However, when The Director set his teacup down with a loud clang, it became clear that more was needed to appease his appetite. After all, he did think he was in charge.

"Back in Cuba," AD added.

"He got a good job as a chef, I presume?" The Director queried.

AD was tiring of the game and decided to give the Director the answer he was looking for.

"Yes, Director. He got a job in Havana at a wonderful restaurant. I hear his Chateaubriand is to die for."

That was the answer the Director was looking for. Chateaubriand was not only The Director's favorite dish, it also clearly told him that the Cuban they turned was now back in Havana and working as a double agent for The Bureau. Under the law, The Bureau was required to turn such a resource over to CIA; it'll never happen. The Director couldn't have been happier, although he had still not reached his objective. He pressed onward.

"Did he go directly to Havana from New Orleans?"

It was probably the first and only time AD ever broke a sweat anywhere, over anything. He knew exactly what the Director wanted to know, and he had the answer, but he also knew he had to be very careful in having that conversation. The Director also knew that, but he wanted to see AD squirm anyway. So the conversation meandered, as The Director continued.

"So, I understand there was a road show. Did our 'Jerry Lee' join the boys in the band and make the show in Dallas?" The Director nonchalantly asked between sips of tea.

This wasn't the first time The Director played these games and while on occasion AD enjoyed the banter, this was not one of those times. The stakes in their current little frolic were much too high. So he decided to put a quick end to it.

"Yes, he did. I am told he was the star of the show, although completely unanticipated, I might add. It was the performance of a lifetime; people will be talking about it for decades. Would you like to hear the details, Director?"

A bright line had been drawn and AD was hovering over it, ready to cross at the slightest encouragement by The Director. Neither wanted that to happen, nothing more really needed to be said. They both knew that their primary objective was to keep Miguel buried deep undercover in Havana. After what happened with that entire missile thing only a year earlier, Castro could at any time again drive the planet to the brink of nuclear annihilation. It was essential for Miguel to keep Castro's trust and an open line to The FBI, at almost any cost.

There was a long silence. Both men remained seated, just staring into their tea cups.

"Some things just have a high price tag," AD nearly whispered into his tea cup, without looking up.

The Director had the final thought on the subject.

"It's not the price they ask—it's the cost you're willing to bear."

Bloomfield Avenue, Newark, N.J.
Sometime Around Thanksgiving, 1964

It was a casual, public eating establishment, but the conversation was all business, very serious business.

"The price is too high?" the deep, familiar voice boomed as it spoke into the receiver of the telephone.

"I understand their problems. Dat doesn't mean dey have to become mine, does it?" The voice paused, allowing time for the person on the other end to respond.

"Okay, okay. When can dey pay up? You gotta tell 'em that we ain't shippin' no more till they fork it up. *Capisce?* Don't make me come out there and get ugly with dat ganga fuckin' thieves." Another very short pause.

"You better fuckin' tell 'em dat. Okay, see you for *torkino* (turkey) on Thursday. *Ciao,* Daddy-0."

With the phone back on the receiver, you could see the face was familiar, but not the same. It was thinner and had a healthier color, but the clothes were the most noticeable difference. No more Italian, double-knit sweaters draped over a protruding belly onto black, shark skin slacks, silk socks and black Italian loafers overstuffed with fat feet.

While it was still the same old Uptown Diner, it was a new Canevecchio. He was sitting in T's old booth, with the telephone cord stretched from the other side of the counter to a corner of the table in front of him. He looked terrific. He must have lost more than fifty pounds. He was renovated from top to bottom: a new, sharp, angular haircut; horn-rimmed glasses; a crisp, white Egyptian cotton shirt with a dark blue and red "power tie"; but no gold pinky ring—just a nice, rose gold Panerai Radiomer on his left wrist. A $500 Armani suit jacket that matched his slacks hung on the hook at the end of the booth. And Salvatore Ferragamo, lace-up wingtips adorned his feet. What a sight. He certainly looked like a legitimate businessman, although you would have to admit, the image was a bit incongruous when surrounded by the chrome stools and the brightly colored Naugahyde of the diner. Little else on the planet could have made him smile more than the visitor who slid into the booth.

"Ciao, Dog?"

It was Frankie. Canevecchio hadn't seen him in almost three weeks.

"I guess that Daddy-0 on the phone was Ron Ron?"

"Yeah, he's on the left coast with the clients," Canevecchio replied, in his home Sicilian dialect.

"You know, Dog, you sound more like Ron Ron every day. Do you even know what the fuckin' left coast is?" Frankie asked, actually knowing the answer, but dying to see if Canevecchio knew.

Canevecchio looked up, smiled and said, "Yeah. It's the one he left to come here, right?"

Frankie looked at him like he was doing an Abbott and Costello routine. It was all he could do not to ask, "Yeah, but who's on first?"

"Yup, you got it, Dog. How is Ron Ron, anyway?

"He's doin great, *Ponte*. He hooked up with these young dudes out there. They do this outta their garage. They're takin' as much product as we can deliver. How you doin' on your end?"

"We're good. We're good. We can keep up with what you and

Ron Ron are sellin'."

"Great," Canevecchio said with a very professional nod. Then he opined, "Ya know, I had no idea you could make so much fuckin' money and have so many laughs goin' legit. These micro-thinga-ma-chips are like fuckin' gold, or even better, if you know what I mean."

"I know what you mean, Dog. And they're called microprocessors. They're gonna rule the planet. Someday everybody will have one. They're gonna take us to the moon. Just like JFK said."

"Yeah, and we're gonna get a fuckin' piece-a every one of 'em. They'll be bigger than Hula Hoops."

"Yeah, Dog, bigger than Hula Hoops," Frankie repeated with a loving smile on his face and a congratulatory pat on the hand for Canevecchio.

"Ain't it funny how it all worked out with Ron Ron and Carmine and all. We really turned the corner, huh, *Ponte*?"

"Ever hear from the kid?" he asked, knowing it was a sore subject for Frankie.

"Nah," Frankie replied with a sad sigh. "Maybe over Christmas, maybe over Christmas," he repeated, not confident it would really happen.

A long silence lingered over them both. It happened regularly. Each of them knew that the other was thinking of T and about how much they missed him.

Canevecchio never could understand what killed him. He finally stopped trying to figure it out. Frankie, on the other hand, knew exactly what happened. He saw it in combat more than once. Sometimes it was as simple as a soldier standing up during a firefight so he could take a German slug in the head and end the pain. Sometimes it was like T. They just didn't crawl out of their foxhole one morning. Instead, they just gave up, left their body in the muddy bottom of that pit and freed their spirit to go someplace better. It was the thought of him being someplace better that kept Frankie smiling when he thought of T.

"Well listen, I gotta go. I gotta go home, pack and get the red-eye out to see Ron Ron and those kids," Canevecchio said, as both of them were glad to break the silence.

"Right. Listen, call me when you get there and keep me posted on what's happening, okay?" Frankie instructed Canevecchio, as both men stood and hugged like only old world *paisani* did anymore.

Frankie stood by the booth as he watched Canevecchio confidently walk out of the diner and climb into his brand new black Cadillac parked out front. Some habits were hard to break. He then slid into the other side of the booth, the side where T always sat so he could see everybody who walked into the joint. Then, in his best T impersonation, Frankie bellowed:

"Hey Louisa, how about a cuppa coffee here, huh? This booth does come with service, right?"

Louisa flashed him a smile, while a dozen cups of coffee were simultaneously raised in silence throughout the diner.

THE END

ABOUT THE AUTHOR

J.A. Ballarotto graduated from Loyola College of Maryland in 1971. At the age of 23, he entered the United States Secret Service as a special agent in the Newark, New Jersey Field Office. He was among the first group of new, college educated special agents, without prior law enforcement experience, that were hired by the Secret Service. Also included in this group were some of the earliest minorities commissioned as special agents, including the first two female special agents commissioned by any federal law enforcement agency. It was a time of change and turmoil in the Secret Service and America.

After leaving the Secret Service, Mr. Ballarotto attended Seton Hall University Law School where he graduated with honors and joined the New Jersey Attorney General's Office. In order to gain experience as a trial attorney, he joined the Essex County Prosecutor's Office and later became an Assistant United States Attorney. He completed his career in public service as Chief of Criminal Prosecutions in the Trenton, New Jersey office.

Since 1987, Mr. Ballarotto has been a criminal defense attorney with offices in both Trenton, New Jersey and Key West, Florida. He continues to assume responsibility for protecting the rights of those wrongfully accused throughout the United States.

This book is dedicated to the men and women on both sides of the criminal justice system, who fight the good fight to protect and defend the constitution every day of their professional and personal lives.

J.A. Ballarotto
143 White Horse Avenue
Trenton, New Jersey 08610
ballarottolaw.com
Worthyoftrustandconfidence.net

36027567R00228

Made in the USA
Lexington, KY
03 October 2014